THE RIGHT WAY

MAY ARCHER

For my family - those related by blood, and those I've found along the way. I love you all.

THE RIGHT WAY

A brilliant, obsessive mind is the heart of Sebastian Seaver's genius. It might also be the thing that costs him everything he's created and everyone he's ever loved. Consumed with the need to destroy Alexei Stornovich, the Russian mob boss who murdered his fiancée and parents, nothing can turn Bas from his plans of revenge until he's eradicated every last one of them. By any means necessary, and at any cost.

Drew McMann learned early that the key to success is control. Control carried him through law school and helped him keep Seaver Tech together through tragedy. It helped him survive the brutal murder of his sister Amy, his parents' divorce, and the revelation that the seeds of their destruction had been planted by someone he had considered family. It's how he's hidden his love from his best friend Bas for more than half their lives. And now it's how he's going save Bas from himself and finally get his family of friends free

from Alexei's clutches.   Drew has a plan for everything...
Until the kiss.

When Drew loses control one reckless, drunken evening
and his true feelings for Bas are revealed, he tries desperately to contain the damage and keep their friendship on
track, even as decades of lies and half-truths seek to tear
them apart. With Alexei targeting them and their friends,
Drew and Bas are forced to rely on each other more than
ever. But as danger closes in on them, can they sacrifice
their needs for logic and control, and recognize that the
only *right* way to move forward is the one in which they're
together?

CHAPTER ONE

October 31st - Almost two months ago…

"TELL me again why I let you get me into these things," Drew sighed, leaning his head against the passenger's seat window.

Sebastian pulled his sleek blue Charger into a spot on the dark, tree-lined suburban street and cut the engine, while Drew glared at the sprawling Colonial across from them. Purple and green strobe lights flickered from the wide-open garage, and through the large front windows, he could see a throng of people milling around.

"Because you never go out and have fun anymore. It's beyond introversion - it's unhealthy."

"This from the man who turned his living room into a cave for months on end?"

"Uh huh. Takes one to know one. And speaking of my brief time as a hermit, you're here because you owe me," Bas reminded him, leaning over to check his artfully messy, dark hair in the rearview mirror. "Two months ago, when my little brother was jetting off to St. Brigitte with that overgrown golden retriever he calls his boyfriend, *you* told me I had to get my ass off the couch and come with you. *Stop wallowing*, you said. *The plane crash happened more than a year ago*, you said. *Your parents and Amy wouldn't want you to be this way*, you said. *Help your brother*, you said."

Drew sighed again.

"And when I wouldn't listen, you yelled at me," Bas continued, flipping the mirror closed. "Cursed a blue streak, called me an asshole, said Cam deserved a brother who wasn't a... how did you put it? Hmmm... A *self-absorbed prick* who was *too busy wallowing in grief to save the only family he had left?*" He nodded. "Yep, pretty sure that was it."

Closing his eyes on a wince, Drew shook his head. "Right, fine. I remember."

"And *then* you hit me." Bas touched his jaw as if the long-healed injury might still be tender. "Hard. Aaaand, I went with you to help Cam. So this is what we call *payback*."

Drew folded his arms over his chest. Bas had conveniently forgotten a few pesky facts, as he tended to do. "Your brother was following a guy who was *not* yet his boyfriend to a remote island. A guy who happened to be an FBI agent *and* was related to the pilot we all thought had killed your parents and my sister. *And* you had just figured out that there was a connection between our parents' oldest friend and the plane crash. I shouldn't have *had* to hit you to get you to come."

"Eh. All that's irrelevant. You did hit me. *Hard*," Bas repeated, blue eyes wide and guileless. "It's not about right or wrong here, McMann. It's about you hitting me, and *payback*."

Drew shook his head and thunked his head back against the headrest repeatedly. "Serves me right for trying to help your sorry ass. And Cam's. No good deed goes unpunished."

"*No good deed goes unpunished,*" Bas mocked, sing-song. "Listen to you. It's a Halloween party, Andrew. With a bunch of old friends we haven't seen in a decade. Costumes, and candy, and spooky music. Hardly a firing squad in sight." He shook his head, pulling the handle to open his door. "I thought we decided a long time ago that I was the pissy, dramatic one in this friendship."

"Who decided that?"

Bas waved a hand in the air. "Who remembers? Point is, it's been that way forever. We can't be changing the rules thirty years down the line. I won't know who I am anymore."

"Yeah, right." Drew opened his door and pulled himself out to stand on the sidewalk. "You'll still be Sebastian Seaver," he said gloomily. "Millionaire heir. Tech genius. Too single-minded to care about other people's boundaries." Or their hatred of loud parties, costumes, and high school 'friends' they hadn't seen in a decade. "But somehow people like you anyway."

He walked around the hood of the car and stood next to Bas for a second, staring up at the house. "Meanwhile, *I* am a humble lawyer..."

"Humble," Bas scoffed.

"A *humble lawyer,*" Drew repeated loudly. "A man who has more than a dozen people reporting to him, a mother to support, and a reputation to uphold - and I'm letting you drag me out, dressed like this." He looked down at the thick work boots, flannel shirt, necklace, and jeans that made up his costume. "Nobody's going to get who we are, you know. I look like a grunge musician, circa 1990-something."

"Okay, first, these are kick-ass costumes!" Bas said, offended. "The Winchesters from Supernatural? Everyone with a brain will get this. And second, I chose these outfits for you because I knew you would want something low-key! You should be thanking me, man. I debated making you come as a Pokémon."

"Like hell. There are limits," Drew told him, leaning back against the car.

"To our friendship?" Bas looked offended.

"To how much I can be guilted."

"Fine. Four hours," Bas said. "Then the debt is cleared."

"Jesus. I smacked your face. Once. I didn't fatally stab you. They're going to be getting drunk and playing games like we're still in high school," Drew argued. "A time in my life I don't need to relive. I'll give you two hours. Tops." Two hours to nurse a drink so he could get them home safely was plenty.

Bas shook his head as he started walking backward across the wide, leaf-strewn street toward the driveway. "The punch was a betrayal, McMann. It wasn't fatal, but the pain ran deep. *And* these people are old friends, so it's not like I'm torturing you in a dungeon here. No skin flaying. All your teeth will remain intact. Three hours, final offer."

"*Fine.*" Drew pushed himself off the car and reluctantly followed his best friend. "Do you realize how often we have followed this pattern? You dragging me somewhere - whether it was summer camp, or some terrible party with warm beer, or that Frisbee golf team - all so you could hook up with a…" He paused, horrified. "Oh, Sebastian. Tell me we're not here so you can hook up with some girl. Please?"

"We're not here so I can hook up," Bas repeated duti-fully, throwing an arm around Drew's shoulder as they reached the bottom of the driveway. Though Bas was stockier than Drew, far more muscular, they were nearly the same height, which meant Drew had to lean toward Bas in order to walk this way. It brought Drew close enough to smell Sebastian - some cologne that smelled like bay leaves, along with the salt and spice that was uniquely Bas. The smell made Drew's heartbeat accelerate, just as it had since they were fourteen, despite all the very important reasons why it shouldn't: their lifelong friendship, Drew's (brief, disastrous) relationship with Bas's brother, Bas's (very brief, tragic) engagement to Drew's sister, and the fact that unlike Drew, Bas was one hundred percent straight.

Drew had to remind himself that it would be weird to sniff his best friend too deeply, that it wouldn't be cool to lean his head on Bas's shoulder, that it was playing with fire to be this close.

"I brought you here tonight for altruistic motives, young Andrew!" Bas was saying. "I think we've both been under a lot of stress. First, we found out the crash wasn't an accident, then we found that Uncle Shaw... I mean, *Senator* Shaw," Bas corrected himself impatiently, "betrayed his own best friends and engineered the crash. And now we can't fucking do anything about it because the Shaw kid won't come forward..."

"Give Cain a break. He's a good kid, and he loves his dad, despite his dad being an asshole. Not all of us had perfect fathers, recall."

Drew wondered if his own father was still in Thailand, where he'd fled after his divorce from Drew's mother was finalized last summer. One thing was for sure - he hadn't bothered to leave Drew any contact information.

"But I get what you're saying," Drew told him. "You want to let off steam."

"No! Actually, I want *you* to let off steam."

"What?"

"Listen. As you so *forcefully* demonstrated, I wallowed for a long while after my parents and Amy died. And meanwhile, there you were, stepping up and helping Cam run things at Seaver Tech."

"It's my job," Drew reminded him.

"Yeah, but that doesn't mean it was easy for you to do it. Not while you were grieving. I mean, Amy was your sister."

Drew nodded, feeling the familiar guilt that hearing Amy's name always provoked. Losing her *had* been hard, even though the only thing they'd had in common besides their last name was falling in love with Sebastian Seaver. Drew missed her gentle laugh, the bright-eyed optimism that ran counter to his own sometimes-cynical world view, and the simple knowledge that someone else on earth had come from the same place as him.

Still, the hardest aspect of her death had been dealing with the emotional fallout as his parents' marriage imploded, as Cam and Bas floundered, and as he wondered why *he'd* lived to pine for Sebastian, while the woman Sebastian loved had been taken from him.

Survivor's guilt was a bitch.

"So, I'm saying tonight is your night to cut loose," Bas told him. "It's your turn to lose that iron control and lean on me for a change."

"Me?"

"Yeah, *you*! Pretend you're not an octogenarian whose idea of a good time is NPR and a hot water bottle. Live a little. Get a little messy." Bas reached over and mussed Drew's hair, looking frustrated when the silky strands fell right back into place, as always. "If that's possible."

Drew shook his head. "I highly doubt it. But listen, I don't want to drink. Better let me be designated…"

"No! Hell no. You're not driving us home tonight." Bas shook his head. "Dude, just have fun. Dance, drink, eat fried food of dubious origin from bowls into which dozens of grimy hands have reached. And I will be here to take care of you."

Drew blinked and stopped walking. It wasn't that he didn't believe Sebastian - in thirty years of friendship, he could count on one hand the number of times Sebastian had disappointed him, and most of those weren't Bas's fault anyway. It shouldn't have mattered to Drew that Bas had kissed him once, back at summer camp, and then promptly lost his virginity to some long-forgotten girl named Rai who worked the movie theater at the mall; or that five years ago he'd abandoned Drew at a charity benefit, so he could go home with Misty Sturmacher, whose breasts grew in proportion to her investment portfolio; or that he'd actually *proposed* to Drew's sister Amy, even though... even though...

Nope. Drew put a mental line under that topic and moved on.

Drew was just used to being the nursemaid, the one who'd make sure his friends got home safely. *Captain Control*, as one of Drew's college friends used to call him. And Drew liked it that way just fine.

"I don't get why it's important to you that I get drunk."

"It's not about you getting drunk. Drink or don't, I don't care. Just don't worry about it if you *do*. Loosen up. De-stress, before you die of a heart-attack." Bas shook Drew's shoulder before releasing him, and Drew took one final inhale of Bas-scented air before straightening up, fortifying himself for what would undoubtedly be a long fucking night.

They made it to the top of the driveway, and a vaguely-familiar, petite, dark-haired woman wearing a skimpy bunny costume greeted them. "Ohmigod! Sebastian Seaver! I can't believe it! I haven't seen you in, like, ten years!"

Bas smiled and stepped forward to press a kiss to her cheek. "At least! Vanya. It's great to see you, too."

Vanya turned to Drew, and she let out a tiny but incredibly high-pitched scream as she launched herself into his arms. "Oh, and oh my god, *Drew!* You guys are still together! How long has it been now? Fifteen years or something?"

Drew blanched. Together? "N-no. No, God. No. *No.* We aren't. No."

Sebastian laughed easily and elbowed Drew in the side as he explained to Vanya, "Lawyer. Makes his living with compelling arguments like that. Defendants quake in fear."

Vanya blinked in confusion, like she was still waiting for someone to answer the question.

"We aren't together," Drew was finally composed enough to explain. "We're just friends. We've only ever been friends."

He debated adding something about Amy, but her engagement to Bas had never made the society pages - it had been too new at the time of the crash - and bringing her up now felt cowardly. An unspoken, *See? Here is the evidence that I have never had untoward thoughts about my straight best friend.* Instead, he added, "Bas is straight."

"Oh. My. *God*," Vanya said again, and Drew remembered this had been her favorite expression back in high school too. One that had a hundred different connotations based on inflection. "But you were always together! Like, literally every time we hung out. I was so sure you guys were a thing! Wait until I tell Keisha and Jen. They will *die.*"

The hairs at the back of Drew's neck shifted uncomfortably. They would die when she told them *what*? That Sebastian was single? Suddenly, Drew was strangely eager to bind himself to Bas for the rest of the night. He absolutely hated... *hated*... watching Bas flirt.

"Come on, Bas," Drew said, clapping an arm on his shoulder. "I really need a drink."

"Yeah, go!" Vanya waved them off with a smile, likely eager to go and tell everyone her new info. "Bar's in the garage. Geller Conroy is mixing drinks tonight and he'll hook you up! The punch tastes like cinnamon red-hots!" She paused for a second. "And I love the sexy lumberjack look, or whatever you two are going for!"

"Yes! Yes, that's it. We're a pair of sexy lumberjacks," Drew agreed, trying to restrain his laughter. He couldn't resist whispering in Sebastian's ear, "Told you so, Dean."

"Not another word, Sam," he warned, steering Drew toward the bright lights of the garage bar, where he accepted a tall plastic cup of deep red liquid.

"Cinnamon red-hots? Your favorite candy in the form of an alcoholic beverage?" Bas said, nudging his shoulder. "Pretty sure this is fate telling you to drink up, counselor."

Drew shook his head as the scent of his best friend's cologne washed over him again, and lust, hot and proprietary, crashed through his bloodstream like a tsunami.

Drew didn't believe in fate. Not anymore. These days he placed his trust in his own self-control - self-control that hadn't faltered around Bas since that fateful day at summer camp almost sixteen years ago.

One drink, he told himself. *You handled Bas and Amy getting engaged and managed to keep your mouth shut about your feelings. You can handle one little drink.*

"Sounds delicious," he agreed. And he tipped his cup back, covering Bas's scent with the pungent smell of cinnamon.

"CINNAMON RED-HOTS are the devil's tool," Drew told Bas nearly four hours later, but somehow it came out garbled, like some component of his mouth was malfunctioning. He carefully ran his tongue over his teeth, and found to his horror that he couldn't feel *either*. "Are my teeth gone or is my tongue?" he demanded, opening his mouth wide for Bas's inspection.

Sebastian, who was sitting next to him on the carpeted stairs that led to the second floor, obediently looked at Drew's mouth. "All still there," he promised, his smile wider than Drew remembered seeing it in a while. "I wouldn't let you misplace them."

Drew nodded, slow and deep - the only kind of head movement he could manage currently. Of *course* his teeth and tongue weren't missing. Of *course* his best friend in the entire universe, Sebastian Seaver, would never let anything happen to him. He went to lean his head on Bas's shoulder, as a sign of his trust… and found that it was already laying there.

Huh.

Bas smelled fucking delicious.

"Uh, thank you?" Bas snickered. "I think. Just don't get any cannibalistic ideas, drunk boy."

"Oh, fuck. I said it out loud when it was a secret!" Drew said in a horrified whisper.

Bas laughed, loud and long. "You have totally repaid any debt you owed me. This is priceless." He braced his hand in the middle of Drew's back, and Drew forgot what he'd been worried about.

"It is the most fun I've ever had in a long, long while! Thanks to *you*." Drew beamed up at Sebastian, who was so handsome, Drew couldn't remember why he wasn't supposed to kiss him. "We can stay longer if you want."

"Long as you want," Bas promised, wearing the smirky grin Drew had loved for years.

Years. *Friends*. No kissing friends.

Drew sighed.

"Aw. Everything okay?" Bas asked. His hand rubbed Drew's back in a slow circle that made Drew's arms and legs prickle with electricity that felt dangerous somehow. "They're playing cards or something in the other room if you want."

"Yes," Drew decided. "Cards." He heaved himself to his feet, pleased to see that he was steady.

"One more water before we go," Bas reminded him, steering him toward the kitchen first.

"Water is *not* delicious."

"So true, McMann. But it *is* gonna help the hangover you are *one-hundred percent* gonna have tomorrow." Bas handed him a plastic cup and Drew sucked it down obediently before tossing the empty cup in the recycle bin.

"Why does there have to be a hangover? Why can't good things just be good and we don't have to… pay?"

Bas blinked, and his eyes got soft as he guided Drew to the living room. "You know, I think I like Drunk Drew. You're so philosophical."

"I'm always phil-sofal. I have thoughts a lot. But I don't tell you because they're so crazy." Drew waved his hand with the coordination of a newborn. "You wouldn't believe it."

Bas looked down at his shoes like they were fascinating, but Drew caught the edges of his mouth tipping up, his lips pressing together the way they did when he was trying to hold back laughter. "Yeah? I thought you told me everything!" Bas joked. Or at least it seemed like a joke.

But Drew couldn't help but reply honestly. "Not everything."

"Sebastian and Drew!" Vanya called out excitedly from a spot in the middle of the room. "Come sit by me!" The living room was large, with two sofas, a love seat, and a pair of chairs all clustered around a low, wooden coffee table. However, none of the seats were in use, as everyone was sprawled on the floor.

Vanya was sitting with her back propped against the front of the love-seat. Her eyes were half-mast and unfocused, but she smiled as Drew plunked down beside her.

"What are you playing?" Bas asked, as he took a seat on Drew's other side.

"Either/Or," a girl across from Vanya said. Drew vaguely recognized her as Vanya's friend Keisha. "You just pick which thing you like best."

"I am *excellent* at picking things," Drew confided. "Gimme one."

"Okay, um… Wear nothing but pink forever, or have pink disappear from the world completely."

Drew blinked. This was harder than he'd imagined. "Wear pink. Nothing should *ever* disappear from the earth," he said with the earnestness of the thoroughly inebriated.

Vanya nodded and held up her hand for a high-five. "Good logic."

"I'm an attorney," Drew said modestly. Beside him, Bas convulsed with laughter.

"Hey, give Bas one!" Drew shouted to no one in particular.

"Ooooh, I know!" Vanya said, her smile sharpening slightly as her eyes lasered in on Sebastian. Drew had never noticed how much she resembled a fox. "Would you rather… Kiss Drew, or lose Drew forever?"

Drew blinked. *What?*

He turned to Bas, who was looking at him seriously, though that same little smile tilted the edges of his lips. That smile *did* things to Drew's insides. "I'd kiss Drew, obviously."

"Prove it," the demon-known-as-Keisha demanded, and even through his alcohol haze, Drew could feel his heart rate climbing, his stomach churning. He wanted it, and he didn't… either/or.

Bas lifted an eyebrow and looked around at the assembled people uncomfortably. "We're not twelve-year-olds playing spin the bottle, people. I'm not kissing him to prove something." He looked at Drew with wide eyes. "Right?"

Drew blinked and nodded. "No. Of course. You don't have to if you don't want to."

"If *I* don't want to?" Bas's eyes narrowed. "It's… I mean, it's not that I don't love you. Just…Not in a kissing way." He laughed, but it sounded a tiny bit strained to Drew's ears.

"I get it," Drew assured him, but somehow Bas didn't seem assured.

"I mean, you feel the same way, Drew." Bas rolled his eyes. "You wouldn't *want* me to kiss you. Right?" *Not again*, was the hidden subtext, the reminder of that long-ago summer and the "*silly, little*" kiss they'd shared.

Drew blinked, caught between what he should say and what he really wanted to say. He was just sober enough to know that there was only one right answer to this question, and just drunk enough - just drunk and *desperately in love* enough - to wonder if he could get away with telling the truth this once.

He hesitated, and in the end, that was his ruination.

"I think he does," Keisha whispered. "I think he wants you to."

The woman next to her, a curly-haired person who might have been called Jen, nodded with alcohol-soaked solemnity. "He totally does."

"Ah, poor boo," Vanya clucked sympathetically, pulling Drew into her side. She smelled like cinnamon red hots, which was far less comforting a scent than it used to be. "He doesn't wanna kiss you, but you don't need him."

I do, though, Drew thought sadly. *He's my best friend. I always need him.*

The women collectively said, "*Awww!*" and Drew realized he'd spoken his thoughts aloud again. *Oops.*

"Jesus," Bas muttered. "Drew, you don't know what you're saying. Maybe it's time we go."

"Hey! Leave him alone," Keisha told Bas, all fiery and defensive. "You've been hurtful enough."

"Hurtful! He's my *friend*. It's not hurtful to say…"

"You look at that face," Jen said adamantly, staring at Drew like she wanted to leap over the coffee table and hug him. "Look at his *eyes*. He's hurt."

"Drew." Bas sounded exasperated, but when Drew turned his head, Bas's eyes widened. "Jesus. Do you want me to kiss you?"

Drew shook his head, and it wasn't really a lie because he didn't want Bas to kiss him *like this*. Not with an audience. Not when Bas wasn't into it.

But apparently, the subtlety of his thoughts was lost in whatever emotion Drew was wearing on his face.

"Oh, fine," Bas said, rolling his eyes. "This is so not a big deal."

Bas grabbed Drew's jaw between his thumb and forefinger, turning Drew's head until they were facing one another. He sidled closer so their thighs were pressed close together, and leaned forward.

Holy shit. Drew could feel Sebastian's warm breath ghosting against his lips. It was agonizingly wonderful and terrifying at the same time. He swallowed hard. If this was his only opportunity to have this, he was going to enjoy every second.

He let his eyes shut as Bas drew him closer, and then, after a decade and a half apart, their lips touched.

It was... well, to be honest it was entirely anticlimactic, which was a little bit heartbreaking. Drew had dreamed of kissing Bas again - and, yeah, fine, a lot *more* than just kissing, if he was being honest - and here he'd finally done it, only to find that it was actually kinda dry and dull. He'd had better kisses from a dozen guys. He'd had better kisses from *Bas's little brother.*

He pulled back, opened his eyes, and cleared his throat. "Okay, then," he said. "I guess you proved..."

But he never got a chance to finish the sentence. Sebastian made a low noise and pulled him forward again, pressing their mouths together once more, firmer this time. Again and again and again, tiny kisses, parting Drew's lips, allowing him to taste Bas's flavor, which was more potent than any Halloween punch. His hands lifted into Bas's hair of their own accord, clasping in the soft strands.

This was the stuff of dreams, the reason he'd never been able to - and never really *wanted* to - fall in love with anyone else.

He darted his tongue out to trace Sebastian's lower lip... And someone - Keisha or Jen, maybe - whistled shrilly.

"That's what I'm talking about! Kiss him good!"

Drew smiled. *This is already good. I have wanted this for so long*, he thought. *God. Years and years and years. Every time I've looked at him.*

Bas pulled back and looked at Drew like he'd never seen him before. "What?" Bas demanded.

Oh, fuck. Drew's stupid mouth had opened and once again, his drunken thoughts had fallen out. Panic began to penetrate the cinnamon-fireball haze, and his mind started to churn.

This was the problem with losing control. *This* was why he should never have allowed tonight to happen. Fuck, fuck, *fuck*!

"What do you mean, *what?*" Drew repeated helplessly. "I didn't say anything!"

But Bas had already turned his head away and was pushing himself to his feet.

The women had gone quiet. Drew noticed in a distant sort of way that they stared, mouths open, like they were watching a train wreck. In a way, they were.

Bas reached out a hand to help Drew up, then wrapped his arm around Drew's waist, but he didn't look Drew in the eye. "I'll get you home," he said stiffly, moving them toward the door and then outside, not pausing to say goodbye to anyone.

"We should… maybe we should…" Drew began.

"God, I can't believe how drunk you are!" Bas said, smiling widely as they swayed down the front lawn. "I would never believe it if I hadn't seen it."

"Not as drunk as I was," Drew told him honestly. "And, Sebastian, I think we should talk about what happened in there. I apologize for—"

"So, *so* drunk!" Bas insisted. "I swear, I was getting a contact buzz for a second there. Ha ha!" He shook his head as they arrived at the car, still smiling that same forced smile. And even though Drew could have held himself up perfectly well - really, there was nothing like a massive dose of adrenaline to make him sober up quickly - he let Bas open his door and ease him into the passenger's seat… which was about when he noticed that Bas's jeans were a little bit snug, and he was pretty definitely sporting an erection.

And that was enough to kill the rest of his buzz.

Was it possible? Sebastian had gotten hard... from kissing Drew?

Oh, they *so* needed to talk about this, and soon. Drew knew his best friend like he knew his own mind, and if he let Bas fall into his thoughts over this, the same genius brain that made Sebastian such an amazing innovator and problem-solver would turn this issue over relentlessly until it came to some crazy conclusion, maybe five or ten years down the line.

Damage control was the name of the game now.

"Hey, Bas," Drew said again, once Bas had gotten into his seat and started the engine. "This was just a silly thing. A stupid game. Don't, ah... Don't hide from me, okay?"

"Hush," Bas said indulgently, patting Drew on the shoulder before turning the heat up high. "I've never hidden. We'll talk tomorrow. Just rest, Drew. Close your eyes, okay?"

Tomorrow. Hell, yes, they would talk tomorrow, Drew thought, steeling himself against the lulling motion of the car and the warmth from the vent as he fought to keep his eyes open.

But when he woke up the following morning, alone and hungover in his bed, his best friend had gone, and he wouldn't be back anytime soon.

CHAPTER TWO

*B*oston was really fucking bleak at the end of December.

Usually the view from his top-floor office made Drew McMann smile, regardless of the season. He was high enough above the city that he didn't see the slush and grime in the winter or smell the baked-in oily fumes that clung to the pavement all summer. From up here, he could pretend the whole city was the glittering harbor, stretching out in endless blue all the way past the horizon.

But not today.

Today, it was all endlessly grey and depressing as hell, but it suited his mood. There was something about the period between Christmas and New Year that always made him feel this way - a kind of lame-duck suspended animation. It was too late to change the mistakes of the past year, and too soon to make the changes he knew he needed to make for the coming year, so for this one week, he would wallow.

"Boss?"

Drew turned in his chair to find his assistant, Peter,

looking down at him, one immaculate eyebrow raised and his tablet propped against his arm. "Hmm?"

"I asked if you were fine with pushing back the Tekko meeting until next week, for Paula's sake."

"Paula?" Drew repeated, his mind as heavy and blank as the clouds outside.

"Paula Drake?" Peter gave a perfectly-calibrated sigh, just forceful enough to rebuke Drew without being overtly disrespectful. Peter was a master at sighing. "Have you even heard a word I've said?"

Drew ran a hand down his tie and grimaced. He hadn't. Not a single word. Zoning out at the office was one of his pet-peeves, generally speaking, and it pissed him off that it had been happening to him more and more often. People tasked with running a multi-national company like Seaver Tech didn't have time for daydreaming and navel-gazing. It was the kind of behavior Drew had given other people shit for in the not-so-distant past - his friend Cam Seaver, in particular.

He was pretty glad Cam had been too busy to pop in on him much over the past few weeks.

"Sorry, Peter," he said, sliding his legs under the desk and looking up at his assistant. "Continue. Please."

Five-and-a-half feet tall and lean-framed, Peter wasn't intimidating physically, but he didn't need to be. He could communicate displeasure with a raised eyebrow more effectively than Drew could in a paragraph of text. He was fiercely loyal to Drew, and one of the few assistants he'd ever had who could counteract Drew's frequent habit of micromanaging. But Peter was way too professional to ever sit around and chit-chat.

Which made it all the more bizarre when, after observing Drew for half a minute, Peter sat down in the chair across from Drew's, folded his hands atop the tablet on his lap, and narrowed his dark brown eyes.

"What's going on with you these days?"

Well. That was a loaded question. Drew could start with the plane crash a year and a half ago that had killed three people he loved, though that was old news. His parents' subsequent divorce and his dad's retreat to Thailand with a woman younger than Drew was also well-known. Hmmm... He could mention how his mother, God love her, had no concept of money other than how to spend it, and needed Drew to handle her life for her, but that sounded too self-pitying. He could talk about the horror of learning Emmett Shaw - one of his father's oldest friends and a man Drew had thought of as an uncle - had financed the plane crash, or the absolute mind-fuck of finding out that Shaw had been acting on the orders of some Russian crime syndicate no one had ever heard of, but both those things were secrets that could get someone killed.

Or, he could talk about what was really bothering him these days: that his best friend Sebastian had stopped talking to him.

Except *that* was just too pathetic to discuss.

He grabbed a heavy pen off his desk, running his fingers over the textured satin finish, feeling the comforting heft of it in his hand. "Not a thing is going on," he told Peter finally. "Nothing at all."

Peter clearly didn't believe him, but he was far too professional to do more than give a small head-shake before returning his gaze to his tablet.

"Well, then, *as I said*," Peter continued with the air of a long-suffering martyr, and Drew felt his lips twitch, despite himself. "Paula Drake's mother fell and broke her hip, so we should probably push back the Tekko meeting until next week, unless you feel the burning need to get yourself up to speed and handle it yourself, in which case I can ask…"

"No. God, no," Drew said, waving a hand through the air. "Wait for Paula. In fact, let's see if we can push it back to the fifth or even later. Give her some breathing room."

Peter nodded and made a note on his tablet. "Done. Ah, Margaret stopped by earlier and mentioned getting a couple of emails from a guy who used to work with Levi Seaver back in the day. Looks like he needs a job or a recommendation? I'm having her forward me copies of the emails."

"A job inquiry?" Drew asked. "Shouldn't that be an HR thing?"

"The guy says he was a close friend, and he's been pretty insistent. She didn't want to push it off without checking."

"Margaret is Cam and Sebastian's assistant," Drew pointed out unnecessarily. "If they're the ones getting the emails, shouldn't she check with one of them?"

"Yeah, but Cam's been crazy busy for the past couple of weeks and hasn't had time to check into it. And Sebastian, well. I guess he hasn't been checking his email." Peter shrugged, once again managing to convey volumes in a single gesture.

Drew rubbed a hand over his forehead and nodded, understanding all that Peter was too diplomatic to mention.

Sebastian Seaver was a genius - with all the wonderful and really, really terrible things that entailed. He thrived on logic, but hated rules. Was single-minded in his focus to the exclusion of all other things, but somehow made intuitive leaps in a heartbeat. He was stubborn as hell, and the funniest, most generous human being Drew had ever known.

He had been Drew's best friend since infancy. His sister Amy's fiancé, before her death in the crash. The one constant force in his life.

And he was the only man Drew had ever loved.

He sighed. "Let Margaret know I'll handle it."

Peter nodded. "Last thing on the list is the Macauley case. Katrina handled the depositions last week. You'll find everything on the drive. But Turner is handing out Federal subpoenas like candy, so I'm pretty sure there'll be another round."

Drew rubbed the spot between his eyebrows where a headache was starting to brew. Never a good sign this early in the day. "Get Devi on it, too," he instructed. "He needs the practice, and Crista's going out on maternity leave in February, so it's time to bring him up to speed."

Peter nodded at his tablet again, and Drew tapped his pen on the desktop impatiently. "I have a bunch of HR stuff to work on today - personnel requests and employee reviews."

"Thought the reviews were due to HR before Christmas," Peter countered. Drew pursed his lips and pretended to make a note on the pad in front of him.

"Mr. Kelley. Consistently. Challenges. Authority," he said aloud, and Peter snorted but didn't move from his seat.

"Something else?" Drew asked, nodding toward the tablet, and Peter hesitated, but nodded.

"You got an email from a Mark Charbonnier."

Charbonnier… the name was vaguely familiar, but Drew couldn't place it. He shrugged as he pulled the top file from the short stack at the side of his desk. "Is he from one of those charity things my mother contributes to? She's in Martinique through the New Year, so they'll have to wait for a donation."

"Not a charity, a *man*. Apparently he met you at *The Station* back in November," Peter said blandly.

Drew's eyes flew to Peter's, a clash of brown on brown, and he felt an unaccustomed blush climb his cheeks.

The Station was an upscale gay bar not far from Union Square. It was, as its name implied, not a place where you'd want to linger, but a quick stopping point between loneliness and a fast fuck. The kind of place Drew generally avoided, except when he was desperately trying to gain a little perspective on the stupid, juvenile, ridiculous brush of lips that had turned his mind inside out on Halloween.

Spoiler: it hadn't worked.

Drew could barely remember the guy who'd approached him that evening - couldn't recall his features well enough to make a police sketch. Had they even exchanged numbers? Had Drew really been distracted and foolish enough to give the guy his full name? *God.*

"What the hell is he emailing *you* for?"

Peter's gaze was implacable. "You likely told him your name and where you worked, and he looked up your email address in the business directory so he could ask you out to dinner. Sounds pretty resourceful *and* dedicated."

Ugh. Or desperate and stalkerish. Drew opened the file in front of him. "I have no idea who he is. Tell him thanks, but no thanks."

For once, Peter remained still, making no move to note anything in his tablet of doom.

"Or forward the email to me and I'll handle it," Drew sighed. It wasn't fair to ask his assistant to clean up his personal messes, after all.

"I have no problem taking care of it. But I'm wondering if... Don't kill me, but there was a picture with the email."

Drew blinked and looked up. "A picture?"

"The guy is quite good-looking," Peter continued matter-of-factly, though his own face burned scarlet. "Like..." He cleared his throat. "Well, if I'm being frank, he's hot as hell."

Drew threw his pen down on the desk and leaned back in his chair. "Oh?" he drawled, reluctantly amused.

Peter nodded, clearly beyond all propriety now. "Insanely so. Hot enough that I forwarded the picture to my boyfriend, who confirmed it."

"Thoughtful of you to undertake independent confirmation," Drew said wryly.

"How long have I worked here?" Peter demanded, sitting forward, his serious eyes locked on Drew. "Never mind, I'll tell you. It's been over a year. And in all that time, while I've been keeping your schedule, do you know how many guys you've dated for any length of time? One: Cam Seaver. And even *I* knew that was some kind of crazy grief-induced interlude."

Drew bristled. After the crash, it had seemed oddly right and normal to him that he and Cam, his best friend's brother, would turn to each other. Comfort each other. Cam had just lost his parents, the same way Drew had lost Amy. And Sebastian... well, Sebastian had checked-out on both of them for a long while.

But Cam had realized how wrong they were for each other long before Drew had - Drew's need to protect and comfort had driven Cam batshit, and the word *control freak* had been tossed back and forth more than once. All in all, Drew was happy that Cam had found his boyfriend Cort, and that their friendship had survived intact, but he didn't appreciate being reminded of his mistakes.

"Your point, Peter? Assuming you have one." The hard, cold voice his friend Cain called Drew's "lawyer voice" was as comfortable as a second skin.

"My point is that I'm concerned about you. I get it's not my place to say anything, which is why I've kept quiet," Peter said in a rush. "I get that you're gonna be all pissy about this.

I'm very, *very* aware. But I like you enough to share this truth with you anyway, which really should count for something when you're writing my review." He cleared his throat, and Drew rolled his eyes. "You spend way too much time working. And when you're not here, you're generally making sure Sebastian Seaver is okay or helping your mother with her charity things. Do you know that you escorted her to seventy-three charity dinners or galas last year? *Seventy. Three.*"

Drew pressed his tongue against the back of his teeth to keep from laughing at the outrage in Peter's voice. "Did you know that figure off the top of your head?"

"Of course not! I prepared notes. Would you like to see them?"

"I don't think that'll be necessary." Drew held up a restraining hand when it seemed like Peter would run back to his desk to retrieve them.

"Right, well. You deserve more. You're young, you're cute... I mean, in a boring way that does nothing for me at all," Peter assured him.

Drew couldn't hold back his snort. "Right. Good to know."

"Dark, puppy dog eyes, perfect brown hair, tall, great shape," Peter said, ticking Drew's attributes off like he was making a list on his infernal tablet. "Impeccable career, really intelligent, funny, patient with employees who overstep boundaries..."

"You hope."

"Oh, I really do," Peter said fervently. "My point is, you deserve to have fun. This Mark guy is cute. And as the keeper of your schedule, I know for a fact that you have a light week this week for social obligations. Maybe meet the guy for coffee. Talk. See where it goes."

Drew cleared his throat, looked into Peter's concerned

eyes, and nodded once. "Your opinion is noted. I'll consider it."

"Excellent! I'll hold off on replying for a couple of days then while you ponder. And, uh, I'll grab you some lunch in a minute too." He smiled the winning smile of a man whose performance review was about to be written, then stood abruptly and strode toward the door, likely before Drew could change his mind.

The second the door closed behind him, Drew dropped his calm mask and stood up to pace, more agitated than he'd been in a long time. Drew wasn't angry at Peter, though. Far from it. He was angry at *himself*.

Angry because, one stupid summer half a lifetime ago, his stubborn heart had decided his straight best friend was the only man for him.

Angry because, despite all the years since then, all the men he'd dated, and the men he'd slept with, he'd never found anyone who made him feel half as strong and vital and necessary, even in the *throes of orgasm*, as Sebastian did while they were playing video games on his couch.

Angry because loving Bas was beyond logic and out of his control, leading him to whisper drunken truths that should never have seen the light of day and fucked up the best friendship he'd ever had.

Angry because, despite all of that, he knew he wouldn't be following up with Mark from The Station, no matter how hot and successful and perfect he was, because he wasn't Sebastian Seaver.

Leaning his head against the cold glass of the window, Drew closed his eyes. There were days he would give anything to wake up and not have Bas be the first thing on his mind - the blue of his eyes, the tilt of his smile. Desperate times, like those first days after Bas and Amy had started dating, when he'd wanted to move somewhere, anywhere, and forcibly eject Bas from his thoughts.

But the practical part of him knew that whatever heartbreak he suffered was simply the opportunity cost for having Sebastian Seaver as his best friend.

Drew couldn't recall a season of his life when Bas hadn't fascinated and challenged and encouraged him on a fundamental level. Bas had sat next to him on the sofa when Drew came out to his parents, tutored him in math and computer science all through college, rescued him from dates gone bad, insisted that he couldn't run Seaver Tech without Drew at his side. And in exchange, Drew had been his confidant, his mouthpiece, the Alfred to his Batman, always making sure that Bas had what he needed while he focused on his work.

Every day of their lives, Bas and his crazy genius brain had made Drew think bigger, dream bigger. And now, thirty-something years after they'd first played together as babies, Sebastian Seaver had burrowed into Drew's skin, changed his goddamn DNA.

He wasn't sure how to move on from that.

He wasn't sure he wanted to.

Drew's problem wasn't finding the right someone to fall in love with; it was that he'd already fallen for the *perfect person* - and he kept falling, over and over and over again.

He turned and leaned against the window, back to the clouds, and ran a hand through his short hair, fully aware that it would flop neatly back into place as though it had never been rumpled. Inconstancy had never been Drew's problem.

A knock on the door startled him, and he glanced guiltily at the untouched reports on his desk.

Christ. He was taking navel-gazing to a whole new level.

"Come in, Peter," he called, sitting down once again.

But when the door opened, it wasn't Peter's head that appeared.

"I snuck past when Peter wasn't looking. Got a sec?" Cam asked, light blue eyes serious.

"Always," Drew replied, summoning what he hoped was a genuine-looking smile. "What can I do for you, fearless leader?"

Cam smirked as he plopped himself down in the seat before Drew's desk. "Question for you."

Drew was used to seeing Camden Seaver as young. Maybe it was because he'd always trailed after Drew and Bas like a puppy back in the day, or maybe it was because his cheeks were still dusted with freckles and his hair a mess of cowlicks, despite his twenty-six years. Even when they'd dated, he'd felt the nagging need to protect Cam from everything. But now, madly in love with his boyfriend Cort, and confident in his job as second-in-command to Sebastian at Seaver Tech, Cam had blossomed into someone Drew saw as an equal… and a really good friend.

"Sure," Drew told him. "Shoot."

"When was the last time you talked to Bas?"

Drew sighed. Maybe he should have foreseen this. He and Sebastian had been joined at the hip for years, and now things had changed. It was crazy to think everyone wouldn't have noticed.

Things had grown tense between them ever since that *stupid* high school reunion Halloween party where Drew had admitted he'd wanted Bas to kiss him for a long time. Their barbs had grown more heated, their friendly get-togethers had become cold-war standoffs, and over the past month, Bas cut Drew out of his life completely.

No more video game nights at Bas's place, no lunch breaks, no Pats games on Drew's sofa. Not a single word spoken since November. No text messages in weeks, even at Christmas. (And yeah, Drew had checked. Rather obsessively.) Being without his best friend was like losing a limb. And all because he'd lost control *one stupid time.*

And the worst part was, hurt and angry as he was, he couldn't even blame Bas entirely. Drew *had* been hiding his feelings for years. And he'd *known* Sebastian would pull this shit if Drew didn't force him to talk so he could brush it all off as a drunken misunderstanding. But he'd been too embarrassed. And then it had been too late.

A hell of a way for their friendship to die, if that's what was happening. Ironic, honestly. It wouldn't be the heartbreak of Bas's engagement to Drew's sister that tore them apart, nor the trauma of the plane crash, but a stupid kiss that would never have happened if Drew had remained in control.

But the last thing he wanted was to cause more tension among their friends by discussing this shit with Cam.

"Hard to say," Drew hedged. "We're both busy. At least, I assume he's been busy. I know *I've* been busy. Spending the holidays with my mother and her friends is enough to drive a person to drink."

"Speaking of which!" Cam said, pointing an accusing finger at Drew. "Since when do you not spend Christmas Eve with us? That's been a tradition since before I was born."

Drew shrugged. "Eh. Things change, Cammy." He waited for Cam to react to the hated childhood nickname, but beyond a slight eyeroll, he remained impassive. "You've got Cort now, and he's got his own family, with Damon and Cain and Damon's long-lost sister…What's her name again?"

"Chelsea," Cam supplied. "And Chelsea's daughter Molly. But none of that matters, idiot! We didn't see any of them for Christmas. The three of us sat around having a

Fast and Furious marathon. At least until Bas managed to drink himself into a stupor." Cam rolled his eyes. "But even if we had seen them, it wouldn't have made up for not having you there."

"That's...well. Thank you," Drew said, unexpectedly touched by Cam's words. "But my mother wanted to spend the holiday with her sister and some friends in New York, so we went down there for a long weekend. And now I'm busy writing the reviews I should have been working on." He gestured from the pen in his hand to the open file on his desk. "So..."

But Cam refused to take the hint. Instead he sat back in his seat and regarded Drew with amusement.

"Your deflection skills are amazing, McMann, but not nearly as potent as my stubbornness skills. Recall that I live with Kendrick Cortland, the man Sebastian says is like Sherlock Holmes and a golden retriever all rolled into one."

Drew snorted. Spot-on. Drew had warmed up to Cort quite a bit over the past few months, but it was insanely off-putting that the man always looked like he was laughing at a joke no one else could understand.

"You and Bas have been dancing around each other for weeks now. Why?" Cam persisted.

"I'm telling you, there's no dancing," Drew lied. There was so much dancing. Fred-and-Ginger-level dancing. "I'm not his keeper, Cam." The lies kept rolling off his tongue. "We're just... at a phase in our friendship where we need a little more time apart."

Cam snickered. "Wow. That was epic bullshit, McMann. First of all, you kinda *are* his keeper. Who got him to leave his apartment when he was totally off the rails with grief after the crash? Who tells him when it's time to leave the computer and join the three-dimensional people again? I don't know if he remembers to eat if you're not around."

Drew looked away uncomfortably. This was true. And just one of the many things Drew had been worrying about over the past month. But when Bas so clearly wanted nothing to do with him, what was Drew supposed to do?

"Plus, there's no way you'd tolerate a *phase* where you couldn't keep an eye on Bas when he was so fucked up over this Russian bullshit," Cam said triumphantly.

Aaaand there was the other thing Drew was worried about.

About a month ago, right around Thanksgiving because life was ironic that way, their friend Cain Shaw had been searching for evidence to prove that his father, Senator Emmett Shaw, had been the mastermind behind the Seavers' plane crash. Instead, he'd found evidence that Emmett Shaw and Levi Seaver had taken money from a Russian criminal organization called SILA to found Seaver Tech, and SILA had been blackmailing them for years. The group, led by a psychopath named Alexei Stornovich, had threatened to harm the entire Shaw family if Senator Shaw didn't arrange to have Levi Seaver killed.

Now, instead of finding closure for everyone involved, they'd been given an even bigger, scarier monster to bring down. A bigger, scarier problem for Bas to *obsess* over, likely making risky decisions in his anger.

Drew was pretty sure Bas hadn't spent any time in his official, executive office across the hall in weeks, which meant that he was either working from home or holed up in his private computer lab down in the basement of Seaver Tech, either working on an actual, billable Seaver Tech project, or plotting some brilliant-but-crazy scheme to get revenge on the Russian criminals. Who the hell knew?

It would be as easy as checking his keycard access to

see where he'd been spending his time, but once again, Drew resisted.

"I love that you think I can control Bas when he's got an idea in his head," he said, instead. "If he feels like he needs space, there's nothing I can do to change his mind."

"Once again, I call bullshit. You can always break through. And I'm worried about him, Drew. Really worried. His spiraling isn't healthy."

Drew sighed and met Cam's eyes. "I haven't talked to him since November."

"I knew there was something brewing the last time we met. You were both so pissy." Cam got quiet for a second. "But that long?"

"Yep. He even sends his work-related communications through Margaret," Drew confirmed.

"What the hell did you two fight about?"

Drew chuckled, once. He had no intention of sharing the particulars with Cam, but… "We didn't *fight*. We never do. Bas just… disappears."

Cam sighed. "He misses you."

"Really? Odd, because here I am!" Drew waved a hand in the air above his head. "In my office. With my working phone." He lifted his cell off the desk and gestured with it. "Not avoiding calls or texts. So he could stop missing me anytime he wanted."

Cam ignored Drew's rant. "At Christmas, he kept hoping you'd show up. He sat in the living room with us, but he kept checking the door and looking at his phone. He was like a sad little island off to one side who refused to interact except to ask for another drink. And he was drinking *vodka*, Drew. You know he only drinks the hard stuff when he's seriously upset."

A pulse of guilt made his stomach churn, and Drew hated it. Hated that he felt responsible when he hadn't been the one to pull away... and hated that Sebastian was unhappy without Drew to help him through it, even as a friend.

"Then why didn't he call?" Drew demanded, but even as he said the words, he knew the answer.

Cam raised one eyebrow, and Drew nodded, rolling his eyes.

"He's so fucking stubborn," Drew said.

"He is. And it's more than that, *you* know it. He doesn't always have the easiest time understanding where people are coming from. You think it's obvious that he could have called you at any time, but maybe he just didn't know how to begin!"

"I'll think about it," Drew said, rolling his eyes at himself. He'd given Peter pretty much the same answer about Mark.

"Good. Because we need to put all of this stuff aside and figure out how we're going to handle SILA."

"Has something new happened?" Drew asked, frowning.

"Not that I know of. It's just... I feel like we've been sitting around waiting for the other shoe to drop. Last time we met at your house after Thanksgiving, Cain said his father had warned Alexei that he wasn't to come after us."

"Right," Drew agreed. "That he had plenty of info on SILA and wouldn't hesitate to turn it over to the authorities if Alexei made a move against us."

"Yeah, but do you really think that's going to hold him off for long?" Cam demanded. "Do you really think SILA isn't planning a way to get around that? Or just plain threatening to kill the Shaw family if Senator Shaw doesn't fall back in line? How long can we trust our safety to Emmett Shaw?"

"We can't. We always knew it was a temporary peace," Drew said, tapping his pen on the desk.

"Right. And for Bas, it wasn't even *that*. He's so damn guilty, like it was *his* fault they all died since it was *his* engagement we were all going to celebrate, that he's probably working round the clock on this. And I'm worried he's going to get careless."

"Bas doesn't do careless," Drew said, but he couldn't deny that his own worry was kicking up several notches at Cam's words.

"Fine, not careless. Risky. Something that might alert Alexei that *we* aren't just sitting around waiting for them to get bored and come at us."

Drew nodded. It was distinctly possible.

"We all need to be on the same page." Cam ran a hand through his hair, his blue eyes troubled. "And we need to end this once and for all. There's a horrible cloud looming over all of us, and we're waiting for the storm to unleash. It's no way to live a life, when you can't plan your future more than a couple of weeks in advance. I have this man by my side who's more amazing than I ever could have imagined. I want to plan a life for us, and I don't want to waste another single day worrying about criminals and conspiracies. I want dogs and kids Cort can spoil and protect. I want Bas to start working on AI so he can finally *build* a woman who can put up with his moody bullshit."

Drew laughed.

"And I want you to meet some hot guy who gets hard from listening to NPR like you seem to," Cam continued with a grin. "Someone you can lean on and build a life with, where your primary job isn't worrying about Bas and the rest of us. I want us all to move on, *together*, and to do that, we have to work together to get past all the stuff that's keeping us in suspended animation."

Suspended animation. Just like this depressing week between week between holidays. Just like the past fifteen years of wanting a man who could never love him.

And *whoa*. Those words hit him like a blow to the solar plexus.

He wanted that future Cam had painted. The nice, hot guy, the kids and the dog. Life was short - the past year or so had proven that with gut-twisting clarity - and he'd spent half of his trapped like one of those insects in amber, waiting for a man who couldn't love him.

It wasn't that Drew hadn't proven his love enough. It wasn't that Drew hadn't made enough effort or sacrificed enough of his life. It was that Bas… wasn't gay.

He. Wasn't. Gay.

One mind-blowing kiss in October didn't change that, and neither would the passage of time or the power of Drew's love.

He'd let their friendship expand to fill the empty places inside him, and had started to *expect* things subconsciously. Like that Bas would finally change his mind or fall in love with Drew? He wanted to deny the idea even to himself, but he couldn't. *God*, what an idiot he was.

But maybe… maybe *somehow*… he could find a way to change things for both of them.

"I'll talk to him," Drew said. "I'll head down to his dungeon in a bit, and I'll invite him to a meeting at my house where we can all get together and talk about this. Let's say, Saturday morning." Drew took out his phone to make a note. "Or we could do afternoon. Check with the guys."

"Are you going to make pumpkin muffins?"

Drew lifted his head in surprise. His eyes met Cam's, which had lost their serious cast now that he was confident Drew would handle Bas, sparkling blue in the overhead light. "Pumpkin's so last month. Double-chocolate says New Year."

"Martha Stewart McMann." Cam stood to leave, a smirk on his face. "Who would've thought. How come you never made baked goods for me when we were dating?"

"My inner baker was still evolving," Drew said drily. "All for the best really. You'd never have broken things off if you'd gotten a taste of the chocolate muffins, and then where would Cortland be?"

Cam grinned hugely and leaned over to ruffle Drew's hair, completely unaffected by Drew's single raised eyebrow. "I'll tell Cort you were worried about him," he said with a wink, then sobered. "And, hey. Good luck with Bas. His mind is a dark and wacky place, but whatever bullshit he's spiraling about, remember he loves you."

Drew raised his chin in acknowledgment, but he sat staring at his office door long after Cam had closed it behind him, thinking not about how to stop Sebastian's fixations, but how to cure his own.

He pressed the intercom button on his desk phone.

"Peter? Get me Mark's email address. I think… I'd love to meet for coffee."

CHAPTER THREE

*S*ebastian Seaver put the finishing touches on the final piece of code, and clicked compile. God, it had been a long morning… or maybe afternoon?

He checked the date and time at the bottom of the computer screen as he reached for the Styrofoam coffee cup on his desk and found it empty.

And *huh*, maybe that wasn't a huge surprise, considering somehow he'd been in this room for more than twenty-four hours. *Jesus*.

As he shifted, every part of his body ached - his neck from holding still too long, his wrists from typing, his back from sitting in the crappy chair that hadn't had lumbar support since sometime in the last millennium. Even his leg ached, a pain he knew from experience was caused by compulsively tapping his foot to the Motörhead drumbeat coming from his speakers. But all of that faded in the giddy rush that rose up from his belly as the machine finished.

It fucking worked.

He took a second to call up his email, ignoring the thousands of unread messages, and tapped off a quick memo to

TJ, his VP of Development. *Solved the "impossible" issue with the Pentex software. Someone owes me lunch for a week.* He smirked to himself as he hit Send, imagining her face as she read it.

And, frankly, he was pretty fucking excited about winning lunches, he couldn't lie. At least this way he'd be sure to get fed once a day. He hadn't realized how much he'd come to rely on Drew bringing him dinner until…

Well. Until he'd stepped back from all the drama he'd caused with Drew.

He rolled his chair back from the desk, dumping the empty cup into the trash because he wasn't a *total* slob, and forced himself to a standing position, ignoring the way his joints popped as he moved. He'd sat down a thirty-year-old man, and stood up ancient, the Rip van Winkle of Seaver Tech. Even his fucking head got in on the act, protesting the sudden lack of blue light as he stepped away from the monitor by providing a thumping counterpoint to *Ace of Spades*.

Unlike his shiny, rarely-used office on the top floor, there was no natural light down here in his lab, and no decoration at all besides a really ugly canvas of a ship-wreck that his mom had painted once upon a time. His father had chosen this basement hideout because it removed him from all the outdoor distractions - migrating geese and sunlight glinting off buildings, ships in the Harbor and snow hissing against the insulated windows. Bas liked it because it saved him from noticing how fucking long every day lasted… and from being disturbed by well-meaning individuals who didn't understand the beauty of focusing on a task for as long as it took to finish it.

He shuffled his way over to the mini fridge on the far side of the room - a setup he'd designed purposely, so he'd be forced to move occasionally, and stuck his hand inside the carton of soda.

Empty. Goddamn it.

The only beverage left was bottled water with vitamins and electrolytes. He made a face even as he twisted the cap. It was like mixing vegetables into baked goods - completely unfair to all parties involved. Probably something Drew, or Cam, or Margaret, his assistant, had brought down for him. But it was either this or tap water from the small bathroom attached to his office.

He kicked the door closed and briefly considered going out for supplies. His candy stash was depleted, and he hadn't eaten since yesterday. The project he'd been killing himself over was technically done, and it might be a novelty to actually experience sunlight for a while…

But as quickly as the idea came, he dismissed it. Now that his project was done, his real work could begin, and that was way more alluring than weak winter sunlight.

He chugged the water in seconds and tossed the empty bottle into the recycling bin, then dropped to the floor by force of habit and executed a series of pushups, hearing his father's voice ring in his head.

Your mind is only as strong as your body, Bas. Letting yourself get weak in one area means weakness in all areas.

Too bad dear old dad hadn't dropped any *really* important knowledge while he was doing the Obi-Wan bullshit, like how to deal with the knowledge that your father was a criminal who'd taken a loan from some Russian mobsters to start his business. Or how to keep your shit together when said mobsters threatened your friends and family. Or how to deal with your messed-up brain when you kissed your drunk best friend right on the goddamn mouth, and he whispered words that both scared the shit out of you and made your dick harder than it had ever been before.

Those would have been some quality Dad-lessons, right there.

Instead, Levi Seaver had left his eldest son pushups and an underground lair.

Bas levered himself up, his heart pumping hard, and took a second to stretch out his arms before walking back to the desk.

He plunked into his seat and checked his email - more from force of habit than because he expected anything urgent. He purposely employed people who could handle almost every aspect of his job for him. He winced when he saw one from Margaret.

Mr. Seaver… several emails, attached below… old friend of your father, Michael Paterkin… progressed to phone calls… please direct me on how you wish to proceed or I will escalate this to Mr. McMann. The woman who'd been his father's assistant and now handled things for both Bas and Cam knew exactly how to motivate him to take action: threatening to tattle on him to Drew McMann. Drew had always been able to coerce or cajole Bas into doing the right thing, without ever having to speak a word. There was something about the force of those deep brown eyes that could break Bas out of his mental deadlock.

Until now, anyway, when those eyes had become the reason for the deadlock.

Had he ever really *noticed* Drew's eyes before Halloween? If he had, he couldn't recall. Like so much about Drew, they were just an accepted, necessary part of his existence, like the air around him. Something he hadn't noticed until it had changed.

Warm lips, cinnamon-spiced and yielding. The mad surge of adrenaline pumping through his veins. Drew's leg against his, excitingly firm when it should have been soft and rounded. The prick of light stubble on a jaw that should have been smooth.

Stop it!

Bas knew that his brain was wired a bit differently than most. That, if left unchecked, he tended to obsess about things nearly to the point of madness, to the point of distortion. It was then that he was often able to tap into something beyond himself - something instinctive and vital that gave him his very best ideas. It was also the point at which he stopped being a capable human and became almost self-destructive.

It wasn't healthy, he'd been told time and again, by his mother and his brother and some lovely therapists. It was a risk he took when it came to his work because his alternative was... mediocrity. And that was absolutely not acceptable.

But there were also the times when it happened in his personal life, like it had after the crash when he'd become a zombie attempting to fuse his body to his couch. That was clearly what was happening now.

What other explanation was there for him thinking about Drew and... *wanting*?

His heart thrumming in his chest just at the fucking *memory*, Bas forced himself to scroll down Margaret's email and view the attachments - emails that Bas hadn't bothered to read when they'd been sent a few weeks ago. A man wanted an opportunity to chat with Sebastian, to remind him of the great work he'd done for his dear friend Levi Seaver, to get Bas's assistance with a project that would be mutually beneficial.

Bas rolled his eyes. The trouble with his last name was that it brought so many *dear friends* out of the woodwork when times got tough.

He wished, for about the millionth time in the last few weeks, that he could talk to Drew about this. Drew - the Drew who was his friend, and not this weird phantasm in his head, taunting him with kisses - would understand perfectly and know just how to handle it. But he'd pushed the real Drew away, and the longer the silence between them lasted, the less he knew how to get out of it, or how to explain it away.

Yeah, sorry for the dead radio silence, bud. I just couldn't stop thinking about kissing you, and I was worried that if I saw you, we'd end up doing more than just kissing. I think about your neck a lot, you know? And your collarbone, which has somehow become sexy. And since I have always been one-hundred percent straight, that would be crazy. So… Game of Thrones marathon?

Cursing himself for the idiot he was, he sent Margaret an email asking her to refer the Paterkin-person to HR. What Bas needed was to focus on a problem that he *could* actually solve.

Then, ignoring the rumble in his stomach, he shifted his attention to the second-largest monitor, waking the sleeping machine with a click. A photograph of his nemesis appeared in living color.

Alexei Stornovich, son of Ilya Stornovich and current head of the Russian crime syndicate known as SILA, which happened to be the Russian word for power. *Fucking pretentious.*

Ilya had been the one to bring Bas's father into the SILA fold in the very beginning, but it had been Alexei - ruthless, power-hungry, and by most accounts, literally crazy - who had called Levi Seaver's bluff when Levi wanted to get out of their arrangement.

Alex was stacked - maybe in his mid-forties, broad and muscle-bound as any bar bouncer, and with the same fuck-off scowl. He was a handsome guy, if you liked them tall, older, and wearing a smile that was borderline-insane, which would *not* have been Bas's type even if he was into guys. That was more up Cain Shaw's aisle, considering he was currently shacked up with Damon Fitzpatrick. Or maybe… maybe Alexei was *Drew's* type?

Which begged the question, did Drew have a type? Was he attracted to the soft looking guys who needed protection? Or the brawny guys who could bend him in half and hold him down?

His brain helpfully superimposed a picture of Drew next to the picture of Alex, his tall, lean frame dwarfed by Alex's bulk…

Gross.

Bas scowled as he shook his head to clear it. He had no clue what type of guy Drew went for, but he was reasonably sure it wasn't Alex. Was it weird that in all the years they'd been friends, he wasn't sure what Drew's type was?

And Jesus Christ, since when did he sit around thinking about which guys were fuckable?

He forced his mind back to studying Alex's picture, and then pulled up the list of crimes he'd been charged with, scrolling and scrolling until he reached the bottom. Decades of charges - weapons offenses and murders, thefts and conspiracies - none of which had ever stuck. And these didn't include the thousands of other crimes he'd never been charged with in the first place, like instigating the murder of Sebastian's parents and his fiancée, Amy.

His hands clenched into fists and he forced them to relax. He knew that Drew and Cam, Cort, Damon, and Cain, thought he was being an idiot for pursuing his own investigation into the Stornovich clan. *Let the authorities handle it*, they said. *Stay out of it. This isn't for you to solve, Sebastian.* But how the hell could he leave this to the authorities, when Alex Stornovich had skated on every charge he'd ever been nailed with?

This was Bas's job, uniquely his. The crash was ultimately his fault, and so it would be his job to make sure Alex was put behind bars – or fucking killed outright. Maybe then the ghosts that haunted him would allow him a little bit of peace.

He cracked his neck from side to side and called up a new screen - one that was never attached to the Seaver Technologies mainframe, nor registered under his name in any way - and began his real work.

For weeks, he'd been building a botnet - a web of computers around the world that he'd managed to, er, *conscript into service*, so to speak, by installing an unobtrusive little piece of software that allowed him to control them all remotely. Yes, theoretically the owners of said computers weren't technically aware that the gaming cheat program they'd downloaded had also contained this hidden string of code, but Bas figured it was karmic payback for them attempting to cheat in the first place. And, he consoled himself, unlike most hackers, he had no desire to keystroke-log the users' credit card numbers and passwords. His plan was far more white-hat... and unfortunately, just a little less easily controlled.

Most people were only peripherally aware that their computers - and the servers that housed their sensitive, personal information - were constantly under attack. Oh, there was a massive outcry in the media anytime someone managed to make a huge breach, of course, but most of the time, software companies were able to make patches within hours after a new virus was launched into the world, and the average user was none the wiser that some unsung programmer had saved their ass once again. But during the time between the release of the virus and the creation of the patch... that Zero Day time... there was a flurry of activity happening online, with computers from all over the world trying to exploit weaknesses and occasionally succeeding.

And the easiest way for Bas to hide his search into SILA's servers was to wait until computers all over the world were also launching attacks, losing himself in the crowd.

Tracking fake invoices that Cain and Damon had stolen from Senator Shaw's office, Sebastian had located at least one of Alexei's servers, and yesterday he'd hit the jackpot, using his botnet to attack Alexei's servers for that vulnerability. He'd managed to access the fucking root directory... and he'd found a whole lot of nothing. Legitimate businesses - or so they seemed - through which Alexei no-doubt funneled his blood money... but not a single shred of evidence Bas could use to tie them to any crime.

And not a single hint of where Bas could look for another server.

Coming up against a brick wall this way was maddening, if only because it so rarely happened. It wasn't cockiness to say that Bas was the best of the best. He'd learned everything he knew at Levi Seaver's knee, after all.

He rubbed his stomach, like he could ease the pain of grief that lodged itself there.

Some days, it felt like his father was still in the room with him - like he should be able to lift his head and see his father, busily and silently working on his own projects on the other side of the lab the way they'd done countless times. The instinctive understanding of complex code, the ability to navigate beautiful logical labyrinths, were traits that he and his dad had shared for as long as Bas could remember, and it hit him every single day that he hadn't just lost his *dad* when that fucking plane crashed, he'd lost the one person who understood the way his mind worked.

But then, Bas couldn't understand how his dad had

been stupid enough, *reckless* enough, to get involved with the Stornoviches in the first place, so maybe they weren't as similar as Bas had thought.

He ran a hand over his head, trying to steady his thoughts. *God.* He had to laugh at himself. Emotions were a bitch. He'd a thousand times rather bury himself in code, in problems that had logical solutions.

As evidenced by the fact that he'd all but checked out on his best friend after the fallout from that stupid kiss.

Ugh. Not thinking about Drew's lips, or those loaded words. Not thinking about how he'd taste when his lips weren't flavored with cinnamon.

Focus, Seaver.

He pulled his chair closer to the desk and set to work, ignoring the growing hungers that clawed at both his stomach and the back of his mind, and lost himself in the simple, serene grace of clearly defined parameters that allowed his imagination to flourish.

SOMETIME LATER, the scent of vinegar and spice began to penetrate his concentration, and his stomach gave an almighty growl. Shifting back to reality was like surfacing from a long spell underwater, and he blinked as he looked around. There was a can of diet root beer unopened on the desk beside him, along with a large brown paper bag, stapled shut, which was the source of the delicious smell. And on the far side of the desk, slumped back in a chair with his nose buried in his phone, was Drew McMann.

Hungry as he was, he couldn't help but stare at the man, drinking him in, nearly giddy just to be in his presence after all these weeks. *Shit*, Bas had missed him.

Drew had cultivated a reputation for perfection - his

clothes were always immaculate, posture straight, smile polite. He was punctual, prepared, and never at a loss for words...

Except, Bas realized, that wasn't really true. Not when it was just the two of them. Right now, Drew's tie was askew and his collar unbuttoned, his jacket missing entirely. His elbows were braced on the arms of a rolling chair, his ass on the edge of the seat, and his long legs spread out before him. His face was puckered in concentration as his thumbs moved across the screen, and Bas knew, *just knew*, that Drew wasn't sending some critical text message, but lost in one of the dozens of mindless jewel-matching games that were his dirty little secret.

He was so fucking happy to see Drew sitting there, Bas forgot any awkwardness existed between them, forgot they hadn't spoken in nearly a month, and grinned.

"Can McMann make the four-ruby combo that will take him to the next level?" he queried the room in his best sportscaster voice. "The audience is holding its breath..."

Drew glanced up and scowled. "Dick," he said without heat.

Bas opened his mouth to fire back with a very middle-school retort, but he thought better of it.

Drew didn't seem to notice. "Pad Thai in the bag."

"Oh! From Sweet Lime?"

"Obviously."

Bas opened the bag and pulled out a container. "Is it..."

"Crispy, with no shrimp and extra peanuts," Drew said, his focus back on his game.

Bas groaned appreciatively. "Fucking awesome. Drew McMann, will you..." *Marry me.* That would've been the throwaway end of the statement anytime over the past decade, but now his tongue tripped over that, too. He cleared his throat. "Uh... will you hand me a fork?"

Drew didn't even look up. "Plastic fork's in the bag."

Right, of course it was. Bas grabbed the fork and dug into the noodles, and holy *fuck*. Better than sex. He couldn't remember being this hungry in… ever.

"How'd you find me?" he asked, though it came out garbled.

Drew did spare him a glance then. "Where the hell else would you be but hiding out in your cave?"

So Drew *was* angry.

Bas gripped the fork tighter and shoved more bean sprouts in his mouth. Suddenly all the reasons he'd started avoiding Drew came rushing back. Ever since Halloween, Drew's sarcasm had gotten just a little too pointed, the tension between them a little too thick. And Bas hadn't known how to handle it, because what he wanted and what he *should* want no longer seemed to align.

"Working, Drew. I've been *working* not hiding," he said. And it wasn't a lie. He'd finished his project earlier, after all.

Drew gave a pointed look at the monitor where Alexei Stornovich's photo was still displayed. "Yep. So I see."

"You got something to say?"

Drew's eyes met his and softened slightly. "Eat first, Sebastian."

"Great," Bas muttered. "Suddenly feels like my last meal."

"Could be because it's dismal as fuck down here. Like a prison cell…" Drew pointed to the painting on the wall. "A prison cell with really depressing art."

"Mmmhmm." Bas turned to look at the painting, his mouth full of noodles, and swallowed. "It's a copy of a Rembrandt painting called *The Storm on the Sea of Galilee*. It's s'posed to be inspiring - Jesus does a miracle and calms the storm or something."

"It's inspiring like *Jaws* was inspiring," Drew said. "It inspires me to never go in the water again."

Bas chuckled. "Yeah. My mom did it during some art class, and my dad hung it up, even though it's seriously gloomy. He was kind of a sap."

"And you're the sap who keeps it."

"Hey!"

Drew smirked at his phone, while Bas rolled his eyes and shoveled more food in his mouth.

"What are you playing?" Bas demanded, when several minutes had passed in silence. It wasn't like Drew to ignore him this way.

"Hmm? Oh, it's called Dragon Puzzler."

Bas frowned. "No jewels?"

"Uh. No, there are jewels," Drew admitted, rolling his eyes when Bas snorted. "But it's not *just* jewels. There are levels and upgrades and…"

"Dragons?"

Drew shot him a glare. "Yes."

Ah, there was nothing like provoking Drew. Even after weeks apart, they had resumed their usual banter with the ease of two people who'd been halves of a whole for most of their lives. Bas finished his meal in a much better humor.

"Alright," he said, leaning back in his chair and cracking open his soda. "I'm fed. Would've been better if there'd been dessert, but I can't complain. Is this the point where you give me the blindfold and last rites?"

"So dramatic. Maybe I came to see if you had made any progress." Drew waved a hand at the computer set-up.

"Sure you did. Well, as it happens, I managed to get into Alexei's server yesterday. Or *one* of them." He sighed in frustration. "I hit a dead end."

"I'm not even going to ask how the hell you accomplished that, because the less I know, the less I have to pretend I don't know," Drew said with a long-suffering sigh. "Does that mean we can't get at them online?"

"It might mean he has another server, in which case I'd need to find its physical location. Or... I guess there's the possibility that he's air-gapped all his sensitive data."

"*Air-gapped* it. Of course. I mean, *pfft*. Doesn't everyone?" Drew drawled.

Bas rolled his eyes. "Air gapping means keeping it on a server that's not connected to the internet, ever. Even I can't hack a server that's not online, believe it or not."

Drew frowned. "Is that likely?"

"It's possible." Bas shrugged and shook his head ruefully. "Actually, it's good business practice, especially with the completely illegal shit he has to hide. I don't want to give the asshole credit for being that smart, but maybe he is." He pulled up the picture of Alexei again and swept a hand at it. "Does this look like a criminal mastermind to you?"

"This is him?"

"Yep. Alexei Stornovich," he said, as Drew came around the desk and leaned over his chair. "I won't bore you with the laundry list of things he's been accused of..."

"Convictions?"

"None," Bas returned, tapping another key. "Just a list of charges that haven't stuck. And there's this."

Drew perused the list of names on the screen. "His known associates?"

"Former associates. All of these people have gone missing."

"Missing doesn't mean he had anything to do with it," Drew reasoned. "Correlation versus causation."

That smooth, polished lawyer-voice of Drew's had always been provoking. In the past, it made Bas want to push Drew's buttons, if only to show that he could rile Drew up. But now, it made his stomach clench uncomfortably with something like… something like… *arousal*. He wanted to throw the man against the wall and kiss him until his eyes crossed.

He swallowed hard, uncomfortable and now fucking annoyed. This wasn't the way things with Drew were supposed to be.

"Right, of course," he snapped. "I'm sure these guys all decided they wanted to run away and join the circus. Maybe start a commune for retired crime lords somewhere in Alaska?"

"Or they moved back to Russia, Bas. Or they went into witness protection, which we would never know about. Or they were fake names to begin with, and now they go by other names."

"Doesn't change the fact that this guy is a murderous shithead!"

"Whoa! Chill, Sebastian. In what *realm* am I saying that he's a good guy? He's a fucking crime boss, and I doubt he offers a retiree pension plan. I'm just saying, he doesn't have an unlimited reach, right? So these associates could have chosen—"

"He's dangerous, and the authorities can't stop him," Bas insisted.

Drew shut his eyes and sighed. "Ah."

"*Ah*? What's that supposed to mean?"

"It means now I understand why you were eager to show me what you were working on." Drew walked back around the desk and flopped back into his seat. "And it means Cam, who specifically asked me to track you down today, was right."

Bas narrowed his eyes. "Right about what?" He was unreasonably annoyed that Drew had sought him out because Cam told him to, rather than because he'd been missing Bas the same way Bas had missed him.

Their friendship had never been like that, ever. But now suddenly everything was fucked up.

"Right about you being on a quest to do everything yourself," Drew continued, drumming his fingers on the arms of the chair. "I mean, not that it came as a shock to me that you're in this up to your eyeballs. I just don't think I really understood just how far you intended to take this *on your own*. Riding off to save the day. All by yourself."

Patience. Patience. Bas's foot tapped restlessly against the floor, and he belatedly realized that the pounding heavy metal he'd been listening to was gone, replaced by Classical bullshit. So fucking like Drew to just come in and take shit over.

"We can't all be like you, counselor, biding our time. Some of us make leaps, take risks."

Drew regarded him with a smirk that Bas wanted to kiss — no, punch. Obviously, *punch* — right off his stupid face. "You want to talk about taking leaps and risks suddenly, Sebastian?"

Bas looked away. Did he? Given the way his heart pounded at the very thought, he was pretty sure he did *not* want to talk about it. Not yet, anyway. Not until he'd figured out why he was suddenly looking at Drew in a whole new way, not until he'd categorized things properly and found a logical solution.

"*And* that's what I figured," Drew said, throwing up his hands, his smile smugger than ever. But after a second he leaned forward with a sigh. "Listen, I didn't come here for a fight."

"Yes, you did," Bas grumbled.

"Fine. Maybe a little," Drew admitted. "But only because I knew you weren't going to like what I had to say." He shook his head. "You promised — you fucking *promised* — back in my kitchen a month ago that you would not go off half-cocked. You agreed that you wouldn't do this on your own."

"As I recall, you threatened to inform on me to the FBI."

"Whatever. In any case, you *agreed*."

Turning his neck to the side, stretching his cramped muscles, Bas acknowledged this. "I did. And I'm happy to have everyone help. Problem is, no one else seems to give a shit."

"Not even a little bit true," Drew countered. "Cort has his FBI contacts, Cain has been talking to his father, who might have more info on SILA. Damon's friend Eli has law enforcement contacts. And all of them are ready to help, but they want to have a plan."

Bas blinked. "I didn't know."

"Because it's hard to stay on top of things when you're living in a fucking bunker." Drew threw up his hands indicating the windowless lab. "And especially when you're avoiding me and anyone who might mention my name."

Bas looked into Drew's eyes, golden brown and simmering with impatience. "I...I..." *Didn't*, he wanted to say, but that would be a lie, and they both knew it.

Drew sighed again. "I seriously didn't come here to fight," he said again, like he was reminding himself as much as Bas.

"Why did you come, then?" Bas's stomach clenched in a way that had nothing to do with the food he'd just shoveled in. He was invested in Drew's answer to this question. He was thinking of Drew's lips.

Drew's voice was warmer when he answered. "I came here to bring you food, since I figured you'd be starving, and to stock your fridge with soda, so the cleaners wouldn't find your desiccated husk hovering over your computer."

Bas grinned, shaking his head. "Like One-Eyed Willie with his jewels in *Goonies*? When we were kids, I always felt a kinship with that dude, hunkered over his treasure for centuries." It was *his* treasure, for fuck's sake. Nobody else's.

"Yes, I remember. How many times do I have to tell you, the possessive dead pirate is not a role-model, Sebastian?" Drew said severely, but he shook his head in exasperation, and for the first time in a while - a month, at least - Bas felt like maybe everything was gonna be okay. Maybe they could get back to normal.

"You came to shut off my rock music and replace it with this piano bullshit," Bas said, rolling his eyes as the concerto coming through the sound system swelled to a crescendo. "Hoping I'd fall asleep? Or just being a control freak, per usual?"

"Right. You caught me. This was all part of my cunning plan to keep your ears functional and your brain from melting. Truly, I'm evil."

Bas laughed, and Drew continued, "I came to tell you that we are having a meeting on Saturday at my place. I'm not sure on the timing yet, but Cam, Cort, Damon, and Cain are coming. It's non-negotiable," he said severely, when Bas opened his mouth.

"I wasn't going to negotiate, counselor," Bas said, hands in the air. "That's your line. I was going to ask if I could bring anything."

"Bring anything?"

"Like… a cake, or something."

Drew hooted. "Would *you* be making the cake?" The tease in Drew's voice made Bas feel lighter than he had in a while.

"Hey! *Rude*. I can make cake. How hard is it? Crack eggs, stir shit?"

"Bas, you don't do well with anything that requires you to follow a plan, and baking a cake is just the smallest example of that," Drew chuckled.

Once again, Bas had no retort, because Drew wasn't wrong. It was annoying to have somebody know you that well.

Annoying and kind of awesome.

And it made him want, very badly, to wrap his arms around Drew, to lock them together so that neither of them could ever fuck things up again.

"Seriously, man, don't work too late, okay?" Drew said, pushing to his feet. "We will talk about it all this weekend. I promise."

Bas nodded. "I'm going to head out in a few. I'm… actually pretty exhausted." He hadn't realized just how true it was until he said it. "I put in a long day." It had been a long fucking *month*, missing his best friend like his lungs would miss air.

"And a night. And another day," Drew corrected. "I checked your key card log earlier. I know exactly how long you've been here." He stood to leave, grabbing his long wool coat from the chair and wrapping it around himself. "Oh, hey!" He reached into the pocket and pulled out a candy bar - the kind with the caramel center that was Bas's absolute favorite - and laid it in the middle of his desk. "Forgot I, ah…got you this."

"You brought me dessert?"

"Yep. It's almost like I know you or something."

Bas blinked, staring up at Drew - at the dark stubble on his jaw, the flush that tinged his cheeks, the light in his eyes that Bas could read like a freakin' road map, the way his bottom lip was just a tiny bit bigger than the top, that impending sense of *something* that hung like ozone in the air before a lightning strike. "Thanks," he said, his voice raspy.

Drew shrugged. "Of course. And I'm not kidding about Saturday. I will hunt your ass down if you don't show." He pointed a threatening finger in Bas's direction, and Bas nodded woodenly as he watched him walk out the door.

Bas sucked in a breath, filling his lungs more deeply than he had in weeks, like Drew was oxygen and his brain had been half-starved. Whatever that meant for their future, whatever doubts were fucking with his head, however freaked out he was by the changes he couldn't seem to stop in their relationship, Bas knew for certain he couldn't stay away from Drew again.

CHAPTER FOUR

*D*rew stared at the computer screen, fingers hovering over the keyboard, but he couldn't make them move.

"This is not hard," he muttered to himself. "Just type, for Christ's sake. It's no different than a work meeting, really." But still the fucking words wouldn't come.

He pushed the keyboard away and read the email once again, searching for subtleties and hidden meanings, re-re-*re*thinking his decision to go down this path at all.

Drew, so happy to get your email! I'd love to meet for coffee - I know a great place downtown with killer scones. Or maybe we could do drinks instead, depending on your schedule? Let me know what works for you. Feel free to give me a call, too. My number is below. - Mark.

Killer scones? Sounded pretentious and possibly dangerous. Also, who said things like that?

Was the "or maybe drinks" Mark's way of pushing things? Drinks were at night, and could lead to dinner, which could lead to sex, or expectations thereof. Seemed like more of a commitment than coffee, which was casual and could be ended with an "emergency" work text when things got awkward. And what was with the phone number? Who called people anymore, for God's sake? Were they married now?

Drew still couldn't dredge up a single solid recollection of his conversation with the guy at The Station, even though Peter had helpfully pulled up Mark's social media accounts and scrolled through shot after shot of the guy sitting at Fenway Park, hanging with friends at a winery, and even petting a little dog that looked like a Jack Russell Terrier. Drew couldn't deny that Peter was right - the guy was objectively *hot*, and yet Drew had been more interested in the dog than the guy holding him.

Operation *Get Over Sebastian* was off to a great start.

Drew leaned his head back against his chair and rolled his neck from side to side. This was fine. This was normal. What else had he expected, really? You couldn't just be hung up on a person for years and then switch gears. There would be an adjustment period. Maybe… maybe even a grieving period. But it would be easier if he had something else to focus on. Mending his friendship with Bas, and testing the dating waters with Mark.

He blew out a deep breath and forced his fingers to type.

Coffee sounds great. I work downtown, so we could meet at lunchtime. Or I'm free this weekend for dinner. -Drew.

He sent it before he could delete it entirely, then re-read it and covered his eyes with his palm. What the hell had he been thinking, suggesting a weekend date? Was that tantamount to an offer of marriage?

You'd never know he made his living crafting words.

He didn't look up when Peter knocked on the door and pushed it open. "You'll be happy to know I've embarrassed the hell out of myself, but I replied to Mark," he mumbled.

"Should that make me happy?" Bas said, strolling over to the desk holding a cardboard tray of coffee. "Who's Mark?"

Drew's jaw dropped open. "Holy shit." He glanced at the clock on the wall, then back at Bas. "It's ten in the morning."

"Uh, yeah. Why?" Bas's brow furrowed as he set the coffee on Drew's desk and helped himself to a seat. "Do you have a meeting? Peter said your schedule was clear this morning."

"Uh, no. I'm free. I'm just stunned to see you." He leaned over the desk toward Bas. "Be honest. Does the sunlight burn?"

"Fuck off," Bas told him, though his lips twitched, and Drew couldn't help smiling in reply. "Bring your best friend coffee, get ready to tell him you've taken his freakin' advice for a change, and what happens? You get mocked."

Drew took the coffee Bas held out to him wordlessly and took a sip.

"Cinnamon?"

"Your favorite."

Drew busied himself taking another sip. To say he was stunned to see Bas was beyond an understatement, but he couldn't deny the way his stomach flipped at the sight.

Settle down. Would you be that excited to see Cam or Cain? Friends don't go breathless when friends walk in the room.

But then again, none of Drew's other friends looked quite as good as Bas did - suit pants hugging his thick, muscled thighs and form-fitting blue dress shirt showing off both his broad chest and his bright eyes. Even the stubble on his jaw - slightly auburn in the sunlight, made Drew's chest seize.

"So, Mark? Is that the guy who says he was a friend of my dad's?"

Drew blinked twice, shaking his head. *Fucking idiot.* "Huh?"

Bas's smirk didn't help Drew's good intentions. God, even when the guy was insufferable, he was the hottest thing Drew had ever seen.

"You said you embarrassed yourself replying to *Mark*, and I was wondering who I needed to thank for flustering Attorney McMann. Was it the same guy who's been emailing Margaret about having us work on a project? Or was that Michael somebody?"

"Oh, right. Peter mentioned that yesterday, but I haven't looked into it yet."

"Yeah, me neither. But the dude is relentless - sent another email this morning! - and he's starting to piss me off. Says to remember *Collier*. Do you know who or what that is?"

"Uh… nope?"

Bas hummed a frustrated noise. "I'll ask Margaret to look into it."

"No need. I can have Peter work on it."

"Where is Pete today?" Bas wondered. "He's not breathing fire at your door." He grinned. "That was a dragon joke. In deference to your game."

Drew rolled his eyes and made a gagging noise. It was possibly the worst joke ever, but Drew couldn't hide his grin.

"A bit oblique, I grant you," Bas said, waving a hand.

Right. Fine. So Bas telling the world's stupidest jokes made his heart pound faster than any of hot-Mark's pictures. *Adjustment period,* Drew reminded himself.

"Peter is sorting out a mess with my mother's apartment, actually," he said with a sigh. "Something about her agreeing to renovations on her condo, but not providing the contractor with signed paperwork before she went out of town." He rolled his eyes. "Peter's lesser-known duties include attending to the daily Mary-Alice McMann drama. He should be back any minute."

Bas nodded. "Your mom is lucky to have you."

"I guess. I think Amy would've handled her better." He shrugged.

"Nah. Amy wouldn't have taken the time you do, and practical things weren't her strong suit," Bas said casually, sipping his coffee like he hadn't just dropped a bombshell. But before Drew could recover from his shock, Bas continued, "If that's not Mark, who is?"

Damn Sebastian Seaver for being so fucking single-minded. "No one important."

Now Bas's smirk turned to a frown, though his eyes still danced. "Is this a *secret*?"

"No." Drew waved a hand in the air. They'd never talked about Drew's dates, and it seemed particularly weird to start now, with Halloween still hovering in the air between them. "What brings you here today?"

Bas shook his head, refusing to be diverted. "You know when you resist, it only makes me more determined. You *have* met me, yes?"

But Drew hadn't graduated at the top of his class in law school because he was easily distracted. "Ah. You came here to bait me? Then surely you've got something to say about my hair cut? Or my shirt?"

The weight of Bas's stare as it moved from Drew's hair down to his lavender shirt was slow, thorough, and nearly palpable.

Uh. Whoa.

Had Sebastian ever looked at him that way before? If so, Drew was pretty sure he would have memorized the date.

More likely, you're misreading things, he told himself firmly.

Seeing looks that aren't there. That messed-up corner of his mind that seemed to live for self-sabotage was trying to derail him from what he knew was the right thing to do.

Well, it wouldn't work.

"You look good," Bas said in a low rumble. "Purple is a good color on you."

Drew blinked. He read people for a living, and he would nearly *swear* there was flirtation in Sebastian's voice. But there couldn't be. Could there?

And Jesus, why *now*? Why was the universe tempting him with hope just as soon as he'd recognized the error of his ways?

"Ah. Thanks?" Drew smoothed down the front of his shirt and couldn't meet Bas's eyes.

"So, I had an idea," Bas told him, sipping his own coffee easily.

Drew darted a look from under his lashes. "Really? You? An idea? How odd."

"Hush," Bas said mildly, refusing to rise to the bait. *Curiouser and curiouser.* "I decided to take your suggestion from last night."

Drew thought back to their conversation last night in the lab - how fucking *good* it had felt to be near Bas again, his resolve to keep things easy and peaceful between them, and then their near argument about Bas's nearly-suicidal insistence on going after SILA on his own.

"Which suggestion?" he asked.

Bas raised an eyebrow.

"It's just that all my ideas are good," Drew said, spreading his hands wide.

Leaning forward into a shaft of sunlight, Bas set his cup on the desk.

"Specifically, the one about getting help before going after SILA."

Drew frowned. "We're calling a meeting for this weekend, right? Baking cakes and all?"

Bas nodded, leaning his elbows on his knees. "But you know I can't just sit still for two more days."

"Uh huh." Drew rolled his eyes. Imagine forty-eight whole hours without obsessing over a single thing!

"I realized I've been going about this all wrong," Bas said, blue eyes serious. "Trying to hack their systems directly, when maybe I need to get a clearer picture of the organization."

"Okay," Drew said, drawing the word out. "Are you planning to join up instead? Get the inside track that way?"

Bas scowled and sat back, folding his arms over his chest. "It's like you forget who's supposed to be the smart-ass here."

"Sorry." Drew mimed drawing a zipper across his mouth.

"You're not going to interrupt?" Bas demanded. "Oh, this will be great. I give you…" He pulled up his sleeve and consulted the thick platinum watch on his wrist. "Two minutes."

Humph. Drew sat back, himself, folding his arms in conscious imitation of Sebastian's pose. He would keep his mouth shut for two minutes if it killed him.

"Excellent," Bas said, eyes alight. "I've waited so long for this moment. I've had so many things to say. Remember that time your dad got you that Bruins jersey? The one you wore for a solid week, until it went missing from your room randomly, and you could never find it again?"

Bas spread his hands out helplessly and hesitated like he was about to make a confession. Drew narrowed his eyes. He'd fucking loved that shirt, and Bas had insisted that he'd had nothing to do with its disappearance.

"I've always felt really sorry for you. And I've meant to tell you that." Bas smiled beatifically. "That's all."

Drew felt his lips twitching, despite himself. God, he had no defenses when it came to this man. No matter that they were talking about something incredibly serious, no matter that they had so much unresolved bullshit between them, he couldn't stop himself from appreciating everything about the man in front of him, even the parts that drove him crazy.

Drew tapped his own watch, raising an eyebrow in challenge, and Bas smiled.

"Right, back on topic. Remember when Cain was filling us in on everything his dad told him, right around Thanksgiving? He mentioned that there was dissension in the ranks at SILA. I was thinking maybe what we need to focus on is finding someone we can turn, finding someone who can be our Trojan horse. So, remember the reporter guy who did the interview with Cain Shaw a month or so back?"

A nod. Drew remembered it well. Cain, the son of a conservative Senator, had been closeted for years thanks to his father's political ambitions, but he'd come out, not just to his family and friends, but spectacularly and publicly, with a well-publicized interview in *The Herald*. Drew remembered that the journalist who'd done the interview had been both fair and sympathetic, garnering publicity for the charity work Cain was doing, to boot.

"His name is Gary North," Bas continued. "And before he covered national politics, he earned a name for himself doing investigative work on a certain Russian crime organization."

Drew's eyes narrowed. He recalled that, as well. Gary had written extensively about the power players within the organization, and although he'd never heard it officially, he wondered if the reason for Gary's sudden shift to political work was really a shift at all. Emmett Shaw had been on SILA's payroll, after all. And though that was an extremely well-guarded secret, it wouldn't surprise Drew much if Gary had somehow learned the truth.

"I sent him an email asking him to meet," Bas said heavily. "I'm not sure how much to tell him, or whether to pretend I have a sudden hypothetical interest in the Russian mob." He shook his head. "That's not my forte, as you know. Which is why I'm here." He shrugged. "Will you come with me?"

Drew gave him a pointed look, glancing at his watch, and Bas let out a bark of laughter.

"You passed the two-minute mark, Attorney McMann. You win."

"What do I get?" Drew asked. "For my fortitude?"

Bas shook his head. "I don't know why I'm surprised that you were able to keep your mouth shut. You've clearly never had trouble keeping secrets."

Drew cleared his throat. Yeah, Bas had mentioned that a couple of times this fall, like he somehow blamed Drew for keeping quiet about his feelings for so long. But Jesus, look at what had happened when he *did* mention it?

Nuclear fallout.

"Anyway." Bas cleared his throat and looked out the window as he sipped his coffee, neatly closing the door on that conversation. "You can have the prize of your choice, if you come along for my meeting with Gary."

Drew took a deep breath, trying to restore his mental equilibrium. "Ah, yeah. Yeah, sure." He shook his head at himself, and called up the calendar on his phone, taking refuge in the simple task. "I'd be happy to. What time is the appointment?"

"This evening," Bas said.

"This...*this* evening?"

"I told you I didn't want to wait," Bas reasoned.

Drew sighed, mentally reshuffling his end-of-day appointments. "What time?"

"Six. We're meeting for drinks at some pub he likes."

"I can do that," Drew agreed. "Want me to meet you there?"

Bas looked at him like he had three heads. "Why the hell would I want to meet you there?"

Because after thirty years, things are awkward between us? Because I can barely hang onto my resolve to keep things platonic when you're in my fucking office, let alone when we're in a car together?

"Because you drive like Wiley Coyote on crack?" Drew offered, falling back on a decades-old joke.

"I drive like a Bostonian," Bas corrected, pushing to his feet. "But that's fine. You can drive." He rapped his knuckles on Drew's desktop and shot him a grin. "That's your prize."

"Lovely," Drew said sourly, but he was actually glad. Much easier to be with Bas when he could focus on the road and there'd be no opportunity for deep conversation.

We're friends. Friends, friends, friends.

"Have a good afternoon, counselor," Bas teased as he strode gracefully to the door.

And Drew kept his gaze on Bas's tight ass as he walked away... just like a friend.

He was so screwed.

CHAPTER FIVE

"*...* *raffic on the threes. There's an accident on 93 North in the left-lane by the gas tank that's tying up your evening commute...*"

The monotonous tone of the radio announcer filled the interior of Drew's Acura, and Bas leaned back in the comfortable leather passenger's seat, closing his eyes and pretending to snore. Any drive, even the twenty-minute ride to the pub where they were meeting Gary, was more fun for Sebastian when he could pester Drew.

He'd missed his friend over the past few months - a fact that had been driven home when Drew had shown up last night, exactly when Bas needed him - and he knew he had mostly himself to blame for the weeks of awkward avoidance. But strangely enough, now it was Drew who seemed to be avoiding conversation.

"Is that a comment on my driving?" Drew pretended to muse. "So smooth and comfortable you could fall asleep?"

Bas snickered, burrowing deeper into his overcoat. It was *seriously* cold tonight. "Right. One of these days, you're going to want to listen to actual *music*, instead of talk radio. Listening to this shit makes me feel old."

"I don't know how to break it to you, but you *are* old," Drew said with fake sympathy. "You own a car and a home, and as your attorney, I happen to know you pay taxes and insurance on both of those things."

Sebastian grimaced. "Don't remind me."

"Also?" Drew continued. "That shit on your business card is not for show; you're the real-life president of a multi-national tech company, which pays you a salary."

"Funny."

"And," his so-called-best-friend continued mercilessly. "You were engaged not so long ago. Engaged to be *married*. You could have had kids by now, a family of your own."

The words fell like an anvil, a conversational dead-end, and for a second, Bas was thankful for the monotonous radio announcer, who at least broke the silence.

"Sorry," Drew said, true remorse in his voice. "That was thoughtless of me, throwing that out there."

Bas shrugged, because it seemed the thing to do. "Amy was your sister."

"Doesn't mean I can tease you about losing the woman you loved. I'm sorry." Drew shook his head. "And that's my quota of apologies to you for this year *and* next."

Though he appreciated Drew's effort to lighten the mood, there were a bunch of things in Drew's statements that just weren't true. And as much as Bas loathed talking about feelings - and truly, it was hard to overstate the loathing - he'd been wondering since last night whether this wasn't a huge part of the issues he and Drew had been having.

He didn't know when they'd started keeping secrets from one another - it hadn't been a conscious choice, at least on his part, but he knew Drew had made some assumptions about his relationship with Amy that Bas had simply let stand. And he had certainly made some assumptions about Drew's feelings toward him that, based on what he'd said on Halloween, were a gross understatement of fact.

So.

Maybe they needed to consciously work toward some honesty.

"I don't know if that's true," Bas told him. "Not about the kids, for one thing."

When Bas thought of his family, he thought of his parents, Cam, Drew... and the collection of misfit toys they'd collected over the past few months, Cain, Damon, and Cort. He thought of the weird family they'd formed *after* the crash.

He missed Amy the way he missed childhood - a vague sense of loss and happy memories, not the visceral heart-break a man was supposed to feel when he lost a fiancée. Maybe he needed to tell Drew that, too.

Drew blew out a breath and nodded slowly. "Uh huh. Okay. Maybe you would have waited a while. Whatever. Did you want to change the radio station? Pick some music."

Drew, deflecting. Bas nearly laughed.

"I'm not sure whether I want kids at all," he continued with a shrug. "And Amy and I never discussed it."

Bas was well aware of what it said about him, about his relationship with Amy, that he couldn't speak with any authority about what she would have wanted on what would have been a huge issue in their marriage. He wasn't proud of it, and that's why he'd never discussed it.

He was ashamed because he'd stumbled into dating her because it was easy and his mother had approved. He'd stayed because it was safe. And he'd asked Amy to marry him when he wasn't entirely sure that he was in love with her, because he wasn't entirely sure what love looked like or if he'd ever experience it personally.

And Jesus Christ, *beyond* shame that he hadn't called it off before everyone got in a plane to go celebrate and died on the way.

"I think she *did*," Drew said, shaking his head slightly. "God, Bas. You *never* talked about this with her?"

Bas shook his head. "When we talked, it was mostly about the wedding. The dress, the venue, the ring. And she was really excited to help my mom with her charity work, since her business school thing didn't work out."

"But you were marrying her, for Christ's sake. She was going to be your *wife*. You... you loved her, right? She loved you?"

Drew sounded legitimately angry, and Bas couldn't say he didn't deserve every ounce of his anger.

"Amy and I were maybe the only two people in the world who could date for months without having a single serious conversation." He had to laugh at himself. "I mean, not that it was hard, given that neither of us liked to talk about deeper issues. But Amy had her friends, and I spent all my time in the lab, as you know. And that was fine for both of us, I guess."

"You. *Guess*."

Bas blew out a breath. He hated this. *Hated* it. "You want the truth, Drew? The truth is, I loved your sister a lot. She was gorgeous, and she was sweet. She got along perfectly with my mom. But..." He ran a hand through his hair. "No. I wasn't *in love* with her. Not... not how I think of being in love anyway. I didn't think about her when she wasn't around. I didn't call her every day."

"*God*!" One single tortured syllable. "Sebastian..."

Bas wished he could see Drew's face better in the streetlights. He was also cravenly glad he couldn't. But there was more he needed to say.

He took a deep breath. "I'm almost positive it was the same for Amy. She liked the idea of me. Of being a Seaver. I mean, it's not like she wanted more time or attention and I didn't give it to her. She was happy enough to see me when I was around, and perfectly fine when I wasn't, and I felt the same about her. She never felt the urge to hunt me down in the lab and force pad Thai on me, or whatever. She... she wasn't my best friend."

I didn't need her the way I need you, he thought but didn't speak.

Amy had been everything Drew wasn't, really. She'd accepted where Drew had questioned, yielded where Drew had pushed, faded into the background where Drew could only ever be the brightest star in Sebastian's sky.

Which was why Halloween still loomed so large in his mind. Drew was unequivocally the most important person in his life, and he *knew* he was the most important person in Drew's. But that was *friendship*. The attraction he'd felt that night had come out of nowhere, and the words Drew said had rocked Bas to the core.

The red brake lights ahead of them illuminated Drew's set face as he steered them off the highway and onto a congested Main Street in Southie. Bas struggled to fill the sudden silence.

"Have you ever just fallen into something? And it took on a life of its own?"

"God, no more," Drew said. "I need... I need to process this, okay?" He slid the Acura into a parking space on the side of the road and shut off the engine, grabbed the keys in one large palm and pushed out of the car.

Bas frowned as he levered himself on the other side, his attention fixed on the keys in Drew's hand. There was something about them that had caught his attention, but he couldn't think what. Key fob, a bunch of metal keys that probably went to his house... and Sebastian's place, too.

Drew slid them into his coat pocket as he walked briskly down the street toward the pub... down the street *away from Bas*.

Sebastian jogged to catch up.

"So, how are we going to handle this?" he asked, grabbing Drew by the elbow as he reached the outside of the low brick building. There were several high windows built into the walls, and the neon glow of beer signs flashed red and blue over Drew's carefully blank face.

"I'm thinking we handle it like we ask him questions and he answers them," Drew snapped back.

Bas rolled his eyes. Okay, so maybe the car ride had been the wrong time to force them into a new level of honesty. Still, Bas was glad they were here together; even pissy Drew was better than no Drew at all.

"Cool your jets, counselor. He's not a hostile witness, he's a reporter. He's gonna be curious about why the hell we wanna know this info, and I want us to be on the same page about what to tell him."

Drew ran a hand through his perfect hair and sighed, and Bas could practically see the wheels turning in the man's mind as he tried to compartmentalize his conversation with Bas and get his head in the game.

Perversely, Bas was pretty sure he no longer wanted Drew to be able to do that.

Last night in his office, when Drew had leaned over his desk, Bas had wanted... something. Something he'd studiously avoided thinking about ever since Halloween. But now that his brain had caught hold of the idea, it had become a problem, like a coding issue but trickier...and he couldn't seem to let go of it until he'd found a solution.

"How do you want to play it, then?" Drew asked, calm as a frozen river.

"Friendly," Bas said. "I think we need to give a little information to get some information."

"Fine." Drew nodded. "Friendly it is." He turned to walk inside and Bas grabbed him by the elbow again, forcing him back.

"Listen, about that, back in the car." Bas hesitated. "I feel like there are a lot of things we haven't talked about, and I don't want that. Not anymore. Things are changing between us, and I won't claim to understand it, but I also know avoiding it isn't going to help anything."

"You're wrong." Drew's serious brown eyes shone in a stray beam from a nearby street light. "Nothing is changing. We are *friends*. But the things you said about Amy?" He shook his head. "Yeah, I'm upset. Just drop it for now so we can talk to this reporter. Okay?"

But Bas was still unsettled. He fucking hated this tension. Hated having Drew be disappointed in him, or whatever. As they stood on the sidewalk, breath clouding in front of their mouths, the door to the pub opened, and two men in jeans and leather jackets spilled out, laughing uproariously.

Drew huffed impatiently, grabbed the door before it closed and stepped inside, leaving no choice but for Bas to follow.

The air inside was set to blast furnace, the central bar area crowded and noisy, and nearly every one of the booths that ringed the room was occupied with people - mostly blue-collar guys still in work gear. Bas opened his mouth to speak again, but Drew had already spotted a well-dressed, brown-haired guy in the back booth. Bas recognized him from his online bio.

"Gary?" Drew said, holding out his hand in a friendly way as he reached the table. "Drew McMann."

Gary stood and shook Drew's hand, then broke out into a wide grin that brightened his otherwise nondescript face. "Yeah, I recognize you. From Senator Shaw's fundraiser a couple of months ago. I was there covering him as a probable presidential candidate. Can't say I'm too unhappy to hear that the chatter about him possibly running has died down."

Though he'd counted Emmett Shaw as family once upon a time, Bas was extremely glad to hear confirmation that the man's political star had dimmed, even if it had been because his son had come out in the press, rather than because he'd been exposed for the murdering traitor he was.

"No?" Drew asked. "I'd have thought a journalist would be excited for an opportunity to get to know someone early in the game like that."

"Ah, maybe. But as a *gay* journalist, I can't be entirely objective about a guy who believes in conversion therapy, you know?"

Drew chuckled and smiled his charming, megawatt smile, a smile Bas realized he hadn't seen from Drew in… a really long time.

"Sebastian Seaver," he interrupted, sticking out his own hand. "Thanks for agreeing to meet with us."

"Oh, my pleasure." Gary turned toward him, shaking his hand briefly, before turning his attention back to Drew. "I was hoping I'd run into you again."

"Oh?" Drew said, his smile dimming somewhat as he shifted back into cagey lawyer mode. "Wanted information about Senator Shaw?"

Since both of the others were ignoring him, Bas shucked his overcoat and slid grumpily into the booth

across from Gary, signaling to one of the harried
waitresses.

"No," Gary said. "God, no. We just didn't get introduced at the fundraiser, and I felt like I'd missed my shot to
get to know you better." The grin he leveled at Drew was
beyond friendly, and something about it made Bas grind
his teeth.

Drew cleared his throat and slid into the booth next to
Bas, while Gary resumed his seat.

"That's, ah… The feeling's mutual," Drew said, and
while Bas watched, his best friend *blushed*.

Drew hardly ever blushed.

"I mean," Drew continued, waving a hand in the air the
way he sometimes did when he was at a loss for words, "I
really appreciated the interview you did with Cain. He's a
good friend of mine."

"Yeah? I like him. A good kid. I mean, *man*," Gary
corrected.

"I know what you mean." Drew's smile was warm,
open. "It was hard for me to stop thinking of him as a kid,
too, even though he's grown up a lot in the last few
months."

Gary's eyes - a plain brown that actually, now that Bas
thought about it, looked kind of beady in the low light of
the bar - gleamed. "Pretty sure his boyfriend would be
pretty happy if I never thought of Cain again, *period*."

Drew laughed, soft and low.

And suddenly Sebastian realized what was happening
right in front of him. They were *flirting*. Gary was fucking
flirting with Drew, and Drew was… Drew was *letting him*.

Bas signaled to the harried waitress once again. "Excuse
me? I could really use a drink over here."

As he did, he spied a man sitting alone at a far table - an
older guy with thinning sandy hair and light eyes - whose

gaze was also locked on their table. Was everyone staring at Drew tonight? Had this always happened, and Bas had just been oblivious until now?

"Jesus. What is *with* this place?" he muttered.

Gary spared him a confused glance, but his gaze returned to Drew with magnet-like accuracy. "So, Drew, what do you do exactly?"

Oh, like nosy Gary didn't know.

"He's the head of the legal department at Seaver Tech," Bas said impatiently. Someone needed to redirect this conversation. They were here for a fucking *purpose*, after all. "And he's here because I asked him to come along. I had some questions about the assignment you were working before the Senator."

Gary blinked, then finally managed to focus on Bas, looking back and forth between him and Drew with undisguised curiosity. "My investigation into SILA?"

"Exactly," Bas confirmed, his voice crisp and businesslike. He ignored the pointed look Drew shot him. "They've recently been mentioned in some business dealings of ours, and we wanted to learn more. Get the inside track, so to speak."

"Okay," Gary agreed, drawing the word out. "What did you want to know?"

"Well," Drew said, faint apology in his tone. "General information would be great, since we can't really talk about *why* we need the info. Anything you could tell us about the power players, rackets they run, or where they operate would be helpful."

"So, SILA 101?" Gary said, just as the waitress finally, *finally* came over to their table. "Um, another Johnny Walker rocks for me," he told her.

"Oh, a whisky drinker?" Drew said with a smile. "A man after my own heart. Same," he told the waitress.

Bas gritted his teeth. What the fuck did that even *mean*, a man after his own heart? God. Drew was being an idiot, but Gary seemed to enjoy it.

"Vodka tonic," Bas said, when the waitress finally turned her attention to him. "Make it a double."

Drew gave him a disbelieving look, but Bas ignored it. "Right, so, what can you tell us, Gary?" he demanded instead.

"Well," Gary began, and once again he looked at Drew as he spoke, like Bas wasn't the one asking the questions, like he couldn't see Bas sitting right in front of him, like Bas and Drew hadn't fucking come here together.

What the hell was taking the waitress so long?

"I'm happy to tell you what I know. But I feel like I need to preface this by saying that everything I know has been learned through anonymous sources who cannot be reached to testify." He looked briefly at Bas before turning his attention back to Drew. "I've already explained this to the police. The main reason I still have my head attached to my shoulders is that everything I've written is technically unprovable. Urban legend I have no interest in proving, for my own safety."

"Of course," Drew said easily. "No, this is strictly for our own knowledge. Nothing concerning a legal matter."

Gary nodded. His gaze narrowed on Drew's face and his lips twitched. "So mysterious," he said smoothly. "I like that."

Ugh. Gary was creeping him out.

Bas cleared his throat. "Drew mentioned power players?" he interrupted, not bothering to hide his annoyance. "What can you tell us about them?"

Gary's questioning eyes flickered to him. "If you want to know about the power players in SILA, you want to know about the Stornovich family," he said.

"Right. I've heard of them," Drew said, frowning in concentration as though the names weren't at the forefront of his brain. "Ilya and Alex, I think?"

"Yes, Ilya Grigorovich Stornovich and his son, Alexei Ilyich Stornovich."

The waitress returned with their drinks, and Gary fell momentarily silent. When she left, he took a sip of his whisky, and Drew did the same. Bas threw back his drink in four quick gulps, then motioned to her for a refill. This meeting was a pain in the ass already.

"Ilya Stornovich was born in the Ukraine," Gary began. "Sometime in the early 1930's. How much do you know about Russian history?"

"Not much," Drew admitted.

"Is this really relevant?" Bas demanded.

"Well, given that I don't really know what you're looking for, I can't say for sure, can I?" Gary said sharply. "But if you want to know generally about SILA, I believe it is." He took a deep breath like he was composing his thoughts.

"The common joke about Russian history is that every chapter could end with '...*and then it got worse.*' But even with that said, the 1930s in the Ukraine were a particularly dark time. Communism was alive and well, and Joseph Stalin had a five-year plan... a plan that involved shipping almost all the grain in the Ukraine back east to the cities of Russia." He stopped and took a sip of his whisky. "Starvation was rampant. It was a time when if you *didn't* look like you were starving, your neighbors would rat you out and you'd be accused of hiding food somewhere, which was how Ilya's father, Grigori, died. Ilya became a thief before he was a teenager just to keep his family fed. And after the war, he got even bolder - moved to Kiev and started smuggling in western goods. That's what landed him in a gulag - a Russian prison."

Drew braced his feet and leaned across the table toward Gary, caught up in the story. Bas couldn't help but notice the way Drew's shoulders shifted beneath the wool overcoat he still wore and how the dim, yellow light of the bar made his hair look more auburn than brown. He wore the sharp-eyed, curious expression Bas had seen hundreds of times, but tonight it somehow made Bas's stomach twist sharply.

God, what was wrong with him tonight? Maybe it was the vodka?

He refocused his attention on Gary, who was still staring into Drew's brown eyes.

"Can we speed this up?" Bas asked. Drew kicked him sharply under the table and Bas turned his head. "What? I'm not here for world history."

"Please continue, Gary," Drew said with a smile. '*I* am fascinated."

Gary winked.

So unprofessional.

"Well, no matter how deep I dug, I was never able to find out exactly how he got from the gulag to the States." He shook his head with what seemed like amused respect. "I'm guessing there's a reason why that story doesn't get told. Being sent to the gulag was pretty much a death sentence, so for him to not only survive but find his way to New York was miraculous and likely required some high-level string-pulling. Ilya had made a lot of friends while he was in prison. Climbed pretty high in the hierarchy of what later became the Russian mafia, or *Bratva*. Learned to hate everything to do with the government, if he didn't already. Learned a certain code of honor that earned him respect. And Ilya put all of that to use when he came to New York."

Once again, Gary paused as the waitress brought Bas his second drink.

"By the time the Soviet Union fell," he continued a moment later, "Ilya had already moved to Boston and had made himself a bunch of high powered friends - the Colombians, the Irish. While the leaders of the Russian underground were busy dividing up their territory back home, Ilya was already here, staking his own claim, founding SILA." He looked from Drew to Bas. "He grew his syndicate, and he consolidated his power. And he kept to his own code of honor - he sold information, weapons, protection. Because that was all government bullshit, right? But he became his own authority - kept his men from committing violent crimes as much as possible, kept drugs out of his neighborhood. He was like a Ukrainian Robin Hood. He was, in a word, beloved."

Drew sat back in his seat, his leg shifting against Bas's, and they exchanged a look. Drew seemed surprised, but Bas was pretty sure every word Gary said was bullshit. The fucked-up deference Gary was showing Ilya, like the man was a folk hero and SILA was his merry band of elves, was ridiculous. SILA was a group of criminals, and Ilya Stornovich was a *murderer*. Anyone who said differently was lying.

Bas gripped his glass so tightly his knuckles turned white, and Drew pressed their thighs together beneath the table - either a private show of support or, more likely, a warning for Bas to keep his mouth shut.

But that wasn't gonna happen.

"Skip to the important part. When did Ilya become a murderous, scum-sucking asshole?" Bas demanded.

Gary blinked, apparently startled by Bas's vehemence. "Well, the short version is… he didn't."

"Bull," Bas said. "You're telling me SILA is a charitable organization?"

"Oh, fuck no," Gary said, shaking his head. His tiny brown eyes - soulless, like a demon's - turned toward Bas for once. "No, the change that occurred in the organization wasn't Ilya's doing, it was Alexei's." Gary's face darkened. "If Ilya is Robin Hood, then Alexei is like that spoiled kid from Charlie and the Chocolate Factory who's obsessed with getting her way, except imagine him with a penchant for violence and firearms. He's managed to fuck things up royally in the dozen years since he's taken over."

"How so?" Drew asked.

Drew's leg was still resting against Sebastian's, not a silent communication anymore but a casual touch. He wasn't sure if Drew was aware of it, but it felt nice - warm and comfortable. The easy familiarity grounded Bas, and soothed something inside him that had felt prickly and raw all night.

It reminded him of the way their legs had pressed together during that kiss back in October — so much so that he fought the urge to put his hand on Drew's back to claim more of his heat. And yeah, maybe also to warn off the weird, sandy-haired dude at the next table, whose eyes kept flicking over to Drew in a speculative way every time he thought he could get away with it.

"Day one of Alexei's regime, he told his men they had carte blanche," Gary said, rolling his eyes. "*We are SILA, we follow no rules but our own.* You can guess, everyone was thrilled, from the lieutenants on down to the foot soldiers. They could now drink, smoke, drug, party, fuck, kill, and steal with impunity. So they did. For *years*. And he managed to lose any respect his father had gained in the community, as well as most of the support from his seconds."

Gary turned his glass on the table in front of him, seemingly absorbed in the way the light played over the amber liquid inside. Drew and Bas exchanged another look.

"It's probably strange that I'm so invested in this, huh?" Gary said, glancing up in amusement. "But I have my reasons."

Reasons. Bas rolled his eyes, but Drew gave Gary an encouraging smile that had Bas tapping his fingers against the tabletop, *thumb-pinkie, thumb-pinkie,* ignoring the look Drew shot him.

Drew bit his bottom lip. "So you're saying that Alexei isn't very popular? There's a rift within the organization?"

This, *this*, was what they'd come here to learn about. Not some history lesson about brave and noble Ilya, but the inside track on how to take the fuckers down for good. Bas barely stopped himself from leaning in to hear the answer.

With inquisitive eyes, Gary looked back and forth between Drew and Bas again, but he was far too smart to betray his curiosity out loud. Instead, he took his time before answering the question. "A rift, no. Grumblings, though, for sure. The lieutenants are tired of cleaning up the messes of foot soldiers who have no control. Hell, even the men, themselves, are tired of wondering whether they can trust their brothers, tired of inspiring fear but not respect. Alexei trusts almost no one. Their computer servers are almost all offline now, and they run each crew with strict secrecy so that only a handful of people understand the larger picture. There's little camaraderie. Alexei has used his men to carry out his personal vendettas, even when it costs money and the lives of his crew. And he's taken their business ventures into shadier and shadier avenues. Sex trade, child trafficking, adoption scams, identity fraud." He smiled grimly. "It's all fun and games until you end up on the terror watch list."

"Terrorism?" Bas said, blinking. "Like bombings and things?"

"Not his crew themselves," Gary said, shaking his head. "Not yet anyway. But they do like to broker technology, that's for damn sure." Bas fought to keep his gaze on Gary, when he really wanted to look at Drew. *Brokering technology?* Like the kind they'd gotten from Seaver in the past? "But they've gotten into stealing identities and using the stolen info to obtain passports for foreign nationals looking to come into the US."

"And the government knows this?" Drew demanded.

"I shouldn't have to explain the difference between *knows* and *is able to prove* to you, Drew," Gary chided. He shook his head. "Law enforcement agencies are likely well-aware that this is happening, but Alexei is…"

"Slippery," Bas finished, using the word he'd been thinking of just last night as he'd looked at Alexei's picture on his computer screen.

Gary nodded. "Indeed."

"Maybe there'll be some kind of internal coup, and Alexei will be dethroned," Drew speculated. Gary and Bas both looked at him, and Drew shrugged, as though he was embarrassed. "What? I can be an idealist and a lawyer at the same time."

Gary smiled like Drew was magic, and Bas resisted the urge to roll his eyes.

"I hope you're right," Gary allowed. "I had heard that one of Alexei's lieutenants was thinking to approach Ilya, see if he could corral his son. I don't believe anything ever came of it. Likely, he recalled Alexei's impressive collection of guns and his talent for using them."

"What's the guy's name?" Bas asked, at the same time Drew demanded, "Why isn't Ilya still in charge?"

"Ilya gave the throne to his son because he wanted to,"

Gary said, answering Drew's question first because he was a kiss-ass that way. "SILA was his legacy, something he'd built so that his family would never starve, and he'd always recognized that at a certain point, his son wouldn't be willing to take orders anymore. He retired to Florida, if you can believe it. Tampa… or something." Gary shook his head. "He stays out of his son's affairs completely - cut ties to everyone in the organization, specifically to prevent anyone from using him to usurp Alexei's power."

He turned to Bas, and his eyes were cold and serious. "As to the name of the lieutenant who wanted to breach protocol? I have no idea, and frankly I wouldn't tell you even if I did. That's the kind of information that gets people killed."

"That's the kind of information that could *save* lives," Bas argued, jaw clenched. "If someone could use it to compromise them from the inside."

"And is that your goal, Mr. Seaver?" Gary demanded.

Bas sat back and glared at him stonily, and Gary smiled.

"Fine. Keep your secrets. But trust me when I tell you, a man could be shot for betrayal just for taking my call. And I won't have more deaths on my conscience."

"Must be nice to have the option to save your own ass."

Gary downed his drink in a single gulp and glared at Bas. "The reason I know all that I know about SILA is that I don't name names. *Ever*. Not to the authorities, and sure as *hell* not to spoiled, rich men who are looking to make deals. Alexei wants people to be scared because he thinks they'll keep their mouths shut. But when they've been threatened with losing too much, when their family members have been raped and beaten, when they live in fear every day, they've gone beyond that. They get to a place where they're too scared to stay silent anymore, because they don't believe their silence will protect them. In exchange for their stories,

I've helped some of them find resources, ways to start over in places outside of Alexei's influence." He shook his head once, quickly. "That's how *I* help save lives."

Bas pushed down an uncomfortable niggling sense of shame as Gary stood and tossed a few bills on the table. He took a card from his pocket and handed it to Drew.

"If you need any more information," he said, and Bas was almost positive he wasn't imagining the emphasis on the *you*, "reach out. I'd be happy to answer any questions you have, maybe over dinner sometime."

Drew smiled and gave Bas a pointed look. "That would be nice. To… talk."

"Or," Gary said, his tiny hamster eyes glinting as he leered at Drew. "We could just not talk at all."

He tossed Drew a wink, gave Bas a brisk nod, and walked away.

Bas barely had time to catch his breath before Drew rounded on him. "What. The. Fuck. Was that?"

"I know! That guy. *Jesus*. Made my skin crawl."

"Not Gary! *You*! That… *thing* you were just doing." Drew waved his hand above the table, his eyes sparkling with fury. "Be friendly, you said. He's not a hostile witness, you said. Jesus, Sebastian. What the fuck?"

"I was fine when we came in!" Bas defended, folding his arms across his chest. "I just refuse to hear him talking about Ilya Stornovich like… like…"

"Like he's a human being? With a history and a past? With reasons for doing the shitty things he does, just like you?"

"Like he's a *hero*."

Drew blew out a breath. "He was not talking about him like a hero, Bas. He wasn't. He was saying that he's better than his son, and I believe that. Remember what Cain told us about his talk with his father? Senator Shaw said that when Seaver Tech took startup money from the Russians, he and your dad originally made their deal with Ilya, and shit didn't start to go bad until later, when Alexei took over."

"So?"

"So, it makes sense that Gary appreciates the concept of honor among thieves. Motive matters."

Bas rolled his eyes, aware that he was behaving like a child, but unable to stop himself. "Yeah, it sure as hell does."

"What does *that* mean?"

"It means," Bas said snidely. "I think you're a little bit biased when it comes to Gary. *Oh, Gary, take me to dinner. Oh, Gary, call me.*"

Drew's face flushed a deep scarlet. "I said no such thing. Fuck you, Sebastian."

"Wouldn't you rather fuck Gary?" The second the words were out of his mouth, Bas knew he'd gone too far. Drew shook his head, disgust written on his face, and stood up from the table.

Bas grabbed his coat and followed Drew through the bar. "Hey, wait!" He paused when the sandy-haired man turned in his seat to watch them leave. "And *you*, keep your eyes in your fucking head." The man's eyes widened and he held up his hands in surrender.

Drew didn't acknowledge Bas, and he didn't slow down. He pushed his way through the crowded bar and threw open the front door, nearly hitting Bas in the face. He stormed down the block.

"Drew! Jesus," Bas said, jogging to catch up to him and grabbing his arm as they reached Drew's car. "You're angry? Fine, whatever. But don't just walk away from me."

Don't let us fall apart when we just started talking again.

"Let me go, Bas," Drew said. His voice was low and

tight, and his eyes in the streetlight were shiny with tears. He wasn't angry, Bas saw. He was *hurt*.

Goddammit. Hurting Drew was the last thing he wanted to do.

Bas dropped his elbow immediately and ran a hand over his hair. "Listen, I'm sorry. I... I was pissed off at Gary, and I shouldn't have taken it out on you, okay? I don't know what my problem is." *Except that conversation about Amy stirred up things I don't want to think about, and I feel like I'm going to lose you, and I really don't want to do that.*

"No," Drew said. "Not okay." He pushed Bas out of his way and strode to the driver's door.

"Are you going to give me a ride?" Bas asked, almost pleading.

"You know what?" Drew said, clenching his jaw. He opened his mouth, then seemed to rethink, and closed it again. "Fine," he said. "Get in."

Bas folded himself into the Acura and barely shut the door before Drew pulled away from the curb.

"Drew, I'm really..."

"I *really* don't wanna hear it, Sebastian."

Goddammit. He couldn't remember the last time Drew had been mad at him. Not like this, anyway. Drew always gave Bas a chance to apologize. That was... that was their *thing.*

His gaze caught on Drew's keyring, and he finally realized what had been bugging him about it earlier. The keys and key fob were there, but his keychain was missing.

"Your sand dollar is gone," he accused, pointing at the key ring.

"What?"

"The blue sand dollar keychain that I gave you back at summer camp. The night I..." *Kissed you for the first time. Told you I wasn't gay. Promised you I wouldn't run away from you again. Fuck.* "The last night of camp. I saw it on your keyring a few months ago, back when you lent your car to Cain and Damon."

"Oh. It broke, Bas," Drew said bleakly. "It's gone."

"Gone? Couldn't we fix it?" It was a stupid keyring, a thing he'd forgotten about for nearly twenty years, but it had meant something to *Drew.* Another of those things Bas had taken for granted, and hadn't noticed until it was missing.

"Not everything can be glued back together, Sebastian," Drew told him, and Bas panicked just a tiny bit.

"Drew, I know you're mad, but you've gotta let me…"

"What, Bas? Say you're sorry? Why? Because that's how it's always been? Bas fucks up, Bas apologizes after a day or a month, and Drew just accepts it?"

Well. It sounded pretty shitty when he put it that way.

"How about 'Bas mouths off, Bas realizes that whatever stupid bullshit he said wasn't an accurate reflection of his true feelings and appreciation for his best friend, Bas apologizes sincerely because he really never meant to hurt Drew, and Drew accepts because he recognizes that his best friend is an asshole who's missing a few wires between his brain and his mouth?"

Drew drove the car for several blocks, red brake lights from the traffic around them giving his face a ghastly red glow.

"The thing is," Drew said, enunciating each word clearly. "That's not a healthy friendship, Sebastian. I sometimes feel like I have more invested in this friendship than you do. It *hurt* when you disappeared. It *hurts* that you didn't tell me the truth about you and Amy. It *hurts* that you're accusing me of throwing myself at Gary North, because that's not what was happening at all and *even if it was*, it would be my business and not yours."

Bas blinked. "Of course it's my business. I'm your friend. And you don't have more invested than I do. You *don't*, Drew." He reached out to put a hand on Drew's arm.

But Drew didn't seem to hear him. "It's not your fault," he went on. "I've let things get skewed, and that's on *me*. Okay? And I love you. Of course I do. And we'll always be best friends. Just… give me a little time to process things, okay?"

"I thought me avoiding you was part of the problem!" Bas argued. "How is you *processing* any different?"

"Because I'm saying *let's not talk on this car ride*, not *see you in February*."

Okay, fair enough. "It's just that I didn't intend to avoid you for a month either," Bas said softly. "Things just get out of hand when you don't talk about them right away. The things we need to process alone become secrets, and then those secrets make things harder later."

Drew was quiet for a moment. "It breaks my heart," he finally offered. "Knowing you were going to marry Amy and weren't in love with her."

Bas sucked in a pained breath at the disappointment in Drew's voice. *This was better*, he reminded himself. *Better than silence.*

"You're my best friend, and she's my sister. And I wanted better for both of you."

"Do you blame me?" Bas forced himself to ask. The question had been weighing on him for a while. "For her death?"

"Christ no! No." Drew looked over at him briefly. "Not at all, Sebastian. If everyone hadn't been going to celebrate your engagement, it would have been something else. I have never for one second held you responsible."

Bas nodded, and he couldn't deny the relief that he felt at those words.

"It's just the idea of you *falling into something* that takes on a life of its own." Drew shook his head. "You're smarter than that."

Bas laughed dully. "You'd think. But I'm finding there are a lot of areas where I'm really fucking slow."

Looking at Drew now, at the hard cut of his jaw and the soft fall of his hair, he was beginning to realize just how slow.

"I'm sorry for what I said about Gary," he offered. "I didn't like the way he flirted with you." He shook his head and admitted, "I didn't like the way you smiled at him."

"I smile at a lot of people," Drew said. "Pro tip: it's generally considered friendly."

"Yeah, thanks. But… you don't give other people that smile. That's the smile you use for *me*. It's… I dunno. Different. Like you're really focused on me. It's special." It was a flirtatious smile, he realized now, a smile of total interest and absorption. And he wanted that from Drew. He coveted it.

Like fucking One-Eyed Willie the pirate and his Goonie treasure.

Drew laughed and ran a hand over his face, but didn't argue the point.

"And there was another guy in the bar looking at you, too," Bas grumbled. "Watching you from afar like a fucking creeper." He shook his head. "Next time I'm going to bring a baseball bat."

Drew looked at him and frowned. "Or you could just let me take care of my own love life, thank you very much. I can decide who I want to date on my own."

The idea of Drew dating made him weirdly anxious, and he really didn't want to think about it. As long as it all stayed hypothetical, he'd try to control himself.

"You're, uh… not planning on dating Gary, though, are you?"

Drew smirked - a sexy, sideways twist of his lips - and pondered a long moment before answering. "No. I don't think so. Although I think he's a very good guy. An upstanding guy."

"If you're into rodent eyes," Bas mumbled, looking out the window.

"You're ridiculous."

Yeah. He kinda was.

He was also able to deny that he was attracted to his best friend.

Drew found a parking place on the street barely half a block from Bas's gate - a minor miracle at this time of night - and neatly maneuvered the car into place.

"Come in with me," Bas said impulsively.

Without turning to look at him, Drew shook his head. "Not tonight, Bas. I'm tired."

"You're annoyed, still. And I deserve it. But we haven't hung out in a long time, and I've really missed you."

Drew contemplated this in silence, his finger tapping on the steering wheel.

"We can order whatever you want," Bas promised. "You got me Thai last night, so you can pick the place. Even that gross pizza with the sprouted wheat crust. And we can play a video game - your choice. I'll let you kick my ass at FIFA. Or we can watch whatever you want on TV, even if you wanna go wild and crazy with CNN."

"Shut up." Drew whacked him on the arm, and Bas took the blow with the same thrill of glad relief he'd have felt if Drew had hugged him, because that teasing slap meant that Drew was forgiving him… probably. As long as he didn't fuck it up again.

"We're getting wheat pizza with extra vegetables,"

Drew said, shutting off the engine. "And you're eating it, too," he warned. "No getting a second one with extra cheese and lard for yourself."

"I will avoid lard and eat the cardboard as penance," Bas promised, pulling himself out of the car.

Drew locked the door and met Bas on the sidewalk, shaking his head ruefully. "One of these days, I will figure out how to stay mad at you."

Bas slung his arm around Drew's shoulders. "I sincerely hope you never do."

CHAPTER SIX

"*J*esus! Can you *not*?" Drew said, swatting Bas's hand away from his ribs. He focused determinedly on the tiny soccer players running across the TV screen and tightened his grip on the game controller.

From the corner of his eye, he saw Bas tilt his head like he was pretending to ponder the answer.

"Nope. Sorry. I'm afraid I've got to," Bas said, before reaching out, with both hands this time, to tickle Drew again. One of Bas's large, warm hands latched onto the faded t-shirt Drew had borrowed, while the other fisted into the borrowed sweatpants riding on Drew's hips.

It was a lot like a fantasy Drew had had more than once, except in his dreams, Drew wasn't one goal away from a victory, and Bas was holding him down for a far more compelling reason.

He elbowed Bas futilely.

"If this were a real soccer game, you'd have to dodge defenders, McMann, and deal with distractions." Bas's voice was breathless with laughter. "I'm just helping to make this more *real* for you."

"No, you're a *real* cheater! Stop! Foul! Penalty!" Drew yelled, squirming to the side and holding his arms clear. He focused on the screen, punched a button, and the crowd on the screen erupted into cheers and screaming.

"No!" Bas cried.

"Yes! Goooooooooooal!" Drew said, jumping off the couch to pump his fists in the air. He smirked at Bas, who'd sprawled face-down and groaned into the cushion when the evidence of Drew's vast FIFA superiority had flashed on the screen. "I'd like to thank everyone who made this victory possible, namely *me*. I dedicate this win to Dragon Puzzler, for the hours of intense strategy and hand-eye coordination."

"You match jewels," Bas mumbled into the pillow. "It's not rocket science."

"*And*," Drew spoke over him. "I'd like to thank all the haters, namely *you*, for inspiring me to be the champion I am today."

"So humble," Bas muttered into the pillow. He slouched back into the deep red cushions and glared at Drew in annoyance. "Such a role model."

"One of my gifts," Drew agreed, resuming his seat. He looked over at his friend and grinned. Pouty Bas was adorable… and Drew had missed him so damn much.

Drew pulled his knee up to sit sideways on the sofa, draping his elbow over the back cushion so he could look at Bas fully. His dark hair was mussed and flopping across his forehead, dark lashes framed his blue eyes. His strong jaw and the broad chest that stretched out his t-shirt made him look like the football player he'd once wanted to be. Up in his closet, Drew knew Bas had a dozen thousand-dollar suits. His garage boasted both a sleek restored Charger and an Escalade. He had some of the most influential scientists, politicians, and businessmen in the world on his speed-dial. But looking at him now, no one would recognize him as a tech genius, or one of the richest men in Boston. With that sulky look on his face, he seemed more like a pissed off teenager who hadn't had enough sugar recently.

And Drew had to curl his outstretched hand into a fist to resist the urge to smooth the hair off the man's forehead.

Fuck.

This plan to get over Bas was stalled at the starting line.

When Bas had invited him in tonight, Drew had been so very close to saying *no* and hurrying back to the safety of his suburban house alone. Even now, despite the fun of beating Bas at FIFA - a joy that never got old, really - Drew wasn't sure he'd made the right decision. He was in a weird place tonight, a little too vulnerable and way, way too aware of the man sharing the sofa with him.

The revelation Bas had shared about his relationship with Amy was fucking with his mind. It hurt that Bas had never confided in him about it, yeah. And it sucked that Bas had been about to tie himself to someone he didn't love. But what Drew hadn't admitted in the car was that it fucking killed him to think of how their engagement had broken Drew's heart… and for *no good reason.*

Drew remembered with painful clarity the gut-cramping grief he'd felt the day Bas had decided to ask Amy out. Their parents had been trying to set the two of them up for years - Amy, with her sweet smile and boundless enthusiasm had seemed like the perfect foil for Bas's intensity and single-minded focus. Bas had always found a way to wriggle out of it, though, telling Drew privately that although Amy was pretty, she was about as exciting and transparent as tissue paper. Bas never planned to settle down - he liked focusing on his work, hanging with Drew, and occasionally hooking up with random girls when the urge struck.

Drew had let himself believe it.

Then one random Saturday afternoon, he and Bas had been sitting on this very couch, playing games, trash-talking, and wrestling just as they'd done tonight, just as they'd *always* done. Bas had pinned him to the couch, childishly pissed about losing a game as he *always* was, and Drew had been overwhelmed with affection for the man. He'd smiled at Bas - open, unreserved, and unrestrained.

Bas had suddenly sat up and brought Drew's mind to a crashing halt with just one sentence.

"So, I'm thinking of asking your sister out."

At first, Drew had laughed out loud. But Bas hadn't been joking.

"It's time I stopped screwing around and got serious. We're getting older, counselor," he'd joked. "And besides, your sister's cute. Like you but, you know, a woman."

And Drew, like the fucking martyr he'd let himself become, had smiled through the blinding pain of that, had nodded and said all kinds of bland, encouraging things, but Bas had known, goddamn him, that Drew wasn't really okay. Because sure enough, Bas had asked Amy out - had started escorting her to events and taking her out to dinner to the delight of their mothers. But he had never done more than peck her cheek when Drew was around. And he'd never discussed her with Drew again... until the day he'd proposed.

"It's time to make things permanent. Amy's ready. But I promise, nothing between us will change, Drew, except that we'll finally be *family*. For real."

Drew couldn't remember ever drinking as much as he had the night he'd realized that the love of his life would be marrying his sister. The only way he'd reconciled himself to the idea even a *tiny* bit was with the knowledge that surely Bas must be deeply in love, even though Bas had never volunteered that information and Drew sure as fuck hadn't asked.

Instead Bas had been a clueless idiot, and so had Amy.

Almost as idiotic as you, Drew reminded himself. Because he wouldn't be tied in knots right now if he'd gathered the... the courage, or the will, or the basic sense of self-preservation... to step away from Bas at any point over the past fifteen years.

Drew sighed and ran a hand through his hair.

"What?" Bas said, his eyes not moving from the FIFA main screen.

"*What*, what?"

With a groan, Bas shifted his head. "What are you staring at me and sighing for? Because you'd better not be pitying me, Andrew. I will have my revenge for this loss." He narrowed his eyes playfully and clasped a hand to his heart like he was swearing an oath.

Drew shook his head and felt his heart skip a beat.

Dork. The man had no business being so adorably goofy or so good-looking.

And *Drew* had no business thinking about Bas like this - not ever, but definitely not tonight, when all he could think about was how shitty it had felt every time he'd let himself lose control with Bas and felt Bas retreat from him.

There were so many reasons why he and Bas needed to never cross that line again. Self-preservation was just one of the biggest.

"I was just thinking no one at work would believe that the president of Seaver Tech was such a child when it came to video games and vegetables."

Bas rolled his eyes. "That's where you're wrong. Pretty much everyone knows how I feel about both of those subjects. You, on the other hand, counselor?" He smirked. "What would all the little lawyer underlings of yours say if they saw you in my baggy sweatpants and raggedy shirt, doing your FIFA victory dance?" He tapped his lip thoughtfully. "Next time, video."

Drew grabbed one of the throw pillows from behind him and aimed it at Bas's head. "Next time, I kick your ass."

Bas caught it, put it behind his head, and smiled smugly. "You could try."

Without warning, Drew grabbed the pillow back, smacked Bas in the face with it, and put it behind his own head.

"Oh, there *will* be video," Bas warned, his eyes crinkling at the corners as he laughed. "I may make it a company requirement that everyone *must* watch it and sign off, just like those sensitivity trainings."

"The irony of that statement…"

"Is not lost on me," Bas agreed solemnly. "But why own your own company if you can't violate your company policies every now and again? I have a legal team to take care of shit like that."

He patted Drew's leg comfortingly, his hand lingering just a little longer than it probably should have. Then Bas leaned forward to grab the remote off the table, and Drew sucked in a sharp breath.

Could the universe not let two minutes pass without testing his resolve?

Bas sank back into the sofa and his t-shirt rode up just a couple of inches, exposing an inch or two of tanned, toned flesh, and a tantalizing line of crisp black hair that began just below his belly button. Drew's throat went dry.

Apparently two minutes was too much to ask.

"I need another. You?" Drew asked, seizing the opportunity to put a tiny bit of distance between them. He jumped off the sofa and walked to the black-and-chrome kitchen behind the living room.

"Please. Hey, you wanna watch TV?"

"Okay." Drew took a deep breath. "So, I was thinking about what Gary said…"

"Hey. I thought you said no talk of Russians, or Gary," Bas reminded him.

Drew sighed and rolled his eyes as he opened the fridge. They'd made that agreement before they'd walked in the door tonight, and Drew wholeheartedly supported it… except that it would have been the perfect distraction right about now.

"Right. Fine. Tabling this discussion until Saturday. You want another Sam? Or the Nitro?"

"Is that an actual question? You know I only buy the Nitro for you," Bas said. "How about watching Stranger Things?"

Drew grimaced, though Bas couldn't see his face, and grabbed the two beers. "You know I can't get into that one." He grabbed the bottle opener magnet off the refrigerator and opened the bottles. "It freaks me out."

"Still think that's crazy. Dude, you've watched every season of Game of Thrones."

"That's death and sex, Bas. Not freaky shit coming out of the walls at me."

He got back to the living room to find Bas scrolling through the menu on the TV, and Drew's eyes were drawn again to that thick line of exposed skin above Bas's plaid pajama pants, like a fucking tractor beam.

Christ. Tongue back in mouth, McMann. It's a *stomach* for Christ's sake.

But it wasn't. It was *Sebastian's* stomach, which made it more erotic than a thousand uncensored pornographic images.

He nudged Bas's shoulder with the beer, and Bas reached up blindly to grab it and drink half of it down in one go. "You lose your shit over the weirdest things," Bas said affectionately.

Oh, Sebastian, if you only knew, Drew thought. But all he said was, "Whatever."

He took a spot at the opposite end of the red sofa from Bas, pushing himself into the corner. Staying as far away from temptation as possible seemed like a wise idea.

"How about this one?"

"Man in the High Castle?" Drew made the mistake of glancing at Bas and noticed a little droplet of beer clinging to the stubble just above his top lip. *Fuck.* He wanted to taste that droplet more than he wanted his next breath.

He forced himself to look away. "Yeah. Uh. Sounds great." He was pretty sure he wouldn't be paying much attention to the show anyway. He settled into the cushion, curled his long legs up, and held his beer in front of him like a shield against impulsive decisions.

Bas settled back into the cushion, propped his feet up on the table, and glanced at Drew. "There a reason why you're all curled up there?" He sniffed his armpit. "I've showered today."

Drew rolled his eyes. "I'm good here."

"Don't be stupid." Bas grabbed Drew's ankle, yanking him until their hips were side by side. "How can I steal your gross beer from all the way over there?"

Drew sighed as he propped his feet up on the table by Sebastian's, and tried, *tried*, with every ounce of will he could muster, to focus on the TV despite the way his best friend's body was throwing off heat just inches away.

Then Bas reached down and scratched at his own thigh, and Drew's concentration snapped. He watched those long fingers brushing back and forth across Bas's flannel-covered leg and had to swallow against the desire clogging his throat. Had Bas always smelled that good? Was he wearing some new cologne?

For years - fucking decades - they'd spent hours together with no tension in the air. They'd roughhoused and wrestled, gone swimming half-naked, and Drew had been fine. *Fine*. Because the line between reality and fantasy, between friendship and sex, had been clearly defined.

One stupid kiss in October, a couple of flirtatious looks Drew had probably misinterpreted, and one apparent jealous fit on Sebastian's part, and suddenly when the guy scratched his own fully-covered leg, Drew could feel himself flushing from head to foot.

He forced his eyes back to the television and locked every muscle in his body in place.

Bas casually reached over and grabbed the beer from Drew's hand, took a sip, and then shuddered. "Oh, yuck. I remember why I hate this stuff."

Drew huffed, refusing to turn his head. Bas put the bottle back in Drew's hand, and Drew couldn't help but think of Bas's mouth on the rim of the bottle, just like... just like...

He cleared his throat loudly. "I haven't been here in weeks, so who were you buying the Nitro for?"

"Oh." Bas settled more firmly into the couch, and his left knee slid to the side, bumping Drew's. "Just force of habit, I guess. When I get some for me, I always get some for you. Just like I buy that disgusting olive hummus you like."

Drew breathed in slowly, calmly, trying to still the butterflies that rocketed around his stomach at the throw-away comment. They were fixtures in each other's lives. Best friends. Buying beer was not romantic. Olive hummus was not a declaration of love.

Sitting here like this was fucking torture. So what the hell was he supposed to do?

Drew's phone chimed on the coffee table with a text message. *Thank you, sweet baby Jesus.*

He could have leaned forward and gotten it, but instead he made a show of putting his feet down on the soft area rug and standing up to grab it, pacing several feet away as he checked the screen.

"That your mom? Say hi from me," Bas said, eyes on the TV. He was well used to Mary-Alice McMann's constant need to check in with her son.

But it wasn't Drew's mother.

[*Hey, Drew. Thanks for your email! I was wondering if you were free Saturday night? We could do dinner? — Mark*]

Drew's eyes snapped up to Bas of their own volition, checking to make sure his attention was engaged with the television. How fucked up was it that he felt like he was some cheating husband stepping out on his man? Answer: very, very fucked up. Unhealthy. Not normal friend behavior.

Having dinner with Mark would be a good thing. Good and healthy. Another baby step along the plan.

He typed back quickly. [*Yeah, Saturday sounds great. You can pick the place.*]

"Hey, you're missing the show," Bas reminded him, flicking the control to pause it. "Come sit down."

"Huh? Oh, right." Drew obediently returned to the sofa, seated himself a foot away from where Bas sat, and held his phone face-down on his chest.

It chimed again, and this time Bas reached over, grabbing the phone from Drew's hand. "Your mom is extra chatty tonight," he said. And then he looked at the screen. "Oh."

"Uh. My mom's in Martinique," Drew said lamely. "Until next week."

Bas nodded, still staring at the phone, his face blank. "So. Mark?"

"Yeah. We, uh, met at a bar a few months back, but haven't met up yet."

Sebastian turned his head, and suddenly Drew was submerged in the blue fire of his gaze. "How ridiculous is it that I didn't know you went to bars? I mean, it makes sense that you do. But…"

"But?" Drew whispered.

"We've never talked about it. You're my best friend and we've never talked about you going out, or dating. I think…"

"I don't know what you're talking about," Drew said, a little bit desperately. "You've met guys I've dated."

Bas huffed. "Cam, yeah. And when we were teenagers, maybe. Or that idiot you dated back in college, Tim."

"Tom."

"Whatever. He was a douche." Bas shook his head. "But somehow along the way we stopped talking about any of this stuff. Like with Amy."

"I guess." The way Bas was looking at him right now — his eyes soft, vulnerable, confused — made it nearly impossible for Drew to keep from spilling his guts. From telling Bas that he hadn't brought up his dates because none of them were important, that the only person he'd ever loved, the only serious relationship he'd ever wanted, was with his straight best friend.

He pushed himself to his feet. "It's getting late. I should go."

"Sit down, Drew."

"Maybe that's not…"

"Please?" Bas's eyes were wide, serious, and as always, irresistible. "Just sit down."

Drew hesitated.

Sit down and torture myself for another two hours? This was the definition of a bad idea, not conducive to restoring the balance in their friendship, nor to making a *real effort* with Mark. How many more times would Drew allow himself to be tortured because he couldn't resist that pleading look in Bas's eyes? He needed to stop this.

Bas took advantage of his hesitation, wrapping an arm around Drew's wrist and yanking him back down so they were sitting side by side, their legs pressed together from hip to knee, then wrapped an arm around Drew's shoulder.

Drew sighed. Apparently he'd be tortured at least one more time.

"So this show." Bas gestured toward the screen with the remote. "It's based on a book."

"Yeah?" Drew sighed.

"It's set in this world where the Axis powers won World War II, and conquered the United States."

"Uh huh. Sounds super uplifting."

"I know, right? You'd think it'd be all post-apocalyptic and stuff. And it is, in a way. But the real mind-fuck is that it looks just like some fifties' sitcom on the surface. There are all these people just going about their business, living their lives even though the Nazis won. They salute the German flag, and they accept that this is the way things are." His voice was low and quiet, intense.

"I mean, I guess that makes sense?" Drew said uncertainly. He didn't understand Bas's intensity. Could barely concentrate on his words. "They didn't know any better, if that was their reality. Right?"

"Yeah! Yes. Exactly. They didn't know better." Bas paused, glanced down at Drew, and repeated, on a whisper,

"They just didn't know there could be anything different for them."

Drew blinked.

"But then they find these films," Bas continued. "Films that show the Allies winning. It freaks them the fuck out. They don't understand what they're looking at, right? It's crazy, and they get *scared*. Because it makes them wonder... *Is there something I should be fighting for? Should I have been doing something else?* It shakes them to their foundations, Drew."

Drew stared at the television, barely able to breathe. Was Bas saying what it seemed like he was saying?

"But even though they're scared, they can't stop thinking about the things that they've seen. And the way it makes them feel." Bas's voice was low, husky, and Drew was ninety-nine percent sure he didn't *mean* to be breathing in Drew's ear the way he was, but Drew's dick didn't seem to get the message. "Like maybe they didn't realize just how unhappy they were until they saw the way things could be."

Drew shut his eyes and exhaled. If he shifted his head a centimeter, his lips would touch Bas's lips. And then... and then it would be Halloween again. Summer camp again.

Bad things happen when you lose control.

He pulled away, bending his knee up onto the seat and twisting to face Bas head-on.

"What are you saying, Sebastian? Flat out, without your sci-fi symbolism."

Bas laughed softly and ran a hand over his face. "I was kinda hoping you'd be impressed by the symbolism."

Drew quirked a brow, and Bas admitted, "Fine. I... I haven't stopped thinking about the kiss on Halloween."

And there it was, point-blank and out in the open.

Drew cleared his throat. "I kinda figured that by the way you disappeared for a solid month."

"I apologized for that," Bas said.

"Yeah, and as I said, an apology makes it all fine, obviously. As long as you had a reason."

Bas rolled his eyes. "Give me a break."

"I have." Drew's voice was hardly a whisper. "That's why I'm here."

"We need to talk about it. About the things you said after— "

"No. Nope, we don't." Drew flung a hand out in dismissal. "We definitely do *not*. Suffice it to say, I was drunk. I should never have said that."

"Was it true?"

Drew swallowed, his throat clogged in a way that beer wouldn't cure.

"Tell me, Drew. Did you mean it when you said you'd wanted it for a while?" Bas's voice was cajoling now, pulling the truth from Drew's chest, and he panicked. "Because I'm thinking I'm not the only one who's been keeping secrets for a while."

Drew jumped to his feet. "It's too late to talk about that. I wanted to explain that it was all a mistake, but you kept avoiding me."

"And you kept sniping at me."

"And so did you!"

"Fine, then. Explain now." Bas leaned forward, elbows on his knees, and stared up at Drew.

"*No!* No." Drew pushed both hands through his hair. "I'm telling you, there's no reason to talk about this anymore."

"There's a lot of reasons." Bas blew out a breath. "Drew, I…"

"You disappeared for a *month!*" Drew exploded, hurt and terrified. "You wouldn't return my texts, you didn't even call me on Christmas!"

"You didn't call me either."

"Not because I didn't want to! You'd made it obvious you wanted to avoid me. That Halloween had made you uncomfortable."

"Because I was…"

"Freaked out? By the kiss? Yeah, shockingly enough, I got that loud and clear. But I don't think talking about it is going to help anything anymore. We've moved past it now. I am going on a date with Mark." Drew's voice was nearly pleading. "So there is nothing to talk about."

"You're wrong."

"No! No, for the first time in a while, I'm thinking very clearly, Sebastian. We are *friends*. Whatever alternate universe you think you glimpsed when we kissed, *you're not gay*. And it would be a really shitty idea for us to dwell on that one event when what we need to do is move on. Get back to where we used to be."

"Where we used to be." Bas spoke slowly, like he was pondering this. "You know, Drew, I wonder if the reason you never talked to me about the guys you dated was the same reason I never talked to you about Amy."

Drew's heart pounded frantically, and his eyes flew to Sebastian's face.

"We both knew it wasn't right," Bas whispered. "I'm straight." He swallowed hard and stood up, just a foot away from Drew. "But tonight when I saw that text from Mark, I was fucking jealous. Jealous at the idea of you being out with him. I think maybe that was part of my problem with Gary too. And maybe Amy…"

"We're not talking about Amy." Drew's stomach lurched with that dreadful combination of grief and relief he felt when he thought of his sister. He'd have given his life to save her, but only because that meant he wouldn't have to see her live her life with Bas.

"I don't know what any of this means," Bas continued,

ignoring Drew's objections. "I have no conclusions, just facts and thoughts and… and I want to kiss you again. The right way, this time."

Drew gaped at him. His eyes flicked to the television as he momentarily considered the possibility that *he* had been dragged into an alternate reality, or had perhaps fallen asleep.

And yet, even in his wildest dreams, he couldn't have conjured the sensation of Sebastian's finger running up from his wrist to his elbow, then dipping under the hem of his t-shirt to hook in his waistband and pull him closer; of Bas cupping Drew's jaw with his other hand so, so gently, as though Drew might shatter or run away; of Bas pressing his lips - warm and strange and *somehow familiar* - against Drew's.

Drew's stomach flipped the way it did on a rollercoaster. His heart was in freefall, the ground was rushing up to meet his face, and it was going to hurt so badly when he hit. But he still fisted his hands on the sides of Bas's t-shirt and let himself fly.

CHAPTER SEVEN

*H*e was kissing Drew. Holy shit. Kissing *Drew.* Drew, who was his best friend, his partner in crime, the person he loved most in the entire world. Drew, who apparently knew how to kiss better than anyone Sebastian had ever locked lips with, because *fuck.*

Every sensation was individually perfect - the lean heat pressed against Bas's chest, the roughness of the jaw under Bas's hand, the power in the hands, locked into fists around Bas's shirt near his waist. It should have all felt strange - the stubble, the whipcord strength, and it did, but there was also a feeling of absolute rightness - homecoming, even - and that made the strangeness *exciting.*

Bas tilted his head down slowly, not wanting to miss a second of Drew's reaction - the way the wide brown eyes Bas loved to look at grew stormy with heat and arousal, the way his lips - *had they always been that smooth, one slightly larger than the other?* - parted slightly in surprise and anticipation.

Drew is beautiful, he realized. And then their lips met.

Bas groaned helplessly, heart in his throat, and tasted

Drew's lips with his tongue. No cinnamon this time, just Drew. Sweet and tangy and perfect.

It was the most natural thing in the world for him to lift his hand from Drew's waistband to cup the back of his neck, to toy with the short hairs at his nape. It required no thought for him to lean in, when Drew's hands moved to splay across Bas's lower back, erasing the last bit of distance between them. And it was total instinct that had him rubbing his erection against the corresponding length he felt beneath Drew's sweatpants, and pushing him back against the wall.

Drew broke away with a tortured moan, and Bas inhaled greedily. Lust had stolen the breath from his lungs. "Christ, yes," he said hoarsely, his lips moving to taste the skin beneath Drew's ear. "Drew—"

He thrust harder, thrilling at the way Drew canted his hips, increasing the friction. He couldn't remember the last time he'd felt so mindless with want, except for those few brief moments on Halloween.

He returned his mouth to Drew's, eating at him like a starving man. The noises Drew was making, whimpers and groans that seemed to come from deep in his chest, spurred Bas on like nothing ever had.

Drew pulled his head back, just slightly. "Oh, fuck. Bas, I'm going to…"

"Yes. *Yes.*" He was going to make Drew come. And it was amazing.

Bas was nearly out of his mind. He thrust against Drew faster, harder, holding him against the door, their faces so close they were sharing breath and their gazes locked together as Drew's brown eyes widened. Bas felt him jerk and shudder as he came, just moments before Bas followed.

For a second, Drew let their foreheads rest together as they panted, undone. But when Bas lowered his mouth for a kiss, Drew's hands came up to Bas's chest and pushed them apart. "Stop. Stop, Sebastian."

"No—" *God*, not now. Not when it felt like they were on the edge of some emotional precipice. Not when he finally thought he could share all the things he'd been thinking about and worrying over, all the dawning hope he'd begun to feel.

"Yes." Drew's voice was breathless but insistent. Firm. "Back up. Please."

Bas shifted back inches, his dizzy mind trying to catch up to Drew's. "What's wrong? *Why?*"

"I have to go," Drew said, pushing Bas back another pace.

"Drew, don't do that. That's the stupid bullshit *I* did. Talk to me," Bas pleaded, grasping Drew's arms. "I know this scenario is…" He moved a hand to indicate the wall, and the damp sweatpants sticking to both of them. "Well, it's not exactly the stuff of dreams here."

Drew laughed, a single huff that was more bitter than amused. "You have no idea, Sebastian. None. But we can't do this." He shook his head, panic in his eyes. "It's fun *tonight*, sure, but what happens tomorrow morning? Or the next day? When the experiment is over and you realize that it's wrong for you?"

"I w—." *Wouldn't*, Bas had been about to say, but that was ridiculous, wasn't it? Because history showed that was exactly what happened whenever they got too close.

Bas closed his eyes and cursed past-Sebastian for the fucking idiot he was.

"You're jealous of Mark and Gary, because you don't want anyone to take your place in my life." Drew continued, his voice fifty shades of reasonable though his eyes were wild. "It makes sense. And what happened tonight?

Kissing is kissing. Friction is friction. This doesn't mean you're really attracted to me, personally."

No, Bas was pretty sure he clued in about the attraction when he realized he could get high from the way Drew kissed, from the feeling of their bodies pressed together, and from the way he wanted to touch Drew's bare skin with his hands.

But a sound like a record scratch halted his thought process while he contemplated the possible next steps. After nakedness came mouths and sex and… all kinds of things that were almost as scary as they were exciting. And he didn't have the first clue about any of them. Not with a guy. Not with Drew.

"There are things we can't come back from," Drew was saying. "We almost lost each other because a single kiss on Halloween freaked you out, and I'm saying right here and now, I cannot handle having you walk away from me again. I can't do it. So, whatever's prompting your desire to experiment, you've gotta ask yourself if it's worth throwing away decades of our friendship."

"Throwing away? Drew, no."

But Drew wasn't really hearing him. His face was closed off, shut down.

"So we, what? Just pretend nothing happened?" Bas laughed. The idea was ludicrous. As long as he lived, he was sure he would never forget what had happened tonight.

But Drew nodded, serious as a train wreck. His eyes were wide, shell-shocked, and he ran an unsteady hand through his hair. "That's exactly what we need to do. We need to back up a-and assess what's happening here." He spun around, collecting the suit and tie he'd laid over the leather side-chair after changing, shoving his feet into his shiny dress shoes, which looked ridiculous with his dirty borrowed sweats and ratty t-shirt.

Bas couldn't remember ever seeing Drew so frantic, so rattled, and for that reason, Bas didn't grab him and force them to talk this through. It'd be useless tonight.

"I'll see you at work tomorrow," Drew said. He grabbed his phone from the couch, giving Bas a wide berth, as though he was a particularly unpredictable form of wildlife. "G-goodnight."

Bas followed him to the door, and after Drew let himself out, Bas let his forehead fall against the closed door with a dull *thunk*. His heart was still racing in his chest, and his lips missed the pressure of Drew's.

Fuck.

He'd just rubbed off on his best friend. And it was messed up just how natural it all seemed. The mystery, really, was how he'd been around Drew for years - seen the lean strength of his body and the sexy tilt of his lips, felt the fiery thrill of his attention - without wanting to kiss him senseless.

Of course, part of the reason might have been his confidence that he was straight.

He let his head fall against the door again, harder this time, as doubts surged into his mind like hunting dogs.

It wasn't like Bas hadn't considered the question of his sexuality, for God's sake. His best friend was gay. His little brother was gay. It would've been strange if Bas *hadn't* tried getting himself off to gay porn once or twice. And he could say with conviction that the stuff wasn't *bad*, it just had never done it for him the way straight porn did. He *liked* breasts, he *liked* pussy, and he sure as hell hadn't been deluding himself about that all these years. So what the fuck was he doing with Drew? A man didn't suddenly become gay after thirty years... did he?

Maybe Drew was right.

Bas turned himself around and leaned his back against

the door, wishing he had someone he could talk to about this shit, but sadly the person he'd call - the one person he knew would always answer and would always talk sense to him - had just walked out.

He went into his bedroom and cleaned himself with a damp towel, shaking his head at his messy pajama pants as he threw them in the hamper and put on a clean pair. *So suave, Seaver.* Then he wandered back to the living room, picked up the empty beer bottles, and took them to the kitchen, rinsing them mechanically, his mind still on Drew.

His gaze caught on a large, framed collage mounted on the kitchen wall - a trio of Seaver family Christmas cards, mounted chronologically from top to bottom, from the years Bas had turned five, fifteen, and twenty-five. A familiar pang of grief twisted his stomach at the sight of his parents. They looked so damn young and happy in the first picture - his mother's hair long and shiny, his father's face grinning enthusiastically. By the last picture, both of them looked so much older, and Bas could see the lines that stress and worry had carved into his father's forehead. He wondered what changes another ten years would have brought.

But there wouldn't be another family picture coming. No commemoration of Sebastian's thirtieth Christmas this year, no pictures with Cort in the family, no grandkids. SILA and Alexei Stornovich had seen to that.

He ran a finger along the edge of the frame, tracing his mother's smiling face as he remembered one of the last conversations he'd had with her.

Sebastian! I can't believe you asked her! I worried you'd never make time to step away from your work and find someone to love. And you do love her, don't you, Sebastian?

I... I mean, yes. Of course! We've known each other forever.

Hmm. I worry about you boys. Sometimes you don't see the forest for the trees until it's too late.

But this time I've done you proud.

You always make me proud, Bas. Always.

Bas's chest got tight.

Alexei Stornovich was still out there, guilty as fuck and biding his time, and Bas had a job to do. If Drew wanted him to back off, Bas would attempt to do just that... at least until they'd brought SILA down for good.

CHAPTER EIGHT

August 2000...

THE HEAVY, humid air was a blanket on Drew's chest, the weathered wood dock solid beneath his back, and if he concentrated, really concentrated, he could tune out the voices in his head and focus on the sounds all around him - the lake water lapping against the pylons below, the drone of the night insects going about their business, the rise and fall of the wind as it stirred the leaves on the trees.

"Drew, you fucking fag."

Okay, so maybe tuning out was an overstatement, because the voices in his head were *loud* and sounded very much like Parker Galbreath's taunts from earlier that night.

The athletic director here at Camp Burgess - a sweet, pretty, unbelievably-earnest college student named Katrina who somehow managed to put up with dozens of idiot teenagers like Parker gawking and catcalling her all summer long - sometimes talked about positivity and intentional breathing, so Drew was trying his level best to *inhale peace and creative life force, while exhaling negativity.* But he was pretty sure there were limits to what yoga breathing could accomplish.

The pain in his stomach made him gulp down a sob, and he pushed himself up to sit, wrapping his arms around his knees and knuckling the moisture from his eyes because he was fourteen fucking years old and he'd be damned if he'd cry, even when there was no one there to see.

The world was wide and ancient, he reminded himself. And his life would be far longer than this one miserable summer, way bigger than Camp Burgess, and filled with guys who were not Sebastian Seaver.

Raucous laughter sounded across the water from the left bank of the lake, shattering the peace of the night, and Drew couldn't stop his traitorous ears from listening for one distinctive voice he'd always been able to pick out of a crowd. Would Sebastian be over there laughing with the other guys? With Parker?

Drew inhaled deeply and turned his head away, not wanting to catch even a glimpse of the bonfire he knew was set up on the beach there.

The Burgess Bonfires were a camp tradition, he'd learned back in July, when his mother and Mrs. Seaver had dropped him and Bas off with lovingly packed suitcases and stern instructions to "be careful." Careful hadn't been the plan for either of them, though. They'd been way too thrilled at the freedom of being off by themselves for a whole summer, away from anyone else who knew them. Bas, Drew knew, had been excited to play a role besides *genius nerd*. Drew had just been excited to spend every free minute with Bas who didn't always *get* social things and relied on Drew to guide him. He'd been confident this summer would be no different.

But it had been.

Drew touched his forehead to his knees as his mind tracked back over the past six weeks, trying to figure out when it had all started to go wrong - what *he* had done to make it go wrong.

There'd been the first dinner - the one where Parker announced that being a Seaver made Bas a *gamer geek*, as if Bas being the stunningly brilliant son of America's richest tech genius was in any way a bad thing. It had been so obvious to Drew that Parker was jealous of Bas - of his famous family, his artfully messy hair, his stunning blue eyes, and the broad-shouldered, loose-limbed grace that had made Ella Flores flirt with him all afternoon, but Sebastian hadn't seen it. And the second Drew had opened his mouth to blast Parker with a witty retort, Sebastian had stopped him with a glare, flushed beet red, and spouted some made-up bullshit about nearly failing a class this past spring because he'd been drinking too much.

Drinking.

When Bas had never had more than a couple glasses of wine *in his life.*

While Drew had gaped across the table at him, and Parker had slapped Bas on the shoulder jovially, Bas's wounded eyes had begged Drew not to deny it, so Drew had kept his mouth shut and hadn't brought it up since.

Then there'd been the obstacle course a few weeks after that, where the campers divided into two-person teams competing to solve problems designed to challenge them both physically and mentally. There had been no doubt in Drew's mind that he and Bas would be an unstoppable team - Drew was a strong athlete, Bas was easily the smartest guy in camp, and they communicated like they'd been best friends forever, because they *had*. So, he'd walked across the green and taken his spot next to Sebastian, who'd been laughing with Parker, Jason, and a bunch of other guys Drew didn't particularly like, and he'd asked, "Who's on our team?" Bas had hesitated, his eyes flickering quickly to Parker and Jason. "Oh, you're on McMann's team?" Jason had snickered, shoulder-checking Parker like he'd made some kind of joke. "Good luck, buddy." Bas hadn't said a word, but his shoulders had gotten tight and he'd barely said a word to Drew for the rest of the day, even when they'd won.

And then things had gotten worse and worse until finally…

Yesterday.

It had been cold and rainy - one of those weird autumn days that crop up in a New England summer - so Drew had let Ella and Colleen drag him to their art thing in the afternoon, rather than swimming in the lake with most of the others. Drew had learned weeks before not to seek Bas out for activities, since he insisted on hanging with idiots, and other than seeing each other in passing in the bunk room or at meals, they barely spoke anymore. So, he'd sat at a table in the community room, silently staring out the window at the rain, while the girls painted seashells and chatted about the bonfire. The one and only reason Drew was looking forward to the party was because then this fucking camp would be over, and maybe he'd get his friend back.

And then Bas had staggered in, drunk off his ass.

Drew had jumped up to help him, but Bas had waved him off and hobbled over to take the seat next to Drew, his bright, flirtatious eyes locked on Ella across the table.

"I fell off the dock," he'd told them, lapping up the girls' sympathetic cries. *"Managed to twist my ankle on the way down."*

Drew had stared incredulously at this guy who looked like Bas and sounded like Bas, but in every other way was a shadow image of the Sebastian Seaver Drew knew.

"And here I hoped you'd decided you wanted to come paint with us," Ella had teased.

"Shhhh. *That may have been the real reason,*" Bas had whispered, grabbing a paintbrush with a wink and getting to work on one of the stupid plastic seashells from the stack the girls were painting.

Ella had giggled, and Drew hadn't been able to stop himself from rolling his eyes. *"Yeah, Bas is a huge fan of art."*

"Fuck off, McMann," Sebastian had groused, but he'd smiled at Drew, really smiled, for the first time in weeks, and that had made Drew relieved… and bold.

"See? So cultured." Drew had smirked at Colleen, and that was why he'd missed the giant glob of blue paint Bas flung at his face.

The girls had promptly moved, screaming with laughter, but Bas was hobbled by his stupid ankle, and couldn't move a muscle as Drew retaliated, red paint splattering on Bas's chin and t-shirt. *"Very Jackson Pollock,"* he'd announced.

"You will pay," Bas had growled, grabbing a fistful of paint in one hand, and Drew's head in the other, before smashing them together, smearing sunny yellow all over Drew's cheeks and mouth.

Drew had pretended to sputter, waiting for Bas to smirk at the girls before grabbing his best friend by the chin, and dragging their cheeks together.

Laughing, giggling, smushing paint all over each other's hair and faces like the little kids they used to be, they hadn't noticed when the rest of the guys came back from the lake.

"Jesus Christ! Seaver's having a homo moment!" Parker had exclaimed. *"McCann got to you? Told you that shit's contagious!"*

Sebastian had jumped away from Drew instantly, flinching like Parker's words were acid and standing so fast he'd had to catch himself on the edge of the table when his injured ankle wanted to give out.

A homo moment? So many things had clicked into place then - a million stupid jokes and side-eyes from over the summer, a thousand curious glances shot his way, and most painful of all, the way Bas had completely shut down their friendship because he didn't want anyone to think he and Drew were… together.

He'd been dimly aware that Ella had come over to stand next to him, heedless of the paint, glaring daggers at Parker until he'd wised up and *shut* up. But Drew hadn't been able to turn his eyes away from Bas, who was frozen with shock and regret, his eyes pleading with Drew while making no move to come near him.

Jesus. Like Drew was a plague victim.

Drew had managed to get to his feet, to shrug off Ella's offer of help, to get back to the bunkhouse and shower, then plead a headache so he could stay in the infirmary overnight. And the whole time, as he'd mechanically gone about those tasks, as he laid in bed that night, he'd asked himself… *Is it true? Am I gay?*

There were some girls at school he knew were hot - a couple he'd kissed, and he'd definitely enjoyed it. And guys - the ones at school, the idiots like Parker - held zero attraction for him. And Bas… was Bas. Essential parts of each other's lives since birth. So maybe he felt a little proprietary, but Drew didn't, like, imagine him naked or anyth —.

Oh.

A hot pulse had shot down his spine as his mind fixed on the image. Sebastian, tall and lean, his chest covered with fine droplets of water, like when he emerged from the lake… Drew's dick had given an encouraging throb before he could shove the picture out of his mind.

So, so stupid. Stupid and *weird* and vaguely *wrong*. The very idea of Bas ever realizing Drew had thought that way about him made him queasy, especially after the way Bas had run from the very idea of associating with him.

Drew snorted. Even if he was gay, he refused to do anything as epically silly as falling for Bas.

The dock creaked and Drew's head spun around as a dark figure stepped out of the woods and onto the worn planks.

"Hey," Bas said hesitantly. He paused, as though unsure of his welcome.

Drew turned back toward the lake. For the first time he could recall, he wasn't sure if Bas was welcome either. He didn't know *how* he felt, except confused.

With hardly a sound, Bas walked forward and took a seat beside Drew, mirroring his position. They sat in silence for a while, Drew focused on his breathing and categorically refusing to think about liking guys, and especially not liking *Bas*. In his peripheral vision, he could see Bas glancing at him from time to time, like he wanted to say something, but couldn't, and it made Drew perversely glad. Drew was the one who'd always talked for both of them.

Finally, Bas had broken the silence with a sigh that lingered in the air like a breeze.

"You didn't stay at the bonfire." His voice was deeper than usual, not a tone Drew was used to.

He was stating the obvious, so Drew didn't reply.

A minute later, Bas tried again, "I told him to shut the fuck up. Parker, I mean. I told him… I told him not to say that shit anymore."

Drew, you fucking fag.

And suddenly Drew knew exactly how he felt. He was *pissed*. And more than that, he was *hurt*.

"I sincerely hope you didn't do that for my sake," Drew said, the impact of his frigid tone muted by the leftover tears clogging his throat. "I hope you did that because

Parker is a homophobic asshole, and no one should talk that way."

"You're right. I know you're right." Bas nodded. "But I mostly did it for your sake."

Yeah, right. After nearly a whole summer ignoring him, trying to impress Parker, pretending to be an entirely different person? Fuck that. But when Drew opened his mouth, all that emerged was a single syllable. "Why?"

"Because you're my best friend, Drew. My... my brother."

That was not a compliment, as far as Drew could see. "You already *have* a brother, and he drives you crazy." Camden's favorite pastimes included playing video games and following Bas around like a puppy. This was still one step up from Drew's own younger sister, Amy, a moody, superficial pain in the ass who'd looked at Drew with nothing but disdain since she'd turned eleven earlier this year.

"Not like Cam." Drew could hear the eye-roll in Sebastian's voice, and fought to maintain his distance. Here, in the dark, when it was just the two of them, it would be far too easy to forgive Bas. "You know me better than anyone else."

"Why now?" Drew demanded. "Why *now*, when you haven't cared all summer?" But then, that was the answer, wasn't it? The summer was over, and Parker would be leaving, crawling back under whatever rock he'd come from. Now Bas wanted to make nice before they went back home, back to reality.

"I did care. Of *course* I cared. It's just..." Sebastian sighed into the night, his pale hand glowing in the moonlight as he ran it through his dark hair. "You don't get what it's like, Drew. To be the odd one out all the fucking time.

To be unable to fit in with people unless my best friend is there to make sure I don't act like an idiot."

"I don't?" Drew interrupted. Indignation had him turning to face Bas at last. "You think I don't know what it's like not to fit in? Jesus, Bas. Was this whole summer supposed to be some kind of punishment?"

"No! *No!*" Bas denied quickly. "It had nothing to do with you. It's just… you know how we are, you and me." His voice was soft, cajoling. "I'm invited to things because you are, and we're a package deal. I'm so in my head all the time that I miss shit socially, and you end up fucking explaining it to me." He sighed again. "My mom told your mom that if it weren't for you, I'd spend all my time locked in my room with my computer like a vampire."

"So? If it weren't for you, I'd be failing math and I wouldn't bother owning a laptop. What does it matter if we help each other?" Drew couldn't keep the annoyance from his voice.

"Maybe because I wanna know I can handle shit." Bas sounded defeated. "I want to know that I'm a competent human, you know? Not just some fucking programming *idiot* who can't relate to people. I don't want to *need* you or anyone. I don't want to imagine a future where I'm going to be tripping over some chick and you're gonna have to ask her out for me because I can't get my shit together." He flopped back on the dock and flung an arm over his eyes.

Drew's throat got tight. He didn't want to imagine that future either… and his realization earlier gave him a whole new insight as to why that future looked so painful.

"So I wanted Parker to, you know, like me. Think I was cool. *Whatever*. To prove that I could *human* on my own." He made a sound halfway between a laugh and a sob. "And essentially all I did was prove that I can't. I'm just not as good at life without you."

Drew snorted. "Looked to me like you were doing just fine. Parker's your *bro* now. You were sitting with his little court at the bonfire tonight." Was sitting there when Parker had caught sight of Drew, standing off to one side of the beach, desperately trying not to be noticed. Was sitting there, and hadn't said a word when Parker had called him out in front of everyone.

Drew, you fucking faggot.

"Yeah," Bas whispered. "And that's what proved my point. Because… that's not the kind of person I want to be, Drew. The look on your face yesterday, and then tonight when you walked off…"

Drew huffed. Walking off was a bit of an understatement. It had been more like running. And he could only imagine that his face had been pathetic.

"You were so calm. So fucking… proud. You know who you are. You don't give a shit about Parker or… or anyone. *You're* the kind of person I want to be."

Bas's hand had moved down, and the words were muffled. Drew wasn't entirely sure that he'd heard that last part correctly. He reached over and grabbed Bas's wrist, moving his arm off his face.

"Say again?"

"You heard me," Bas whispered. "I want to be like that. Just, waving a middle finger at every asshole who tries to bring you down."

Drew licked his lips. Bas's interpretation of events was so far from reality it was comical. It was also really, really appealing. But it didn't let Bas off the hook.

"I *don't* give a crap what Parker thinks," Drew confirmed. "But I care what you think. And it was really shitty that my best friend didn't defend me."

"I did, though," Bas said, pushing himself up to sit next to Drew. Drew realized he was still holding Bas's wrist and let go of it immediately. "I told him to fuck off, and that he didn't know shit about you. I pushed him into the water." He shrugged. "Better late than never?"

He could almost feel Bas's gaze on the side of his face, all hopeful and eager as Drew looked out at the moonlit water, like things could go back to normal just that easily.

Drew swallowed.

"Thing is, Bas," he whispered, oily nausea racing up his chest, threatening to choke his words. "Maybe... maybe Parker was right about some things."

The words dropped into the night, and the whole world ceased motion for half a second... or at least that's how it seemed to Drew. His breath caught in his throat, the breeze stopped blowing, the night animal orchestra ceased playing, and the entire universe hung in suspended animation, waiting for Bas's reaction.

His totally anticlimactic reaction.

"You mean, because you're gay?" he said, a shrug in his tone, and Drew turned to look at him in surprise. "Dude, come on. You can't have thought that I would care. I mean, my mom volunteers at the LGBT youth center. They're both pretty liberal."

"But your dad is all... man's man *whatever*."

Bas shrugged. "Well, I mean, if it was *me* he might care." He chuckled, as though the very idea was laughable, and Drew's chest went tight. "But he definitely supports equality and stuff. And besides, I'm not totally like my dad just because I'm smart like him."

Drew nodded slowly. "So it doesn't, like, freak you out if your best friend is gay?"

"No!" Bas said staunchly. "It doesn't. And I swear to you, Drew, I will never let what anyone else thinks come between us. Not again."

"There will be a lot of people who think it's weird for a

straight guy to have a gay best friend." Drew shook his head. "We'll have to be careful how we act."

"Who gives a shit? You're my best friend. Hanging out with you doesn't make me gay. Nothing between us ever has to change!"

"I don't know…"

"I do." Bas insisted. Then he leaned over and kissed Drew.

The whole thing lasted about thirty seconds - ten seconds of soft, hesitant barely-touching contact, followed by ten seconds of Drew's lips being smashed against his teeth. No other part of their bodies touched, and Drew noted in some distant corner of his mind that the scent of Bas - bug spray mixed with the dank odor of pond water - was anything but romantic.

And then Bas pulled back and smiled, wide and open, like Drew was the greatest thing on earth and Bas was thrilled and proud to have proven himself. And those final ten seconds - the seconds when Bas smiled - were the ones that changed Drew forever.

"I'm a pretty good kisser, eh?" Bas said. "My game's pretty epic. Try not to fall in love with me." He nudged his shoulder into Drew's, inviting Drew to laugh along.

But all Drew could do was smile and nod and think *Oh my God. I love Sebastian Seaver.*

And he could never, ever know.

Bas held out his hand, palm up, directly over Drew's lap, and Drew glanced down to see the brightly colored sand dollar Bas had painted the day before, illuminated by the moonlight.

"Peace offering?" Bas said. "It's a keychain. For next year, when we get cars. It's, like, the only artistic thing I'll ever do, probably, which makes it an exclusive collector's item. And it can be yours for the low, low price of forgetting what an asshole I've been for the whole summer and being my friend for the rest of my life."

His gaze implored Drew to take the shell, to accept his apology, to take things back to the way they'd always been.

Drew hesitated for only a fraction of a second before closing his fingers gently over the sand dollar. "Friends," he said solemnly. "Always friends."

And he willed the half-formed dreams of *more* to fly away on the breeze across the water.

CHAPTER NINE

*D*rew ignored the phone chiming on the counter and instead concentrated on measuring coffee into the coffee maker - *one, two, three*. It was surprisingly difficult.

Or maybe not surprising.

He hadn't been able to focus on one damn thing all day yesterday either, fucking up practically every piece of paperwork he'd touched until Peter had - politely and respectfully, of course - told him not to send another email or sign a single document until after the holiday weekend, when he'd hopefully be "better rested."

He didn't have the heart to tell Peter that all the sleep in the world wasn't going to solve Drew's problem, not when his brain kept replaying Thursday night's frantic make-out session on a constant loop until he could practically feel the weight of Bas's lips on his, the slide of Bas's fingers on his skin.

And now he'd fucking lost count of the coffee again.

"Fuck!" He slapped the countertop hard enough to

make his hand sting, then dumped the filter out and started over.

Bas would arrive any minute now and Drew was dreading it. Yesterday it had been *Drew* locking himself in his office and actively avoiding any possibility of confrontation, like the world's biggest hypocrite. He was annoyed with himself.

It wasn't like him to be a coward, but honest to God, the things Bas had said the other night were things Drew had only ever dreamed of hearing him say. It was all too good to be true, and he couldn't help worrying about when it would all go bad. Past experience had shown him that.

Drew didn't believe for a second that Bas had any idea what he really wanted in this situation. And after they'd kissed more, after they'd slept together, or dated for a week or two, and *then* broke up? They'd never be friends again. The dead radio silence of the past month had been painful, but it would be *nothing* compared to the nuclear-winter-agony of losing Bas for good.

Getting involved with Bas romantically was *beyond* risky. And anyone who knew Drew could say with confidence that he was risk-averse.

His damn phone chimed on the counter, and Bas dusted his hands on his jeans before grabbing it, hoping and fearing that it was something from Sebastian... but no.

Mark. Again. Texting about their date tonight.

Hey, you! You didn't reply earlier. Excited for later?

Drew sighed and rolled his eyes. Excited in a dreading sort of way, maybe.

He felt slightly guilty for feeling that way, but he'd already figured out yesterday, after a bunch of back-and-forth texts, that he and Mark were not going to work out. They shared a bunch of interests, sure, but the guy's endless compliments were borderline-creepy, and his neediness would drive Drew crazy in a heartbeat.

"You didn't reply earlier?" the man had said? Seriously? It had been twenty minutes for God's sake, and Drew had a life of his own and a crisis to focus on.

But, it was too late to cancel without being insanely rude. And maybe, just maybe, it was a step he needed to take if he wanted to get the distance and perspective he needed to figure out what to do with Bas.

Busy morning. Yes, looking forward to tonight. 6:30 at West Kitchen.

It was perfect timing, since it meant their meeting today couldn't go too late, and he would have the perfect excuse not to chat with Sebastian afterward.

Oh, the hypocrisy.

He tossed his phone down on the counter and opened a glass-fronted cabinet to take down a set of red ceramic mugs.

Mark texted again a second later. Annoying, since Drew had pretty much finished with this conversation.

I can't wait. I think I'm going to wear green, in case you wanted to coordinate. What are you doing this afternoon? There's a seminar on Biodiversity in Fruit Trees at the Museum of Natural History that I'm thinking of attending if you're interested.

Drew rubbed away the beginning of an ache in the center of his forehead. Jesus. Bas made fun of his old-man radio stations, but this was a whole other level. He tried to keep the snark out of his text as he replied, *That sounds very educational. Sorry to miss it, but I'm afraid I have plans. Enjoy!*

A second later, Mark's answer came with a picture of his dog attached. *I'll take notes and share them with you later! Felix says hi!*

Felix looked like he was asleep on a white carpet in a pool of winter sunshine and couldn't give a shit about Mark or his texts. Drew felt like he and Felix might be kindred spirits in this.

THE SECOND BATCH of chocolate-chocolate chip muffins was cooling on the counter a little while later when the doorbell rang, and he opened his front door expecting Cam, Cort, Damon, or Cain - someone who *didn't* have a key to his house.

Instead Sebastian stood on the front stoop, looking hot as hell in worn jeans and a thick knit sweater, a white paper bag dangling from his wrist and a polite, distant smile on his face.

"Hey," Drew said, his throat suddenly dry for a lot of reasons. "Forgot your key?"

"No, I have it."

Drew blinked, something cold slithering through his stomach at the tightness in Bas's voice, the thin thread of *hurt* Drew could feel there, but he nodded and stepped back, letting Sebastian pass.

"You're, uh, the first one here," Drew said lamely, following Bas to the kitchen.

"Figured. No other cars in the driveway." Bas put the bag on the counter and started removing boxes stamped with the name of their favorite bakery.

"Panadería Pascal?"

"Yep." Bas didn't pause or look up, but the muscles of his back were visibly tight beneath his sweater. "Figured you were right about me baking a cake." His voice was flat. "I don't do so well with following rules. So."

Drew closed his eyes. Had he wounded Sebastian's pride by rejecting him? For the umpteenth time, he berated himself for the drunken idiocy that had started them down this road. "Sebastian, listen, I didn't want…"

"No, it's cool," Bas said, holding up a hand. "We don't need to rehash anything. You made your feelings pretty clear the other night. You want to be friends. I respect that."

I made my feelings clear? Drew almost laughed. In that case, he kinda wished Bas would explain them to *him*, because Drew couldn't say what he was feeling, except unsure, guilty, and a little bit nauseous.

"It's just that you mean more to me than anyone, and I —" Drew threw his hands up in the air, lost.

Bas grinned at Drew's eloquence, and though the smile didn't quite reach his eyes, it was a start. "Nah. It's fine. You were right."

"I was?" Of course he was. And *of course* Bas had realized it. Drew ignored his racing heart.

"I've hurt you a lot. So we'll chill for now. Be friends. See how things go. And focus on SILA, getting justice for my parents and Amy."

"Right," Drew agreed, though his voice sounded hollow to his own ears. "We can… chill."

"So, you have a particular plate you want me to put these sweet rolls on, Martha?"

Drew cleared his throat. "Ah, anything in the cabinet to the right of the fridge." The doorbell rang again. "Cavalry's here."

But Bas was busy looking in the cabinet and didn't turn around as Drew left the room.

He desperately wanted to tell whoever was on the other side to go the fuck away, and then sit down with Bas so they could eat and talk and laugh, and get back to normal. *Fuck*, but he was tired of dealing with this bullshit. Evil politicians who betrayed their friends, Russian mobsters who'd killed people they loved and could come after them at any moment. He wanted to scream.

Drew took a deep breath to collect himself before answering the door. He was being irrational, yeah. He fucking knew it. And he knew it wasn't going to get him anywhere, either. But the section of his brain where his calm, logical center lived - the part he'd relied on for years - seemed to be stubbornly silent this morning. Control Freak Drew, where did you go?

"Hey," he said, opening the door to Cam, who carried a platter of something that smelled deliciously of onions and herbs, and Cort, who had his arm wrapped around his boyfriend's waist and appeared half-asleep. "Come in."

"Sorry we're late," Cam said, stepping inside. "This one was up until all hours working on a security issue."

"You're fine. Cain and Damon aren't here yet." But he stopped when he saw Damon's beaten-up truck pull into the driveway, and traded a grin with Cort as he passed by. "Never mind."

Cain hopped down from the passenger's seat, cradling a plastic container, and waited for Damon to make his way around the front of the cab. Damon's leg, which had been injured in the plane crash and then again as he and Cain ran from some of Alexei's thugs a month ago, had healed significantly, but he still walked with a noticeable limp. That didn't stop him from grabbing the container from Cain's arms and holding it aloft as they made their way down the walkway, despite Cain's attempts to jump up and snatch it back.

"Morning, Drew," Cain said, pointing at the container. "We brought cookies."

"McMann," Damon greeted Drew, his voice sandpaper-rough as always. "I'll have you know, my sister and niece baked these cookies and sent them to us. I'm bringing them under duress." He turned his head to glare at Cain.

Cain glared right back, folding his arms across his chest. "He has three dozen more back at our apartment," he told Drew, rolling his eyes. "And he's already eaten two dozen in the last two days. He's going to be the size of a house if he doesn't learn to share."

"He's mad because I ate the last macadamia one last night," Damon confided.

"Yes! Because you knew they were my favorite!"

Damon smirked at Drew and handed Cain the container. "Which is why I put a couple in the freezer for you, *kid*."

Cain's narrow-eyed expression, a combination of outrage, amusement, and absolute love, made Drew's heart twist with want. "You were holding out on me?"

Damon shrugged at his boyfriend as they walked in the door, eyes glinting. "A little denial is good for the character."

"Hmm." Cain said, squeezing past Damon to head to the kitchen. He turned his head to smirk back over his shoulder. "We'll see how you feel about denial when you're on the receiving end."

Damon blinked. "But…I saved you cookies!" he yelled as Cain disappeared.

Drew shook his head. "Come on," he said, giving Damon a consoling pat on the back.

The others were already arranged around the huge farmhouse table that took up one side of Drew's kitchen, and someone - likely Sebastian - had arranged platters of food and a carafe of coffee in the center.

"Thanks," Drew told Bas, nodding at the table as he took the end seat.

"Yeah, sure," Bas said. He was looking at Drew strangely.

"What's wrong?"

"Nothing's *wrong*. I just found…" A phone chimed, and Bas shook his head, fishing his phone out of his pocket to check his messages.

Another day, another interruption.

"Okay, first things first," Cort said from the far end of the table, where he was seated between Cam and Damon. "I think we need to make notes. Kinda consolidate everything we know right now in one spot." He grabbed a muffin from the platter. "And we can share the info with Sean Cook, my old boss at the FBI."

Up and down the table, heads nodded as everyone filled their plates with food. Drew stood and grabbed his tablet from the counter, along with his phone. "Okay, I'll make notes."

He resumed his seat, and saw that Bas was scowling at his phone, typing away.

"I was thinking pencil and paper," Cort sighed, his hatred of technology clear. "But whatever. Let's go through everything we know starting with the crash?"

"I think we should start chronologically," Drew suggested. "From back in the last millennium, when SILA first started working with Seaver."

"That makes the most sense," Cain agreed. "According to my father, their association started back before Seaver Tech was even officially founded. Levi had ideas, but no capital, and Ilya Stornovich offered Levi and my father the money to start the company, at a pretty high interest rate."

"Loan sharks," Cam said dourly.

"Essentially," Cain agreed. "But Seaver Tech never had a problem making the payments. They were successful right out of the gate, and paid back the initial loan quickly."

"And in the meantime, SILA grew. The little neighbor-hood crime gang Ilya Stornovich founded became a huge regional crime organization," Sebastian said.

Damon snickered and Drew glanced up. "It's just... the parallel is strange, isn't it? His business grew just like Seaver Tech grew, successful from the start."

"If you're making comparisons between my father and Ilya Stornovich," Bas said heatedly, but Drew held up a placating hand.

"Nobody is doing that, Bas. Your dad made the choices he made - choices that Senator Shaw and my own dad were complicit in, by the way, so no one here is casting stones - because he wanted to build something for his family. In his own way, that's what Ilya did, too."

Bas's nostrils flared and he folded his arms across his chest.

"Anyway, yes. Ilya grew his business," Drew said as he typed. "And then he retired and left it to his son."

"Alexei," Cam spat. "Who wasn't content with having the loan repaid in full. He decided he wanted to extort my dad, get him to provide technology."

"Which he did, if we believe Uncle- I mean, Senator Shaw." Bas's voice was heavy, resigned, and so fucking weary. "I wish I knew exactly what he gave them. Projects he worked on for other clients? Or new tech they wanted developed? It's almost impossible. If dad kept files on this stuff, I can't find them anywhere."

"Would they be paper files?" Cort asked, somewhat hopefully.

Cam patted him on the knee. "No, baby. My dad was a tech guy. He didn't do paper and pen if he could help it."

Bas's phone chimed again, and he scowled as he retrieved it.

"Everything okay?" Drew leaned over to whisper, nodding at Bas's phone.

"Nothing to worry about now." He set his phone face-down, and shook his head, refocusing on the conversation.

"I can ask my father," Cain was saying, looking at Damon. "See if he remembers any names?"

"You want to do that?" Damon wrapped a supportive hand around the back of Cain's neck, and Cain nodded.

"I think I should." He looked up and down the table. "I talked to my parents at Christmas. Things aren't great, especially with my mom. I don't think she'll ever forgive me for coming out publicly and ruining her standing with her lunch club." He sighed. "But my dad is trying. He... I don't know how to feel about it." Cain spread his hands in front of him, almost a pleading gesture. "He's a criminal. He killed people. You know? I don't know how to forgive him for that, or how he can make amends."

Bas sighed. "Cain, I'm the first person to tell you, your dad *is* a criminal. And he deserves to be punished for what he did. But, hey, seems like my dad was, too, huh?" He gave a half-laugh and shook his head. "Point is, no one can tell you how you're supposed to feel about it. It's fine to be confused. And it's fine to forgive him, if that's how you feel."

"Yeah?" Cain whispered.

"Yeah." Bas cleared his throat. "You need to make your own right path - one that's true to who you are. And trying to love people, trying to forgive them for being blind and stupid, that's generally always the right way. I don't always get there, myself, but... if you can, go for it."

Drew looked up from his tablet and stared at Bas, stunned.

"What?" Bas demanded.

"Nothing." Drew shook his head, even as his chest

warmed with pride and... yeah, fuck it, *love*. "That was just... really profound."

"Yeah, well, every once in a while I get something right. Don't look so shocked." Bas rolled his eyes, and Drew ducked his head as he smiled, afraid of what Bas might see if he looked too closely.

"Okay," Damon said. "So Cain will talk to his dad about projects. What's next in our timeline?"

"Next is that my dad said *no*," Cam said, a note of pride in his voice. "For whatever reason, he got fed up and didn't want to give them information anymore."

"And Alexei didn't take too kindly to that, because he's a miniature despot who trusts no one." Drew filled them in on everything they'd learned about Alexei from Gary. "So he forced Senator Shaw's hand and had him arrange for the Seavers' plane to crash."

"Which I don't get," Damon interjected. "He's a man with a hundred henchmen on his payroll. Why get the senator involved at all?"

"Leverage," Cort answered. "If Alexei's men did it, the senator could get all remorseful at any point and blow the whistle. This way, Shaw can't come clean without implicating himself."

Bas laid his hand on the tabletop, his fingers clenched into a fist. "Such a fucking prick."

"He really is," Drew agreed.

"And so, the senator had his assistant Jack Peabody sabotage Damon's plane, causing the crash," Cam continued.

"And I survived, much to everyone's amazement," Damon interjected.

"But the others didn't." Bas stared at his fingers, and Drew couldn't help lifting a comforting hand to his shoulder.

"I figured out Jack was involved, and we confronted him. He told us he'd taken orders from the senator and was arrested, but never made it to trial." Damon's jaw tensed. "Because he was killed in prison."

"Which my dad claims he had nothing to do with," Cain reminded them all with a shrug. "According to him, that was all on Alexei."

"Figures," Drew said. "And then you and Damon confronted your father, who explained that he'd only gone through with it because Alexei was threatening your family. Is that pretty much all we know?"

They all nodded.

"Is there a way we can leverage what you just told us about Alexei's lieutenants being unhappy with him?" Cort's eyes were narrowed in thought.

"I don't know." Drew shrugged. "Not without names, and Gary didn't feel like he could share."

"What about their side businesses? ID fraud and all that," Cort wondered. "Could we nab him on a lesser charge?"

"Get a murderer on ID fraud?" Damon asked dubiously.

"Remember they got Al Capone on tax evasion," Cort reminded his brother. "Stranger things have happened."

"It could work." Drew looked at Bas, who was scowling at his screen. "What do you think?"

Bas looked up from his phone, startled. "Huh? I'm sorry. What were you saying?"

"That maybe we could get Alexei on ID fraud, if we can't bring him down on something bigger."

"No." Bas shook his head, putting his phone down. "In fact, *fuck* no. I don't want to get Alexei on ID fraud, or possession of drugs, or jaywalking, or whatever misdemeanor we can come up with. I want to get him on *murder*.

He had my parents killed, Drew. He had your sister killed. He needs to answer for that. Anything else is unacceptable."

Drew sighed. "Sebastian, if we *can* do that, we *will*, but isn't it more important to remove him from power and stop him from killing anyone else?"

"No! I mean, yeah, that's important, but getting him on ID fraud… that's a stopgap, and not a guarantee that he'll even see prison. Besides, how the hell are we even going to do that much?" he demanded, glaring at each person around the table in turn.

"I agree," Damon said. "He ruined my life…" He glanced at Cain, and his expression softened as he stroked the column of Cain's neck with his thumb. "Or he tried damn hard to, anyway. I want him to pay for that."

"That would mean my dad coming forward and going to prison," Cain said woodenly. "He'd have to confess and, as much as he's trying to be helpful now, I don't see that happening."

"I just want this to be over." Cam crossed his arms and stared around the table. "I want to know that no one is coming after us. Will getting them on ID fraud be enough to ensure that?" he asked Cort.

Cort grimaced and shook his head. "I don't know, babe. It would depend on whether someone pleads out, and how generous the prosecutor is being. I still have a lot of friends in the FBI, but investigators don't have the final say on plea deals. If a prosecutor feels like they could turn Alexei? Use him to get a RICO charge on another organization, or hunt down an even bigger fish…"

"He wouldn't spend a minute in an orange jumpsuit," Bas growled.

"I still say it's worth pursuing," Drew insisted. "I mean, if we could get information from Gary on just that aspect of the organization - just finding a couple of fake IDs that were used or whatever, maybe we could…"

"Could *what*? Is that going to dismantle SILA?" Bas demanded as his phone chimed again. He glanced at the screen and swore under his breath.

"What's going on?" Drew demanded.

"I told you, it's nothing." He caught Drew's glare and sighed in frustration. "Nothing *pertinent*, okay? Just that asshole who's been emailing me at work. Michael Paterkin."

Drew narrowed his eyes, trying to recall the name. "Wait, is that the guy who was sending you weird emails insisting you get him a job?"

"Yeah, said he worked with my dad. Well, he's gone from insisting to threatening. Not a big deal, just annoying."

"Threatening?" Cort said, his gaze sharp. "Explain."

"Not threatening like he's going to kill me. Just obviously pissed off. A crackpot. It's noth—."

"Don't say it's nothing, Sebastian. Remember this is my *job*, yeah? Head of security for your company?" Cort reminded him mildly.

"What idiot promoted you to that position?" Bas demanded, rolling his eyes.

Since everyone knew that Sebastian had created the position for Cort himself, Cort didn't bother to dignify this with a response.

"Hand me the phone," he demanded, and Bas passed it down with a mighty sigh.

"My dearest Mr. Seaver," Cort read aloud. He glanced up and down the table. "Anyone else creeped out already?"

Cam snorted and leaned in, putting a hand on Cort's thigh. "Keep reading."

"I am sure you have received my several recent messages regarding a most important opportunity for us to work together, but I have to date not seen your reply."

"It sounds like one of those Nigerian phishing scams," Cain said, frowning. "Does he want your bank information?"

"It's the English," Cort mused. "A little bit stilted, the words out of order and way too formal. Ordinarily, I'd ignore it, but the dude goes on to say that he enjoyed working with your father many times in the past, and appreciated the brilliance of their work together on the *Collier Project*." He glanced up at Bas. "Any idea what that is?"

"None." Bas shrugged. "Must've been before my time."

"Can we check out what it was?"

"Already on it, babe," Cam said, typing out a message. "I'll have Margaret look into it."

"Okay, good," Cort said. He frowned at Bas's phone. "He says if he doesn't hear back from you today to discuss the details, he'll be 'forced to take actions you would not enjoy.'"

"What the hell does that mean?" Drew demanded.

"It means he's a lunatic who wants a job," Bas insisted. "If I got agitated every time someone asked me for a hand-out, I'd already be dead of a heart attack. What's he gonna do, really?"

Cort shook his head. "You might be right. It might be nothing. But it's worth looking into. I think we need to play along with him and find out what the hell he wants before we dismiss him." Cort handed the phone back to Bas. "Reply and ask him for more information."

Bas flushed. "I, uh… I already sent him a reply."

"Oh, lord." Drew covered his face with his hand. Of course Bas had already replied, no doubt with his usual tact.

"I told him to fuck off and stop contacting me," Bas admitted.

Worse than Drew had thought. *Jesus*.

Bas's phone chimed again. "It's from him." He swiped his finger across the screen and looked at Cort, eyes worried, then read aloud. "Mr. Seaver, you remind me of your father. He, too, was an intelligent man who died for his arrogance. Thus far, I have attempted to be friendly and helpful. But in the end, you will come to me, offer to work with me, offer me anything I want. Indeed, you'll be begging for my help. And please know, I'll be waiting to hear from you." He swallowed hard. "It's signed Michael Paterkin, but... Jesus, Cort, is that Alexei?"

Cort ran a hand through his mop of hair. "I don't know." His voice, usually so open and joking, had morphed into the cold, tightly-controlled voice of a trained operator, and that change more than the chilling words of the email, sent a chill up Drew's spine. "I'm going to call Sean and have him run this guy's name." Cort stood up and walked into the living room, sliding his cell phone from his pocket.

Drew looked at Cain, Damon, and Cam in turn, and saw the same anxious resolve in their gazes that he imagined they'd see on his. Their peaceful interlude, thanks to Senator Shaw's intervention, was over.

It was time to end this standoff for good, one way or another.

Taking a deep breath, Drew turned to look at the man on his left, who had hardly moved since he finished reading the email. Every muscle in Bas's body was locked, from his jaw down to his torso. His phone was still clutched in his hand, and though the screen had turned black, he continued to stare at it with wary absorption, as though Alexei might appear on it at any moment. Drew was nearly afraid to touch him in case he shattered like glass, but he knew from experience that beneath the surface, that genius brain was whirling a mile a minute.

"Hey," Drew whispered, sliding the phone from Bas's hand and setting it on the table. He leaned closer, not quite whispering. "This is…" *Going to be okay*, he was about to say. But then, no one knew better than the men sitting around this table that there was no guarantee of that whatsoever. Too many lives had been lost and ruined thanks to Alexei Stornovich for Drew to spout platitudes. "This is exactly what we knew would happen. We are going to do everything we can to handle this. Together. Understand? You're not alone. None of us are."

For a moment, Drew thought Bas wouldn't react, but eventually his gaze slid right, and those fiery blue eyes locked on Drew's. "Yeah?"

"Yeah."

Bas nodded slowly and took a deep breath as Cort came back into the room.

"Cooksy's running the name as we speak," he said, coming to stand behind Cam's chair so he could rest his hands on his boyfriend's shoulders. "But he's fairly confident, and so am I, that this is a threat from Alexei or someone who works for him."

Drew inhaled sharply, lifting his chin to the ceiling at this confirmation. "So what do we do?"

"Well, the first step is that I'm meeting with him this afternoon to discuss the possibility of pursuing a lower-level investigation on Alexei. I know what you're going to say," he interrupted himself, holding up a palm toward Sebastian. "It's not good enough. I know. But from everything Gary told you and Drew, Alexei's grudges are his own. There's every reason to believe that if we can take Alexei out, our dealings with SILA will be over and done with." He glanced up and down the table. "I know just how much that asshole has cost every single person in this room. I know how badly you want to get justice for the people you loved." He squeezed Cam's shoulders. "And to get your fucking life back." He nodded at Damon, who wrapped a shoulder around Cain and pulled the man practically into his lap. "But we need to consider the future."

"Whose future?" Bas demanded.

"All of ours," Cam said hotly, glaring at Bas. "What will it take to get justice for Mom and Dad and Amy? Is it worth sacrificing your life? Mine? Drew's?"

Bas's gaze shifted to Drew. He glanced away. "Fine."

"Okay, good. Everyone needs to be extra cautious from now on," Cort continued. "I'm doing updated background checks on all Seaver Tech personnel, and I'll have a core group of guys I trust handle security for the building round the clock. But I'm more worried about personal safety." He looked at Damon, Cain, Bas and Drew. "Those security systems we installed in everyone's home are top-of-the-line, but it goes without saying that they only work when you use them." He ran a hand over Cam's hair. "Even when it's the middle of the day, and the door is locked, and you're wide awake."

Cam blushed and glanced up. "It was one time, Kendrick."

Cort stroked Cam's cheek with a tenderness he didn't often display in public. "One time too many, babe."

Cam shut his eyes tightly and nodded.

"I don't think any of us need to curtail activities right now - we can go to work, go to the grocery store, and continue our normal routines as much as possible. As long as Alexei thinks Bas is treating his email like a crackpot threat, he'll think he has us at a disadvantage." He looked around the table. "But we'll need to be hyper aware. Better to pair off as much as possible, and not take any unnecessary risks."

"That makes sense. Drew can stay at my place," Bas said.

Drew's eyes widened. Oh, the last thing they needed right now was proximity. There was *no* perspective in proximity. "Uh, no. I can't."

"Fine," Bas conceded with a sigh. "We can stay at your house then. But the commute is gonna be…"

"I'm not living with you, Sebastian." He turned to Cort. "I'm *not* living with him."

"You're joking!" Bas spluttered. "That's ridiculous! You've slept at my house a hundred times. More! Christ. We've shared tents and fucking sleeping bags, McMann. We can share this house if it means keeping you safe!"

Cort frowned. "Bas is right. If you could…"

"I can't." His voice was loud and unequivocal, and maybe a tiny bit desperate.

"Uh. Okay, then," Cort agreed, clearly surprised at Drew's vehemence. Drew's control-freak reputation was suffering hit after hit this week. "It's less than ideal, but if that's what you think you need to do…"

"It is," Drew insisted. He couldn't bring himself to look at Bas. He could feel surprised anger and hurt radiating off the man, and nearly wavered in his resolve.

"Fine. Sebastian, you can come and stay with your brother and me — ?" Cort offered.

"No. It's not *me* I'm fucking worried about!" The tension in Bas's voice suggested he was two seconds away from meltdown, and Cam clearly recognized this.

"New Year's Eve is tomorrow. I'm not sure what everyone has lined up, but maybe we need to cancel those plans," he suggested. "You guys can come to our place and hang out, or everyone can stay home."

"Great idea," Cort said.

"We had no plans anyway," Cain agreed.

"Speak for yourself," Damon informed him, waggling his eyebrows. "I had lots of plans for you."

Cain turned beet red and slapped a hand over his boyfriend's mouth, but somehow reserved Damon had managed to cut the tension around the table, and everyone laughed.

Everyone except Bas.

"Stay with Cam and Cort tonight, then," he told Drew, unable to let the subject drop. "Or Damon and Cain."

Drew shook his head. "It's not that I don't want to stay with you in particular, Sebastian." It was. It totally was. "I have…a thing."

"A thing." Sebastian's voice was as icy-cold as the air outside, heavy as lead.

"A *date* thing. With Mark." He looked at the others. "A guy I met a couple of months ago."

Damon looked at Bas and winced, and Cam whispered, "Oh, Jesus," under his breath.

"Not a big deal. I do date from time to time," Drew said hotly. Though not recently, for damn sure.

Bas sucked in a breath through his nose. "You really think that's wise?"

Drew's neck muscles clenched as his temper soared. No, it *wasn't* a fucking wise idea. It was an exercise in futility. Worst-case scenario, he was leading on a guy who already seemed way more interested in him than he would ever be in return. But he was scared. So damn scared that he would fuck up their friendship further if he stayed.

"It's not up for discussion," Drew said, still without looking at Bas. The tension between them was a thick cord, frayed and straining.

"Really? Because you *just said* not five minutes ago, that we were all going to stick together."

Drew looked at Bas, shocked. "But I was talking about

you going off doing…" He swallowed, and Bas nodded grimly.

"Doing stupid shit? Yeah. That's exactly what this is about." He ground his teeth together. "You're like the one idiot in every horror movie who insists on going off on their own. People are covering their eyes and peeking through their fingers saying, 'No, Drew! Don't be a fucking idiot!'" Bas's voice was high, mocking, then turned to a growl as he spat, "They should save their breath. Andrew McMann doesn't need anyone's advice! Christ, why would he when he already knows everything? He doesn't need anyone to worry or give even that first *shit* about his welfare. He can run his life *and* yours. Hell, he even knows what you're *feeling* better than you do."

Drew's stomach dropped. No, that wasn't what he was doing! That was ridiculous!

Wasn't it?

Bas stood, his chair squealing against the hardwood floor, and stared down at Drew so their gazes locked. His eyes were glazed over with a molten combination of anger and pain, and Drew was horrified to realize that he was the cause. "Isn't that right, Drew?"

"No," Drew whispered, his stomach churning. "I never said…"

"That's right. You never said *anything*." Bas pushed his chair in roughly, jostling the table, and the others sat back, silent. "For years, you said *nothing*. Your choice. Your terms. You always had to be in control… until that one time you weren't."

"Bas," Damon said, a warning note in his rough voice, but Drew barely registered it. His throat was clogged with anger and tears, and he couldn't think of a fucking thing to say. Bas was wrong, so wrong. Everything he'd ever done, every action and every conscious choice not to act, had been designed to preserve their friendship, for God's sake.

He wet his lips. "And what happened then, Sebastian? I lost control one time… and then I lost *you*. For weeks you ignored me. Turned your back on me, easy as that. And I'm supposed to forget it just because you say so?"

"I was confused!" Bas yelled.

"Uh huh. And you had to solve your problem by yourself, didn't you?" Drew stood, smacking his palm on the table. "You could have talked *to me*. I begged you to talk to me. Spiraling and spiraling, never letting anyone in. *It's all my fault*," Drew mocked, pressing the back of his wrist to his forehead. "*I'm responsible for everything, and only my great genius can save us.* But what did it solve, Sebastian? All that time in your little cave, searching for answers alone, and Alexei is still after us. All that time spiraling about Halloween, and you still don't even know what you want! Not really."

"It's not me who's scared, Drew. It's not me who—"

"Whoa!" Cam interrupted. "Guys, seriously. If you're talking about what I think you're talking about…"

"Shut up, Camden," Bas and Drew said in unison, their gazes still locked like dueling wands.

"Hey now," Cort interjected. "This isn't the time or the place. If you wanna flay the skin off each other, do it in private. And for Christ's sake, don't do it when we already have a fucking psychopath crime boss gunning for us!"

A muscle in Bas's jaw flexed and finally, finally he looked away. "You're right, Cortland. I don't think I have anything more to say to Counselor McMann at all." He grabbed his phone from the table and slid it back into his pocket, while Drew watched wordlessly, chest heaving. "You want company when you meet with Sean Cook? I can give him the names of the companies I got from Alexei's server. Might do some good to someone, even if it's not admissible evidence."

Cort and Cam exchanged a glance. "Yeah," Cort said. "That'd be good. You can drive us and Cam can take his car."

"Actually, Cam, I have a gift card and I need to buy some…ah, video games?" Cain said, after a wordless communication with Damon. "Why don't you come back to our place and you can help me teach Damon to play?" He shrugged. "Safer that way?"

Damon rolled his eyes, but stood and rounded the table to extend a hand to Cam. "Right. I just love me some video games. We can call it brother-in-law bonding."

"Perfect." Cam stood and kissed Cort soundly before following Cain and Damon to the hall.

Damon turned back before he'd gone two steps and walked back to the table to snatch up his tin of cookies. "Shame to waste them," he told Drew with a wink and a one-shouldered shrug. "Take care, McMann."

Drew nodded, the only response he was capable of.

"Cam, phone on at all times!" Cort called after them.

Cam turned to give his man a brilliant smile and a lazy salute. "Yes, sir." He gave Drew an apologetic half-smile. "Thanks for the brunch, Drew!"

"Yeah, thanks for the brunch, Drew," Bas said roughly, stalking his way around the table without a backwards glance. "Enjoy your *date*."

Drew gripped the back of his chair so hard he wondered if he could crack the polished hardwood.

"Listen," Cort began hesitantly when everyone else had left. "I don't know exactly what's going on with you two…"

"Join the club." Drew huffed out a laugh. But then he shook his head. "That's a lie. I know, I just don't know what to say or do about it."

"You're a lawyer, McMann. You know how to talk your way out of a million scenarios." Cort folded his arms over his chest and watched Drew steadily.

"Yeah? Well, not this one."

"Then maybe…" Cort cleared his throat and winced. "Christ, I hate giving advice, but… If you don't have anything to say, maybe you should start listening instead."

Drew's eyes met Cort's green ones, surprised at the amount of sympathy that shone there.

"You love him," Cort said. It wasn't a question, and Drew didn't pretend to misunderstand the context. Cort meant *in* love, far beyond friendship. Drew only hesitated a second before he nodded.

"For years."

"Do you trust him?"

"Of course I do!" He grabbed plates of food from the table and moved them over to the island. "I've known him for decades. I'd trust him with my life. What kind of question is that?"

"Thing is, Drew, you're a smart guy. A problem solver. You're good at it, which is why you're an excellent attorney… and a much better friend than I gave you credit for the first time we met in that hotel bar."

Drew snorted, thinking back to their disastrous first meeting, and Cort grinned.

"The only problem is, you're busy trying to make things the way they *should* be for everyone you care about, and sometimes that makes it hard to hear when people tell you how things really *are.*"

Drew dropped a plate of muffins on the island with a clatter. "Pretty sure you're trying to tell me I'm a control freak."

"But in the nicest possible way."

"Huh." Drew leaned his hands on the edge of the sink

and watched as his fingertips went white. "Don't feel so in control these days, Kendrick."

"And maybe that's a good thing," Cort shocked him by saying. "Dude, make some time to meet with him. Soon. Like, *tomorrow*. Let him talk, and when he does? Listen. Believe him."

Believe him. Trust him.

Drew shook his head. "That sounds deceptively easy."

"No way. Listening *is* easy. But believing?" He grinned. "Some of us have harder heads than the rest of the world, McMann. Takes a little longer for shit to penetrate. But if I can get there, you can."

From outside, a car horn sounded, and Cort chuckled. "Jesus, first I'm giving advice, now I'm stuck with *that one* for the evening."

"And you're letting him drive." Drew shook his head. "Is your health insurance good?"

"I'm winning all the karma points today." Cort clapped his hands together once. "Anyway, you be careful tonight."

"I will," Drew promised. "It's honestly not going to be a late night, I can tell you already. I just felt like I needed to... Well." He didn't need to explain himself to Cort. The man he owed an explanation was currently in the driveway, impatiently tapping out *Shave and a Haircut* on his car horn.

"I'm going to West Kitchen," Drew said quickly. "At six-thirty. I'm meeting a man named Mark Charbonnier. And I'll have my cell. Call if you need me."

"See? Smart guy," Cort said with a wink. He strolled out the door toward Sebastian, leaving Drew to contemplate a date with a man he didn't want, and a reckoning with the man he did.

CHAPTER TEN

"*Yeah!* You see that? Everybody see what my man Brady did there? He just performed a fucking miracle on the field! Nobody else coulda thrown that pass. Greatest of all time, baby!"

The drunk guy at the bar was cheering loud enough to be heard over both the din of the packed restaurant and the cheering of the crowd on the bar's big-screen TVs, which was of course tuned to the late-season Patriots game. The guy's absolute glee was enough to make the three men seated in the back booth roll their eyes and trade grins.

"Glad somebody's happy," Sean Cook remarked, staring down at the page of notes he'd made over the past two hours of sipping beer and talking Russians.

"You're not happy to be here, Cooksy?" Cort demanded, tilting his beer bottle to his lips. "That hurts, man." He set the bottle down and clapped an offended hand to his chest.

"Yeah, yeah," Sean sighed. "Just once, Cortland, I wish you'd call and offer to buy me a beer that didn't come with a side order of me doing semi-legal investigations for you. That's what got you canned in the first place, remember?"

Cort grimaced. "I promise you, after all this bullshit is over and Cam is safe, Seaver and I are going to take you out for *twelve* beers. And we'll even cart your drunk ass home to your wife," he vowed.

"Hell yes. Twelve imported beers," Bas agreed. "And the biggest steak in Boston." In truth, he'd offer to pay Sean a fucking fortune for the help he was giving them, if he thought the guy would take it.

"Also, just for the record," Cort added with a smirk. "I was never officially canned. I quit."

Bas rolled his eyes at the man sitting next to him. "A technicality, as I heard it."

"No shit. You quit like two minutes before you would've been canned. And I'm taking you up on the twelve beers and the steak." Sean hesitated, then added, "But, ah... Stacey moved out."

"Are you kidding?" Cort turned serious. "You're separated? You guys were solid!"

"I thought so too. But it's been a long time coming, I guess. Too much stress at the job and then coaching the kids' sports teams in my off time, never made time to spend with her, never took an interest in her work. The whole nine." Sean waved a hand through the air. "Pretty sure we've all heard this song before."

Cort nodded, brow furrowed. "Yeah. A career in law enforcement takes its toll on a marriage. But I'm still sorry."

"'Preciate that," Sean said with a sad smile. "Between that shitstorm at home, and Agent Porter breathing down my neck at work, it hasn't been a fun few months. But the new year is almost here, right?" He raised his beer bottle in an ironic toast and took a deep drink. "Onward and upward."

Bas and Cort exchanged a look, and Bas made a mental note that when this thing with Alexei was over, he was going to find Sean Cook a very high-paying job at Seaver Tech. Maybe he'd make him Cort's boss, just to mess with Cort. The idea had him fighting a grin. He'd have to ask Drew how they could accomplish that, next time they...

His brain stopped short.

Next time they, what? *Hung out?* Yeah, right.

With a sigh, Bas sipped at his own beer. Given the way he'd completely lost his cool at Drew's house earlier in the day, he couldn't imagine they'd be having another pleasant video game night anytime soon, and the thought of that - of losing something so essential he'd always taken it for granted - made him panic. He'd spent the afternoon trying to make his mind focus on the conversation, to take solace in logic, planning, action, but it wasn't working.

"So, the Paterkin guy mentioned something called the Collier Project?" Sean tapped his pencil against his paper. "What do we know about that?"

"Not a damn thing. My assistant checked our archives, and there's nothing by that name," Bas told him. "Besides which, Margaret's been at Seaver since my dad founded the place, so if it were a big thing, she'd remember. It's possible that Collier was a contractor we worked with, or a contact person for a company. We'll need to dig deeper. Margaret offered to get started this weekend, but I didn't want to worry her. I told her it could wait until Monday."

Sean frowned. "There's nobody else at the company who could research it for you?"

"Maybe? I have a few people I trust completely, but it'd be like looking for a needle in a haystack for anyone who hasn't been at the company since the early days. And there are several long-term employees who might recognize the name, but if Paterkin is actually Alexei or works for

Alexei, and the Collier project is probably one of the jobs my dad did for SILA, I really don't want to call attention to it."

"Right." Sean tapped his paper again, then looked up at Bas and grimaced. "Then I think you need to tell Margaret to work this weekend."

Bas lifted his eyebrows in surprise, the knot of tension he'd been carrying in his stomach all afternoon tightening a fraction.

"Do it. Buy her a yacht, if it makes you feel better," Sean said grimly. "But this doesn't look good."

Cort sighed. "You think Paterkin - or Alexei - will threaten to go to the press with info on Seaver Tech's dealings with SILA?"

Bas stared at Cort. "What? You never mentioned that as a possibility."

"I was hoping Cooksy would have a different read on it."

"Actually, I do. It sounds to me like he was initially trying to recruit Sebastian, much the way he did with his father."

"Recruit me? Yeah, right."

"No, seriously." Sean leaned back slightly in his seat and looked at Bas fully. "It's better for Alexei's image inside his organization to show that he can make you kneel to him than to actually crush you. If he could acquire you as an asset, he could still get tech from you. Best case scenario, he could have lured you into working with him by offering you money."

Bas snorted. He was confident he could buy and sell Alexei's organization ten times over.

"Okay, fair enough. Not a huge inducement for you," Sean agreed. "So, second-best scenario, he *threatens* you and gets you to work with him that way."

Bas's stomach shifted uncomfortably. "Threatens me how?"

"Well, it could be with a media scandal about your dad, like Cortland suggested." Sean shrugged. "Whispers about your father's connection to SILA could cause some trouble for you - stock prices dropping, losing government contracts, that kind of thing. But Alexei can't say too much without implicating himself. And your father's death absolves him of most guilt in the court of public opinion." His mouth twisted in sympathy. "And I think Alexei knows that."

"So, what then?" Cort demanded.

Sean rubbed a hand over his chin, scratching at the stubble. "Well, I suppose the best thing would be to threaten you some other way - a physical threat maybe? Breaking your kneecaps unless you comply? Because he knows you won't risk involving the police, and once he gets you to do even one thing for him, he'll own you the very same way he owned your dad."

Christ. The very idea made him sick.

"Senator Shaw has information on Alexei and SILA," Bas reminded Sean. "Enough that they've backed off for a few weeks now."

"Yeah, but that information implicates Shaw, as well as Alexei. Will he use it to prevent a scandal for Seaver Tech?" Sean shook his head. "To save his kid's life, sure. Maybe the guy has the stones to hang himself to save his kid. I know I would. But to keep Seaver Tech from going under? Nah."

It made sense. Frankly, he was surprised Shaw had even pushed back against the Russians to save Cain. The guy wasn't exactly warm and fuzzy... *or* particularly loyal.

"So, if we think he'll plan to beat me into working with him, maybe I need to get him to make a move? Come at me, try to force my hand, and trap him when he…"

"Wow, ready to jump right in!" Sean said. He downed the rest of his beer and wiped his mouth with the back of his hand. "Sadly, this isn't a Lifetime movie, and the FBI doesn't like to use civilians as bait unless it's the *only* option. Besides, Alexei's likely had Plan B and Plan C in his pocket, ready to go. The very best thing you can do is stay vigilant, and don't take chances."

Chances, like Drew going out on a date. Bas felt his anger rise again, along with something else that made his stomach clench. Something pitifully like jealousy.

Was Drew really so excited about this Mark guy that he couldn't cancel or at least *postpone* his love-fest while they were being hunted by a psychopathic Russian criminal?

Bas ground his teeth together and breathed through his nose, remembering the sand dollar keychain he'd seen hanging from a hook in Drew's cabinet that morning. Drew *had* kept the damn thing, even after it broke, though he'd let Bas believe it was gone. Kept it, and put it back together almost seamlessly, so you could hardly see the crack. That had to mean something, didn't it?

But if it did, why the hell was Drew out on this date?

Emotions were fucking impossible. No logic, no clarity, no way to forge a path through them. He could barely get a handle on his own feelings, let alone trying to suss out Drew's. He needed to stick to the things he was good at.

"Cook, I can help. I can try to access his system."

"I thought you already did that, and there was no sensitive information online."

"Well, yes, but I can try again. Maybe bribe someone to get me some login credentials. Or better yet, someone to gain me access to the offline server where the real goods are kept."

"What?" Sean stopped himself, shaking his head. "Let me make sure I understand what you're suggesting here before I go off. You want me to let *you*, an untrained civilian who's so well-known his face is plastered all over checkout stands from coast to coast, gain physical access to SILA's headquarters and their servers?"

Well, when he put it *that* way…

"No way," Sean continued firmly. His eyes pinned Sebastian in place. "You think he's not monitoring you, waiting for you to do just that? No. If you want me to help you - and I want to help, Sebastian, I do - you need to let me handle this *my* way. I don't want you to do anything more strenuous online than updating your Facebook status. No hacking. No traces. Not even a Google search about this. Got it? I can operate with a certain amount of anonymity, look into shit and make it seem like the low-level kind of surveillance we're always doing on organizations like SILA. But some anonymous hacker starts knocking shit around, it's going to look suspicious and Alexei will know it was you."

"What? Knocking shit around? You're kidding me, right? I'd be in and out before they knew I was there. I did it before."

"You wanna bet your life that your luck will hold? Your friends' lives? Come on, Seaver. Work with me."

Bas fumed. "I need an outlet, Cook. I need something to focus on. Let me help." *Before I have a nervous breakdown and do something stupid, like kidnap Drew from his date and hold him prisoner until we work out our shit.*

Maybe naked.

"The only help I need from you is contacting Margaret and asking her to send me information on every project your dad worked on - nothing his team handled, only the projects he spearheaded himself - for all the years he was in contact with Alexei. I'm pretty sure your dad would have wanted to be the only one with eyes on the projects he was sharing with SILA."

"Fine. I'll do it now," Bas said, pulling out his phone and typing a brief message to Margaret.

"Good. Once she gets me the information, I'm going to cross-reference it with all of Alexei's known aliases and associates, including this Paterkin guy, and any mention of a Collier project."

"You need help?" Cort asked. "That's a big job."

"Nope. The fewer people in the loop on this, the less likely I am to attract notice from the powers that be." Sean rolled his eyes. "And besides, I have a lot of free time in the evenings these days."

A waitress in a dark-green *Lola's* t-shirt approached their table and started loading their empty bottles onto her tray. "Get you boys another round?"

"Yeah," Cort said, glancing at Bas. "I'll have another. And maybe an order of guac and chips."

Bas nodded.

"Not me. I'm out. I'm picking up my kids from a birthday party and bringing them to Stacey's. All hyped up on sugar and ready to play." Sean smirked as he reached for his wallet.

"No way are you paying," Bas said, putting a restraining hand on Sean's arm. "Jesus. You're risking your career helping me out."

Sean looked at Bas for a minute. "I'm risking my career because it's the right thing to do."

"Either way," Bas said quickly. "I'm buying your beer."

Sean snorted. "Have it your way, Seaver." He stood, shoving his wallet back in his pocket. He grabbed his jacket from the seat and his notes from the table. "I'm not kidding. You guys need to stay out of this and let me work. Trust me. Do *nothing* about this, hard as that is."

Bas studied the wood-grain print of the Formica table for a second, then looked up at Sean. He *did* trust the guy, not only because Cort trusted him or because he'd helped them in the past, but because there was something innately trustworthy about him. That didn't mean he agreed with everything the man said.

"Yeah, okay. Twelve beers," he reminded Sean, extending his hand.

"Counting on it," Sean said, shaking Bas's hand firmly.

Sean clapped Cort on the shoulder, then lightly slapped the side of his face twice. "Stay safe, boys."

After he'd walked away, Bas sank deeper into the fake-leather cushion and sighed. Cort moved to sit across from Bas and studied him for a moment.

"He's a good guy," Bas offered.

"The best. You gonna do what he said?" Cort wore a knowing smirk.

Bas sighed, then nodded, making up his mind on the spot. "Only because he managed to convince me that I'd put everyone at risk if I didn't. But I don't like it," he added sourly. "Being benched when this is something I do better than…"

"Better than everyone else?" Cort finished, when Bas cut himself off mid-thought rather than sound like an asshole.

Bas flushed. "Well, yeah. It's not conceit, Cortland. It's what I do."

Cort nodded, then looked at Bas thoughtfully. "You know, before we met, I had this whole idea of you in my head as an arrogant, entitled asshole."

"And then I proved you wrong."

"Well, first you proved me *right* by being a total jerk when we were back on St. Brigitte," Cort told him, eyes dancing. "But yeah, then you've proven to be not so bad."

The waitress delivered their beers at that exact moment, and Bas glared across the table at the man who was almost his brother-in-law before replying. "If it makes you feel better, I thought you were an insensitive idiot who was either gonna get my brother killed or break his heart."

Cort smirked and took a pensive sip of his beer. "And yet, I'm the guy who'd protect Cam with my life, and you aren't particularly arrogant or entitled."

Bas batted his bottle back and forth across the table, from hand to hand. "But still an asshole?" he joked.

Cort closed his eyes briefly and smiled. "Sometimes."

"Sometimes I feel like one." He narrowed his eyes. "You know why everyone was on the plane the day of the crash?"

"Fate?" Cort suggested.

But Bas shook his head. "They were there to celebrate my engagement. To Amy." Cort blinked, and Bas elaborated. "Amy McMann, Drew's sister."

"Yeah, I know. Cam's talked some about it. I've seen pictures."

"Right." Bas took a sip of his beer.

"Must've been hard for you," Cort said slowly. "Losing your fiancée on top of everything. But what does that have to do with you being an asshole? You didn't cause the crash, Seaver."

"No. Nope. I didn't. But if it hadn't been for me getting engaged, they wouldn't have been there. Drags at me, you know?" And maybe it always would, even though Drew didn't hold him responsible.

Cort cut him off with a shake of his head. "You and your brother. Seriously. Buncha martyrs."

"Pardon?"

"You know, the first night I met Cam, he told me he was guilty because *he* was supposed to be on that plane!" Cort said, almost amused. "Like if he'd been there, he could have psychically known the engine had been tampered with."

"That's stupid," Bas said, stunned. "I had no idea he felt that way."

Cort shrugged. "I think it was mostly just some latent guilt. I think he knew it wasn't reasonable even then. Whereas you seem to have convinced yourself that it's totally reasonable." He shook his head. "It was a tragedy, Bas. It was *murder*. It wasn't your fault, even a little bit. If he hadn't seen this opportunity and taken it, maybe he would have had Jack tamper with a car instead, and killed a bunch of innocent people on the road along with your parents. Or something else entirely." He shook his head. "There's no knowing."

Bas stared moodily at the table. "That's what Drew said," he admitted.

"Yeah? Then why are you so determined to make this about you?" Cort wondered.

"I'm not *determined*. It just…" Bas blew out a breath and looked Cort in the eye. "I wasn't in love with Amy."

He wasn't sure what he expected to happen. Maybe for Cort to narrow his eyes in judgement, maybe for flames to erupt… something dramatic and scary.

Instead, Cort just nodded sadly. "That sucks. Was she in love with you?"

"I don't think so, no," Bas said. "We had things in common. Friends. Family expectations."

"People get married for lots of reasons," Cort said. "Bas, you didn't cause the crash because you weren't head-over-heels for her."

Bas bit his lip. It sounded so ridiculous when Cort said it like that. "I know," he said finally. "I do. But I still feel like I need to get justice, you know? Like I owe them that. Before I can do… anything else."

"Anything else, like… fall in love?" Cort guessed, and Bas's eyes flew up to find Cort watching him steadily. "Sebastian, you don't owe anyone penance here," he continued quietly.

"Feels like I do."

Cort shook his head. "So, like I said, I used to think you were an arrogant, entitled asshole."

"We're back to that?" Bas rolled his eyes and sipped his beer.

"It was easier for me to think that, back when I thought Damon was dead and maybe you had paid someone to cause the crash and kill your parents."

Bas winced. He remembered when Cort had accused him of that a few months back. It wasn't any easier to hear it now.

"It's easier to have someone to blame," Cort continued. "No matter how illogical it was. But that doesn't make it true. You need to get this idea out of your mind. The crash wasn't your fault. Getting engaged to someone for practical reasons wasn't wrong. And regretting the engagement… well, that's not wrong either. Forgive yourself for being human, and move on."

Yeah. Maybe. But even if he could, he'd fucked up the only thing he most wanted to move toward.

"I lost it at Drew's today," he told Cort instead.

"I was there. But it was a very stressful day, in a stressful week, in a stressful year," Cort said. "Tensions run high, and things spill over."

"Maybe." Bas played with his bottle for another minute, then looked cautiously at Cort before confessing, "Our argument wasn't about Alexei, though. Not entirely."

Cort sighed and cast his eyes toward the ceiling like he was asking for divine intervention. "Love advice, twice in one day?" he muttered to the heavens. "Really?"

"What?"

"Nothing. The universe is out to get me." Cort shook his head like he was resigning himself to something. "So you and McMann."

"Yeah. Me and Drew." Just saying the words felt *right*. Him and Drew. It had always been him and Drew. "We kissed."

Cort's eyes widened and he leaned closer. "Reeeeally? You and the counselor finally hooked up? Do tell! I've been watching you two dance around each other for months now. Pretty sure all of us have."

"Don't be an ass."

"Tiger can't change his stripes, Seaver," Cort said, pointing his beer bottle at Bas. "So, when did this kiss happen."

"Uh. Which time?"

"More than once? Damn, Seaver. *Damn*."

The laugh that bubbled out of Bas's chest surprised both of them. "The first time was on Halloween. Well, no, the *first*-first time was back while we were kids in summer camp, but ah... that doesn't really count." He frowned. "I don't think. Does it?"

Cort scratched his temple. "I... guess it counts only if you want it to?" he suggested.

"Right. Okay, so then that was the first time. And the second was on Halloween."

"Halloween," Cort repeated. Bas watched him connecting the dots mentally, no doubt thinking of how tense things had been between Bas and Drew for weeks, and then how Bas had disappeared off the grid altogether.

"I didn't take it well," Bas admitted. "The first one, when we were kids... that was mostly a joke. Or, I let it be one." He pushed both hands through his hair, grabbing at the strands.

"And I thought this would be the same, but it got *real* pretty quick. Drew had been drinking, and he told me... he told me he'd wanted to do it for a long time." Bas lifted his eyes to Cort's. "I didn't expect it to be like that. Threw me, you know?"

"Didn't expect it to be what?"

"Well... awesome. *Hot.*" Bas looked away.

"But it was."

"Yeah." Bas sighed. Bas fell silent as the waitress returned with their food and departed again. "Messed me up how hot it was. Drew and I have been best friends forever. Longer than Cam has been alive, even. And in all that time, I've never been attracted to him."

"But you are now."

"I... Yes." He thought of Drew's lips, of his brown eyes when they were hazy and unfocused with lust. "Yes, now I definitely am."

He looked up at Cort, waiting for a reaction - shock, confusion, maybe even *anger* or disbelief that Bas could suddenly feel this at his age.

But Cort just nodded and dipped a chip into the guacamole, like straight men admitted having crushes on other men every damn day in his world.

Bas wasn't sure how to feel about that.

"Damn!" Cort said, crunching the chip. "This shit is good! You know, I never liked guacamole when I was a kid, and then Cam convinced me try it again a few months back. Fucking delicious."

"Uh. That's good?" Dealing with Cort's conversational shifts was like herding kittens. Freakin' exhausting.

"Anyway, back to what you were saying." Cort washed down his chip with some beer. "I'm not seeing the problem. You're attracted to him, he's attracted to you. You're practically married already, you're so close. Grab some lube and go for it." He shrugged and pointed a fatherly finger at Bas. "Be safe, kiddo."

"Are you being deliberately obtuse? I am *straight*, Cort. *That's* the issue!"

Cort blinked in surprise, then his gaze softened. "Evidence would suggest otherwise, Sebastian," he said softly.

"I've dated women. Had sex with women. *Enjoyed* sex with women, even." Bas's voice sounded bewildered to his own ears.

Cort grinned and winked. "Me too. Lots. Not that I'm one to kiss and tell."

Bas folded his arms over his chest. "It's not a joke."

"No." Cort sobered. "It's not. I'm sorry. I've known I was bi since high school, so I forget how scary it can be to make these realizations. But it's gonna be fine, dude. There's not a single person we know who will think any differently of you. And if I can help you in any way…"

"That's not it! It'd be fine if I was gay, Cort. Or bi. Or what-the-fuck-ever. But I'm… I've got to be straight. I've *always* been straight. People are *born* the way they are!" Bas took a deep breath before he started singing Lady Gaga in the middle of the crowded bar.

Cort frowned. "Well, yes, in the sense that it's not a conscious choice to be gay or to be straight. But sexuality isn't black and white, anyway; it's more like a spectrum. And it's not a fixed thing, either. Your attractions can evolve over time. I'm not attracted to the same people I was when I was younger." He shrugged. "Hell, if my taste in snack food can evolve, why can't my attraction to different people?" He popped another chip into his mouth.

"Because…" Bas shook his head and ran a hand through his hair. "It's not that simple."

"I *agree*," Cort said intently. "It's not simple at all. It's actually super complex. Sexuality doesn't necessarily follow any rules or develop fully in a specific time frame."

"I'm a thirty-year-old adolescent?" Bas rolled his eyes to cover his frantic thoughts.

Cort snickered. "So tempting to give you shit, but no. And also…" He licked his lips as if debating whether to say something.

"Spit it out." Bas crooked his fingers in invitation. "While I'm already reeling."

"Maybe think about whether it *is* a new thing, or whether maybe it's been happening for a while and you're just ready to come out to yourself now." Cort's voice was low, soothing, like Sebastian was a skittish horse.

And maybe that wasn't too far from the truth. His mind was practically dancing, realigning and re-categorizing information based on this new data, thinking about all the times he and Drew had been physically close and he'd run away.

"Have I been lying to myself all this time?" he said, horrified. "When Cam and Drew have always been so honest about who they are? God."

"Bas, it doesn't work like that," Cort insisted. "I mean, I'm not some gay guru, okay? But if there is one thing I know, it's that it's a process, an evolution. *There are no rules.* Everyone has their own truth, and they recognize it in their own time. There is no right way to do this. Or maybe it's better to say, *any* way you do it is right. Any time you accept yourself for who you are, it's a win. And it's not fair to say, 'I should've realized I was gay when I was a preteen like Camden,' any more than it's fair for me to say, 'I should have realized avocados are delicious when I was a kid.'"

"Could you shut up about the damn guacamole?" Bas sighed.

"It's an *analogy*, Seaver. Yeesh. Follow along here." Cort

winked. "Right, lemme break it down for you with no snack references." He counted off on his fingers. "First, give yourself a break. Second, you don't need to label yourself. Maybe you're a straight guy who likes kissing Drew." He shrugged. "Weirder things have happened. Don't feel like you need to label yourself *anything* unless *you* find it helpful. And third, it should go without saying, but I won't share this with anyone, even Cam. He wouldn't expect me to. You can talk to other people about it if or when you're ready. Yeah?"

Bas nodded, too overwhelmed to speak. Maybe he was bi. *Or maybe I'm a straight guy who likes kissing Drew.* He ran a hand over his eyes and huffed out a laugh. Fucked up as it was, the idea was a revelation. For a man who needed to sort data, to evaluate and categorize and, yeah, *label*, the idea that he didn't have to label himself at all was... fucking revolutionary.

Sebastian took a sip of his beer and took a second to appreciate the fact that he was discussing Drew - his *romantic feelings for Drew* - without a nagging worry in the back of his mind. What if... what if he could just *be* with Drew. Kiss Drew every fucking day. Have... *Oh, Jesus. His dick pulsed in his jeans before he could even complete the thought...* Have sex with Drew.

His chest felt lighter than it had since October.

"So, maybe you need to share this revelation with Drew," Cort suggested, his eyes teasing.

"Well, the thing is, I kinda tried. I...we hooked up the other night." He held up a hand before Cort could open his mouth. "Yeah, it was hot. *No*, I'm not giving you details for your prurient fantasies."

Cort snickered.

"But Drew told me he doesn't want it to happen again. He's scared that I'll figure out this was all a mistake at some point. That I'll pull away again to sort my shit like I did the past month. And it'll ruin our friendship permanently."

Cort grimaced. "Do you blame him?"

"No. It wasn't my finest moment."

"Typical Seaver though. Gotta puzzle it out in that genius brain of yours." He rolled his eyes. "When all along, what you've had is a heart problem, not a head problem. You were using the wrong machine.

"I guess maybe I have." Another stunning idea.

"Falling for someone is scary shit. Believe me." Cort's mouth tilted up at one corner. "I avoided love for three decades, before it fell on my head like an anvil in a Roadrunner cartoon. It kinda makes sense that you'd wanna avoid that - something you can't control or think your way out of."

Something he couldn't control or think his way out of? Yeah, that was his relationship with Drew, alright. So maybe it did make sense that he'd hidden behind Amy, behind his straightness…

Bas blew out a breath and looked at Cort across the table. "You're a fucked up kind of Dear Abby, Cortland. But shit, you're good." He couldn't believe he'd ever thought Kendrick Cortland was insensitive.

"Uh huh." Cort sighed. "So I keep telling your brother, but he just rolls his eyes and reminds me he said *I love you* first."

Bas snickered.

"So. You want Drew?"

"Yeah," Bas whispered. It was rather frightening how badly he wanted Drew.

"You love him?"

"I've always loved him." No surprise there. And maybe… Maybe he'd been *in* love with him for nearly as long. Damn.

"Then tell him so, genius."

"How do I convince him to take a chance on me, though?"

Cort grinned so widely that his eyes crinkled at the corners. "Oh, Seaver." He shook his head. "I am pretty sure that won't require much convincing."

"You think?"

Cort's eyes flashed with humor. "Care to make a wager?"

Bas snorted and Cort relented.

"A blind man could see it, Seaver. He wants you."

With a shaking hand, Bas combed through his messy hair. "Fuck, I wish I knew where he was. I kinda wanna camp out on his doorstep. How stupid is that?"

"Extremely stupid," Cort agreed. "Since I happen to know that he's meeting Mark Charbonnier at West Kitchen, a lovely establishment not two blocks from here."

"Are you… are you kidding?" Bas blinked and pushed himself out of his seat before his brain was aware of the movement. "Oh, Kendrick Cortland, I could kiss you!"

"Your brother would take you down if you tried," Cort declared smugly as Bas reached for his jacket.

"I wish I'd had the Mark-dude's name when Sean was still here," Bas said. "I would've given him one more name to run."

"Yeah, I don't think that's legal or even advisable," Cort began. "It's kinda borderline-stalker." Then he stopped himself and shrugged. "Oh, who am I kidding? I'd totally do the same thing." He grabbed his phone and winked. "I'm texting Cooksy and having him add Mark's name to the list. Just in case dude's got a long line of defrauded ex-boyfriends or unpaid parking tickets to his name."

"Perfect. I owe you, big-time."

"Nah. No debts among family." Cort looked up after

sending the text and heaved a long sigh. "But since this advice thing is apparently addictive after the first hit, I've got one more piece for you. Talk to him, Bas. Explain everything you explained to me. You guys have that symbiosis thing happening, but don't assume that he's actually inside your wacky mind and can read your thoughts, yeah?"

Bas laughed. "Yeah. Okay, I promise."

"Then have fun storming the castle," Cort said, waving his hand airily as he finished the last of his beer. "Go get your prince. I'll call an Uber and go get mine."

CHAPTER ELEVEN

"*D*o you like calamari? Because they do a calamari, grapefruit, and avocado bruschetta antipasto that is *to die for*, I swear!"

Drew rested his elbow on the table, and cradled his chin in his hand as he watched his date pore over the menu with the same obvious excitement he'd shown for Drew's simple attire of jeans and a deep green cashmere sweater, the rustic but elegant restaurant decor, and the football game, which apparently the Patriots were winning at the half.

West Kitchen, a fairly new fusion restaurant Drew had eaten at several times, was impressive as always - dark wood tables, snow-white linens, twinkling fairy lights, and conscientious servers. Mark was as *objectively hot* as ever in a dark blue suit, to the point where Drew almost wanted to take a selfie to send Peter.

But sadly, the most interesting part of the date for Drew thus far was the comical way Mark kept over-pronouncing the Italian words. He couldn't help but wish that Sebastian were here, if only so they could share a commiserating glance every time Mark trilled out "brrrruschetta."

Mark glanced up at him expectantly, and Drew realized he'd missed a question. He quickly backtracked, forcing out a smile. "Uh, yeah. Yes. I like calamari."

"Oh, that's great! See, I knew we would get along!" Mark beamed. His phone beeped and he slid it out. "Pats scored again!"

Drew nodded, drawing a pattern on the linen tablecloth with his forefinger. "That's great."

"Celebration time!" Mark announced, and Drew stifled a sigh as Mark lifted a finger to signal their waiter.

"A bottle of Cristal, please. Something from before… let's say, 2006." Mark smiled wide, like the world's most pretentious shark, and Drew imagined what Bas would have said about celebrating a football score with a $200 bottle of champagne.

"We have a 2005, sir," the waiter offered.

"Perfect," Mark agreed, delighted. He looked at Drew and blinked as the waiter departed. "Oh, I suppose I should have checked with you! You do like champagne, don't you?"

All the blinking made him look like a turtle. A turtle wearing a curly brown wig. And his dirty-green eyes seemed dull and… even a little bit smug. Nothing like the intelligent fire in a certain pair of blue eyes.

"Not much, no. But then, I don't really drink that often, and hardly ever on a first date," Drew told him with a small smile. "You go ahead."

Mark pouted, sticking his lower lip out. "But champagne's no fun unless you share it. You'll have one glass, won't you?"

"Oh. No, I really…"

"One tiny little glass," Mark insisted. "It's just that I feel like I've been waiting forever to get you on this date. You have no idea. We need to celebrate!"

Ugh. Drew had been afraid of exactly this - encouraging Mark by agreeing to this date. He didn't want to hurt the man's feelings, but as he'd once told Bas, he could only be guilted so far.

"One glass," he agreed, firmly intending to dump the glass into the small potted tree that the universe had conveniently placed just inches from their table. He cleared his throat and cast around for polite conversation. "So... how was your holiday?"

"Perfect," Mark said. "I went skiing with some friends!"

He pantomimed holding a set of ski poles, complete with swishing sounds, while a tiny part of Drew's soul died.

"That's, uh... perfect," Drew agreed.

Mark checked his phone again, frowning.

"Did the other team score?" Drew asked. It was a good thing he had little invested in this date, or else he might have been slightly offended.

"Pardon?"

"Your phone," Drew said patiently. "Is it the score?"

"Oh. Uh. Yes. Yeah, the score." Mark put his phone away again and focused his brilliant, sharky smile on Drew. "What were we saying?"

"We were talking about Christmas. I spent my holiday in New York. With my mother."

Mark's eyes widened. "Oh, wow. Your mother? I had no idea she was still alive. That's so great!"

Only a decade spent in and around courtrooms prevented Drew's jaw from dropping open. *Who said shit like this?*

He cleared his throat. "So, Mark. I'm afraid I forgot some of the details from our first meeting, but tell me more about your work." And then Drew put his chin back into his hand and nodded without listening as Mark launched into what any fool could predict would be an exhaustive rundown of the financial services "game."

So much for trying to put honest effort into your date. This was what came of trying to do the right thing.

Bas's words from earlier echoed in his head. "Sometimes you need to make your own right path - one that's true to who you are. And trying to love people, to forgive them for being blind and stupid, is generally always the right way." The words had stunned him at the time, but as he thought about them now, he realized they were not only true, but completely *Bas*. Sebastian Seaver was not a person who played well by other people's rules, and he sometimes played fast and loose with legalities. But when it came to his family, to Drew, that meant there was no limit to what Bas would do to keep them safe.

And Drew was starting to believe that there was no limit to how many times they'd find their way back to one another, either. They'd done it back when they were stupid teenagers, for God's sake. After Bas had proposed to Amy. After Drew had dated Cam. And then again after Halloween.

Drew was a fortunate man in many ways, but if it had been the sum total of his life's luck to simply be born in Sebastian Seaver's sphere, then Drew would still have been the luckiest bastard on the planet.

Drew clenched his fingers under the table, thinking of the way he and Bas had left things, how angry Bas had been. And with good reason, considering Drew had been a total hypocrite. *Stay safe, Bas. Don't take risks, Bas. You have nothing to prove, Bas.* And yet here was Drew, suffering through the world's most boring date while somewhere out there, Bas was worried about him.

Mark's droning cut off as his phone sounded *yet again.*

"We can reschedule, if you want," Drew offered. *Please say yes, please say yes.*

He checked his own phone to see if he had any messages from Sebastian, but there was nothing.

"Oh, no!" Mark said. "No, not at all." He gave Drew an apologetic smile. "In fact, I'm going to shut my phone off and leave it right here." He winked. "So I won't be tempted. And you know what?"

He reached out and snagged Drew's phone from his hand. Before Drew could protest, he placed both phones face-down in the center of the table, a set of twins with matching jet-black cases. "Now both of us can concentrate on our conversation," he said happily, then leaned forward, like Drew might just reveal the secrets of the universe. "Tell me more about what makes Drew McMann tick."

"Excuse me, sir. Your champagne?" the waiter said. And Drew could almost imagine the server giving him a sympathetic glance.

"Yes, yes," Mark agreed excitedly, and Drew looked longingly at his phone as the waiter poured their champagne and they both sipped cautiously.

"Perfect!" Mark enthused. "Isn't it perfect, Drew?"

"Very good," Drew told the waiter. "Thanks."

The waiter nodded. "Are you ready to order?"

"I think we need some more—" Mark began, just as Drew said, "We're ready."

"Oh," Mark said. "But we hadn't even talked about getting a variety of entrees to share."

Kill me now. "You know, I'm really just in the mood for a steak." Drew gave an apologetic shrug. "Maybe another time."

"Yes! Yes, *next time*," Mark agreed, waving his arms so enthusiastically that he knocked his menu into Drew's water glass, sending it spilling across the table and onto Drew's lap before rolling onto the floor and shattering.

"Fuck!" Drew said, jumping up and mopping at his jeans with his napkin.

"Be careful sir," the waiter warned, picking up the larger pieces of glass. "I'll get a broom."

"Here, let me help," Drew offered, bending down to help him despite the waiter's protests.

"Oh, I'm so sorry! So, so sorry. So very sorry!" Mark was bleating, and Drew could only sigh. There were signs, and then there were *signs*. He should excuse himself before the universe intervened any further, he thought wryly, because someone might get hurt.

"Listen, Mark," he said, resuming his seat as the waiter hurried away for a broom. "I really think…"

But Mark was guzzling his glass of champagne, nearly in tears. "I'm so very sorry, Drew! God, I looked forward to hanging out with you for so long, and now *this*. I can't believe I've ruined everything."

"You didn't," Drew assured him, and it wasn't a lie, since the date hadn't been going anywhere, anyway. "Really. I'm just tired tonight."

"You haven't even had any champagne!" Mark wailed, and moisture trickled from the corner of his eye.

Fuck.

Drew lifted the glass to his lips and took a deep sip, barely suppressing his shudder. He really *didn't* like champagne, and this bottle was particularly bitter. "See? Yum," he said. "But I really am tired. Maybe we could…"

"You might feel better if you get some food in you," Mark said. "Really! Perks me right up."

Drew sighed, then smiled tightly. "Alright. Fine." He really *was* hungry, and West Kitchen did a great steak. "Just a quick dinner."

Mark's sharky smile reappeared and his eyes glittered intensely - so intensely that Drew was sure he'd misread them. He glanced back at Mark curiously, but Mark had already turned his head, like he was appreciating the decor once again.

The waiter reappeared, tidying their mess and taking their dinner order. Drew got his steak, and Mark ordered some complex octopus-and-fennel dish in his faux-Italian accent.

"Gosh, this is good!" Mark said, pouring himself a second glass of champagne. "Have some more," he encouraged Drew.

Drew looked at his nearly-full glass and wished he'd asked the waiter to bring him a new glass of water. He took a small sip of the bitter bubbly, knowing that Bas would mock him relentlessly if he could see Drew now, wearing soggy pants and sipping disgusting champagne.

"So! You work with Sebastian Seaver," Mark said, and for a moment Drew wondered if he'd spoken Bas's name out loud.

"Uh, yeah. For quite a few years now," Drew agreed. "Seaver Tech is a great company to work for."

Mark shook his head sadly. "Your loyalty is commendable," he said. "I don't think I could do it."

"Do what?"

"You know. Work with a man like… *that*."

"Pardon?" Drew employed the lawyer voice at its most-frigid.

But Mark didn't seem to get the message. "A man like Sebastian Seaver. Is it true about the fits?"

"What the hell are you talking about?" Drew said angrily. He was attempting to keep his temper, but he could feel his temperature rising. He yanked the sleeves of his expensive sweater up to his elbows and took a deep drink of the champagne, shuddering as he swallowed.

"Calm down," Mark said, all wide-eyed innocence. "I just meant that the press says he's... you know... *unstable*."

"No, I don't know! I have never heard a single thing about that. And it's absolutely, categorically untrue!" Drew shook his head, and anger made his vision blur, the tiny white lights of the restaurant flashing intensely in his peripheral vision. "Sebastian Seaver is a genius."

"Alright," Mark said mildly. "If you say so." He smiled his stupid fucking smile, the one with way too many teeth, and watched Drew's escalating anger like he was watching a fascinating display at a zoo. "I heard that he lost his mind after his parents died, is all."

"You read the tabloids?" Drew demanded. "How does this not surprise me? Well, if you did, then you know I lost my sister at the same time he lost his parents. So how about a little respect?"

Mark put his hands up. "I apologize!" he insisted. "I'm just repeating what I've heard. He's insane, but everyone covers for him because he's a money-maker."

Drew pushed himself to his feet, shaking with anger. *No one* was allowed to talk about Sebastian that way. Ever. He braced a hand on the table, leaning toward Mark.

"You just repeat what you've heard?" Drew mocked softly, dangerously. "Then let me give you something new to repeat. Sebastian Seaver is the best human being I have ever known. He's loyal, he's loving, he's kind. He would do *anything* to take care of his family. And yeah, he's a goddamn genius, but that is the smallest part of what makes him amazing. Any person would be lucky, *lucky*, to have him in their life. I love him more than anything in this universe, and I'll be damned if a twat like you runs him down in my hearing." Drew's knees swayed as temper had blood pounding in his ears. "And? He knows how to fucking pronounce bruschetta, you pretentious prick."

Drew straightened with difficulty, and Mark seemed almost amused by his distress... until he caught sight of something over Drew's shoulder.

"Fuck," he whispered.

A warm, strong arm wrapped around Drew's waist, holding him up when he would have sunk back into his seat.

"Did you mean that?" a voice whispered in his ear — the best voice in the world, the only voice Drew wanted to hear.

"Which part?" Drew whispered, leaning back against Bas without thought. And sure enough, Bas's solid strength held him up, supporting Drew when he would have fallen.

Bas had rested his face against the crook of Drew's neck, and Drew felt the warmth of Bas's breath on his skin as Bas chuckled. "I kind of expected you to be pissed that I was crashing your date."

Drew stiffened and glared at Mark, who was staring around the restaurant, as if praying for reinforcements. "This date was over anyway," he told Mark, disgusted.

Bas turned him around. "We need to talk," he began, then he looked into Drew's eyes and frowned. "Are you okay?"

"Ye-Yesh," Drew said. His lips weren't working properly. "I'm just pissed off."

Bas shook his head. "I've seen you pissed off, McMann. Your cheeks get flushed and your eyes go cold. Right now your eyes are glassy and your skin is..." He lifted a hand and cradled Drew's cheek. "Icy."

He turned to glare at Mark, and in all their thirty years of friendship, Drew couldn't remember ever seeing Sebastian so angry or so dangerous. "What the *fuck* did you do to him?" he demanded.

"Me? I… Nothing! He had, like, half a glass of champagne!" Mark squeaked, scraping his chair back from the table in an attempt to get away. He pushed himself to his feet. "I didn't do anything!"

"If I find out differently, fucker…"

"Let's go, Bas," Drew said. He looked around the restaurant quickly and saw that every eye in the place was on them, some more overtly than others.

"Drew, you're on a date with *me*," Mark said, stepping forward. "If you're not feeling well, I can help you home."

"No. Way. In. *Hell*," Bas informed him. "You're not going to fucking *touch* him. And if I find out that you were attempting to get him drunk—"

"He wasn't," Drew said, torn between outrage, amusement, and bone-deep satisfaction at Sebastian's overprotectiveness. "I barely had two sips of champagne." He smoothed a soothing hand down Bas's chest, dimly aware that this was not usual for them, but it felt right and it seemed to work.

"You haven't even had your steak!" Mark bleated, and Drew almost, *almost* felt guilty again. "You need to stay!"

Drew fumbled for the wallet in his back pocket, and Bas helped him extract some cash that he threw in the center of the table. "Really, this is for the best," he told Mark over his shoulder. He added apologetically, "You're not my type."

Bas snorted, grabbing Drew's jacket from the back of his chair and helping Drew's heavy arms into the sleeves. He wrapped an arm around Drew's waist, supporting him to the door.

"Oh." Drew patted his pockets. "My phone. It's in the

middle of the table." He rolled his eyes. "Could you grab it for me?"

"Happy to," Bas whispered, and Drew focused all his attention on standing straight. His head was way fuzzier than it should have been.

He heard Bas say something to Mark in a low voice, and Mark's angry reply. He turned his head just in time to see Bas punch Mark in the jaw, sending him sprawling on the floor.

The other patrons gasped and cried out, but the waiter ran forward to "assist" Mark, while really keeping him pinned to the floor. He turned and gave Drew a nod, and Drew smiled in reply.

Bas grabbed something off the table and hurried back to Drew.

"Feel better?" Drew asked. He could still feel the tension coiled in Bas's body, but it seemed to dissipate somewhat as he let Bas take more of his weight.

"Not really," Bas muttered. "What were you thinking? That guy is an asshole."

"I was thinking that was the best I could expect of anyone who wasn't you," Drew admitted.

Bas squeezed his eyes shut for a second, then pushed the restaurant door open. The air outside was hard and painfully cold, frigid enough to penetrate some of the cotton wrapped around Drew's brain. He paused as Bas towed him down the street toward Drew's own car. "How did you get here?"

"Cort," Bas said succinctly. He pushed a hand through his hair, his breath suspended in the air like fog. "Keys?"

Drew extracted them from his coat pocket and handed them over.

"I don't know what's wrong with me," Drew told him slowly. "I'm so sleepy."

"Fuck." Bas opened the passenger's side door and helped Drew into the seat, leaning over him to fasten his seatbelt. "We should call the police."

"No." Drew shook his head, sucking in a deep breath when the action made him nauseous. "No police."

"Drew," Bas began, squatting on the sidewalk by the open car door. "Baby, listen. He must have put something in your drink."

"Couldn't," Drew said. "It was champagne." He made a face. "Disgusting shit."

"It would only have taken a drop of something," Bas insisted.

Drew shook his head again. *Whoa. Jesus.* Everything spun. "He's just so pretentious. I wanted you there to laugh with."

"Shhh. It's okay," Bas told him, stroking a hand over Drew's face. His fingers were so warm, and his touch so proprietary, Drew closed his eyes to savor it.

"I wanted you there," he insisted, because it was important that Bas understand. "I wanted you. With me."

"I know. I wanted to be with you, too," Bas said hoarsely, sliding his fingers back into Drew's hair. Drew arched into the touch. "But are you sure you don't want to call the police?"

"No police," Drew insisted. He shook his head again, which seemed like a massive mistake as what little he'd eaten earlier that day seemed to revolt. He'd barely had time to unbuckle his belt and push Bas back before he vomited on the pavement.

He curled around himself, chest heaving, and let Bas shift him back into the car and shut the door. He was vaguely aware of Bas starting the engine, turning the heat on high, rubbing his hand lightly over Drew's back.

"I'm okay," Drew whispered, not sure if he was talking to Bas or to himself. "I'm fine."

"I should have hit him harder," Bas mumbled.

Bas's phone chimed, a different sound than Drew had heard earlier, and he wasn't sure why that bugged him, but it did.

"What's wrong with your phone?" he demanded.

"Not my phone. Yours," Bas said.

"Not mine."

Bas took the phone from his pocket and looked at the screen, then up at Drew. "Mark's," he whispered. "Fuck. Did I take the wrong one? It looks just like yours."

Drew nodded. "They looked the same."

Bas's face reddened as he read whatever message had popped up on the screen.

"Whass it say?" he forced out.

Bas sighed, and Drew could see that he didn't want to tell him, but he did. "It says 'Our date should be ready for action now. Lead him out the back.'" Bas cleared his throat.

Drew resisted the urge to vomit again, breathing shakily through his nose. It *had* been intentional.

"I am going to make that man's life a fucking misery," he vowed. "Plaster his face all over social media. He will never have another moment's peace for the rest of his life."

Bas's eyes, when he turned them toward Drew, were molten. "That won't be very long," he swore. "I'm going to fucking kill him."

Drew laid his hand atop Sebastian's, where it rested on the steering wheel, and felt the shudder that moved through Bas at the simple contact. "I'm fine, Bas."

Bas's nostrils flared, and he nodded once. "You will be," he promised. He flipped his hand over and threaded his fingers with Drew's.

For a moment, Drew wished he were a little less foggy-headed, so he could commit every second of this to memory - the warm slide of Bas's palm against his, the way their fingers knitted together perfectly. But it wouldn't be the last time they held hands; Drew would make sure of it. He was through resisting. If Sebastian wanted to experiment, Drew would gladly donate himself to the cause.

"Where are we going?" Drew asked, noting that they weren't heading toward his house.

"That guy has your phone," Bas said, shaking his head. "I have no idea whether he's capable of opening it…"

"It was locked, I think," Drew said, rubbing his free hand over his forehead.

"It's okay. I can wipe it remotely," Bas told him. "But just in case, I don't want to take you back to your place. We'll spend the night at mine."

Drew swallowed hard. *We.*

Bas squeezed his fingers. "That okay?" he asked, glancing at Drew. But it felt like he was really asking something different. Something bigger. Something like, "Do you trust me?"

And the answer to that was the same as it had always been.

A clear and unequivocal "Yes."

CHAPTER TWELVE

"*W*hat do you mean, *drugged?*" Cam screeched. "Why the heck are you home? Shouldn't you be at the hospital? This isn't the kind of thing you mess around with, Sebastian!"

Bas pulled the phone away from his ear slightly, for the sake of his eardrums, and propped his ass against his dresser, settling in for Cam's tirade. He'd pretty much expected this exact response, knowing how protective Cam was of everyone in their odd little friend-family, but he was glad he'd waited until Drew was out of earshot before calling.

"He's okay, Cam," Bas soothed when it seemed Cam was winding down. "I promise."

"But what if—?"

"I told you, he said he didn't want to go to the hospital," Bas reminded his brother, rubbing at the tension that had lodged in the back of his neck. "We need to respect his decision." Bas would, and would make sure everyone else did too, even though he was privately just as outraged as Cam.

"Well, you tell Drew that's ridiculous!" Cam sputtered.

"This Mark person could be doing this to other guys! He needs to be stopped. Put Drew on the line!"

There was a brief scuffle in the background, and then a deep, raspy voice came on the line.

"Bas? It's Damon. Cam and Cort are still at our place. Cam's a little bit, uh, *worried*, but Cort's got him. Sean already called with some news you'll wanna hear, but not tonight, eh? We'll take care of things, and you just take care of McMann."

"Yeah," Bas agreed, not even the slightest bit curious about any other news Damon might have for him. As far as Bas was concerned, taking care of Drew was the only priority right now. Everything else could wait. "Tell Cam it's under control. We'll check in tomorrow."

He disconnected, then checked the time on his phone. Drew had been in the shower for at least thirty minutes - time enough for Bas to cook up a batch of pancakes, make a call to get Drew's phone wiped remotely, and contact Cam. *Not* enough time, however, for Bas to have calmed down, and the only thing that kept him from barging into the bathroom to check on Drew was the certainty that Drew would kick his ass if he tried.

Drew had been patient with Bas's fussing to a point - letting Bas help him out of the car, even though he'd insisted he was feeling better after throwing up the contents of his stomach, and could walk by himself; letting Bas help him out of his coat and shoes; even letting Bas run the shower for him and agreeing, after a pointed eye-roll, to keep the door ajar in case he needed help. Bas was pretty sure Drew's patience with the coddling was done.

Which meant Drew was just gonna have to suck it up, because Bas's need to take care of Drew, to reassure himself Drew was okay, was nowhere near satisfied.

They had a fuck-ton of things to say to one another... or

maybe it was more accurate to say there were a fuck-ton of things Bas was finally ready to admit to and discuss openly, thanks to his conversation with Cort earlier. And then, please God, he wanted to get his mouth back on his best friend.

The only thing that shocked Bas at this point was that he'd waited as long as he had.

The water cut off sharply and Bas straightened, opening his mouth to let Drew know the food had arrived. But before any sound came out, Drew emerged from the bathroom with one towel wrapped low around his hips and another draped across his neck.

Bas sat back down *hard*, and tried not to swallow his tongue.

Jesus Christ. Just look at him.

Bas had seen Drew half-naked dozens of times over the years. Maybe hundreds, if he counted every beach trip, every swim class, every locker room. He knew the long, lean line of Drew's torso by heart, knew the tan skin lightly dusted with brown hair over his pecs, and the three tiny moles arranged in an obtuse triangle a bit below and to the right of his belly button, just above the ridge of his pelvic muscle. None of that was a surprise. But years of cataloging Drew's features in no way prepared Bas for the sight of Drew now. Not now, when every twitch of those muscles begged to be touched, and every stray droplet of water gliding down that flat stomach begged to be followed.

He hadn't lied when he'd told Cort that he'd enjoyed sex in the past, but the wanting had never been this consuming, this overwhelming. Maybe he'd always held something back. Maybe it was because none of them had been Drew. The man he was in love with.

It was like his conversation with Cort had kicked down

a mental barrier he hadn't realized existed, and suddenly his emotions were tripping over themselves, trying to get out.

He wanted Drew.

He loved Drew.

He was *in love* with Drew.

Drew stared at Bas uncertainly and lifted one end of the towel to dry his hair. "What?" he asked slowly.

Bas looked away and cleared his throat. "Nothing. Ah, how are you doing?"

"I'm fine. I told you so when we got here and you insisted I needed a shower anyway." Drew rolled his eyes, but he was smiling. "If you thought I smelled like vomit, Seaver, you just had to say so."

Bas folded his arms over his chest and watched Drew steadily, until finally Drew rolled his eyes and put the towel over his head, rubbing his hair vigorously.

"Fine, fine." His impatient voice was muffled by the towel. "I do feel better after the shower," Drew admitted.

"Uh huh. And now you need to eat." Bas pushed himself off the dresser and walked to the nightstand where he'd left Drew's dinner.

"Eat?" Drew removed the towel from his head and glanced at the table. "I *do* feel better, but I really don't want... Pancakes?" He stared at Bas, wide-eyed. "You made me pancakes and bacon?"

"Pancakes are your favorite comfort food," Bas told him. But when Drew continued to stare without moving, he asked, "Aren't they?"

"Yeah. Yes." Drew sounded breathless — breathless in a *good* way, like Bas had stumbled into doing something very right somehow — and it took all of Bas's self-control not to grab him and kiss him senseless.

He went back to rubbing at his neck and motioned

Drew to take a seat on the bed. "And I figured they'd be kinda light on your stomach."

Drew gave him an amused glance, but obediently sat and grabbed a slice of bacon. "You really didn't have to go to all this trouble," he said.

Bas folded his arms and leaned against the wall near the table. "Right."

"You didn't," Drew insisted, glancing around. "You cooked me dinner?"

"It's pancakes, McMann," Bas grumbled. "I didn't fetch you a lobster fresh from the ocean." Which he totally would have, if he'd thought Drew would want it. *Eat.*

"I'm eating, I'm eating," Drew told him, forking up a bite of pancakes. "You don't need to stand there and supervise, Sebastian! Who were you talking to?"

"Oh, Cam and the whole crew." He didn't want to make Drew uncomfortable by watching him eat, but without anything else to focus on, his gaze kept returning to Drew's broad shoulders, to the scruff on his jaw. He could feel his pulse kick up. "I told them what happened, and that you're safe for tonight. They're all worried, and they all, you know, love you."

Drew raised one dark eyebrow. "They said that?"

"Eh." Bas scratched at the back of his neck. "It was understood."

"Uh huh."

Drew shifted slightly in his seat to grab the water glass Bas had also placed on the nightstand, and his towel slid open to reveal a thick triangle of pale skin high on his thigh, a place where the sun never reached.

Bas coughed to cover the sudden tightness of his throat and gripped his arms more tightly. He could be patient about this, he could. Hell, he'd waited decades, so he could wait a few more minutes.

"So," Drew began. He turned his head so that his warm, oh-so-amused brown eyes met Sebastian's, and deliberately licked maple syrup from his lips. "How are *you* doing?"

"Me?" Bas shrugged his shoulders against the wall. "*I'm* fine. It's not *me* I'm worried about."

Drew nodded. He put his fork down and grabbed his water glass again. "You sure?"

No. Nope. He wasn't sure at all. His entire body felt stretched thin and hummed with tension. The collar of the thick cable sweater was suddenly restrictive, the fabric of his jeans too rough against his skin.

He wanted to talk, and he didn't. He forced himself to stand against the wall, when he wanted to be three paces away, clutching Drew against him.

He was scared to death - not of taking the next step with Drew, but that he wouldn't be able to convince Drew to give him, *them*, a shot. And he was angry, though he was trying really hard to push that down for Drew's sake, at what that fucker Mark had tried to pull earlier tonight on *his* man.

"Yeah," he said brusquely. "I'm sure."

"Okay, because your hands are kinda telling a different story."

"My hands?"

"Yeah." Drew stood, putting his plate back on the night-stand. He tightened the towel around his waist, and stepped forward, placing his palm over Sebastian's forearm. "You kinda look like you wanna kill someone."

Bas glanced down, and saw that his crossed arms were balled into fists. He immediately relaxed them. But Drew didn't step away.

"I wish you would call the police," Bas admitted. "If only to make sure that this asshole pays for what he tried to do to you."

Drew shook his head. "First of all, nothing happened." He held up a restraining hand against the argument Bas had opened his mouth to make. "Nothing happened, in the sense that there was no secondary crime. We can imagine what he was planning to do if he'd gotten me out of the restaurant, but he can't be prosecuted for what we *think* might happen. Plus, we don't have the champagne from the restaurant."

"*Champagne,*" Bas scoffed. "Asshole didn't have the first clue about what you like."

"Not the first clue," Drew agreed. He was rubbing his thumb over Bas's forearm - the simplest touch, but Bas could hardly concentrate on anything else as Drew continued, "We can't prove there was anything in my drink in the first place, and since I got sick, it's unlikely there's anything in my bloodstream at all anymore. So, getting them involved would be useless at best... and at worst, it might call the authorities' attention to us when we don't want it."

Bas swallowed. "So that's it? There's no way to stop him from doing this again? No way to punish him?"

Drew smiled. "Oh, no. I told you earlier. I want to make this guy's life a living hell. I have his Facebook profile, I know where he works. Hell, I know his stupid dog's name. And..."

"And?"

"*And*, I happen to know a guy who will hack every electronic device Mark owns, starting with his phone." Drew brought his other hand up and touched Sebastian's waist. Even through his sweater, the touch burned. "Pretty sure he won't even be able to win a round of Dragon Puzzler by the time you're through with him."

Bas laughed and shook his head. "You know I will." He lifted an unsteady hand and ran it over Drew's head, loving the way Drew's breath caught, like he was every bit as shaken by the touch as Sebastian was. "But how can you be so calm? God, baby! Weren't you scared?" He stared into Drew's eyes. "I can't stand the idea of you being hurt."

"I didn't have time to be scared then." He stepped closer, until only centimeters then millimeters separated them. "You were there saving me before I even know anything was wrong."

"And now?" Bas demanded, fingers tangling in Drew's damp hair while his other hand tentatively reached out to touch the smooth skin of Drew's flank.

Drew laughed. "Sebastian, how could I have the mental space to think about being scared when you just called me *baby*?"

Bas grinned. "Did I?"

"You did," Drew confirmed. "But I won't hold you to it. You can take it back if you need to. Think it over. Take things as slow as you want, okay? This... *us*... whatever happens will be at your pace."

"I don't want to take it back," Bas breathed. "And I sure as hell don't need to think things over. I'm not scared of this anymore."

Drew slid his arms around Bas's back, locking their torsos together and smiled gently. "Then how come you're shaking?"

"Because..." Bas swallowed, and he was shocked - fucking *shocked* to find himself on the verge of tears. *So ridiculous.* He hadn't cried since shortly after his parents had died, for God's sake. "I wasn't sure I would be able to convince *you*. I was worried I'd fucked things up between us."

"You haven't." Drew shook his head. "I promise you haven't, Bas. I don't think you ever really could." Drew lifted a hand to Sebastian's jaw, traced the curve of Bas's lips with his thumb. "I was thinking about you earlier."

"While you were on your *date*?"

"Yes, yes, while I was on my godforsaken date with the self-absorbed *criminal*." Drew rolled his eyes and wrapped both arms around Bas's waist again, shaking him slightly. "But can we agree that we never, *never* need to bring this up in conversation again?"

"What?"

"Do not act innocent with me, Sebastian Seaver. I know very well the next time I beat your ass at FIFA, you're going to bring this up and say at least *you* never dated Mark Charbonnier."

Bas considered this, a tricky proposition given the fact that all the blood in his body was rushing below his waist thanks to Drew's proximity and the heat rising off all that hot, damp skin. "Yeah, that's not going to happen," he croaked. "This isn't funny, and it never will be." He tugged Drew's hair. "But feel free to tell me more about how you were thinking of me."

"Well, I was thinking about what you said earlier. About how the right path isn't always obvious, so you need to find your own right way of doing things."

"I said that?"

"Mmm hmm."

"Huh. I'm pretty damn smart."

"Occasionally," Drew agreed. "And I couldn't help thinking I was letting my fear prevent me from finding that right way. Because the truth is…" He took a deep breath and the look in his brown eyes was one that Bas hoped to see every day for the rest of his life. "The truth is that I don't think we *can* be fucked up, Sebastian. Not as long as we stick together, not as long as we're fighting for each other and putting each other first."

Bas sucked in a deep breath. He was *not* going to cry, goddamn it. Not when he was about to get everything he'd never imagined having. "That, right there, is proof that we are perfect for each other," he told Drew. "Because you're pretty damn smart, too."

Drew laughed, leaning forward to rest his forehead on Sebastian's chin. His warm breath tickled Bas's jaw.

"Clearly not *that* smart, though," Bas mused, and when Drew pulled back to spear him with a narrow-eyed glare, Bas cupped Drew's jaw in one hand and whispered, "A truly smart man would have kissed me by now."

Drew's eyes widened. "You… you're sure."

"I'm sure."

"Definitely sure?"

Bas rolled his eyes, and without waiting another second, took Drew's mouth with his. There was no hesitation this time, and definitely no finesse. All the tension that had been building today – hell, building through the entire *lifetime* that some part of Bas seemed to have been waiting for this - seemed to crash through him at once, and he pillaged Drew's mouth, claiming it, owning it.

Drew moaned and pulled Bas even closer, until they were pressed together as fully as possible. He ran a hand up under Bas's sweater - a sweater that was suddenly way too warm and confining - and the t-shirt below.

Bas let his hands roam over Drew's back - tracing the smooth muscles, the ridges of his shoulder blades, the bumps of his spine… and then further down until his hand hovered just above the edge of Drew's towel. Bas hesitated for just a second, letting the moment sink in. This was when their friendship would change forever. There would be no coming back from this… no running away, no pretending it hadn't happened. And Sebastian found he was totally fine with that.

But the fact remained that, practically speaking, he

didn't know exactly what he was supposed to do after the towel came off.

Drew pulled back, like he could sense Bas's hesitation.

"At your pace, Bas," he reminded Bas breathlessly. "There is no rush."

"I know."

"*Seriously*. My God, if we just keep kissing like this all night it will be the single most fulfilling sexual encounter I've had in the last decade."

"Drew…"

"Or, you know," Drew mused. "Maybe *ever*."

"Andrew!" Bas lifted his hand to tickle Drew's ribs, a move guaranteed to gain the man's attention. "Are you listening to me?"

"Quit!" Drew yelled, writhing against him. "We were having a *moment* here."

Bas wrapped his arms around Drew's waist again. "We were! So let's get back to it."

Drew leaned forward and deliberately bit the edge of Bas's jaw. "I just don't want you to feel pressured," Drew whispered, and Bas squeezed his eyes shut briefly.

Clearly, Bas's track record of running away from this shit had left scars, and only time would heal them.

Time, and honesty.

"I have no clue what I'm doing, so you're gonna have to guide me." Bas ran a hand up Drew's back, loving the way his palm fit perfectly into the space between Drew's shoulder blades. Had they always been perfectly aligned this way? Had Bas just failed to see it? "But I promise you, I have never been more sure of anything than I am of you. And the only pressure I feel is happening, ah, under my clothing." He glanced down significantly.

Drew laughed shortly, but his eyes went molten. "I'd

better see what I can do about that then, huh? As your… guide."

His hands came to Bas's waist, rucking up the sweater and t-shirt simultaneously. Bas lifted his arms, letting Drew pull the clothing off completely and throw it on Bas's empty dining chair. Then he stepped closer, pushing Bas back into the wall until their naked chests brushed - intentionally - for the first time ever. He grabbed Bas's wrists and lowered them, pinning them to the wall near their hips, while his lips blazed a trail of kisses along Bas's jaw and down his neck. Every individual sensation shot straight to Bas's cock and he closed his eyes, absorbing it.

"Did that help?" Drew asked innocently. He trailed his lips across Bas's smooth chest, flicking his tongue over a nipple - a sensation so unexpected it made Bas's eyes fly open as he cried out. The warm, knowing glint in Drew's gaze was everything Bas had been missing during sex, without even knowing it.

"I'm afraid not," Bas murmured. "In fact, I think you're making it worse."

Drew made a tsk-ing noise. "Shoot. We can't have that, can we?"

"Not… *Oh, Jesus.*" Bas's thoughts broke off as Drew let go of Bas's left hand and his fingers wandered slowly over Bas's abdomen to toy with the button of his jeans. "Not if you want to be a good guide," Bas bit out desperately.

"And I do," Drew crooned, all fervent innocence. "What kind of a friend would I be if I let you suffer when I could help you?"

"A *terrible* kind," Bas groaned, breath hitching as Drew's fingers traveled lower, tracing the ridge of Bas's erection. "*Oh, God.* The *worst* kind."

Drew chuckled softly. "Show me where it hurts, Sebastian. Is it right here?" He pressed the heel of his hand into Bas's cock and Bas let his head fall back against the wall.

Holy fuck, that felt amazing. He thrust helplessly against Drew's palm and heat seared him from the inside out. "Please, baby," he breathed. "Please."

Drew dropped all pretense and tugged open Sebastian's fly, pushing his jeans and boxer briefs down to his thighs in one movement. Bas's erection jutted out, hot and hard, and as he watched, Drew trailed a single finger up the length of it, then over the head.

Bas shuddered at the contact, and for the life of him he couldn't seem to draw a deep breath.

Drew wrapped his hand around him and lifted his burning gaze to Sebastian's...

Then sank to his knees.

Oh God, oh God, oh God.

"Is this okay?" Drew whispered, and Bas nodded solemnly. He couldn't imagine a circumstance where a blow job *wouldn't* be okay, but *Jesus Christ* this was Drew.

Andrew McMann is on his knees for me, he thought to himself, but the words simply wouldn't compute. So he anchored himself the way he always had, dragging a hand through Drew's nearly-dry hair, and letting the warm, solid presence of his best friend ground him in reality... even as he took Bas apart.

Drew's mouth closed over him, enveloping Bas in wet heat.

"*Fuck.* God, Drew."

Their gazes remained locked - Bas couldn't have looked away if he tried - as Drew grabbed Bas's free hand and directed it to his head, also, encouraging Bas to hold him, to use him. Bas's eyes widened as Drew's meaning became clear, but there was no way in hell Bas was going to do that to Drew. He would *never* hurt him, but especially not tonight. He shook his head frantically, clutching Drew's hair tighter as he fought the urge to thrust *hard*, to take everything Drew was offering him.

But Bas should have remembered that Drew McMann had never been one to accept defeat easily. He wrapped one strong arm around Bas's thigh, holding Bas in place, and bobbed his head forward, taking Bas until he choked once... then twice.

"*No!*" Bas said, even as his eyes crossed from the obliterating pleasure rushing down his legs and up his spine. "Easy!"

Drew's eyes watered, but their expression was as stubborn as Bas had ever seen it. Bas pulled firmly on Drew's hair, forcing him back slightly.

"You want me to take control?" he demanded.

Drew's moan was the most depraved thing Bas had ever heard.

"Fine. Then we do it my way," he whispered. He held Drew's head in place and thrust just slightly, then harder because he couldn't fucking help it and because the way Drew moaned around his cock when he did it was incredible.

Meanwhile, Drew's hand was moving beneath the cursed towel, stroking himself to the rhythm of Bas's thrusts, and *oh, God*, the connection of it - of Bas *inside* Drew's mouth while Drew got them both off in synchronized movements - stole his breath.

It was all happening too fast - the orgasm ready to drag him under with the force of a tsunami, even before he'd told Drew about his own revelations, or put his hands on Drew... hell, before he'd gotten a single peek under that cursed *towel*.

"Move the fucking towel," he croaked. "Please. I wanna see you come. I want to watch."

He hadn't thought Drew's eyes could burn any hotter, but somehow Drew managed it. He moved his hand off Bas's thigh and stripped the towel off himself, flinging it away.

Bas tugged on Drew's hair, forcing his head back so Bas could get a better view.

And *holy hell* what a view. Drew's cock was dark purple and - Bas swallowed - *massive*. His fingers ached to touch it.

But Drew was done with games. He swallowed Bas back into his mouth and sucked, swirling his tongue in a way that had Bas seeing stars, while his own hand jerked himself once more in a relentless rhythm. And Bas was a goner.

"Please! Oh, God, I can't stop it." He was pleading - loud, rough, inarticulate noises.

For Drew to back off.

For Drew to continue.

For Drew.

For Drew.

Always for Drew.

And then before he could draw breath to scream Drew's name, Bas came in a concussion blast of pleasure that hollowed out his mind, obliterating every wall and obstacle, every doubt and concern, until Drew was the only truth left.

CHAPTER THIRTEEN

*D*rew woke up, disoriented. The house was dark around him and he was so, so warm under the blankets. A heavy arm fell over his waist and he startled before the night before came crashing back to him.

Oh, shit. He was naked under the covers. And the arm belonged to *Sebastian*. Sebastian, who he'd given a blowjob.

"I can practically hear you thinking," Bas mumbled, voice thick and rough. "Go back to sleep."

"But we need to…"

"Drew? It's like four o'clock in the morning, and everything is fine for right now." Bas's arm tightened, pulling him closer until his back was flush against Bas's chest. "Just fine. I promise you."

"We should…"

"Hush, baby. There'll be time enough for everything. Go back to sleep," he instructed, and Drew obediently closed his eyes and fell back into a world where Bas would call him baby all the time.

WHEN DREW WOKE UP AGAIN, light was streaming in
Sebastian's bedroom window, and despite the indentation
Bas's head had left on his pillow, the bed beside him was
cold. Dread pooled in his stomach.

*You fucked it all up again. No matter what Bas said, he was just
confused and scared last night. You pushed too hard, and now he's
running, and it's no more than you deserve.*

When will you learn?

But when he rolled over, he found Bas sitting in a
comfortable red chair next to the bed, dressed in only a pair
of black plaid pajama pants, his bare feet propped atop
the duvet.

"Good morning, sleeping beauty."

"Hey," Drew croaked, then cleared his throat. "Has the
apocalypse come? Is that why you're up earlier than me?
Preparing for your New Year's resolution to start tomorrow?" He pushed himself to sitting, propping his naked
back against the headboard.

Bas pursed his lips like he was trying to stop himself from
smiling and rubbed a hand over his jaw. "No. Everything's
fine. But I kinda worried you might think it *was* the apocalypse, once you'd processed what happened last night. So I've
been sitting here staring at you for the past two hours, trying to
figure out all the arguments you'd come up with for why it was
all a mistake we should never repeat, so I could counter them."

Drew blinked, eyes wide. He'd imagined a variety of
things Bas might say - *Sorry, this experiment got out of hand*, or
Let's keep things light and have more blowjobs, or *I'm gonna need to
think about things for the next three months before we can talk
again* - but this one, the idea that Bas might feel like Drew
still needed to be convinced to continue being physical now
that they'd started, was so laughable he would never have
come up with it on his own.

"Don't give me that innocent look," Bas told him. "You made it pretty clear the other night that you didn't want to pursue things with me anymore for the sake of our friendship. And then you woke up in the middle of the night, already *thinking*. You're nearly as bad as I am when it comes to that shit."

Drew swallowed the instinctive denial on his lips and thought about it for a moment. "You might have a point," he conceded.

Bas had said last night that he was sure - had repeated it about a billion times. And yet, this morning Drew had still been preparing for the worst, expecting Bas to run off at some point and ready to mitigate the damage.

"Whoa. Score one for me," Bas said, licking his finger and making an invisible hatch mark in the air. "I'd expected this to be way harder."

Drew folded his arms over his chest and contemplated his best friend… his *lover*; holy shit. He resisted the urge to pinch himself. "Let's hear what else you've come up with," he challenged.

Bas nodded, taking Drew at his word. He dropped his feet to the floor and leaned forward, bracing his elbows on his knees. "Okay, well… first of all, it was really good. Last night, I mean."

Drew snorted. Yeah, *good* would be an understatement. Drew had had *good* any number of times. Last night was… was….

"Wasn't it?" Bas frowned, looking at Drew with concern, and Drew blinked, realizing that Bas had misinterpreted his snort. Like maybe *he* needed reassurance.

"Yeah, Bas. It was so far beyond good that they don't exist in the same realm," Drew told him quietly, and Bas smiled, nodding. "But that doesn't mean…"

"No. No, I know," Bas said quickly. "That was just my… *whajamacallit*. My beginning thing. Like at a trial."

At a trial. Drew pressed his lips together to keep from laughing at the comparison. "Your opening argument?"

"Yes. Exactly." Bas licked his lips. "Right. So, I know I hurt you in October because I couldn't wrap my head around shit. I need you to know, that's not happening again."

"It's not?"

"Not again," Bas repeated, his bright blue eyes as serious as Drew had ever seen them. "I'm going to tell you things from now on. Communicate. And if I need to slow down or process things, I'll… you know… I'll do it *with you.*"

"Oh-kay," Drew agreed, stunned. *Was this really happening?*

"I have a bad track record, okay? I know this. What Amy and I had was pretty much a cautionary tale."

"One you *fell into*," Drew couldn't help but interject.

"Yeah, exactly. Yes. I *knew* you were gonna say that," Bas told him excitedly. "That you'd worry maybe I'm just falling into *this*, with you."

Drew nodded. The thought had occurred to him more than once.

"But I'm not," Bas said, pressing his palms together. "I'm not. And you know how I know?"

Drew shook his head wordlessly.

"Because it's not easy!" Bas was triumphant. "Coming to terms with being something different than I've ever been… or maybe just allowing myself to realize it? Whichever it is, it's fucking *hard*. It's making me question every feeling I've ever had. Every girl I kissed, every date, every time I've had sex. I don't want to do that, believe me. I don't want to think that I wasn't…" He ran his hands through his hair in obvious frustration. "I dunno, *smart* or *self-aware* enough to figure this shit out earlier, like you did. Like Cam did."

"Bas," Drew interrupted. "It doesn't go like that."

"I know! No, I know. I talked to Cort about this yesterday afternoon."

"To Cort?" Drew repeated. "Are you kidding?"

Bas smiled. "Nope. And he told me the same thing. But knowing that here," he tapped his temple, "is not the same as believing it here." He pointed at his chest. "And I think it's gonna take me longer to wrap my mind around *that* than it is for me to get used to having a boyfriend."

Boyfriend. Drew finally *did* yield to the urge to pinch himself then, and it hurt. A lot. He tried to speak, but the only sound he was capable of making was a brief puff of air. "A…"

"Boyfriend," Bas supplied, and his eyes crinkled at the corners as he took in Drew's shock. "Did you think this was gonna be some casual thing? You've been my best friend forever. Best friends who love each other more than anyone else and sleep together are pretty much the definition of boyfriends, aren't they?"

"I… guess?" Drew looked out the window, taking in the clouds, the cold sunshine on the bare tree limbs. It appeared to be a normal morning. He didn't *think* he was still drugged. "Out of curiosity, if I'd been transported into one of those alternate realities you were telling me about the other night, what would be the signs?"

"There!" Bas said, pointing an accusing finger at him. "Right there. *That* is exactly what I'm talking about. Nobody would sign up to deal with that snark unless they were head over heels for you, Drew. Because you are *anything* but easy."

Drew snorted.

"I'm serious! You're going to make me crazy before we're forty." Bas moved to sit on the edge of the bed at Drew's hip. "And it's not *falling*. I'm not just letting this happen. Not ever again."

"Oh." Overwhelmed with the words Bas was saying, with his warm and *naked* chest within touching distance, this was the most intelligent thing Drew could come up with.

Bas's face broke into a grin. "That's the level of intelligent argument which sways juries, ladies and gentlemen." He notched another imaginary point, and Drew rolled his eyes.

"But since you brought up the alternate realities," Bas said.

"Oh, God. Please tell me your arguments don't involve alternate realities," Drew pleaded, massaging his temples with both hands - both *shaking* hands. "I can barely keep up with you as it is."

"Two *hours*, Andrew. I sat here for *hours*. I have plumbed the depths of my brain," Bas reminded him. "And you know better than anyone how deep in the weeds I can get in an hour."

Drew blinked, because he *did* know.

"But I was thinking, I don't know if alternate realities are a thing, but there are *choices*, you know. Choices that dictate the way things work out, the paths we take. I can't go back and change anything that happened to cause the crash." He laughed without humor. "Cort kinda showed me that, too."

Cort was getting a magnum of champagne, if Drew had anything to say about it.

"And even if I could," Bas paused, took a deep breath, and looked Drew in the eye. "Even if I had the power to change things, I don't know if I would. That crash brought

Cort and Damon into our lives. It brought a lot of truths out into the open. And it's giving us the chance to maybe make things better for a lot of people by taking SILA down."

Drew bit his bottom lip and nodded, knowing exactly how much it had cost Bas to say all of that - to give meaning to the senseless deaths of the people they loved.

"I had a choice that summer when we were teenagers." Bas glanced out the window and his brow furrowed. "I had another one in October. All of those things have brought us to where we are, and I guess I wouldn't change those either, because they brought us here." He glanced at Drew and smiled. "But I'm tired of taking the path that leads me away from you. The only right way for me from now on, is the one where you and I are together."

He swallowed hard and gave a nervous chuckle. "I'm nervous as hell," he admitted. "I have no idea how to be in a real *relationship*. I have no idea how to have sex with a guy. I am a total noob at all of this. So, believe me when I tell you, I'm not falling into anything here. I'm choosing. I'm choosing *you*."

Whoa. Drew's eyes filled with tears and he sniffed loudly as he reached for Bas's hand and wound their fingers together.

Bas blew out a breath. "That's, uh… that's it. That's all I came up with." He licked his lips. "I want to be with you. I love you. I don't have the first idea what I'm doing, but I *will* be all-in when it comes to figuring it out."

Drew ran his free hand over his mouth. So many things he wanted to say to this man. So fucking many things he'd been storing up since he'd first realized he was in love with his best friend the summer he turned fourteen, and they all toppled over one another in his mind, paralyzing him.

"So… what do you think?" Bas asked, his beautiful face stark with anxiety.

Drew shook his head and said the most important thing. The only one that really mattered.

"I love you," he whispered, and as Bas blinked, disbelieving, Drew figured out what he needed to say. "Sebastian? At the risk of quoting that old movie, you kinda had me at *good morning*."

Bas laughed, a helpless sound that seemed forced from him.

"I'm serious," Drew said. "Knowing you were still here this morning, I think maybe I started to believe you were serious about everything you said last night. About wanting me. And you've gotta know, I've wanted you forever." He swallowed hard, squeezing Bas's hand and looking up at the ceiling as he admitted, "I've been *in love* with you forever. You've been the star of every fantasy I've had for the past fifteen years. I've never needed to be convinced that we're perfect for each other, Bas. I just needed to be sure that you were sure."

"And you are now?" Bas whispered.

Drew looked at him. "I'm getting there."

Bas nodded, looking down at their joined hands. With the fingers of his free hand, he traced the ridges of Drew's knuckles tenderly. Then he looked back up wearing a smug grin.

"Get back to the part where you love me. And the fantasies."

Drew laughed.

Love with this man would never be precious. No sparkling hearts, no dancing fairies. And that was absolutely perfect.

"I love you," Drew told him, and Bas's smile was glorious.

"Now that I think about it, there were clues," he said, and Drew's brows shot up.

"Besides the kissing? And the frottage the other night?"

"That's sex," Bas said. "Not love. But the sand dollar gave you away."

"Pardon?"

"The sand dollar. The keychain?" Bas explained. "The one I gave you when we were kids at camp."

"Right. What about it?"

"I saw it on your keychain when you gave your car keys to Cain and Damon a couple of months back. When they went to Tennessee."

"I remember," Drew said. And he'd wondered at the time if Bas had understood the importance of it. *Apparently so*.

"After everything that happened on Halloween, it just cemented to me that you'd had these feelings for me for a while. Messed with my mind that you hadn't ever said anything." He played with Drew's fingers. "When I'd thought we were really honest with each other about everything."

"We *have* always been honest…"

"Not about the things that counted, though." Bas dipped his head and gave him a self-deprecating smile. "I never told you I was questioning things with Amy, and you never told me about your feelings. We've both held back."

Drew nodded quietly. Bas was right.

"Anyway, it was all symbolical to me." Bas rolled his eyes. "Like this thing you'd been keeping forever, this reminder of me. And uh, I worried, after I saw your keys the night we met Gary at the pub. You didn't have the sand dollar there."

"It broke," Drew told him. "Came back unscathed from

Cain and Damon being shot at in Tennessee, and then fell out of my cabinet onto the counter and cracked."

"You told me it was *gone*," Bas reminded him, and Drew rolled his eyes.

"Well, it was," he said defensively. "Gone from my key ring, anyway." He sighed, and in the spirit of their newfound communication, he admitted, "And maybe I told you that because I was afraid it would give away too much if I told you I spent a whole night, while we weren't speaking, supergluing the thing back together."

"I kinda wish you had." Bas's voice was raw. "Maybe it wouldn't have changed anything. Maybe I wasn't ready to hear it then. But I wish we'd gotten to this place earlier."

"The place where we have sex?" Drew joked.

"Honesty," Bas said, thwacking him on the thigh. "Love." He moved his hand to Drew's knee below the blanket. "But yeah, the sex is pretty good too. And you mentioned fantasies?"

Drew leaned back further into the pillows as Bas climbed on top of him, straddling him through the blanket. Despite the seriousness of their conversation, Drew felt a bit like he was suspended in a dream and vaguely hoped he'd never wake up.

"Naturally, you remember that part," Drew fake-scolded, his voice a little breathless.

"So, what were they?"

"Which one?" Drew demanded. "There were dozens. Hundreds, maybe. Some of them were just lame, teen-romance shit... probably fitting, since I was a teen when I came up with them. Like, in one of them, you met me at my locker in high school and walked me to lunch."

"Scandalous," Bas said, nipping at Drew's collarbone.

"Well, it was. We were *holding hands* while we walked

into the cafeteria. And you were smiling at me. And everyone stopped what they were doing and stared at us."

Bas lifted his head to look at Drew. "And this is a *happy* fantasy?"

"Mmm hmmm." He lifted a hand and dragged it through Bas's dark hair. "Because I wrapped my arms around you and we kissed right in front of everyone."

"Of course we did," Bas said, resuming his kisses with a smile in his voice. "I wanted everyone to know you were mine."

"I'm pretty sure the motive went the other way around, in my fantasy," Drew warned him. "Fantasy-Drew was a very possessive boyfriend."

"And real-Drew isn't?"

"Real Drew hasn't had a lover he wanted to possess," Drew admitted quietly. *Until now.* "But... there is some scary potential there.

"It's only scary if the man you're with doesn't want to be possessed. You don't scare me one bit, McMann." Bas sucked hard at Drew's neck, and Drew cried out at the sudden flash of pain. That was going to leave a mark. "Tell me another fantasy."

Drew's heart was pounding recklessly at the feeling of Bas's teeth ravaging his skin, and the utter lack of anxiety on Bas's part. He'd never imagined Bas would be a possessive partner, and the idea lit him up in a way he'd never imagined.

"Uh. Hmmm. The hot tub on the deck at the Shaws' cabin in Tennessee?" he said, ending in a gasp when Bas moved lower, nipping at a particularly sensitive spot on his neck just below his ear. "Just the two of us, naked, with hardly anyone around for miles. I wanted to trap you in the water and kiss you until you forgot your name."

"Hardly anyone?"

Figured Sebastian would have noticed that slight tell. "There are no neighbors," he whispered. "But there's always the possibility someone else could see us."

Bas shuddered. "We will make that happen," he promised hoarsely. "It might not be in that cabin, but I will *buy* us a cabin where we can do that if I have to."

Drew snorted, tilting his neck to give Bas better access. "I might let you," he whispered. "Oh, and when we stayed in St. Brigitte? I imagined you coming to my room at night…"

"Yeah?"

Drew nodded. "You knocked at my door."

"In a sexy way."

"Obviously." Drew snorted. How was it possible to be amused and so fucking turned on at the same time? "And when I opened the door, you grabbed me around the waist."

"I'm very *caveman* in your fantasies," Bas noted, nipping at Drew's collarbone while Drew ran his hands along the warm, smooth skin of Bas's back. "I like it."

"Oh, please." Drew slapped that sexy back once, lightly. "Like you're not all caveman in real life. *Must protect family. Must kill bad guys. Eliminate threat.*" He grunted theatrically, and felt Bas's shoulders shake with laughter.

Bas's blue eyes danced as they met his. "I think you're getting off-track, counselor. Caveman-me knocks at your door in the sexiest possible way, grabs you around the waist like King Kong, and…"

Bas dipped his head and licked at Drew's Adam's apple. Drew momentarily forgot what he was saying.

"Uh. You walked me backwards into the suite and pushed me up against the bed. And then we… you know." Drew could feel his cheeks burning.

"Do I know?" Bas teased. He bit his lip and pretended to think. "Oh! Did we play Xbox?"

"Exactly, yes." Drew sank his hands deeper into Bas's hair. "Naked Xbox."

Bas chuckled. "Sounds hot." He bent his head and licked at Drew's nipple, then rubbed his face over the hair that covered Drew's chest. "Did I win?"

Drew laughed. "We both won," he said.

"Mmm." Bas nuzzled Drew's pec again. "Have I ever mentioned how much I love your chest hair?"

"Uh, you know very well you haven't ever mentioned it."

"Well, I do." Bas looked at him again. "I really, *really* do."

Drew flushed further, feeling a lingering piece of anxiety fall away at this proof that Bas was turned on by something so... well... *masculine.* "I'm really, *really* glad."

Bas smiled hugely, satisfied and teasing all at once. "So tell me the specifics of Naked-Xbox," he demanded.

"Huh?"

"What happened after I backed you to the bed?"

Drew opened his mouth and closed it, a fish out of water in every sense. He'd never had to talk about his fantasies with a lover before, because all of his fantasies had always been Bas-specific. And he wasn't sure he wanted to do it now, either. What if Bas freaked out? What if it was all just a little *too* gay for him?

"We had sex," Drew hedged.

"Yes, and I'm guessing there was no actual Xbox involved," Bas said blandly. He stacked his palms on Drew's chest and propped his chin on them, like he was settling in and waiting for Drew to talk. "Be specific."

Oh, damn.

"You, uh... kissed me. You kicked off your shorts, and pushed me onto the bed."

"Were *you* naked?" Bas asked, his eyes alight.

"I... I don't know. I think I was already naked? Believe me, I wasn't concerned about how I got naked," Drew said wryly. "That was the least compelling part of the fantasy to me."

"Alright," Bas allowed. "I'm gonna fill in the blanks for you, then."

"You're co-opting my fantasy?" Drew couldn't help but laugh. That was *so* Bas.

"I'm *assisting you* in working out the details," Bas corrected. "Because the hows and whys of you getting naked are extremely interesting *to me*. So... I kicked off my shorts, like you said, and then I stripped off your t-shirt."

Drew swallowed. "You did?"

"Slowly," Bas confirmed. "So I could slide my hands up your skin. Like this."

He demonstrated, pushing up onto his knees so he could run his hands up both sides of Drew's torso.

Drew sucked in a stuttering breath.

"And then I ran my hands over your chest, like this, because it's fucking fascinating. The hair, the muscles. Different," Bas told him. "Familiar, because it's *you*, and I know every single piece of you. But different because I'd never touched you *that way* before. Like I wanted to make you want me. Like I couldn't keep my hands off you because you were the hottest thing I'd ever seen." The light in Bas's eyes was searing. "*Then* I pushed you down on the bed," he whispered. "What happened next?"

"I..." Drew licked his dry lips. "Then you, uh... Kissed me."

"Did I?" A breath against Drew's chin. "How did I kiss you? Like this?"

He pecked at Drew's lips. Licked gently at the seam of them.

"N-no. Harder."

"Like this?"

Bas levered forward, braced on one arm, and leaned in, pressing their mouths more firmly together, sucking on Drew's tongue. Then he sat back.

"That... that's closer," Drew told him.

Bas smiled. "Tell me, Drew. Tell me *exactly* what you wanted in this fantasy."

"You held me down," Drew blurted. "You climbed on top of me and pinned me down, because you're heavier than me. You held my wrists down because you're stronger than me."

"Oh, *fuck*," Bas said. "Fuck yeah, I did."

He gripped Drew's hands, forcing them down into the pillow beneath Drew's head, and slid his knees down, bringing his weight flush against Drew's. Both of them moaned.

Their lips met again, and Bas didn't hold back this time, thrusting into Drew's mouth with bruising intensity until they were both panting and writhing.

"Then. *What*?" Bas demanded, breathless.

He was sprawled against Drew, with only the sheet trapped between their cocks. Drew could feel Bas's rigid length pushing against his, and he could barely think.

"Then... Then I wrapped my legs around yours and flipped you over," Drew said, honestly. "Because I wanted to show you that you're not always in charge."

Bas's eyes widened, a combination of arousal and apprehension. Arousal won. "Yeah? Do it."

Drew kicked the sheet down, and Bas lifted himself slightly, then brought his weight back down. Drew whimpered at the glorious sensation of them skin-to-skin. He could barely string his thoughts together.

"Flip us," Bas breathed, bringing his hands up to cradle Drew's jaw. "If you can."

The challenge in his tone, in his eyes, ratcheted Drew's arousal even higher - and he truly hadn't known that was possible. He locked his leg over Bas's, braced the other, and pulled.

Bas wouldn't move.

"Maybe," he drawled. "We need to amend this part of the fantasy. Maybe there's a reason why I should be in charge. Maybe you want me to be in control. *Maybe* you like it better this way."

Drew blinked, then lifted his head so he could bite Bas's lip - part tease, part distraction.

It worked. This time when Drew pushed, Bas was caught off-guard and rolled. Drew landed on top of him, pinning *his* hands this time, so they were sideways on Bas's bed.

"In my fantasy, you weren't this cocky," Drew complained, leaning down to nip at Bas's jaw this time.

Bas snorted. "Then it wasn't *me* you were fantasizing about."

The very idea made Drew laugh. "It was definitely you. But I do like your version better."

Bas laughed, his dark hair falling on his forehead and blue eyes wild. "Uh huh. So, once you got me where you wanted me, what happened?"

Drew opened his mouth to answer, then hesitated. "It doesn't really matter from that point. We can do whatever we…"

Bas thrust his pelvis up into Drew's, a reminder that, unlike fantasy-Bas, the real thing was infinitely bossy and determined. "Fuck that. You have the whole fantasy laid out. I can see it in your eyes."

"Fine!" Drew swallowed. "Fine. I… I turned you over and fucked you. Hard."

Bas's eyes widened.

Cue the freakout in 5, 4, 3…

But Bas didn't freak out.

"Oh," he said. "Okay, yeah, we can… we can do that." But his eyes had gone unfocused just slightly, and his voice carried an audible thread of hesitation.

"Sebastian?" Drew released Bas's hands and squirmed until he was sitting on Bas's thighs. He wanted to rid Sebastian of his uncertainty, but he still had to take a second to marvel at the position in which he found himself.

I'm sitting on Bas's lap. Talking to him about sex. And he's not freaking out. Bas's naked cock was inches from his own.

For the first time ever, Drew was absolutely fine with his reality. All the alternative realities could fuck off.

"Bas." He stroked a hand over Bas's cheek. "Do you *want* us to do that? Or do you think you *should* do that?"

Bas thought about it. "How about… I want to *want* that? I want everything with you, I just…"

"It's scary?"

"Yeah."

"Yeah, it is!" Drew agreed. "It's a lot. And honestly? Many guys aren't into anal *at all*. Ever. It's not like some requirement in order to be with a guy. It's all about what you like."

Bas nodded, then looked away for a second before meeting Drew's eyes again. "But, uh… do you like it?"

"Yeah," Drew told him. "I like it. Not in the sense that I have to have it, though, Bas," he hurried to add. "Like I told you last night, just having *you* - in my bed, in my arms - it's better than any fantasy. So, you know…"

"Giving or receiving?" Bas interrupted.

It took Drew a second to make the connection. "Both," he told Bas. And then, because Bas was being one hundred percent honest, Drew couldn't help but add, "Receiving hasn't been my favorite in the past. But I would be open to that. With you." In fact, Drew had almost always preferred to top, since it meant he could control the situation. But the very idea of having Bas with him - *inside him* - that way made his cock throb happily.

"Yeah?" Bas's eyes lit up. "I want that. I mean… if you want to."

Drew leaned in and kissed Bas, slow and gentle. Then he rolled back to his original position and flopped to the mattress, spread-eagle.

"You're gonna have to help me embellish this part," he told Sebastian with a wink. "So, what's your fantasy?"

CHAPTER FOURTEEN

*W*hat was his fantasy?

Now that was a hell of a question, since he hadn't considered Drew in that light until Halloween, and then had tried to *prevent* himself from thinking that way until just a couple of days ago. Bas would have to make this up as he went along.

Which was perfect, really, since that was how he did his best work.

He pushed himself up to his knees, and then sat back on his feet, contemplating the man before him.

Drew was laid out in his bed like an offering. His brown eyes were shut, but his mouth was smiling - a plump, rosy curve above his stubbled jaw. With his arms stretched to the side, the lean muscles of his shoulders and chest were on prominent display beneath his thatch of chest hair. His abdomen was firm, sculpted, despite his relaxed state, and below his belly-button, another fine line of hair ran south, down past the line where his tanned skin turned paler, to the dusky, hard base of Drew's swollen cock. His legs were slightly parted, but there was no disguising the thick strength of them beneath the coarse, brown hair.

All in all, there could not be the slightest doubt in Bas's mind that the person laid out before him was *all male*. And Bas had to grab the base of his cock, hard, because the sight absolutely overwhelmed him.

"Where to begin?" Bas mused out loud. "It might be logical to start at the top." He laid a kiss over each of Drew's closed eyelids, enjoying Drew's breathy chuckle on his cheek. "I could make my way down…"

He licked at Drew's nipple, then bit it lightly. Drew cried out - a thin, reedy sound Bas would never have associated with his best friend.

He moved lower, swirling his tongue once around Drew's belly button, and every muscle in Drew's body locked down.

"But, then again," he said thoughtfully, sitting back again to ponder once more. "Maybe that's not the best path."

Drew let out a breath that was more like a shiver. "You could get on with it," he whined. "Not that I expect you to listen to… Ahhhhh!"

Leaning forward, Bas braced his hand by Drew's hip and licked a broad stripe up the underside of his dick, all in one smooth movement, catching Drew totally off-guard.

Excellent. Score.

And fuck, the taste was incredible. Salty, musky… delicious.

"So, explain to me how points are awarded in Naked X-box," Bas said. "Because I am determined to win."

Drew's brown eyes flew open, dazed with lust. "Has anyone ever told you that you're *too* competitive?"

Bas grinned. "My best friend tried to tell me that once. But I don't believe it." He stroked a single finger up Drew's cock, shocked by the way the smooth length twitched beneath his fingertip. He gripped the length firmly in his palm and stroked, just a little *too* gently. "He used to have some bullshit dad-ism…"

"It's not about winning or losing," Drew croaked out, eyes clamping shut as he thrust into Bas's hand. "It's about having fun and playing the game."

"That's the one! But Andrew…"

Drew's eyes opened again, and met his.

"I promise you, you'll have fun if I win."

Drew shook his head, but as he looked at Bas, a broad grin broke across his face, like he was stunned, over and over again, to find Bas here with him.

Bas knew the feeling.

He was elated by their new relationship and terrified that he'd fuck something up, relieved they'd started being honest with one another, and worried that somehow he'd waited too long. He'd never considered *making Drew happy* before - but wasn't that what boyfriends were supposed to do?

All he felt qualified for was loving the man… and hopefully that would be enough.

He leaned down and kissed that smile, letting Drew's happiness soak into him.

"So, where was I?" he asked against Drew's lips.

"Harder," Drew said. "You were going to do it harder."

"No… nope. I'm pretty sure that wasn't what I was going to do. Maybe I need to start over again from the beginning. Try to figure out where I left off."

Drew groaned in frustration. "Sebastian Seaver. I don't care how long you've been open to touching someone else's cock. You've had one of your own for over thirty years, and you fucking *know* how cruel you're being right…"

Bas snickered, then leaned forward and put his mouth

on Drew's erection once again, this time, taking the whole thing into his mouth. Well, not the whole thing - not even close - but enough to stretch his lips wide, enough to make him almost gag.

He pulled back, then bobbed up and down, sucking as he pulled off and firming his lips on the way back down.

Beneath him, Drew writhed.

He pulled off, replacing his mouth with his hand and stroking slowly again. "You know, this is a remarkably good way of quieting you," he told Drew conversationally. "I feel like I should get points for that."

"You will never win at FIFA again," Drew threatened hoarsely. "No baked goods ever. I will hide cauliflower in your pizza crust."

Bas chuckled. "Damn, counselor. Is this how you typically handle negotiations? Because I'm worried about Seaver Tech…"

"Sebastian!" Drew grabbed a pillow, drew it over his face, and screamed into it.

"Hush! I'm considering the logistics here. It's simple physics," Bas told him. And he was. There had to be a way he could take Drew in fully, all the way to the root, like Drew had done to him. He wanted that - to feel all of Drew inside him, to watch Drew when he did. The very idea had Bas squeezing his own cock and stroking hard.

"Fuck you!" Drew moved the pillow. "We're having *sex*, Bas. Concentrate on the subject at hand."

"I am!" Bas told him.

"What fucking physics could possibly be pertinent right now?"

"How to take more of your dick in my mouth," Bas told him.

Drew's eyes flew wide. "What?"

"It's physics," Bas said, his hand closing more tightly

around Drew, his fist pumping faster in a way he was pretty sure would drive Drew crazy.

He was right.

"Oh, *fuck*," Drew said, thrusting his hips off the bed. "I am so screwed."

"Not yet, but you will b— "

"Never," Drew interrupted, laying a hand over Bas's mouth. "Never in all my fantasies, did it occur to me exactly what would happen when I got a single-minded perfectionist into bed with me. You just can't help yourself, can you?"

"Well," Bas started, but his voice was mumbled by Drew's hand.

"Yeah, you think through the angles and the physics and the logistics on your own time, Bas. For right now, I am *dying*, and the mission of this round of Naked Xbox is for *you to make me come*."

Bas laughed. He gripped Drew's wrist and pulled his hand away from his mouth.

"I love you," he said, bending down to kiss the man who knew him better than anyone on the planet and somehow loved him anyway. "I really love you."

"And I really love you," Drew told him, as Bas straddled his lap and reached into his nightstand drawer. "And I would love you even more if you…"

Bas threw a tube of lubricant and a condom on the bed. "If I…?"

"Fuck me," Drew moaned breathlessly.

"Show me," Bas told him. "Show me how to get you ready."

And Drew did, squeezing lube onto his own fingers, rubbing it over his hole as Bas watched and then inserting first one finger, and then a second, inside himself.

Bas's gaze moved like a ping-pong ball, from Drew's

fast-moving hand, to the sheer ecstasy on his face. *He* wanted to be doing that for Drew, making Drew feel whatever it was that had him closing his eyes and biting his own lip.

He rolled the condom onto his cock, grabbed the lube, and slicked it over himself. The sound was loud and nearly obscene. Drew's eyes flew open and he watched with dilated pupils as Bas stroked himself over and over.

"Oh, fuck," Drew said. His voice was broken, shaking, wrecked with lust, and it was maybe the single best sound Bas had ever heard. "How is this real? How is this happening?"

Bas shook his head and coasted his hand down the flat plane of Drew's stomach to grasp his cock once again. "How did this never happen before? Christ alive, I must have been blind."

This thing was so far beyond lust or arousal, Bas had no way to categorize it. It wasn't want but need. Not desire but *requirement.*

A tremor wracked Drew's body and he made a frustrated noise, halfway between a moan and a sob. He clutched at Bas. "Now. Please, Bas, now!"

There was no finesse to the way Drew spread his legs, no art to the way Bas kneeled between them. Drew grabbed a pillow and propped it under his ass, and Bas could only be glad that Drew knew what he was doing because Bas was no longer in any sort of control.

He lined himself up at Drew's stretched entrance and paused, staring down at Drew.

"I'm nervous," he admitted, "but I don't think I can wait another minute."

"I *know* I can't," Drew told him, bending one knee up to his chest. "Please, fill me up."

Bas leaned forward, so that his chest was pressing

against Drew's bent leg. He lined his cock up and slowly, relentlessly pressed forward.

Drew inhaled sharply, pushing his neck and shoulders back into the bed, and Bas froze.

"Is it okay?" Bas demanded. "Am I hurting you?"

"In the best way, baby," Drew croaked, eyes shut like he was praying. "I promise."

Baby. Bas had said it to Drew several times, but hearing it on Drew's lips was powerful magic. He shuddered as the absolute *rightness* of it settled in his stomach. He and Drew were always meant to be this way. A thousand alternate universes, a thousand times Bas had chosen the wrong way, and still, *still*, this had been as unavoidable as gravity.

A second later, Drew was clutching at Bas's shoulders, urging him to move. Instinct had Bas leaning forward, propping his hand beside Drew's shoulder on the bed, and snapping his hips, pushing himself further into the scorching heat.

Oh. Shit.

It was beyond anything he'd ever felt. The thought sounded trite even inside his own mind, given that he'd had sex - good sex - with a number of women over the years, but that made it no less true. Because he'd never had sex with anyone he'd ever loved before.

He'd never had sex with *Drew* before.

And tears stung his eyes as he realized that this was just like having sex for the first time, not because it was his first time with a man, but because it was the first time he'd ever felt connected to the person beneath him.

"Open your eyes," he growled. "Open your eyes, Drew and watch me. Watch us."

Drew's eyes flew open, the brown nearly amber in the wash of light from the window and burning with intensity.

Bas looked down to where he and Drew were joined, and felt a rush of heat through his body.

"Oh my God," Drew whispered putting a hand up to touch Bas's cheek. "Sebastian. Oh my God."

The second Drew touched his face, any semblance of control Bas was attempting to exert over himself snapped.

Drew had called him a caveman earlier, but it had never been truer than it was at that minute. There was nothing civilized about the way Bas rocked his hips, pushing himself into Drew over and over like he could somehow rearrange the molecules of their bodies, forming them into one single being.

Mine, mine, mine, mine, Bas chanted in his head.

Drew was chanting, too, but his were breathless pleas of "Don't stop, don't stop, don't stop." If Bas had had the breath, he would have told Drew not to worry - he was fairly certain there was no force on earth that could have made him stop at that moment.

The focus of his entire consciousness was currently his dick, and the uninhibited cries of the man beneath him. He wanted to make this good for Drew, and he seriously hoped it was, but he could feel his orgasm racing up his legs, the electric burn of it more powerful than anything he'd felt since the first time pre-teen Bas had realized what his dick could do.

He reached a hand between them and grasped Drew's erection, which was leaking precum all over his stomach, and slid his thumb over the head. *Christ*, but Drew was gorgeous, in this and every other way.

And *he* was the lucky bastard Drew wanted.

"Drew, baby? I need you to come for me," Bas breathed. "I'm so close."

"Touch me, I need—. Yes!" Bas jerked him firmly, not slowing his pace at all, and only a few seconds later,

Drew was shooting all over their stomachs and all over his chest.

The orgasm made his hole spasm, and that was all it took to send Bas over the edge along with him, filling up the condom inside him.

Inside.

Drew.

He collapsed onto Drew, their chests heaving in syncopated rhythm as they attempted to catch their breath.

A second later, Drew's gasps turned into laughter, and Bas pulled back, propping himself on one arm to look down at him. "Something amusing?"

Drew shook his head, but laughed harder, tears streaming from his eyes, but he looped his wrists around Sebastian's neck and pulled him down for a kiss.

"Sorry! Sorry, it's just… if you had told me last week… or hell, even *yesterday*, that we would end up like this today," Drew gasped. "I never would have believed you."

"Didn't anyone ever tell you it's impolite to laugh when a man still has his dick inside you," Bas whispered, nuzzling at Drew's neck. But Bas couldn't be too upset - the marks he'd left on Drew's skin earlier were blooming bright against his tan, and it soothed something primal inside him.

Bas slid out carefully, removing the condom and tying it off, before throwing it to the floor someplace near the trash. He flopped on his back in the bed and pulled Drew into his side.

"Guess you'll have to teach me some manners," Drew sighed, nuzzling the hair of Bas's armpit- a sensation that should have been odd, but wasn't.

"Guess I will. Starting now. I'm deducting all of your points," Bas said. "Meaning, I officially win this game."

Drew snorted and started laughing again. "I wasn't aware I had won any points in the first place!"

"You did," Bas whispered. "I awarded you all the points, because that was the most epic sex that has ever occurred."

"And it was all my doing, naturally," Drew agreed. "But I'm not sure it's fair that I get penalized for breaking a rule when I wasn't advised of the rules in advance."

Bas sighed, long and gusty. He picked up Drew's hand, where it lay on his chest, and toyed with his fingers, feeling happier and more at peace than he had in a very long time.

"Well, *fine*, if you insist on bringing the law into it."

"I do," Drew said solemnly, lifting his head to prop his chin on Bas's shoulder. "It's my job."

Bas looked at the man beside him, all sweat-dampened skin, sleepy eyes, and hair tangled into gravity-defying brown clumps that rivaled some anime character's.

Oh, shit!

"I take it back. I win all the points. I have achieved something I believed was impossible."

Drew snorted. "Remind me never to play this game for money." But he rolled his eyes and sighed. "Fine, fine, tell me what impossible thing you've done."

"McMann," Bas said. "Your hair, your un-messable hair is a total fucking mess. And I take all the credit."

CHAPTER FIFTEEN

"Hey, Bas?"

Drew shook the blanket covered lump still curled up in the middle of the king-size bed. It appeared Bas hadn't moved since Drew had gotten up to take a shower half an hour ago.

He slapped what might have been Bas's ass. "Wakey, wakey, Sleeping Beauty."

A tired moan emerged from the duvet. "I want another round, Drew. You know I do. I just need, like, thirty more minutes of sleep."

Drew snorted. "This is the kind of stamina I have to look forward to?"

"Fine. Twenty minutes."

Amused, Drew pulled the blanket down to Bas's shoulders, baring his dark head and one corner of his stubbled jaw. No one should look so sexy when they first woke up.

"Hey!" Bas whined. "It's fucking cold. Climb back in, if you want."

"I wish. I'm afraid it's time for you to climb out, baby. I

got a call from Cam. He and the guys are on their way over."

Bas rolled over onto his back and stacked his hands behind his head, blinking sleepily. He looked Drew up and down, his gaze traveling over Drew's naked chest so intently that Drew could feel it like a physical touch, then he narrowed his eyes.

"You look way too awake right now, McMann. I'm rethinking this whole relationship."

Drew ran a hand through his clean, mostly-dry, perfectly tidy hair. "A shower and coffee will do that for you, too."

"You made coffee?" Bas perked up.

"Yep. Yours is in the kitchen." Drew smirked when Bas scowled. "I purposely didn't bring it in, because I know you're more likely to get up for coffee than because I'm telling you to." Bas's eyes narrowed further, and Drew winked. "The downside of being with someone who knows you too well, Seaver."

Bas's lips quirked, like maybe he didn't think that was a downside at all. He ran his hands over his face and sat up. "So they're all descending on us? Right now?"

"Right now. Apparently they have some new develop-ments to discuss." Drew stood and glanced down at Bas's naked chest. *Do not get distracted!* "My jeans from last night are fine, but I kinda wanna burn that sweater. It smells disgusting."

"Take anything you want," Bas said, throwing the covers aside and rolling out of bed with a deep sigh. "You know my closet better than I do." He stood by the bed and stretched fully, the lean, naked length of him fully on display.

Drew forced himself to look away and busied himself pulling open the t-shirt drawer in the dresser at the foot of the bed, cursing Cam and the whole crew for interrupting what otherwise would have been a long, lazy Sunday morning, segueing into a delightful New Year's Eve. "You don't seem very excited," he noted. "I thought you'd be dying to know what new developments they found."

Bas stalked forward, wrapping his arms around Drew's waist from behind, and their gazes met in the mirror above the dresser. "Damon mentioned something about news last night but didn't get into details." Bas put his mouth at the juncture of Drew's neck and shoulder, sucking lightly, and Drew shivered. "I figured we'd hear from them today."

"Wait." Drew grabbed a shirt from the drawer without looking at it, and held the folded fabric against his chest. "You mean they told you last night they had stuff to discuss?"

"Mmmhmm. When I called to let them know what happened to you."

"And you didn't want them to come over last night to talk about it?" Drew demanded.

"Uh, *no*." Bas said immediately. "Baby, you'd just been through the wringer! I wanted to take care of you. I wanted to be alone with you." Confused blue eyes watched Drew. "Did you want me to have them come over?"

"No! I… no. I'm just surprised." Stunned, actually. Since when was anything more important to Bas than stopping Alexei? "And you didn't ask what it was?"

Bas's eyebrows went up. "Nope. I told you, I had more important things on my mind. Are you upset?" he demanded, arms tightening.

Drew shook his head slowly, then turned in Bas's arms and gave him a brilliant smile. "Not even a little." He pressed his mouth to Sebastian's, but just as Sebastian gave a little moan and started to take the kiss deeper, the doorbell rang.

After a final brush of lips, Drew pulled back. "Go. Shower. I'll get them settled."

"Don't let them drink my coffee," Bas warned over his shoulder.

"Never," Drew vowed on his way out the door. "I've got your back."

He pulled the t-shirt over his head as he made his way down the hall. The hardwood floors were chilly against his bare feet, and he thought longingly of the warm, rumpled bed he'd left, and the even warmer man currently in the shower.

"Hey," he greeted, throwing the door wide and stepping aside for the four men bundled up in coats and scarves.

Cam was the first in the door. "You okay?" he demanded, laying a hand on Drew's bicep. "I cannot *believe* that guy drugged you!"

"I'm fine," Drew promised. "I didn't drink very much of my drink, and I vomited what little I did. I'm not actually sure if I was drugged, or…"

"From the way Bas described things, it sure sounded like it. And I can tell you more later," Cort said, stepping in behind Cam. He carried Cam's laptop bag slung over his shoulder. "Glad you're okay, man."

"I am," Drew said. He stretched out his arm, inviting everyone to head into the living room.

"Looks like you're a little *better* than okay," Damon remarked, stepping in after Cain. He raked his gaze from Drew's wet hair down to his bare feet and gave him a wink.

Cain elbowed his boyfriend lightly, and Damon gave him the boyish smile he reserved just for Cain. "Hey! Just sayin' what we were all thinking!"

Drew pursed his lips, unsure of how to respond and annoyed with himself for being unsure. He and Bas hadn't discussed how they were going to play off the new development in their relationship, and really, Drew should have seen this inquisition coming. He didn't want to out Bas before he was ready, and this crew was worse than a gaggle of old women when it came to gossip.

Cort was his unlikely savior. "Not a social call, brother," he yelled from the living room. "You can grill Drew, *or not*, another day."

Damon gave Drew an apologetic shrug and let Cain tow him into the room. Drew followed, watching as Cam and Cort pulled the two side-chairs and the ottoman closer to the coffee table, while Cam set up his laptop.

Cain pushed Damon into one of the chairs, and pulled the ottoman over to prop up Damon's injured leg. Damon scowled. "I told you it's *fine*, baby."

"Uh huh. And I told *you*, you're gonna rest it."

"But—"

"Stop arguing," Cain said, plopping himself down on the ottoman by Damon's leg.

Damon shook his head, but grinned. "Stubborn."

"It's no wonder, living with you," Cain grumbled, but the way he smiled and leaned back against Damon's leg took any sting out of his words.

Drew wondered whether he and Bas would reach that level of comfort with their relationship. Speaking of which...

"Uh, Sebastian just jumped in the shower before you came. He'll be along soon." He frowned. "I have no idea what food he has in the kitchen," Drew said, frowning. "But there's coffee, if anyone wants some. Do we have enough chairs?"

"Hey, guys!" Bas said, lifting a hand as he entered the room. The others all greeted him distractedly, but Drew watched in surprise and, yeah, excitement, as Bas came directly to Drew's side and put his hand on Drew's lower back. It was proprietary, claiming. *Soothing*.

"Calm down, babe," he whispered, low enough that only Drew could hear.

"I'm calm," Drew whispered back, but Bas shook his head.

"Nope. When you go into hyper-Martha mode, it's a sure sign you're stressed. When things get tense, your need to take care of people goes through the roof."

"It does not!" Drew argued. "I just like to cook. And make sure things are set up properly. Some people wouldn't remember to eat for days if I didn't…"

"You're cute when you're hyper," Bas said, low and intimate. Drew was pretty sure no one else could hear what they were saying, but they could sure as hell hear the *sex* in Bas's tone and see the hot glint in his eyes.

Drew swallowed. *Well, then.* Apparently they weren't hiding anything.

Another knot of Drew's tension loosened.

"You guys have all been here a hundred times," Bas said, addressing the others. "You don't count as guests anymore. Just help yourselves to coffee, or whatever else you want. I'm about a gallon low on caffeine, and judging by the looks on your faces, I'm gonna need it."

"You, sit." Bas pushed Drew into the other side chair, leaving Cam and Cort to sit on the sofa. "Need more coffee?"

Drew shook his head. Between Sebastian Seaver and the upcoming conversation, he was already wired.

Bas nodded once. "Be right back."

"Okay, *so*," Cort began, raising his voice slightly so Bas could hear him. "Sean was sufficiently worried that he put in some time last night, running the company names Bas gave him."

"The ones he found on Alexei's server," Cam clarified.

"Right. Not shockingly, all of them seem to be legit, just like the dummy companies Cain and Damon found in Senator Shaw's records last month."

"Figures." Bas came back and perched himself on the arm of Drew's chair, one foot up on the seat next to Drew's thigh. It was incredibly distracting - every cell of Drew's body was warmed by the proximity.

"They've all got an online and/or physical presence. They all filed taxes for last year," Cort continued.

"Why isn't that a shock?" Damon demanded. "I know *good* people who don't pay taxes."

Cain snorted. "Let me guess what tinfoil-hat-wearing mountain man you might be thinking of."

Damon nudged Cain's back with his foot. "Hush."

Cain grinned. "I bet the difference is, Eli's not a criminal. If the government does come after him, the most they'll get him on is failure to file taxes. But for Alexei…"

"Exactly," Cort confirmed. "Alexei doesn't want anyone poking around in his files. He doesn't exactly have receipts for his expenses."

"There have to be other servers where he keeps his black-hat accounting information," Bas said, shaking his head.

"Air-gapped," Drew said, repeating the new vocabulary word Bas had taught him. "So there's no way to get at the information unless you can access the server physically."

Bas pursed his lips and looked like he was thinking about something.

"Which you're not doing," Cort told him. "We've already discussed this, Sebastian. So seriously get any idea you have of infiltrating SILA right out of your head. We don't even have a clue where the server might be kept."

Bas sighed. "Yeah." The agreement was grudging and unconvincing at best.

"And," Cort continued, still staring at Bas like he'd heard the reluctance in his voice. "As we have discussed in the past, Sebastian, obtaining information from SILA that way would only damage any case against them. None of the evidence would be admissible in court. I know you want to take down the organization, but—"

"But that's not the way. Fine," Bas said, frustrated. "I get it."

Cort nodded, satisfied. "Yesterday, Cam had Margaret comb through all of the Seaver Tech projects your father took the lead on, searching for Michael Paterkin and/or *Collier* - the project that Paterkin mentioned in his emails. Sadly, both searches came up empty."

Cam spoke up. "And it's worth noting that Margaret's memory is long, and she doesn't remember anyone by that name."

Drew pushed a hand through his hair. "Great. Tell me you didn't call this meeting to tell me that all we have are dead ends."

Cort's grin was positively feral. "Would I do that to you? No. Darling Margaret, the love of my life, who deserves a raise by the way—" He pointed to Bas and raised an eyebrow. "Was brilliant enough to notice that there was a client your father handled who generated quite a bit of income for Seaver Tech over the years. So much income, in fact, that she was shocked she couldn't remember the details of the project, or the contact person. She can't remember handling any of the billing. And? There are no notes or files in the project folders. No contact person listed. It's like they've all been removed."

Bas frowned and rubbed at his chin. "I guess it's possible there was a glitch. That something got archived..."

"It *might* have been possible," Cort allowed. "But it wasn't. Show them, Cam."

"The name of the company is Storm Surge Enterprises," Cam said. He turned his laptop around to show them the screen, where a very, *very* basic website of white text on a black background was displayed. The only visual interest on the entire page was a picture in the header bar.

"Is that Comic Sans font?" Cain demanded. "Was this created by a thirteen-year-old?"

"More like a fifty-year-old who wanted to stay under the radar, I'm pretty sure," Cam answered, ill-concealed excitement in his voice. "The contact information at the bottom is bogus except for the email, which is listed as R. Van Rijn at Storm Surge."

Drew blinked. "Who?"

"Van Rijn?" Cain asked, leaning forward to look at the website more closely. "Isn't that the painter Rembrandt's last name?" When Damon shot him a look, he said defensively, "What? My mom made me take an art appreciation class back in the day."

"Ding ding ding!" Cam exclaimed, pointing at Cain. Then to Cort, he said, "See? I told you someone else would recognize it."

Cort rolled his eyes. "Literally, *one* other person. You and Cain."

"Not to be a kill-joy, trivia fans, but I'm still not getting why this is important," Damon interjected in his rough voice.

"Look, Bas," Cam said offering up the laptop. "Look at the picture on the site."

Bas grabbed the laptop and sat back down on the chair arm, enlarging the painting on the website so he and Drew could look at it."

Holy shit.

"Bas, isn't that—?" Drew began, but Bas was already nodding.

"*Storm on the Sea of Galilee*," Bas confirmed. His jaw was set, and Drew could feel the tension coming off him, even as he handed back the laptop. For the others, he explained, "My mom did a copy of that painting - an amateur thing - in one of *her* art classes, and it's hanging on the wall in the private office my dad and I shared."

"This has to be some kind of... *thing*," Cam said, gesturing with his hands. "A secret message or a clue or something. Dad is trying to tell us something."

"Like what?" Drew asked.

"I don't know," Cam admitted. "But if he was bringing in money off the books, it makes sense that he'd want to push it all through a dummy company." He grimaced. "Sort of like Alexei, in a way."

Bas rubbed a hand over his eyes, sorrow stark on his face. "But what would the painting have to do with anything?"

Drew lifted a hand to the base of Sebastian's spine and rubbed gently. Hearing these things about Levi Seaver, a man Bas had always looked up to, had to be killing him, and he was infinitely glad that now, *finally*, he had the right to touch Bas this way. To comfort him. Bas flashed him a grateful smile.

"Is it possible that there's a safe behind there? Maybe with all the project notes and files that are missing?" Damon asked. "If this were some James Bond movie..."

"My dad was no James Bond," Cam said. "More like Q, the tech dude."

"Yeah, you said he wasn't a pen-and-paper guy," Cort mused, drumming his fingers on the table. "But then again... Maybe that would be the last thing anyone would expect."

Cam blinked and looked at Bas for direction.

"It's possible," Bas allowed. "It's not exactly a secret that the painting is there - the cleaning people have access to the office. But my dad never conducted meetings down there, so I can't imagine anyone would have connected the dots." He shrugged sadly. "I think at this point, neither Cam nor I can claim to be an authority on what our father would or wouldn't have done."

Cam huffed sadly, and Cort pulled him into a sideways embrace.

"So, we need to get into your office and look at the painting," Cain said, looking from face to face for confirmation.

"That's easy enough," Bas said. "I'll go over right now."

"And I'll come with you," Drew told him.

"You might wanna wait a minute," Cort told them. He licked his lips, looking between Drew and Bas. "You, ah, remember the final name you wanted Sean to run for you yesterday, Seaver?"

Bas frowned for a second, then his face cleared. "Oh, right." He looked down at Drew guiltily. "Mark Char-bonnier."

"You had Sean run the name of the guy I went on a date with?" Drew demanded. "Before or after the date?"

Bas cleared his throat. "Uh, it might have been before?" He spread his hands. "I just got a bad vibe off the whole thing."

Damon snorted. "A bad vibe called *jealousy*."

"Well, it turned out he *is* a criminal, so it was justified," Bas said with a nod, though his eyes sought Drew's as though he worried Drew might be upset.

In truth, Drew was far from upset. The idea of Bas being *that* jealous turned his insides to putty, and the worried look in his eyes made Drew want to laugh. But he knew admitting it would only make Bas even more of a caveman, so he pressed his lips together and tried to look stern.

"You have a handy way of making up rules to suit your purposes," he remarked. "Try to control that."

"Or don't," Cort said. He glanced at Cam, and then at Cain and Damon, who all nodded solemnly, before turning back to Drew and Bas. "I'm afraid Mark Charbonnier isn't just your garden-variety asshole. The financial services company he runs *is* on the list of businesses from Alexei's server."

"What?" Bas jumped to his feet, running a hand through his hair. "Are you fucking kidding me?"

Drew was paralyzed by shock. He was vaguely aware of Bas's agitation, but he could barely process it. *Mark?* The fucking idiot who looked like a turtle? *Mark*, with the stupid dog? He'd hardly processed the idea of that self-absorbed creep being the kind of person who'd drug him, though he knew logically that date rape wouldn't be so rampant if you could tell that sort of thing about a guy by looking.

Still. To think he'd been texting with someone who worked with Alexei was nauseating. He had to swallow before he could force out the words, "What the hell could Alexei want with *me*?"

Bas sat back down and wrapped an arm around Drew's shoulder, and Drew *knew* that Bas was pushing down his own anger to give him the support he needed.

Drew leaned into his solid body, and thanked his lucky stars for Bas's caveman instincts. They'd saved him from... God only knew what.

Cort raised his eyebrows at Cain. "This is your part of the show and tell, bud." He looked at Drew and Bas. "Damon already called and filled me in on this part, so I could get the ball rolling with Sean. But I wanted you to hear it straight from Cain."

Cain nodded. He looked down at his hands, which were clenched tightly in his lap, the picture of nervousness.

Damon pulled his leg down from the ottoman and leaned forward, bracketing Cain's body with his own. He leaned his chin on Cain's shoulder. "Remember, baby, everybody here knows you're not your father. And nobody blames you for the shit he's done." He glared at everyone else in the room, as though challenging them to disagree.

But of course, no one did.

"Damon's right, Cain," Cam said encouragingly. "You're braver than all of us put together."

Cain snorted, but he leaned back against Damon, looked directly at Drew, and said, "I heard from my father this morning."

Drew looked from Cain to Cort and back. "And that's a bad thing?"

Cain had mentioned that his dad had been trying to "salvage" their relationship, calling at Christmas and even inviting Cain to bring Damon if he agreed to visit his parents. Cain had also told them that he didn't feel right cutting off his parents completely, though he wasn't sure there was any relationship there to "salvage."

"Yeah. He wasn't calling to chat. He was calling to warn me." He rubbed the back of his fist over his mouth. "Alexei made contact with my dad last night."

Bas's hand clenched on Drew's shoulder, but otherwise his body locked down. Drew wanted to soothe him, but couldn't. He could tell from the look in Cain's eyes that whatever he was about to say was going to be bad.

"You know the way my father and Alexei left things after Damon and I had that confrontation with the senator." He looked at Damon. "Alexei has information on him, he

has information on Alexei. They agreed on a standoff. A
'you don't fire, I won't fire' kinda thing, with the understanding that none of us would move against Alexei either."
He nodded around the room.

"Another Cold War," Cort said. "Or so we thought."

"Right." Cain agreed. "And we knew it wouldn't last
forever, because Alexei Stornovich is a crazy bastard. But
we hoped it would last long enough for us to find the information to take SILA down. Acting under the radar."

"But that changed?" Drew asked.

"Well, yes and no. I think it's safe to say that Alexei was
running his own game under the radar all along. He wanted
Sebastian to work with him again." Cain looked at Bas. "If
he could get you to make the same mistake your dad made,
he'd own you, just like he owned your dad. You'd never be
able to move against him without ruining Seaver Tech and
sending yourself to prison."

Bas shook his head in disgust. "That's what those emails
were about?"

"Yup. But you didn't take him seriously," Cain said.

"Because I didn't even know that Michael Paterkin had
anything to do with Alexei!"

"Maybe he thought your dad had shared more of that
with you," Damon suggested. "I mean, he was leaving you
and Cam the company the way his dad left him SILA. It
stands to reason he would have shared this big, dangerous
secret with you."

"But he didn't!" Cam said. He shook his head once,
sadly. "Maybe he thought he had time. Or that he could
resolve things himself."

"Or maybe he never intended to tell us at all," Bas said
harshly. "Because he was too ashamed."

Drew leaned his head against Bas's chest.

"In any case, you didn't respond favorably to his

requests, so he came up with a backup plan. Getting to you through Drew."

"Me?" Drew demanded, but then he understood. "Mark."

"Yeah," Cain said. "Seems that way, putting together the other stuff we figured out today. He was going to blackmail you somehow."

Drew frowned. "I'm no saint, but I haven't committed any felonies that I'm aware of."

"Maybe it wasn't going to be that kind of blackmail," Cort said, looking from Drew to Bas, clearly uncomfortable. "If you had gone out with him, *maybe slept with him…*"

Beside him, Drew felt Bas tense, and he defended himself. "I didn't!"

"No. But if you had," Cort said in a low voice. "If he'd gotten compromising pictures of you? Threatened to publish them?"

"Then, whatever! I wouldn't have gotten involved with SILA, even if my junk was all over the nightly news!" Drew said hotly.

"He wouldn't have gone to you," Cort said, looking at Bas.

Bas nodded once. He sat upright and folded his arms over his chest. "Cort's right. If he'd come to me with those pictures… I don't know what I would have done."

"Are you fucking kidding me?" Drew demanded, pulling away to glare at Bas. "You would have signed your soul over to Alexei? Jesus Christ, Bas. We weren't even *together* then."

Bas turned his head, blue eyes hard. "Yes we were. We just didn't know it yet."

And what the hell was Drew supposed to say to that?

"But Drew didn't date the asshole back in November," Cam prompted.

"Right," Cain said. "And then Alexei figured out that we weren't sitting quietly by."

Drew frowned at Sebastian, still more than a little annoyed at his earlier declaration. "Did he figure out you hacked his server?"

"Impossible," Bas declared. "And that's not bragging. It would be impossible to track me through the botnet. At best, he'd be guessing I was behind it."

Cain nodded. "Sebastian's right. No, somehow he figured out you'd met with the reporter."

"Gary North?" Now it was Bas's turn to frown down at Drew. "I told you we couldn't trust that guy. He was all about getting in your pants!"

"No way!" Drew demanded. "Gary didn't like Alexei at all! He wouldn't have…"

"Jesus, could you two can it for a second and let my guy finish?" Damon demanded.

Drew hung his head for a second, trying to release the tension from his muscles, while Bas muttered, "Sorry, Cain. Go on."

"I don't know how he knew about you meeting Gary," Cain told them. "I didn't get that deep into it with my father. Although I also wouldn't be surprised if he was paying people to follow us. Remember he's a paranoid freak."

Drew nodded. "Fair point."

Bas blew out a breath. "There was a guy at the bar that night, watching us. At the time, I assumed he was interested in Drew."

Drew shook his head. Beyond ridiculous.

"However he found out," Cain said, his voice stronger now, "he knew you had the meeting. And that's when he upped his game. Namely, with you, Drew."

"With Mark, you mean." Drew was pretty sure that

date was the biggest mistake of his life. "Fuck. If he drugged me..."

"I don't know that we need to say *if* anymore," Cort interjected.

"Fine. If he'd gotten me out of that restaurant after he drugged me, he could have a billion blackmail pictures."

"Worse," Cort said. "He'd have *you*. And I don't even need to ask Sebastian what he'd be willing to do if he thought your life was in danger, Drew, because it's the same thing I'd do if it were Cam, the same thing *any* of us would do if the person we love was threatened." He smiled grimly. "We'd sign over our souls. In a heartbeat."

Drew pushed his lips together and nodded. Risking himself was easy enough, but risking Sebastian? Cort was one hundred percent accurate. It would take *less* than a heartbeat for him to sacrifice anything and everything if Bas needed him.

He looked at the unsmiling man beside him and put a tentative hand on his leg. "But that didn't work either," he said. "Because Sebastian saved me."

"Which brings us to my father," Cain said.

"Finally," Damon muttered. "No more interruptions from any of you. It's hard enough for Cain to get through this."

Cain gave him a grateful smile, but it disappeared quickly. "Since Alexei can't use you, he wants to 'tie up loose ends.'"

Drew and Bas exchanged a glance. That sounded ominous.

"My father said he wouldn't be involved in hiring out another murder. But Alexei said he didn't need a 'trigger man.' He just needed to get everyone in one spot. And my father agreed... and then called to tell me everything."

The strain in Cain's voice was mirrored on every face in

the room. They'd known all along that Alexei was danger-ous, but to hear Cain speak it aloud - to confirm that Alexei literally wanted to kill them all - was terrifying.

"Did he say how?" Drew croaked.

"Yeah. There's a black-tie charity auction being held by the Cambridge Collaborative," Cain continued. "They're a great organization - a reputable one I'm pretty sure isn't connected to Alexei in any way. The senator is supposed to get us all to go."

"That's not quite what he said," Damon growled. "He specifically said that *you* don't have to be there, Cain. That you *shouldn't.*"

Cain shrugged. "Irrelevant. If you're going, I'm going."

"We'll see about that," Damon muttered.

"Whoa, wait a minute." Bas's scowl was fierce. "*Nobody* is going to go!" He turned to Cort. "Right? We're not all gonna traipse along to some party where we know we'll have targets on our backs!"

Cort winced. "I agree with you," he said, but not as firmly as Drew would have liked.

"Tell them," Cam insisted, nudging Cort. "Tell them what Sean said."

"Camden, I told you, I don't give a shit what Sean said. Not about this."

"Fine, I'll do it then!" Cam said, ignoring Cort's glare. "Sean said we should do it. He'll get a team on-site. Maybe claim there were threats about the auction or something. The team will be our security, but they'll also be there to watch for Alexei or his 'trigger man.' If they can nab him on a weapons charge, they have probable cause to get a warrant and search his premises. If they can nab his guy, they can lean on him to talk, and *then* have probable cause for a warrant. Either way, Alexei goes down." He dusted his hands off. "And we are finally *done.*"

"If we *live*," Bas exploded standing up to pace once again. "Do you hear the words you're saying right now, little brother? You're talking about using yourself, using *all of us*, as bait!"

"What's the alternative?" Cam said coolly. His eyes, a paler version of Sebastian's blue, were resigned.

Drew leaned forward, bracing his knees on his elbows, and ran his hands through his hair. This was the stupidest thing he'd ever heard. He couldn't imagine Sean would go along with it. And yet…

"I can't think of one," Drew said dully.

"No!" Bas said, turning to glare at Drew. "You're on board with this, too? Is everyone in this room crazy?"

"Don't put words in my mouth! I'm not on board with it. I just said I can't think of an alternative!"

"The thing is," Cain said softly. "It's not like we have the choice to just stay home and stay safe. You know? If the senator doesn't get us there, Alexei will ruin him. Or, for all I know, kill him." He rubbed his palms on his jeans and said softly, "And maybe that's justice. But that's not going to stop Alexei from coming after us, too. It's personal now. And if he doesn't come for us this way, he'll come for us some other way. A way we can't predict, and can't take action to prevent."

The room fell silent after that. Drew looked at Bas, who was staring at Cain, seemingly frozen. And then suddenly, Bas exploded into motion.

"I can't handle this right now," he announced. "I'm going to Seaver Tech. I'm going to see what's behind that fucking painting."

"But Bas," Cam argued, pushing to his feet. "We need to agree so we can plan…"

"I'm not agreeing to a goddamn thing, Camden!" Bas insisted. His eyes were wide, and he was shaking his head like a madman, but his voice was very precise as he bit out, "I'm going to see what's behind that painting. And when I know, I will call you. But I'm warning you right now, no force on earth is going to make me change my mind."

Drew shook his head. Bas, when he'd made his mind up about something, was an unstoppable force. Unfortunately, Alexei Stornovich was an immovable object.

He felt a spurt of anger in his chest. Anger, and hurt, too. They didn't have time to deal with Bas stalking off in a huff until he could wrap his mind around an issue.

Not now. Not again.

Not after he'd fucking promised to communicate.

Bas stomped to the front door. Drew turned in time to see him grab his coat from the peg that hung there, and reach for the door handle. But just as Drew opened his mouth to protest, Bas stopped with his hand on the knob. He didn't turn. "I'll be in the car. If you're coming, Andrew, you can borrow a pair of my socks."

Drew let out a relieved breath he hadn't known he was holding and stood. "I'm stealing your sweater, too," he told Bas, then hurried to the bedroom.

CHAPTER SIXTEEN

"*I*t's weird just sitting here without playing around on my phone."

Bas gripped the steering wheel tighter. They'd been driving for nearly ten minutes and were almost at Seaver Tech, but with the tense silence stretched between them, it had seemed much longer.

Christ, but he was *angry*. And he had no idea what to do with it. He couldn't recall a time he'd felt such a fierce emotion with no outlet. Even after the crash, grief-stricken and heartbroken as he'd been, he'd been able to concentrate on figuring out who'd been responsible, making sure someone paid the price.

But now… Now there was no one to blame, except Alexei, and no useful task he could throw his energy into. So it simmered in the air around him. He could almost feel it.

"I had your phone wiped remotely," Bas told him. "Last night. There's no way they could have gotten anything useful off it. We can get you a new one."

From the corner of his eye, he saw Drew nod. "RIP, Dragon Puzzler. I was on Level 37. Nearly a mage."

Bas snorted, almost against his will, and glanced at Drew. "Nearly a mage?" he mocked.

"Mmm. I was going to put it on my email signature." He swept a hand out in front of him like he was reading an invisible title. "Head of Legal Department… and Mage."

Bas shook his head, some of the tension leaching from him even as he tried to hold onto it. "Are you being ridiculous on purpose?" He put on his turn signal and headed into the underground garage.

"Depends," Drew said, as Bas flashed his keycard at the scanner. "Is it working?"

"No." He sighed. "Maybe."

Drew reached over and put a hand on Bas's knee. "I don't want to fight with you, Sebastian," he began.

"Then let's not talk about the auction," Bas told him. He pulled into his designated parking spot next to the elevator and cut the engine. "You're not going to change my mind."

Drew sighed like he was disappointed. He got out of the car, slamming the door behind him, and Bas wished they could rewind this day by six hours, to the part where they were totally on the same page and confessing their love to one another.

But honest to God, what did Drew expect? That somehow Bas would be okay with them all risking their lives on the slim chance they might be able to nab Alexei? No fucking way.

There was irony there. Drew was forever accusing him of going off half-cocked, despite the risks. Where was Drew's levelheadedness now that they really needed it?

Despite the lingering tension, Drew was waiting next to Bas's door as he got out and locked the car, and he took Bas's hand in his as they walked inside.

"So, what are you hoping we'll find behind the painting?" Drew asked as they made their way across the lobby toward the elevator.

Bas shrugged. "What do I want to find? Some evidence of Alexei committing a felony? Maybe a nice clear color photo of him with a gun in his hand." With his free hand, he jammed the button that would take them to the basement. "But what do I *think* we'll find? I don't know. Something incriminating, no doubt."

"*Air gapping* on steroids," Drew said. "Your dad was smart." Bas shot him a look that had Drew raising his hands innocently, "Just practicing my new vocabulary."

Sebastian snorted. Drew had always known how to get around his moods, and he appreciated the effort, but it wasn't gonna work today.

"If he was *really* smart, he would've stayed out of all this mess and there wouldn't have been any information for him to hide," he countered. "I think we're going to find hard evidence that my dad took money from SILA. Maybe more details about the specific projects he gave them." He looked at Drew. "Proof of his guilt, essentially."

"Ouch." Drew frowned as the doors opened and they stepped out into the hall.

"Yeah, well." He unlocked the door to his office and pushed it open, flipping on the light. The place seemed darker and smaller than usual - not a lair, but a cage.

"Wait a sec. You can't just drop a bomb like that and move on." Drew pulled at his elbow. "Talk to me."

Bas shook his head even as he let Drew turn him. Apparently Drew didn't get that Bas wasn't in any mood to talk. "Can we just do what we came here to do? Please?"

"In a minute! Bas, you keep talking about choices and alternate universes. How... how people find themselves in situations that are wrong, but they don't even realize how wrong they are. Maybe your dad—"

"No." Bas held up a hand. "Nope. I'm gonna stop you right there. What my father did - getting involved with fucking criminals, *continuing* to be involved with criminals for years - was wrong. Flat out. It's not subjective." He shook his head. "And you have no idea what it feels like to...*God*. To look back at this guy I *idolized*, and to doubt every fucking thing he ever taught me. Who was he? Did I even know him?"

Drew stepped closer, wrapping his arms around Bas's waist, pressing their chests together. Bas closed his eyes for a moment, shocked all over again at how good and *right* it felt.

"Has anyone ever told you that you can be stubborn as hell?" Drew demanded. "Not everything can be put into one category. Was he *good?* Was he *bad?* Nobody's all one thing or the other. I'm not. Neither are you." He cupped Bas's cheek in his hand. "Baby, sometimes you can't think your way through something, because it won't make sense no matter how hard you try. You just need to accept it."

Bas ground his teeth together. "I'm aware of that."

"Are you?"

"Yes! Just because I prefer logic - things I can under-stand and... and *control* doesn't mean I think everything works that way! Look at us for God's sake! There's no logic to that."

Drew raised an eyebrow, and Bas flushed as he replayed his words. "Not like that!" He squeezed Drew around the waist. "I just mean, I tried to logic my way through it, but I couldn't make it fit into any of the boxes in my mind. And now... I dunno." He stepped back, frus-trated that he couldn't articulate the truth he knew hovered at the back of his mind. "I've never been really good with emotional stuff. I wonder if… if the reason it took me so long to see the truth of what you and I could be, was because I knew it *wasn't* going to be logical or reasonable." He huffed out a laugh and looked into Drew's serious brown eyes. "I don't seem to have any reason or rationality at all when it comes to loving you. It's beyond everything."

Drew's smile, when it came, was soft and slow.

"You think it's any easier for me? Sebastian, I fell for you while believing you were straight. That… that it was doomed. And I tried so hard to think my way out of it, to distract myself with other guys." His gaze grew sharp and he pointed an accusing finger at Bas. "And if you bring up Mark right now I will drop you where you stand!"

Bas widened his eyes. "I would never."

They both knew he was lying.

"Uh huh. Anyway, we both made dumb choices." Drew smirked. "I think that's the theme of our whole friendship. Put it on a t-shirt. 'Loving each other and making dumb choices, since 1987.'"

"Yeah, I'll get right on that."

"But we were both doing what we thought was best, right? In these hard situations. We did the best we could, given your overwhelming stubbornness…"

"And your insatiable need for control."

"Yes, fine, and me being a control freak." Drew rolled his eyes. "Can you not give your dad the same benefit of the doubt? I mean, looking back, we can see that he totally fucked up getting involved with Ilya. But put yourself in the shoes of a man who is mortgaged to the hilt with no idea how he'll support his wife and kid. He's got a great idea, and no one will give him a loan. Was he supposed to let you starve? Forget all of his talent and dreams so he could get an *honorable* job working at the grocery store?"

Did he think that? Would that have been better? Bas didn't know.

"Look." Drew pulled Bas close again, and pressed a kiss to his jaw. "He took a calculated risk with Ilya Stornovich. He had no idea how it would end up. You or I might have done the same thing in his position."

Bas shook his head. "I hear what you're saying. I do. And maybe I even get it logically." He gave Drew a wry grin, acknowledging the irony. "But I don't know how to forgive him when his choices harmed innocent people and destroyed my family." He wrapped his arm around the back of Drew's neck and spoke the ultimate truth. "His choices put *you* at risk. How can I forgive him for that?"

"But imagine he *hadn't*," Drew said. He braced his warm palms on both sides of Bas's neck, and his thumbs stroked Bas's jaw. It felt so damn good. "If he hadn't started the company, our fathers wouldn't have worked together for years. We wouldn't have grown up together. We wouldn't have been friends. We wouldn't be together now."

Bas wanted to fight against Drew's words, against the truth in them, but he couldn't. Logic and emotion *both* insisted that he was right. If his father had made a different choice, everything might have changed and that... that was unthinkable.

"He just always seemed larger than life. He had a solution for every problem," Bas told him. He looked around the office, at the bank of monitors where he and his father had spent so many hours together. It had been a long time since he'd allowed himself to remember the good times they'd had here. The laughter they'd shared. The joy of discovery and challenge.

"He was a lot like you," Drew said, and Bas knew that was true, too. And maybe he was blaming his father because he would have made the same choice.

"So you're saying I need to put this behind me, huh?"

"No way. It'll take time to get through it. To grieve for the man you thought he was. I'm just saying maybe it's time to stop *blaming*. Forgive him for being human. For your sake. For the sake of our future."

The need to kiss Drew was overwhelming, and Bas didn't bother trying to resist. As he lost himself in the taste of Drew's mouth, in the heat of his embrace, he sent up a silent message to his father.

I forgive you. I'll live well. I'll take care of Cam. I'll love Drew until I die.

Because that was a choice Bas could make.

ALL TOO QUICKLY, Drew made a noise in the back of his throat and pulled back slightly, his lips clinging to Sebastian's.

"Jesus. We need, like, an entire week when this is over. Just us. No phones. No family. No work."

"No clothes?" Bas asked, ducking his head to claim one last kiss. "Are you sure a week will be enough?"

"Did I say week?" Drew sucked in a breath and ran his hand down the front of Bas's sweater, which peeked out from his open coat. "I meant *month*."

"Noted."

With a sigh, Bas let him go and moved over to the painting, moving the edge cautiously. It was surprisingly light and had been mounted with a single wire draped over a screw in the wall. It lifted off easily.

"Well, that's fucking anti-climactic," Drew said, coming closer as Bas set the painting on the floor.

The wall behind it was completely bare, but Bas ran a hand over the smooth surface anyway.

"Total waste of time," Bas said, looking up at the ceiling. "*Fuck.*" What the hell were they going to do now, without any other strings to tug or leads to follow?

"It'll be fine," Drew said, coming around to console him. "We still have things we can...Wait! Bas! Look at the back of the painting!"

The painting was just a stretched canvas on a frame, with no paper backing. And nestled against the bottom edge of the frame, held in place with a single strip of duct tape, was a tiny thumb drive.

Bas watched as Drew knelt to peel away the tape. His mouth was suddenly dry and his gut churned.

"Got it!" Drew said, brandishing the stick. He looked at the row of computers and frowned. "How do we load this up?"

Bas took the drive from his hand. "I can do it." He shucked his coat, sat in his chair, woke his machine, and inserted the flash drive, tapping his fingers restlessly on the desktop all the while.

"Hey." Drew leaned over him from behind and laid a hand on Bas's, stopping its motion. "It's gonna be fine. Whatever's on there, it'll be okay."

Bas nodded, but he wasn't sure he believed it. Everything he and Drew had talked about was a hypothetical. Now he was going to see the reality... and learn exactly how much blood Levi Seaver had on his hands.

He called up the directory on the drive and scrolled through it. "It's a bunch of notes," he told Drew. "Names and dates. Contacts. Amounts paid, all in cash and untraceable. Shit, he made a lot of money from SILA."

"What are those?" Drew pointed at the screen.

"Those are... Huh. Those are charitable contributions," Bas said. "It... it looks like he made anonymous contributions for the same amounts Alexei was giving him."

"So he wasn't profiting," Drew said softly.

"I guess not."

And did that make Levi Seaver's actions okay? Maybe not. But, yeah, it made Bas feel somewhat better. He kept digging.

"Are those emails?"

"Yeah. Dozens. Between my dad and Michael Paterkin. And notes from my dad's conversations with him." He turned to Drew. "Use my cell and call Cort."

As Drew got Cort on the line, Bas skimmed the emails, excitement and anxiety thrumming through his blood in equal measure the further he read.

The FBI-agent Cort used to be was evident in his no-nonsense voice as Drew put the phone on speaker and set it on the desk. "We're here. What did you guys find?"

"A flash drive," Bas said. "With all the missing project notes from Storm Surge. For a paranoid man, Alexei... or Michael Paterkin, as he calls himself here... was remarkably stupid about the things he put in writing."

"Yeah, probably because he knew we couldn't connect Michael to Alexei," Drew said.

"What kinds of things, Seaver?" Cort demanded. "What have you got?"

"I can tell you what tech my dad sold Michael over the years. I can tell you how much he paid - in cash - for each thing." Bas kept reading. "And... oh, damn. I can tell you who Collier is."

"Collier's not a project?" Cam demanded. "I thought when Alexei... or Michael... whoever... emailed you, he referred to the Collier Project."

"He did," Bas said, shaking his head even though he knew his brother couldn't see him. "Looks like Alexei had Dad feeding him information on some surveillance programs that Seaver Tech developed for the government.

Collier was an undercover agent trying to infiltrate SILA about three years ago. But using the tech Dad passed him, Alexei was able to find and eliminate Collier before he could get any info on Alexei."

"Jesus," Cam breathed. "So when he was going on and on about how well they worked together on the Collier project…"

"He was essentially implying that Dad had a hand in the guy's murder. Yeah," Bas confirmed. He was sickened by the idea. "But that's where it ended for Dad. After this, he refused to pass on any more information. There are no new deposits here, even after… Huh. Even after he reminded Dad about the terrible car accident Drew and I were in, and how he hoped we'd learned to be more careful." He glanced back at Drew, who looked shaken. "Son of a bitch."

"Dad said no?" Cam repeated quietly.

"Yeah, bro. That was the line he wouldn't cross. And, uh. For what it's worth, it looks like he donated all of the money Alexei paid him to charity. Anonymously."

Drew's hands came up to thread through his hair and Bas let some of the tension he'd been holding bleed out of him. "See, it's not black and white," Drew whispered, low enough that only Bas could hear.

Bas nodded and grabbed one of Drew's hands so he could press a kiss in the center of his palm.

"So, it sounds like you have plenty there to connect *Michael Paterkin* to a whole host of crimes," Cort said. "And it's all been obtained legally. But you've got two problems. One, giving all this information to the authorities is going to cause serious problems for Seaver Tech."

"I don't care," Bas said quickly.

Cam's answer was slower, more reluctant, but no less heart-felt. "Yeah, Bas is right. I hate to see my dad's legacy go down in flames like this, but if it means putting Alexei away, there's no question."

There was a rustle on the other end of the line, and Bas strongly suspected Cort had wrapped Cam up tightly, just as Drew was now doing with him. Thank God they had both found men who loved them for far more than their last names.

"Well, the other problem is that we need to find a way to connect Michael Paterkin to Alexei," Cort said.

"And the only way to do that is to get into Alexei's money. And we can't do *that* unless we can get into his fucking server." Bas groaned. "So, we've traveled in a circle and found ourselves right back where we started."

Someone, likely Cort, sighed. "Seems that way. Don't suppose that drive contained any contact information for people who'd love to testify against Alexei?"

Bas snorted. "'Fraid not."

"Figured. Well, I'll give Cooksy the update. Decide whether you wanna give him a copy of the drive for safe-keeping, just in case."

"Right. I'll consult my attorney," Bas said, winking at Drew.

"Your attorney is overworked," Drew replied. "The answer is no. We're not turning anything over to the FBI, even unofficially. But we'll give *you* a copy, just in case, Cort."

"Fair enough," Cort agreed. "So, uh. What should I tell Sean about the auction? It's in less than a week and he needs to prepare."

Bas opened his mouth to tell Cort exactly what Sean could do with his stupid fucking idea, when Drew slapped a hand over his mouth. "Tell him we're still considering," Drew said. "Give us New Year's Eve to think about it. We'll get back to him by tomorrow."

"Fine." Cort seemed to hesitate before he continued. "For what it's worth, Bas, I share your concerns. But I agree with Cam. The alternative is waiting for Alexei to come for us another time, another way, and that's unacceptable."

"We'll talk to you tomorrow," Bas said.

"I, ah, take it you won't be coming to our place to hang out tonight, then?" Cort teased. "How am I not surprised?"

"Uh huh. Happy New Year to you and Cam, too!" Drew said brightly, then he leaned over Bas again to disconnect the phone.

"Smooth," Bas remarked.

"Sebastian," Drew said, turning Bas's chair around to face him. "Did you hear what Cort said a minute ago?"

Bas wrapped his hands around Drew's lean hips and brought him forward until he was straddling the chair. "The part where he totally knows why we're not going to his house tonight, or the part where he's still trying to convince me to fall in line with this asinine plan?"

"Neither." Drew shifted until he was sitting sideways on Bas's lap - not the most comfortable position in this chair. But when Drew leaned down and brushed his lips against Bas's neck, Bas decided it was his new favorite. "I meant the part about knowing someone who'd testify against Alexei."

Bas rubbed his hand up Drew's back, distracted by the warm breath on his skin. "What about it?"

"Well, we do know someone who knows them," Drew whispered.

Bas pulled back. "Who?"

Drew licked his lips. "Well. Gary."

"Gary," Bas repeated dryly.

"Gary North."

"I know which Gary you meant, McMann. The Gary

who wants to get in your pants. The Gary who flirted with you relentlessly. The Gary who refused to give us any more information on Alexei because he wouldn't betray his sources. *That* Gary."

"Fine. Point made. Forget I mentioned it." Drew looped his arms around Sebastian's neck. "Do you know how many times we would be sitting in meetings and I would think about this? You'd get all cranky about... something or other. I mean, it never took much."

"You're calling me a drama queen?"

"Never!" Drew laughed. "But I'd stare at you and wish that I could push back your chair and sit on your lap. Tease you. Relax you. Kiss you. Like this."

He pressed his warm mouth to Sebastian's, and even though Bas *knew* he was being played, he couldn't bring himself to give a shit. He threaded his fingers into Drew's hair and took the kiss deeper.

"That was supposed to relax me?" he asked when he finally eased back some time later.

"Didn't it?" Drew asked innocently.

Bas took Drew's hand and pushed it against the front of his jeans. He was already half-hard and debating the wisdom of taking Drew against the floor or having Drew suck him off right in the chair.

"You know tonight is New Year's Eve," Drew commented. "If you had told me even three days ago that you and I would be spending it together, like this, I wouldn't have believed you."

"I know," Bas said. He traced a finger around the curve of Drew's neck which, three days ago, had just been a neck, and now was almost unbearably erotic.

"And you know what's even better than that?"

Bas shook his head. He literally couldn't think of anything better. He wouldn't have been able to imagine *this*.

"What's even better," Drew whispered. "Is thinking about the way we'll spend *next* New Year's Eve. And all the nights between now and then. Together. Safe."

Bas ran his tongue over his teeth and stared into the intelligent, *crafty* brown eyes of the man he loved.

"You want me to agree to go to this auction," he surmised. "Plying me with kisses is low, McMann."

"Please." Drew snorted. "That won't sway you. My argument will." He dropped another kiss on Bas's lips. "I just like to kiss you because *I can.*"

And fine, Bas could hardly argue with that. But as to the rest…

"Okay, let's talk about this, then." He shifted position, holding Drew more firmly. "I know I've been the one pushing this for months. All I could see was Alexei and SILA. Getting revenge." He ran his hand up Drew's back, feeling his muscles bunch and flex under the soft cotton of his own t-shirt. "And part of that was guilt, because things began to change on Halloween. I started to think of you in a different way and I… felt like maybe I didn't deserve that. After Amy."

"Bas," Drew sighed, his brow creased with worry. He started to tense and pull away, but that was the last thing Sebastian wanted. He squeezed Drew tighter.

"I shouldn't have asked her to marry me. I didn't love her."

"But…"

"Hush," Bas said. "I know it doesn't make sense, but it's true. And this shit with my dad… I think I hoped by catching Alexei, I could somehow make up for the bad choices my father made. Which also doesn't make sense," he added, before Drew could interrupt. "I know that too."

He wished he had Drew's gift for words, his way of crafting convincing arguments, but the best he could do was state the bald truth. "Now that you and I are together, Drew, none of that matters anymore. None of it. The best revenge is living well, isn't that what they say? And that's what I want. To love you, to take care of my brother and the weird-as-fuck family we've made for ourselves. That's how I'll honor the people who died."

Drew was silent, watching him, so he took Drew's hand in his, toying with his fingers. "So… maybe we walk away. Run off to some island, or some tiny town in the middle of nowhere. I don't know. Just… the right way is the one where we end up together, remember? And to do that, we need to survive this."

Drew shook his head. "You know, I've loved you for a long while. But every time I think I can't love you more, you prove me wrong."

Bas laughed. "So… we leave town?"

"Sebastian, you have no idea how tempting that is. But, baby, we're too well-known to hide. Especially you. This is a personal vendetta for Alexei, and he's never gonna stop searching for us. We'd be looking over our shoulders for the rest of our lives. And there's my mom. I'm the only one she has left." Drew paused for a second. "Plus, I know you're not jazzed about the idea of having kids, but maybe… maybe we'd like to, someday."

Wow. Yeah. Bas hadn't had any desire to have kids of his own in the past. But having kids *with Drew*? That was a whole different ballgame. "Damn, baby," he breathed.

"Listen, no one likes this plan, Bas. No one is eager to be bait! But if we trust Sean and his team, if we stick together, that's our best hope of catching Alexei. You *have* to agree, Sebastian. Please. Because we need to end this."

"Since when are you the risk taker?" Bas asked wryly.

"After thirty years, I feel like it's time for us to shake

things up. From now on, I'm the dramatic risk taker and you're the calm voice of reason."

"God help us," Bas said, and Drew laughed.

"Fine. We'll play this your way," Bas finally said. Reluctant didn't begin to describe his feeling about this, but he also knew Drew was right. "We're stronger together, right?"

Drew pressed a kiss to his lips, soft and gentle. "Right. And when this is over - *when* Bas, not *if* - we are absolutely taking that month off."

"I'm holding you to that," Bas said against Drew's mouth. "But for now, let's go home and ring in the New Year together."

And if Bas had his way, it would be the first of many.

CHAPTER SEVENTEEN

"*I* think that went well," Peter said, pushing Drew's office door halfway shut behind them. "You got everything that we wanted from Tekko and let them think they were getting a good deal."

"Mmmhmm," Drew agreed, setting his folders and a paper coffee cup down on his desk. He took off his suit jacket and hung it over the back of his chair, and fished his brand-new cell out of his pants' pockets. He was dimly aware that Peter kept talking, even as he plopped into his seat to check his texts.

There was a new one from Bas. *Working alone isn't satisfying. Text me when you're back from your meeting.*

And Drew couldn't help grinning as he replied, *Back,* and then sat and watched the bubbles dance as Bas replied.

God, this schmoopy, hearts-in-eyes thing was so unlike him. He remembered mocking Cam and Cort relentlessly when Cort had first come to work for Seaver and the pair had been unable to sit through an entire meeting without making eyes at each other over the conference table. He'd prided himself on the fact that *his* feelings for Bas were virtually undetectable to the casual observer, which was really how relationships *ought* to be conducted.

And now, here he was, waiting for a reply from his boyfriend — the same boyfriend whose bed he'd crawled out of only a few hours before, sex-drunk and famished, and who'd driven him to work — with all the eagerness of a lovesick wife whose sailor had gone off to sea years before.

It was getting out of hand…but he'd be damned if he'd do anything to stop it.

Sounded ridiculous to say he'd missed Sebastian while he was in an hour-long client meeting — they were hardly co-dependent, generally — but it was the sad and sappy truth. And he was more than half hoping Bas would grab his laptop and move himself into Drew's office to work this afternoon, just as he had every day that week. Drew was getting pretty addicted to seeing Bas's blue eyes and broad shoulders every time he looked up from his keyboard.

"Okay, what's with you?" Peter demanded.

Drew slapped his phone face down on the desk and cleared his throat. He'd actually forgotten Peter's presence entirely.

"I'm sorry, were you saying something?"

"I asked you if you wanted me to set any follow-up meetings. With Tekko," he added, when Drew didn't respond right away.

"No, I think things are settled. Check in with Paula and make sure she doesn't need any additional face-time."

Peter nodded, but his gaze remained fixed on Drew's face and a slow smile began to dawn at the edges of his mouth. "You're flirt-texting!" he accused.

"What?"

"You. Are. Flirting. With a man. Over text." He perched on the edge of the chair facing Drew's desk and put his chin in his hand. "Don't bother to deny it."

Drew raised an eyebrow at this serious over-familiarity... but he was pretty sure he was blushing, which probably killed any air of authority he might have achieved. "I'm not discussing this with you," he said instead. His relationship with Sebastian was personal, and he wanted to be discreet about it as long as possible.

"That's fine!" Peter said, throwing both hands up innocently. "I'm just going to assume that Mark is just as hot in person as he was online." He tossed Drew a wink.

Oh. Oh, no no no.

"I'm *not* texting with Mark," Drew said.

"But I thought..."

"Yeah, we had a date. Let's just say it was an absolute disaster. If he ever tries to contact me again through you, let me know immediately."

Peter nodded, his brow furrowed. "Yeah. Of course. But if not him, then..."

Bas stuck his head in the partially opened door and knocked on the doorframe. "Hey, counselor?"

Peter and Drew turned to look at him in one synchronized movement, watching as he pushed the door open fully and walked in. Sure enough, he was carrying his laptop under his arm.

"Oh, sorry, Peter," Bas said. "I just needed a moment of Drew's time." He glanced at the phone on Drew's desk and said archly, "You didn't answer my text."

Peter's eyes flew to Drew's face, then back to Bas, and grew wide as comprehension dawned.

Drew shook his head and huffed out a laugh. *So much for discretion.*

But Drew was surprised to find he didn't really care all that much. Alexei's threat hanging over their heads was enough to put every other problem into perspective, and besides, he and Bas weren't a temporary thing. Even just six days into this new phase of their relationship, he could say with confidence — a confidence he couldn't have imagined even a week ago — that this was forever.

Bas was right - he really *was* evolving into a risk taker all of a sudden.

"Sorry," Drew told Bas. "Peter and I were just finishing up."

"Yeah," Peter jumped to his feet. "We're all done." But he was staring at Bas like the man had grown an extra head… or suddenly acquired a gay boyfriend overnight.

The thought was so amusing, Drew had to cover his mouth with his hand to keep from laughing out loud, and Bas narrowed his eyes, like he was missing the joke.

"I'll just… take my lunch now," Peter said as he reached the door. "I'll be gone an hour or so. I could, like, lock the door?"

"Not necessary," Drew said, not taking his eyes from Bas as he came closer, laying his computer on the desk top.

"Right, okay. Well, I'll just close it then, and I'll see you… much later."

Bas shook his head, still staring at Drew as Peter shut the door. "What was that?"

"That," Drew said, standing and bracing his hands on the desktop as he leaned toward his boyfriend, "was my assistant figuring out that you and I are dating."

Bas leaned in and brushed his lips over Drew's once before sinking into the kiss with a sound of relief. Drew understood it completely - being together was a lot like puzzle pieces sliding together, satisfying and right. It had always been that way between them, but now they could show it openly.

"Dating?" Bas asked, pulling back so his teasing eyes could meet Drew's. "Is that what we're doing?"

"Oh, yeah. Taking it slow. Keeping it casual." Drew

gave him a final peck, pressing a smile to Sebastian's lips, and then sat back down.

"Oh, thank goodness," Bas said, taking Peter's seat and propping his laptop on Drew's desk. "I was a little worried when you took me to your mom's two nights ago. Kinda *forward* to introduce me to your mom this early on."

Drew pressed his lips together to hide his smile and nodded solemnly. His mother had been introduced to Sebastian when he was in diapers.

"Which part worried you, exactly? Was it the way she jumped up to hug you the minute we arrived? Or the way she made you promise we'd visit her weekly before she let us leave?"

Bas seemed to think about it, his eyes gleaming all the while. "You know, it might have been the way she stared at me the entire time, like I might evaporate if she looked away? Or the way she looked like she might faint from happiness every time you and I touched?" He pantomimed fainting back against the chair, his wrist at his temple.

Drew burst out laughing, because Bas wasn't lying. His mother had always loved Bas, but she was overjoyed to hear they were together. And Drew couldn't deny that he was relieved - his mother was a stickler for what she deemed "propriety," and he'd worried that she might not approve of him falling in love with his sister's former fiancé.

She'd brushed his worries aside with a wave of her hand.

"I was shocked when he and Amy got engaged," she told him speaking in hushed tones in the kitchen while he'd helped her prepare coffee. "Thrilled, of course. But shocked. I'd always thought he was for you." She'd patted his cheek. "And now he is."

And now he is.

For however long they had left.

Bas gave him a bright smile before focusing on his laptop. Drew turned his phone over, checking the display.

His missed text from Bas flashed up at him. *I missed you. I'm coming over there. We can finish up fast and take off early. It's Friday.*

He looked at Bas out of the corner of his eye and bit his lip. They really were moving quickly with their relationship, even for two people who'd known each other their whole lives. He didn't regret it in any way, but he knew part of that was because neither of them wanted to waste a second, given the uncertainty of the coming weekend and their plan to finally, finally end things with SILA for good.

Things seemed to have quieted down on that front. No new emails had come in from the mysterious Michael Paterkin. No new threats had emerged. It seemed like Alexei was biding his time, as well. Waiting for their high-noon showdown Saturday night.

And Bas seemed to have become reconciled to it, as well, though Drew knew he was still far from happy with the plan Sean had laid out. He and Bas hadn't discussed the auction at all since Sunday, which was one of the reasons Drew had avoided telling Bas about the phone call he'd made the day before.

He dropped his chin to his chest, stretching out the tension in his neck. If the situation was reversed, he'd be mightily pissed at Bas for not speaking up, even if Bas's intentions were as pure as Drew's own. He sighed.

"Bas, I need to tell you something," he began.

"Hmm?" Bas looked up from the computer and watched Drew closely. He closed the laptop screen. "What's up?"

"I called Gary North."

"For what?" Bas scowled, looking more confused than upset, which was promising.

"Well, you remember our conversation down in your

lair the other day? When Cort joked about us knowing someone who would testify against Alexei?" Drew shrugged. "I figured it was worth a shot to ask him."

Bas nodded slowly. "And?"

"*And*, it pretty much went exactly the way you thought it would. He refused to even mention the subject to his SILA contacts at first. I told him that our lives were on the line - in fact, I essentially told him everything we knew about Alexei and the plans he had to neutralize us, including the auction Saturday. I even told him I didn't expect him to volunteer information that was given to him in confidence, just that I'd really appreciate it if he could contact his sources and see if anyone was interested in talking." He shook his head. "Said he'd think about it."

Bas looked at him evenly, his fingers drumming on the sides of the chair. But then he lifted one shoulder. "I'm sorry, babe. I know that must have been disappointing."

Drew blinked. "That's it?"

"What did you want me to say?"

"Nothing. I don't know. I mean, last time we met with Gary, you had a fit. And even when I brought up his name Sunday, you didn't seem to want me to have anything to do with him."

Bas raised an eyebrow. "So you thought I'd be jealous, and you decided to call him anyway in a sneaky way?"

Ouch. Trapped by his own words. Way to go, counselor.

"It wasn't sneaky," he defended himself. "I just didn't want to spoil our time together because you were jealous. And I also didn't want to get your hopes up if it didn't turn out." He gave Sebastian a rueful grin. "And it didn't."

"Drew, I told you that I was making a choice by being with you. I trust you're doing the same thing. I don't *like* the way the guy flirts with you, because I swear to God part of the reason he does it is just to provoke a reaction."

Drew nodded. He suspected the same thing.

"But Gary can't touch what we have. And even if I massively disagree with you on something, we can't hide things from each other."

"I promise," Drew said. He stood and walked around the desk to sit on Bas's lap. "Not again."

Bas wrapped his arms around Drew's waist and pulled him to rest against his chest. "Good. And in the interest of being open and honest about all things…"

Drew snickered. "Yeah?"

"I can't stop thinking about New Year's Eve."

Despite burying his face in Bas's neck, Drew could feel himself blushing. *Blushing!* Thank God he wouldn't encounter Peter or anyone else for a while. "Is that right?" he croaked. "Which part?"

"Mmmm. All of it. But especially right at midnight. I hadn't really understood how hot that position could be, but taking you from behind like that…"

Drew ran his hand up Sebastian's chest and around his neck, his memory thrown back to that epic night. With the emotional one-two punch of learning Alexei's scheme *and* finding the flash drive, all coming right on the heels of them admitting their feelings for one another, the sex they'd shared was like nothing he'd ever dreamed of. Bas had reached for him over and over again, ringing out the old year, and ushering in the new in the most life-affirming and love-affirming way possible. But the time Bas was referring to, when Drew had knelt on the bed with his hands braced on the headboard, and Sebastian had taken him from behind, destroying him slowly and methodically until he'd been a babbling mess… Drew was pretty sure he'd never, ever forget that.

"I want to do that," Bas said. He gripped Drew's hair and repositioned his head so that he could run his teeth along the side of Drew's throat.

Drew shivered uncontrollably.

"We could lock the door," he offered.

And yeah, discretion was totally flying out the window if he was considering letting Bas fuck him in the office, but he was already half-hard and he wanted Bas *now*.

"I have a better idea. Let's just *leave*." He pulled Drew's hair again, a sensation that Drew had already begun to associate with incredible arousal, and his blue eyes bored into Drew's. "The first time I feel your cock in my ass, I want us to be at home, in our bed."

Drew blinked. "My... your... Your ass?" he repeated.

It was a good thing he'd already had the Tekko meeting today, because his mind was obliterated to the point where he might have given away the whole company if he'd had to speak coherently after this.

"You heard me," Bas said with a nod. He leaned in and whispered, "Your cock. My ass. Now."

Drew swallowed hard and forced himself to stand, adjusting the front of his pants. "I'll get my coat."

Later, he wouldn't remember the drive home - he had no idea how Bas had been able to keep his Charger on the road, if his pulse had been pounding half as loud as Drew's. He vaguely recalled spending the entire time gazing at Sebastian's profile as he drove, occasionally reaching out to run his thumb along the firm line of his jaw, and imagining the fulfillment of a fantasy.

He remembered *very* clearly the way the two of them had stumbled through the front door of Bas's place - likely Bas's choice because his house was simply closer to Seaver Tech than Drew's - and raced to the bedroom without a word. There had been no careful undressing, no teasing kisses, no tender caresses as each piece of clothing was removed. It was as if they'd both realized that arousal was a powder keg ready to explode between them, and they avoided even *looking* at each other for too long, lest they spontaneously combust.

When Drew was finally naked, he couldn't help but reach down and touch himself, stroking firmly as he watched Bas throw his remaining clothing haphazardly on the floor.

Christ, but he was beautiful, in every single way, from his broad shoulders to his hard, jutting cock. But maybe most of all because he was looking at Drew with nothing but love and trust and searing arousal in his eyes.

"I love you," Drew said, the words torn from him. "So much."

"I love you, too, McMann." Bas's face, which had been tense with arousal, softened as he looked at Drew. He moved across the short distance until they were pressed together, chest to chest, cock to cock. Drew couldn't help but moan at the sensation. "But please, Drew. Don't go slow. I'm burning up."

Drew nodded. He understood the feeling. Still, he took a moment, running his hands up Sebastian's taut stomach to his chest, and then back down again. He licked his palm and grabbed both their erections in his hand, stroking them together and admiring the way Bas's eyes rolled back in his head at the sensation. "I'm going to make this good for you," he promised.

"It couldn't be any other way," Bas whispered. Drew stroked again, and Bas gasped, the cords of his neck standing out as he threw his head back. "I've been hard since we were in your office. Every pothole in the fucking road was making me rub against my pants. And I swear, Drew, if you don't get inside me soon, I'm going to come just from this." He lowered his head and caught Drew's gaze. "And I don't want to come this way. Not today."

"Then get on your knees in the bed," Drew told him, releasing his hold.

He moved to the nightstand to retrieve the bottle of lube that had been well-used over the past week and rummaged around for a condom.

There was only one left, and he threw it on the bed next to the lube.

He kneeled on the bed behind Bas's gorgeous ass, and bent to lick a path up his spine.

"Sebastian?" he said. "What do you think about getting tested? So we don't have to use condoms anymore, I mean."

Bas turned his head. "I've been tested. And I haven't had sex with anyone at all in a year and a half."

"You... what?" Drew had known he hadn't dated anyone serious since the crash, but he'd never suspected this. "Really?"

"Yeah, really." He smirked. "So, I'm ready to go when you are."

"I... I've been tested. And I've never had unprotected sex before." Drew swallowed. "Is that something you want, though?"

Bas sat back on his heels and twisted, cupping Drew's face in both his hands. "If you haven't figured it out, Andrew, there's *nothing* I don't want with you. I want everything." He leaned in to bite Drew's bottom lip firmly, and Drew's cock jumped.

Bas chuckled. He grabbed the condom from the bed and tossed it like a Frisbee so it landed on the dresser. "Come on," he said, turning around and bracing himself once again.

Drew didn't require any further convincing or discussion. He quickly dribbled lube over his fingers and Bas's hole, teasing him and stretching him. They'd played that way several times in the past week, but they'd never moved beyond… until now.

"Oh, fuck," Bas groaned, as Drew eased a finger inside him. "More. Please, more!"

But Drew would never hurt him, even if he demanded it. With measured thrusts that took every bit of his control, Drew worked him, with one finger and then two and three, until Bas was moaning, panting, *begging* for Drew's cock.

It was surreal, and Drew wondered if it would ever be something he took for granted, having Sebastian want him in this way. After fifteen long years of wanting him with hopeless passion, he really doubted it.

He eased his fingers out and slicked more lube on his aching cock as a wildfire burst of lust and anticipation snaked its way down his spine. *Forever*. That was how long he'd wanted this. And now it was finally his.

He nudged the head of his cock against Sebastian's ass and pushed slowly forward.

Bas's hiss of pain broke through the clouds of arousal that blanketed his mind. "Are you okay?"

But Bas's voice, when it came, was groggy not with pain but with desire. "Very okay," he said. "Oh my God, Drew."

Drew knew the feeling. There should have been nothing new for him in this experience - he was no virgin, and the feeling of sinking into tight heat should have been familiar. But it wasn't. This was *Sebastian*, Sebastian *bare* without a condom, and so everything was brand new.

He set a fast rhythm, because he simply couldn't help it, couldn't give a thought to drawing out the experience when Bas was pushing against him, thrusting back eagerly even as Drew thrust forward. The knowledge that there was nothing between them, that soon his cum would fill Bas's hole… it was overwhelming and perfect.

He pushed Bas's shoulders down so his chest was against the mattress, his ass in the air, and leaned over him, seeking Bas's mouth for a kiss. Bas turned his head, his eyes wide open and totally lost, and Drew pressed their lips together, hard and messy, thrusting his tongue in time to his hips.

Bas's orgasm seemed to take him by surprise, and he cried out into Drew's mouth as he came, untouched, all over the sheet beneath them.

Oh, fuck.

If there was a better sensation in all the world than Bas's tight hole clenching as Drew fucked him through orgasm, Drew couldn't imagine it… and was confident his brain couldn't survive it. As it was, he had to squeeze his eyes tightly shut and dig his fingers into Sebastian's shoulders as the overload of sensation made his rhythm falter.

He pounded Bas harder, faster, with Bas spurring him on the whole way, widening his bent knees, lifting his ass higher, his breath pushing out in staccato moans with every thrust of Drew's hips. They were the same creature - two people merged temporarily into one being greater than either of them could be together, feeding off each other's pleasure.

Drew shouted his release - a hoarse cry so loud the neighbors could have heard it, and he kinda hoped they did - as he came inside of Bas. He looked down, as he gave a few final thrusts, and saw his cum leak out of Sebastian's hole. Claiming Bas, owning him. Because Bas had let him.

Holy, holy shit.

He grabbed Sebastian's hand from the bed and brought it back, pushing it against the place where they were joined. He not only heard Bas gasp, he felt it from the inside. Bas turned his head until his eyes met Drew's.

"I *love* you," he said fiercely, his voice still wrecked and

breathless, his eyes practically glowing with love and satisfaction.

Drew closed his eyes and committed that vision to
memory. When the end of days came, no matter how soon
or distant from now that time might be, and the most important moments of his life began to flash before his eyes, he
knew with absolute certainty that *this* moment would make
the highlight reel.

CHAPTER EIGHTEEN

Bells. Bells were ringing. It was like church, but not quite. Like… like…

Like a door.

Bas recognized the warm weight partially draped over his chest and burrowed into his neck. He reached out a finger to poke at it. "Door?"

"Okay," Drew mumbled into his neck, cuddling closer, and Bas allowed himself to drift back to sleep.

And then Drew's cell phone began ringing.

"Seriously?" Bas demanded of no one in particular. "I thought everyone agreed we were all going to sleep in. Enjoy the day." Or, more accurately, to gear up for the danger that awaited them at the auction that evening. "If that's my brother…" He shrugged, unable to think of an appropriately dire consequence.

Drew draped himself further across Bas's chest - a change in position Bas would have heartily approved of under other circumstances - and reached for his phone on the nightstand. "It's not your brother," Drew told him. He rubbed the sleep from his eyes, checked the display again, and looked up, blinking. "It's Gary North."

"Jesus. The man is seriously not endearing himself to me," Bas complained, burrowing his head back into the pillow. The man had the shittiest timing.

"He just texted to say he's outside, and to get my ass down there." Drew blinked at Bas again. "How'd he even know I was here?"

Bas shook his head. "I haven't the foggiest idea."

The bell rang again, repeatedly. "Fine!" Drew touched his forehead to Bas's chin for one long moment, then threw the blankets back and rolled out of bed.

"Hey!" Bas said as the cold air hit him.

"Hurry up!" Drew told him, already grabbing sweat-pants from Bas's drawer and pulling them on sans underwear.

For half a second, Bas seriously considered letting Drew go meet Gary alone.

And then he realized Drew would be *meeting Gary. Alone.*

"I might hit him," Bas said. He rolled out of bed and grabbed the slacks he'd stripped off the previous afternoon, which were still handily strewn on the floor next to his side of the bed. He caught the sweatshirt Drew threw at him, took a second to pull it on, and followed Drew to the door.

"Alright, alright." Bas heard Drew muttering as he unlocked the door. He reached the hallway in time to see Drew throw the door wide. "What's the emerg... Oh! Oh, Christ."

Gary stood on the doorstep, bundled in a thick wool overcoat and black winter hat. His cheeks were pink with cold, the morning air fogged around his face...

And he wasn't alone.

Beside him stood an older man - barrel-chested, broad-shouldered, and a couple of inches shorter than

Gary. He had improbably snow-white hair above a care-worn face and he sported the impeccable tan of someone who'd spent the autumn months sitting in the sun. He probably had.

"Pardon me for interrupting," Ilya Stornovich said, his dark eyes grave. "But when Garik called to tell me your troubles, I knew I needed to speak with you most urgently."

Drew threw Bas a look that clearly said, "I don't want to let the Russian gangster into your home," and Bas shrugged in a way that he hoped conveyed, "Neither do I, but what else are we gonna do?"

In the end, Drew stood back and ushered both men into the living room.

"I apologize for the short notice," Gary said. He unbuttoned his jacket before taking a seat on the sofa. "I wanted to call you last night, but Ilya persuaded me that it would be better for all concerned if we had the element of surprise on our side."

"Well, you certainly achieved that," Bas said. He extended his hand toward the other end of the sofa, encouraging Ilya to take a seat. Then he seated himself in the side chair Drew had occupied during their meeting with Cam, Cort, and the others.

He pulled Drew to sit on his lap.

Drew immediately popped back up again. "Coffee?" he offered. "I'm going to brew a pot."

"Please, do not trouble yourself," Ilya said, holding out a hand. "I am afraid I cannot stay long."

"Uh. Okay," Drew agreed. He allowed Bas to pull him back down onto his lap, even though he sat stiffly at first.

Despite the mind-blowing seriousness of having Ilya Stornovich in his living room, something primal in Bas awakened when Gary acknowledged their seating position with a raised eyebrow and a smirk. *That's right, fucker*, Bas thought, pulling Drew more firmly against him. *Mine mine mine.*

"So. What brings you by?" Drew asked, as though this were a social call. Mary Alice McMann would be so proud of the ingrained manners that had him treating Russian criminals with the same polite deference as Boston's social elite.

"I called Ilya earlier this week and told him what you'd told me - that Alexei has plans to kill all of you tonight, that it's become a personal mission for him. Ilya is prepared," Gary said, leaning forward and knitting his fingers together with the polished charm of a high-powered defense attorney. "To make your problem go away."

"Make it go away?" Drew looked at Gary, dumb-founded. "How?"

"Mister Seaver," Ilya told Bas. "First, let me tell you condolences on loss of your father, yes? Levi was a good man. A very good man. We work together for many years. He did not always like me, I will not lie. And I did not always like him. But we were same in many ways. Both men with... with... *chest.*" He looked to Gary impatiently. "Garik, what is this word in English?"

"Er... *honor*?" Gary said quietly.

"*Da!*" Ilya agreed, giving Gary a fond smile before turning the weight of his stare onto Sebastian. "Honor. Both men who did what must be done to make our families strong. You understand this?"

Did he understand that? Honor was not the first word that came to mind when thinking of his father. But by Ilya's definition, he supposed the word applied to both men.

"Yes," he whispered.

"Yes," Ilya repeated with a more confident nod. "*Yes.* But my son, he is different." Ilya's voice was low. Sad. "He is…" He waved a hand before him, as if searching for the correct word. "*Ruthless*. He thinks this shows power, yes?"

Bas inclined his head. It certainly seemed that way.

"When I came to this country, I wanted to give power to the powerless. A voice to the voiceless. That was idea for SILA."

"You committed a lot of crimes along the way," Bas commented, not willing to fully exonerate Ilya, no matter how tempting it was.

"Crimes," Ilya scoffed, smiling broadly. "Means many things to many people, *да*? Government takes money from poor people, uses it to make rich men richer. Is not a crime. I take money from rich men and use it to help people." He shrugged.

"Yes, you're a regular Robin Hood," Drew said wryly.

Ilya's laugh was loud, booming, and unexpected. "If Robin Hood had lovely home in Florida and a sports car!" he chuckled. "I am not a saint, Mister McMann. I have never claimed to be. But I am not a killer of innocents." A shadow moved over his face. "Never on purpose."

Drew shot Bas a look he couldn't quite interpret, then turned his attention to Gary.

"This is all very interesting. And I admit, enlightening, as well. But… how can this help us?"

Gary looked at Ilya and raised a single eyebrow.

Ilya smiled and patted Gary on the knee. "Yes, yes, Garik. I'm coming to the point." He rummaged in the chest pocket of his coat and removed a flash drive. He turned it over in his hand thoughtfully. "This is information I retrieved last night from the server in my son's home. On here, you will find the information you need to connect my Alexei to several of his alternate identities. This is a service he runs, providing immigrants and others with the names and identities of deceased individuals." He shook his head like he was disappointed. "Alexei does not use this service to help the desperate, you understand. Only those who can pay. Men who have killed and raped, women who have sold children like livestock. That information is on here, as well." He sucked in a deep breath and let it out, then set the flash drive on the coffee table with a decisive *click*.

This time, it wasn't difficult to read the incredulity in Drew's expression. Bas knew it *had* to be mirrored on his own face.

"Is one of the names Michael Paterkin?" Drew whispered.

Ilya nodded. "Yes. That is one of his favorite… *aliens*?" He turned to Gary as if checking the word.

"Aliases," Gary corrected, and Ilya nodded.

"Yes, exactly."

Drew moved to retrieve the flash drive, as though he worried Ilya might change his mind. Bas didn't blame him, but he was too stunned to move, himself.

"Why?" he whispered.

Ilya watched him for a moment, his mouth turned down in a frown.

"Garik tells me that you wish to make repayment for the sins of your father," he said at length. "That you feel responsible in some way. But this is not so. Sons should not be held responsible for their fathers' crimes. Fathers, on the other hand…" He spread his empty palms before him. "I believed I was doing the right thing in leaving my organization to Alexei. I moved to Florida, refused contact with my lieutenants, so that my power would never overshadow his." He looked up once again. "I had not realized how that power would corrupt him. How it would make my son lose sight of important truths."

"You understand that we are going to use this information to have Alexei arrested?" Drew asked. "That, between this and the information we have already collected, we have enough for a conviction?"

"I understand." Ilya's voice was heavy with sorrow. "I also know if he continues along this path, someone will kill him. They will have no choice." His eyes were pleading. "I don't want my son to die. And so, I find myself making a seemingly impossible choice: working with his enemies to send him to prison, instead."

Gary reached out and laid a comforting hand on Ilya's shoulder, and Ilya lifted a hand to pat it. "You are a good boy, *malysh*. Thank the stars that we were fated to be friends."

He looked at Bas and Drew again. "Prison will be the making of Alexei. He will understand what it means to be truly powerless, a lesson I could never teach him. I plan to hire him an excellent attorney - someone who will get him a short sentence and an early parole." His words were part challenge, part warning, and ironically, they made Bas feel even more confident in Ilya's sincerity. He wasn't switching sides, or working against his son; on the contrary, he was doing what all good fathers do, and giving his son the medicine he *needed*, even when it wasn't what he *wanted*.

He could grudgingly admit Gary was right when he suggested that Ilya was a decent person, despite the bad things he'd done... and the monster of a son he'd placed in power.

"And what will happen with SILA?" Drew asked, ever practical. "Will you hand the reins to one of your lieutenants?"

"*Nyet*. I will take them myself, hold them for my son. With help from my nephew Dmitri, of course."

Gary's nostrils flared and he cast his eyes to the heavens.

Interesting. Anyone who made Gary look like *that* was

someone Sebastian wanted to get to know better, even if he was part of a Russian crime organization.

One corner of Ilya's mouth turned up. "Retirement was boring anyway." He slapped his hands on his knees and stood. "Well. I thank you both for meeting with me. I know you will take care of the information I gave you. Good luck tonight."

Wait, *tonight*? There was no need to attend the auction tonight if they had the information they needed. He and Drew exchanged another wordless glance.

"Ilya… Mister Stornovich," Drew began gently. "We won't be attending the auction tonight. Just being there would be a tremendous risk, and if the information you gave us is enough to incriminate your son, we have no reason to go."

Ilya raised his eyebrows and frowned once again. "Ah, but you must. My son is a man of many resources. Simply being able to make a case against him isn't enough to keep you - any of you - safe. As long as he is free, he's a danger to you."

"But you could tell us where he is," Bas protested. "You could let us tell the police…"

"No," Ilya said calmly, as though he'd anticipated this turn of events. "This I will not do. You'll find that the information I have provided to you contains nothing that will incriminate my organization. It is all information on Alexei's dealings alone. I will not invite the authorities to poke their noses into other information, you understand? SILA has no quarrel with any of you."

There was a sly glint in Ilya's eye, a hard cast to his jaw, proving that this man, though he looked more like someone's doting grandfather than a criminal mastermind, was not someone they could afford to take lightly.

Bas clenched his teeth. So *this* was the compromise?

They had gotten the information they needed to prosecute Alexei, but at the expense of being able to dismantle SILA? Fine, then. So be it. Revenge was the furthest thing from Sebastian's mind - all he cared about now was keeping his family safe.

But their safety was no more guaranteed now than it had been yesterday, and *that* pissed him off. In order to arrest Alexei, they needed to be able to find him. They could use Ilya's information to obtain a warrant and search for Alexei at his known locations, but he was unlikely to be sitting there waiting. And, if Alexei learned about Ilya's flash drive, he was likely to become even more enraged and unpredictable... even more dangerous.

They needed to make sure he was arrested as soon as possible, and that meant continuing with their plan to attend the auction.

"Yeah," Bas said. "We understand."

But if he was annoyed by the turn of events, Drew looked resigned... and reluctantly impressed. Probably the admiration of one born negotiator for another. "Thank you for the information," he offered, and Ilya nodded.

Bas stood, following Gary and Ilya to the door.

"Come on, Ilya. I'll give you a ride," Gary said, buttoning his coat.

"Thank you, Garik." Ilya placed a hand on Gary's shoulder. "But I believe I will walk for a bit. Boston winter is like mild spring day in Siberia. It will not do for me to grow soft in my old age." He winked, then turned to extend his hand to Drew and Sebastian in turn. "Mr. McMann. And Mr. Seaver. A pleasure."

Bas couldn't return the sentiment, but he nodded and shook Ilya's hand anyway.

"I'm sure we will see each other again," Ilya said as he departed.

A chill went up Bas's spine at the casual words, a chill that had little to do with the cold waft of air through the open door. He could not imagine anything good ever coming from a second meeting.

"Thank you," Drew told Gary as the three of them watched Ilya walk down the steps.

"Don't thank me, thank him," Gary said, nodding in Ilya's direction. "He's risking everything, including his own life, to do this." He sighed, jamming his hands in his pockets. "Just like I suspected he would."

"Do you think his own son would harm him?" Drew asked, surprised.

Gary sighed. "Possibly, if he thought his father had betrayed him. Ilya and Alexei have a complicated relationship. Alexei covets his father's approval, but he's never really understood the kind of man his father is."

Not like Gary clearly did.

"You care about him a lot. More than I expected."

Gary turned to give Bas an appraising look.

"Not all of us were fortunate enough to have good fathers of our own. We can quibble about your father's ethics all you like, but from everything I've heard, he loved you and showed it."

Bas frowned but nodded, and he felt Drew's hand snake around his back in a gesture of support. Gary was right. Whatever kind of businessman his father had been, Levi had been a loving father. He and Ilya *did* have something in common.

He extended his hand to Gary. "Drew's right. Thank you. For setting this up. For letting him risk himself. I owe you."

Gary's eyes sharpened and his smile turned shark-like. "Exclusive-interview-level gratitude?"

Sebastian barked out a laugh. "We'll see." Assuming they lived to tell the tale.

Gary and Drew exchanged goodbyes, and the moment the door was closed behind him, Bas leaned back against it, exhausted.

Drew took out his phone. "Twenty minutes," he said, stepping forward to burrow his face in Bas's chest.

"For what?"

"That's how long we've been awake! *Twenty minutes*, and the world's turned upside down." Drew looked vaguely shell-shocked, and Bas snickered. His little control-fiend was having a rough couple of weeks.

"But at least now we get the fun of waking up Cort and Cam to share the news."

Drew pulled back to give him a fulminating look. "You take way too much pleasure in winding them up."

"Nonsense," Bas argued. There was no such thing as too much. And if Bas had learned anything from this nightmare with Alexei, it was to take his pleasure where he could find it. Speaking of which…

"We could probably wait and call them in half an hour," he offered, coasting a hand down Drew's back to glide over his ass. He had no underwear beneath his borrowed sweat-pants, which were conveniently loose.

Drew's teasing smile was wide and gorgeous, familiar and brand new. "I think that would be the considerate thing to do," he agreed, and he lifted his lips to kiss Sebastian.

CHAPTER NINETEEN

"*Y*ou all understand how this will work, correct?"

With a squeak of leather, Sean Cook turned in his seat to regard the six tuxedoed men - *six*, despite Damon's incredibly loud and curse-filled threats of retribution against his lover when he insisted on accompanying them - in the back of the limo.

"You've been over it enough times," Damon said, his gravelly voice made even rougher by suppressed anger and worry.

Cain took Damon's hand and leaned into his side, undeterred by his grumbling, and Damon laid a fervent kiss on his temple. "The entire event is being held in one room. We walk into the room together," Cain recited. "We take one walk around the perimeter to observe the items for auction, also together."

"If one of us stops, to bid or to chat, all of us stop," Cam said flatly, slouching in his seat. Cort reached over and took his hand, pressing a smiling kiss to his knuckles.

"Right." Cain nodded.

"After the first circuit around the room, we find our table, which will be in the back corner, furthest from the door and without a direct sightline from any windows," Bas said. Though he held tightly to Drew's hand, his jaw was hard and his gaze was turned resolutely out the window, maybe watching the lights shimmer on the Charles River as they approached their destination. His displeasure at the whole scene was visible in every line of his body.

"We eat the special meals that will be delivered by Agents Derrick and Marquez," Cort said, taking his turn. "Who have already warned me against asking for extra ketchup with my steak tartare." He sighed comically.

"I appreciate you reminding Carl and Nat why they really shouldn't miss you all that much," Sean said soberly. "What else?"

"We don't leave the room for any reason. Not to use the bathroom. Not to take a phone call," Drew said. "If we have an emergency situation, we find one of the agents we know and inform them."

"Good," Sean said. "Excellent. Everyone's phones are on and charged?"

A chorus of yeses, along with Damon's, "I already fucking told you it was!" filled the air.

"We've got a dozen agents working behind the scenes in that room - some as waiters, others as guests. They will be monitoring *you* at all times, keeping in proximity and ready to jump in if something happens. We have a safe room set up in one of the unused maintenance shops just down the hall from the main area. We have taken every precaution to make you as safe as possible."

"Except one," Bas said, finally turning his head only to glare at Sean. "Because what you're not saying is that Alexei has likely anticipated all of this. He knows we'll have agents in there with us, thanks to Cort's connections if nothing else. He knows you guys have run checks on all the guests, and will be doing tight security screenings at the door. And he still chose to do this here and now. Which means he must have thought of something we haven't."

Sean scratched his cheek. "Sebastian…"

Bas shook his head. "I don't wanna hear it. I appreciate the effort you're putting in on this, Sean, but you know it's true. *I* know it's true. No matter how much smoke you try to blow at us."

To Drew's surprise, Sean grimaced and nodded slowly. "You're right, Bas. You're absolutely right. And yet, this is the best plan because it's the only plan." He shrugged. "You can still back out."

Bas squeezed Drew's hand more tightly and turned his gaze back out the window.

Sean took this as the silent capitulation it was. "Alright, then. We're pulling into the covered parking area as we speak. This is the spot where our position is weakest, and the time when everyone needs to be on high alert. Listen to the agents and stay vigilant."

He turned around and was out of the passenger door practically before they'd come to a complete stop. A second later, he was opening the rear door and ushering them out into the cold, damp night.

Bas emerged first. An agent dressed in a tux came forward to usher him inside, but he hung back, holding out his hand for Drew.

Drew shook his head, even as his heart soared. Trust Bas to defy orders in the most romantic way possible.

He gave Sebastian his hand, gripping it tightly, and walked quickly into the lobby of the hotel - a large atrium twenty-seven stories tall, ringed on all sides by walkways that overlooked the space below.

Even to Drew's untrained eye, this situation appeared

incredibly unsafe. He held his breath as Cain and Damon were ushered inside, followed by Cam and Cort, and the agents tasked with shepherding them to the function room formed a loose ring around them, two women dressed in simple but elegant gowns, and four men in black tie. The twelve of them moved together, spread out just far enough that they didn't attract much notice from the other guests, but close enough that no one else could approach them.

When they made it to the relative safety of the ballroom on the far side of the lobby - a place with a ceiling, granting them safety from *above*, if nothing else - Drew breathed a sigh of relief.

And then, as his heart rate began to settle, he noticed dozens of eyes turning in his direction, watching him enter the room.

No, he realized, recognizing the direction of their collective stares. *Not* watching *me*. Watching *us*. They were focused on Bas's hand clasped around his.

Drew swallowed and glanced at Sebastian. He seemed wholly unaware of the gazes focused on them, and he probably was. His mouth was turned up in a polite smile, his posture relaxed. Only someone who had studied his face since childhood would have recognized the slight tension in his jaw, the squeeze of his hand, that indicated Sebastian was not nearly as laid-back as he appeared. Nor was he likely to relax at all until Alexei was in prison. Not unless Drew stepped in.

Drew stroked the inside of Bas's wrist with his thumb, and Bas turned to look at him.

"You know, it's not exactly a high school cafeteria," Drew began. "But it's pretty close."

It was a sign of just how distracted Bas was that it took him a few seconds to catch on. But when he did, he smiled -

small, but intimate and *real* - and turned to face Drew, bracing a hand on his waist.

"Drew McMann," he said, batting his eyelashes. "Will you go steady with me?"

Drew snorted - the least-elegant noise he'd ever made in his life - and he could only be glad that he'd convinced his mother to miss tonight's gala for safety reasons, or else he'd never live it down. He shook his head. "Sebastian Seaver, you are murder on my reputation."

Bas pulled him a fraction of an inch closer - not nearly as close as either of them would have liked - and bit his lip. "Nonsense," he said. "I'm trying to make an honest man of you."

Drew ran his tongue over his teeth. "Ask me again when this is over and I *might* let you."

Whatever reply Bas was about to make was cut off as one of Cort's friends, Agent Carl Derrick, approached them in his waiter garb wearing a faint scowl.

"Sirs, if you need a drink, you can find one *on the perimeter of the room*," he told them, his eyes all but flashing the words *Stick to the plan.*

Oops.

Bas cleared his throat. "Right, yes. Excellent."

From behind them, they heard Cam snicker. "Bas is the first one to forget the plan. Raise your hand if you're surprised. Anyone? Anyone? No? Me neither."

Bas shot a narrow-eyed glare over his shoulder. "Is it past your bedtime, Camden?"

"Let's move it along," Damon groused, moving forward with his arm around Cain's waist. "Sooner we get to the table, the sooner we can fucking leave."

Drew and Cort exchanged a glance. Not *quite* how it would work, and Damon knew it, but neither of them wanted to remind him of that fact. They'd be in this ballroom until Alexei made his move, or the party came to a peaceful end... and he wasn't sure which outcome he was hoping for.

They strolled around the outside of the room, looking at the items that had been donated for auction. Golf lessons with a PGA champion, a brand-new Jaguar, a one-week rental of a house with ocean views in Ogunquit, Maine. Drew stopped to look at that one, transfixed by the pictures of the pounding surf on the jetties, and before he knew it, Bas was making an offer that was double the retail price.

"What was that?" Drew demanded. "Thirty thousand dollars for..."

"That was me, planning for our future," Bas said firmly. Drew shut his mouth without another word and clasped Sebastian's hand more tightly.

They had nearly completed the circuit of the room when Lydia Tyndall approached them.

"Well! If it isn't the handsomest group of men in the whole room. Sebastian, Drew, Camden... and Camden's young man! Oh, and Cain, you look so distinguished." She stepped forward to exchange kisses with everyone except Damon, who she regarded with unconcealed curiosity. "And who might you be?"

Damon looked at Cain, who grinned proudly. "He's my partner, Damon Fitzpatrick," Cain said.

"Oh, the young man mentioned in the *Herald* article." Lydia gave him an appraising look, then nodded. "I approve," she said.

If Damon was surprised to be called a young man, or to have earned the approval of a woman he'd never met, he didn't show it. He simply returned her nod and smiled with unusual restraint.

Drew coughed into his fist to cover his laugh. Love made people do the strangest things.

A waiter, likely another FBI agent in disguise, approached with an offer to help them find their tables, reminding them pointedly that dinner was about to be served. They said goodbye to Lydia and shuffled off to their table at the back. Drew had to admit that he felt somewhat relieved as they took their seats. They might be no safer when seated, but he felt less like an open target.

Drew's phone vibrated in his pocket just as the first course was served. He panicked for half a second, before realizing that if he was the only one receiving a call, it was unlikely to be related to Alexei. As he took it out to glance at the screen, Bas leaned over to read with him.

"Gary," Drew told him. "No message."

Bas rolled his eyes. "Was it unclear earlier today that you and I are together and he has no shot?"

"Hmm. Yeah, the lap-sitting was kind of ambiguous. Maybe next time you need to pee in a circle around me or something."

Bas rolled his eyes, but his lips quirked. "Whatever. Call him back."

"Now? At the table? That would be rude. And I can't leave. I'll text him."

"Fuck rude. Call him. Maybe he has more information to give us. Maybe Ilya's changed his mind and we can all go home."

"Yeah, right." Anyone who'd seen the man's eyes earlier today knew *that* wasn't going to happen, but Drew called Gary back anyway.

"Hey. We're at the auction," he whispered the second the call was engaged, not waiting for Gary to say hello.

Which was fine, because Gary seemed to have no time for politeness. "Have you seen Ilya?"

"Seen him?" Drew glanced around the room involuntarily. "Of course not. Why would I?"

"Because he's missing," Gary said frantically. "He was supposed to call me this evening when Alexei left. He'd been working on his lieutenants all day, making sure that none of the guys who were loyal to him accompanied Alexei tonight. Now he's not answering his phone."

"Don't panic. That could mean a lot of things," Drew said in his most soothing voice, but inside his mind alarm bells were ringing.

"Find someone," he mouthed to Cort. "Get Sean."

Cort blinked, then looked around the room for one of the FBI agents. Spying someone he recognized, he stood up and hurried off.

"I should go with him," Cam said, but Damon held him down with a hand on his forearm. "Not a chance, Cam."

"That's not the worst part, Drew," Gary said in his ear. "Ilya's nephew Dima — I mean, Dmitri — the one he mentioned today?"

"Yeah?"

"He just called me from the fucking *hospital*. Alexei beat the shit out of him, broke his arm in three places, dislocated his shoulder and his jaw. He can barely *talk*, but he called me," Gary repeated, his voice shaking. "Because he wanted me to find his uncle. And because... because he's pretty sure Alexei has a bomb."

Drew's entire body flushed cold in the space of an instant. He looked up and saw the room, the loud and claustrophobic buzz of conversation and pressed bodies, in a whole different light. They were *all* sitting ducks here. They always had been. If Alexei had a bomb, it could be anywhere in this room.

Anywhere.

How long would it take to evacuate the guests? Lydia Tyndall, with her brash humor and kind eyes, all the other men and women picking at their salads and talking about their New Year's resolutions, never dreaming —.

"Drew? McMann, are you there?" Gary demanded.

Drew didn't answer. Couldn't. The buzzing in his ears was growing louder, the amorphous anxiety that had been weighing on him all night had just been given a very real and credible focus, and panic threatened to swamp him. Controlled, rational Drew was gone.

The men around the table - his friends, his *family* - stared at him. Concern was etched on their faces, but he had no idea what to tell them. He'd agreed to this plan tonight. Hell, he'd *encouraged* it - disregarding Damon and Cort's objections, talking Sebastian *out* of his objections. And now...

Now...

He'd pay the price for always thinking he knew best.

He looked at Bas and swallowed, his eyes filling with tears he couldn't hide.

"What *is* it?" Bas demanded. He wrapped one large palm around the back of Drew's neck. "*Tell me.*" But Drew could only shake his head.

Cort returned to the table with Sean Cook in tow, and Drew passed over the phone without a word.

Sean took one look at Drew's face and grabbed the device from his nerveless fingers. "Sean Cook." He listened for a moment, his face an impassive mask. "How sure are you?" Whatever Gary said made Sean's jaw clench. "Do you have any specifics?"

Cort watched his former boss with a growing sense of horror. Though Sean's reaction was outwardly calm, apparently Cort could read his tells the way Drew could read Sebastian's. He wrapped an arm around Cam's shoulders and pulled him closer, practically yanking him out of his chair, though Cam didn't protest.

"Drew, what's going on?" Cort asked, his voice a rumble of sound barely audible across the table.

Drew inhaled a breath and mouthed a single word. "Bomb."

"Jesus fucking Christ," Damon said, his eyes wheeling around the room. Like Drew, he seemed torn between getting to his feet and causing a panic, and sitting down to wait for Sean's command, which felt infinitely riskier.

Sebastian gripped Drew's hand so tightly Drew thought he might lose circulation, but he didn't protest, he just tightened his own grip.

Sean waved Cort in the direction of the waiters serving meals. "Get Nat and Derrick," he whispered.

Cort hesitated, clearly loathe to leave Camden behind. In the end, he didn't need to, since Natalie Marquez appeared at just that moment in her tuxedo waitstaff uniform.

"What's happening?" she asked. "You guys are about as subtle as a three-legged elephant."

Sean beckoned her closer and whispered in her ear. Her eyes grew large. "But boss, we swept this place. That should be impossible."

"Stand by, Mr. North. I'll be sending a team to take you into protective custody just as a precaution," Sean said into the phone before disconnecting the call. To Natalie, he said, "Yeah, we did. But I'm not taking any chances. We need to evacuate. Someone's reported a *gas leak*. Get on your comms and alert the team. Have Derrick call it in and get us back-up. Hear me? We're gonna do this nice and orderly."

"And these guys?" Nat looked at them and hesitated. "This could all be part of a plan to get them out of a secured room and on the move."

"I know," Sean said grimly. "You and I are going to take

care of these guys ourselves. Now get moving, and then get back here for Plan B."

She nodded once, tapping her earpiece to sound the alert even as she jogged off to find Derrick.

"Okay, listen up," Sean told them, drawing their undivided attention. "We have a contingency for this. I didn't think we'd need one," he admitted. "Bombings have never been Alexei's MO, but we went over the room shortly before the auction began anyway, *and* we've scanned most of the guests. Still, it's possible something slipped through. So. Simply out of an abundance of caution, we're going to take you down the hall to the monitoring room and hang out there until we can sweep the room and confirm it's clean."

Drew heard Sean's comforting words, but he knew better than anyone that words were only part of the story, and the disquiet in Sean's eyes was more telling than any of his platitudes. This *wasn't* expected. And it was very likely real.

Nat returned to their table. "All set."

Sean nodded. "Out we go. Marquez, give Cort your backup weapon," he instructed. "Just in case."

Natalie bent over and pulled up her pant leg, retrieving a small-caliber pistol from a holster attached to her calf. "Be gentle with her," she told Cort.

Cort seemed to relax somewhat once he had the weapon in his hand, and Drew was bizarrely jealous. He didn't have the first clue how to shoot, but he wanted to be doing something *active*, rather than waiting politely for death to find them and rip Sebastian away as it had Amy and the Seavers.

"Let's go," he said, jumping to his feet, his hand still firmly locked with Sebastian's. He couldn't wait around another second.

"Follow me," Sean said.

Behind him, Drew could hear the murmurs and shocked gasps of the other party attendees as they were informed of the gas leak. Panic seemed to grip the whole room at the same time, as the people who *hadn't* been informed of the leak yet jumped from their seats to follow those who were obviously evacuating.

"Oh my God! Is it a bomb?" a feminine voice yelled.

"It's a terrorist!" someone else screamed.

Sean led them out into the hall and toward the back of the building at the very moment that the fleeing revelers began streaming out of the room and heading back toward the lobby. No one seemed to notice their small party heading in the opposite direction.

Two twists down the back hallway, and they reached a door labeled *Janitorial Supplies*. Sean touched his earpiece and murmured something Drew couldn't hear. The door opened a second later by a gray-haired woman wearing a pantsuit.

"In," she said, her eyes on the hall as she ushered them into a tiny room, barely big enough for the six of them to stand in. There was a bank of laptops set up on a folding table against one wall, and rows of monitors tapped into the various security cameras stationed around the premises.

"I'm Deb Gutierrez," the woman said as she closed the door and locked it behind her. "We've got the situation under control, boss." She nodded firmly in Sean's direction.

"Pull up the cameras from the auction room," he told her, and she tapped at the keyboard until three separate views of the ballroom appeared on screen. They watched the empty room for a moment as a team of men entered the room and fanned out."

"Bomb disposal is on the scene," Sean narrated.

Sebastian wrapped his arms around Drew from behind,

pulling Drew back against his chest. "We're safe now," he whispered.

And Drew nodded past the tightness in his chest. They *should* be safe in here, with weapons and trained agents all around them. He tried to force air into his lungs.

For several tense moments, they watched the disposal team in their padded suits as they walked around the auction room. And then one of the men stopped at the table *directly next to* the table where his family had been sitting and looked beneath it. He motioned frantically to another person, who came rushing over, and the two had a brief consultation, while Bas's arms squeezed him tighter.

"Looks like they found something," Sean said, equal parts resigned and incredulous. "They'll dismantle it."

Drew turned around and buried his face in Bas's neck, inhaling the comforting scent of bay leaves and spice. There *had* been a bomb. It was a relief and a nightmare brought to life, all at once. Thank God they'd found it, but Drew still couldn't fully process the danger they'd been in.

Sebastian ran a hand up his back, and it was warm, even through the tuxedo jacket.

"I love you," Drew said, overwhelmed with relief because he'd gotten another chance to say those words. He would say them over and over and over.

"Yeah, it's Cook. Go ahead," Sean said into his earpiece.

Bas's mouth caressed his temple. Somewhere to one side, he could almost swear he heard a sniffle, followed by the rough rumble of Damon's voice. He tuned out everything but Sebastian.

"Oh, Jesus. Yeah, I'm seeing it," Sean said, and Drew twisted his head to look at the monitor. Off to the side of the auction room, something had caught on fire. Thick gray smoke roiled around the room, and the sprinklers turned on.

"Yeah," Sean continued. "Okay, yes, I'm on my way. I'll bring Nat with me. No, hold off until I arrive! I wanna see this bastard's face when we take him down."

"Looks like there was a small incendiary device in addition to the bomb we found," Sean told them. He waved his hand to the ceiling. "Idiot didn't realize the place is covered in sprinklers! Anyway, remote detonators on both devices, and we traced the mobile phone used to detonate those bombs to the roof of the Parkside across the street. You guys?" he said, his words tight with tension. "We've got him. And now we're gonna go seal the deal."

Drew sensed Bas's arms tightening around him, felt Bas's hot breath against his ear whispering sweet, filthy words, though he could barely hear them. He pressed his eyes closed and thanked God that it was all over.

"Open the door, Deb," Sean said, strapping a vest over his tuxedo like James Bond in Kevlar. "Then lock it behind us, and no one leaves until we clear the scene. I'm meeting up with the team across the street and Alexei and I are going to have a little chat." He smiled at the others. "Firefighters are on the scene to help the bomb unit finish clearing the place. You wait here and I'll text you a picture of his pretty face when Nat and I have read him his rights, okay?"

"Yeah," Drew said. "That's more than okay."

CHAPTER TWENTY

"How much longer do you think this might take?" Bas demanded of the one remaining agent in the room. Sean had left over an hour ago to apprehend Alexei, and though Drew kept checking his phone for the promised text, none of them had heard anything.

Then again, Deb wasn't as keen on sharing information as Sean had been. Her primary job seemed to be compulsively scrolling through the video feeds, ignoring all the men in the room.

"It'll take as long as it takes," Deb said, like she'd come up with something profound and philosophical. "It's impossible to predict."

Bas clenched his teeth against a stinging retort. It might have been impossible to predict Sean's return, but it didn't take psychic powers to realize they didn't have time to wait around. One look at the security monitors showed thick, black smoke clogging the ballroom, effectively blinding the cameras in there. Though it was impossible to tell exactly what was on fire, the situation was obviously not under control and seemed to be getting worse. Other screens showed smoke billowing from the ballroom, filling the hall-way, moving steadily closer to the supposedly *safe* room where his family was holed up.

He leaned back propping his ass against the desk, pulled Drew against his chest, and surveyed the room. Cort had moved to sit against the wall using his tuxedo jacket as a headrest. Cam was curled up in a ball with his head on Cort's thigh, while Cort carded his fingers lovingly through Cam's hair. Meanwhile, Damon was sitting against a wire shelving unit with his feet flat on the floor, knees bent and spread wide to accommodate Cain, who was leaning side-ways against his chest. It couldn't have been a comfortable position for Damon, even if he had a full range of motion in his legs, but given the way he and Cain were staring at each other, he didn't really care.

Bas gathered Drew tighter, taking comfort in the solid weight pressed to his chest. The emotional whiplash of the evening - panic, to relief, and back to nagging worry - was taking a toll on all of them, and he knew they were all beyond ready for this night to be over.

He brushed a kiss over Drew's temple and felt Drew's responding shudder to the tips of his toes. If there was a silver lining to this cluster-fuck of an evening, it was exactly this - a pliant Drew in his arms. It was so rare - unheard of, almost - for Andrew McMann to show vulnerability and let himself be comforted, and Bas accepted it as the honor it was.

And he was ready to take his man to bed for the solid month Drew had promised him... assuming they didn't all die of smoke inhalation first.

He watched on the screen as smoke crept down the hallway like a sentient being. It was unnerving.

"Agent Gutierrez," he tried again, more deferentially this time. "I'm not sure we're safe here anymore. We need to weigh the slim danger of Alexei slipping away from Sean Cook's team against the very real risk of fire. If you could contact Agent Cook…"

She shook her head stubbornly. "Orders are not to hail unless there's an emergency. Your boredom doesn't count. Please, Mr. Seaver, calm down."

Bas exhaled and exchanged a glance with his brother-in-law on the floor. *Can you do something?*

Cort inclined his chin. "Hey, Deb? I think what Bas is trying to ask is, what's the protocol in case the smoke gets worse or the fire flares?"

"Same as usual." Deb turned her chair to face them and pursed her lips. "Firefighters are on the scene, and they know where we are. If the fire becomes a real threat, we follow the orders of the guys in the masks and boots. But there are no flames to be seen."

Bas and Cort exchanged a look of disbelief, and Cort grimaced as the first tendrils of smoke began to curl beneath the door near his leg.

Still, Cort was polite as he said, "I have no idea what's causing this smoke, but I think it might be worth hailing the FD, if you don't want to bug Cooksy, so we know what we're dealing with. Remember Cooksy appreciates people who take the initiative."

Bas gave Cort an approving glance. Bonus points for dropping Sean Cook's nickname, a reminder that he was close friends with her boss.

It seemed to work. "Fine," she sighed. She paused her compulsive scrolling to glare at Cort. "But you heard Agent Cook. We're staying in the room until he makes contact." She touched her earpiece and requested a member of fire personnel report to the surveillance room to assess the situation.

Bas rolled his eyes. Assess? *Please.* The situation was

fast approaching critical. On the monitor, a pair of fire-fighters came down the hall, half-crouched - probably for better visibility - and wearing full gear, including oxygen masks. He could imagine what their assessment would be.

One of the firefighters knocked on the door and Cain shuffled to his feet to pull it open for him. The men stepped inside, shutting the door against the smoke, and the one in front removed his mask.

"Hey, I'm Greg Prada from Engine 4. This is Jack Rodi from the One-Three." He hooked a thumb over his shoulder at his partner who lifted a hand in acknowledgement. "Situation's pretty bad out there. Damage from the initial device was inadvertently compounded by the sprinkler - some kind of alkali reaction occurred. The device was placed right by some wall hangings, and the fire got into the soundproofing foam in the ceiling. We're getting it under control, but we're evacuating the entire building as a precaution. That includes you folks."

Deb folded her arms over her chest. "These men are targets. They need to stay here as a precaution until my superior verifies that the person who planted the bombs has been caught. It's nonnegotiable. I can't guarantee their safety out there."

So much for her taking direction from the men in masks and boots.

"With all due respect, ma'am," Prada said, as the acrid tang of smoke began to fill the room. "We have an emerging situation happening. I can't guarantee their safety if they stay."

"I'm not abandoning my post," she argued, sweeping a hand at the monitors. "We need to keep an eye on the situation."

"That's your choice, but the others in this room don't

need to risk smoke inhalation!" Prada's eyes were tired and his mouth grim.

Damon tapped Cain's arm, and Cain scrambled to his feet before turning to offer his boyfriend a hand. "I think we'll take our chances out there," Damon rasped.

Drew straightened and looked at Bas with one eyebrow raised. Bas nodded, linking their fingers as they'd done before. A team, always. "We're going too."

"Same," Cam agreed, standing up. He looked back down at Cort belatedly. "Aren't we?"

Cort shook his head, hesitant. "I don't like it," he said. "Sean should have been back by now."

"Well, maybe the processing part is taking longer than he thought." Cam shrugged, coughing slightly.

"Or maybe Alexei had a gun and it's taking longer to subdue him than anticipated," Bas suggested. It only made sense, really. It had seemed impossible to him that, after all he'd put them through, Alexei would go down without a fight.

"Maybe," Cort said, but it was clear he didn't believe it. "If you're determined to go, I'll go with you." He pushed himself to his feet and grabbed the tuxedo jacket he'd been using as a headrest, tossing the folded fabric over his arm.

They walked out and let Rodi and Prada lead them down the hall, away from the smoke.

"There's a back entrance this way," Prada told them, turning around to walk backwards. "Through the laundry room in the basement. Leads to a parking area where a bunch of other folks were already evacuated. I'll get you out there, and then come back for your agent friend." He rolled his eyes. "She's prickly."

"She's dedicated," Cort corrected. His eyes followed Rodi as he turned right and pushed through a swinging door labeled *Laundry*.

"Sure, sure," Prada said, pushing open the door and holding it wide as they all filed through. "Reminds me of my—"

But whatever comparison Prada was going to make was cut off in a sickening gurgle as a bullet hole ripped open his throat. His eyes widened in shock for one second before he collapsed to the floor.

For a second, Sebastian's entire world seemed to have entered a state of suspended animation as his brain tried to process the jumble of his sensory input. *Shot. Dead. Bomb. Smoke. Danger...Drew.*

A crazy thought danced across his panicked brain - *Is this how mom and dad felt during the crash?* And then instinct took over and time sped up as Jack Rodi swung his gun in their direction.

"Holy shit!" Drew cried, just before Bas tackled him to the ground, covering him with his own stockier body.

"Touching," Jack Rodi mocked as he removed his helmet and tossed it aside with one hand while holding his gun aloft in the other. "Truly, your selflessness is impressive." He removed the mask from his face and tossed it, too, aside.

The man looked directly at Bas and smiled - the same insane smile Bas had pulled up countless times on the computer in his lair, the one that made SILA lieutenants cower. "You were right, Seaver. I *do* have a gun. And I'm going to be very, *very* difficult to subdue."

ALEXEI MARCHED them all to a storage area at the back of the laundry room, and shut the door behind them with the sharp *clang* of a lock snapping into place. The room was lined with shelves of various chemicals. A pile of rags lay in one corner, and two large white bins full of linens were pushed to one side. The tiny room had the distinct odor of bleach and fabric softener.

There was nothing in here to fight back with, no way to escape, and nowhere to hide. He wrapped his arms around the man he loved, burying his face in Drew's hair.

Alexei had brought them here to die.

"You!" he said, motioning toward Sebastian with the gun. "Against the wall. The rest of you, too. Hands flat against the wall!"

Bas looked at Cort. If anyone here had any idea how to get them out of this, it would be him. But Cort seemed to only have eyes for Cam as they lined up their backs against the cold cinderblock.

"Ah! So perfect. All the faggot lovers stood in a row." He grinned. "Alexei Ilyich throws the best parties. Just one thing missing!" He stalked to the corner, keeping his eyes and the gun trained on Sebastian the entire time, and kicked at the pile of rags.

"*Batya*!" Alexei called. "Wake up! You don't want to be rude to our guests!"

As Bas watched in horror, the pile of rags shifted and moaned. "Alyosha?"

"Who else would it be but your one and only son? Look what I brought you."

The pile shifted again, rolling slowly and tentatively, and a face emerged from beneath a bulky blanket.

Bas sucked in a breath.

The hair that had been snow-white this morning was now caked with dried blood, and the tanned, lined face was covered in bruises. Ilya Stornovich, a force to be reckoned with, had been brought low. His eyes were clouded with pain as he surveyed the men against the wall before finally focusing on his son.

"What," he began, pausing to swipe his tongue over swollen lips. "What's happening here, Alyosha?"

"I am so glad you asked!" Alexei reached down and yanked the blanket away from Ilya entirely, revealing his bloodied, rope-bound hands and what appeared to be a knife wound on his left flank.

Drew turned his head away, like he couldn't stand the sight, and Bas moved his hand slightly so he could graze Drew's thumb with his pinkie finger - the only comfort he could offer.

"I brought you a present," Alexei told his father. "And I'll have you know, I went through a fuck of a lot of trouble to get it for you. You tell me I'm weak? You say I force my men to do evil deeds in my name?" He reached down and grabbed his father by the hair, making Ilya cry out. "Not this time! *No one* did my work for me. *I* made the bombs, *I* planted them, *I* shot the firefighter, stole his gear, and hauled his carcass to the roof of the Parkside to throw the fucking Feds off my trail. So what do you say now?" he screamed. "What do you say *now*?"

"Alyosha," Ilya cried, shaking his head in confusion. "Where has this come from? I do not even recognize you in this moment. Stop! Stop this madness!"

But Sebastian wasn't sure Alexei *could* stop it. There was an unholy light in his eyes, a manic energy gripping him, and though he yelled and ranted like a lunatic, the gun pointed at Bas was held steady, and his finger was poised on the trigger.

Bas swallowed and moved his hand another fraction of an inch, placing his hand atop Drew's. Drew's brown eyes - terrified and beautiful - lifted to his.

"Madness?" Alexei scoffed, throwing his father back down to the ground so that his head hit the wall behind him with a dull thud. "There's no madness here. There's ambition.

Determination. All the qualities you told me a good leader needed. Remember, *batya*? Remember what you told me?"

"I remember," Ilya whispered sadly.

"The family comes *first*," Alexei railed. "First, last, always. That's what you told me. That's what you *taught* me. But then you betrayed me, betrayed our family. You turned my own cousin against me, got him to lie for you. You talked to that fag reporter, telling him all your old war stories like he even gave a shit, like he wasn't just using you to make a name for himself." His nostrils flared. "I'm going for him as soon as I'm done here. And I will make him pay."

Tears spilled down Ilya's cheeks. "Alyosha. *Alexei*. My son. There is no need for this."

"There is every need!" He stood, pacing in front of Bas and the others. "Now I see the truth - that I am the *only one* who will protect our family name. The only one I can trust is myself."

Bas had the frantic thought that surely all of them, working together in close quarters, could take down *one* man with a handgun. But what if he got off a shot? What if one of them was killed as a result? He'd learned there were some things that weren't worth risking.

He chanced another glance at Cort, and saw the man's eyes were trained on Alexei, not in fear, like the rest of them, but in cold assessment. His jacket was draped over his right hand, hanging off his wrist in an odd way. And at that exact moment, Bas remembered that Natalie had given Cort her backup weapon.

Cort had a gun.

Bas swallowed and forced himself to look away.

"So now I will take care of SILA," Alexei said, crouching by his father, who was openly crying now. "It's mine now, and I will destroy anyone who threatens her, just like you taught me. And then you'll be proud." He slapped Ilya's cheek with his palm. "Won't you, *batya*?"

Ilya shook his head.

"Which one will I shoot first?" he demanded. "What would you have me do, hmm? This one?"

He pointed the gun at Damon, who stood closest to him, and Damon swallowed hard. "This is the one who couldn't just *die* in that fucking plane crash like he should have. He's been living on borrowed time already. Maybe his time has run out?"

He thrust forward with the gun and Cain cried, "No!" throwing himself in front of Damon's body.

But Alexei hadn't fired, and now he laughed out loud. "Oh. Oh my god. The child jumps in front of you to protect you?" he asked Damon, as Damon shoved Cain roughly behind him.

"*Piz'dyulina!* This is one of the *men* you betrayed me to protect?" he demanded of his father. "Pathetic. So, tell me which one first, Ilya Grigorovich? Shall I kill the brave little angel?"

"Shoot *none* of them, Alyosha. Please. This isn't a show of strength, I tell you."

Alexei ignored him, turning his mocking smile on Cain. "Your father isn't here, sweetheart. He can't save you from me. How brave are you with no one to stand in front of you?"

Cain wisely didn't answer.

But Bas saw Alexei turn his attention on Cort next, and knew he had to do something to distract him. The gun in Cort's hand might be their only hope.

"You know they're coming for you!" Bas said. It sounded like a cheesy line from a movie, but it worked. Beside him, Drew froze in place, and Bas could feel the angry disbelief radiating off him as Alexei turned to glower at Bas.

"Ah! Ah, ah, ah," he said, punctuating each syllable with a jab of the gun. "Sebastian Seaver. Of course! You're the one who caused all of this trouble in the first place, you and your father. A pair of geniuses, and I'll have killed you both." He smiled, almost pleasantly. "Does that make me smarter than both of you?"

Bas set his jaw, but didn't answer.

Alexei turned the gun on Drew. "I *said*, Sebastian, does that make me smarter than you?"

"Yes," Bas said quickly. "Much."

If the man really thought Bas's pride was more important than Drew, he was a bigger idiot than Bas had imagined.

Alexei smiled. "You hear that, *batya*?" he said, still staring at Bas. "I've outsmarted two geniuses. Does that please you?" When Ilya didn't respond, didn't even lift his head, Alexei turned and took two strides across the floor, lifting his father's head by the hair. "I *said*, 'Does that please you?'"

For just a second, Alexei's rage made him incautious. He turned his back to them, and Cort brought out his gun to take aim.

But Alexei was holding Ilya's head, forcing him to look up, and when he saw the gun in Cort's hand, his eyes widened. It was the smallest flinch of movement, but it was enough to alert Alexei.

He turned and fired without missing a beat, and Cort cried out as a red stain blossomed on the front of his shirt and his gun skittered across the floor.

"Cort!" As Cort sank to his knees, Cam sank with him, pressing his hands to the wound in Cort's side.

Damon sank to the floor on his other side, but Alexei

brandished the gun in his direction, elbow locked, and Damon stood again, holding his hands in front of him.

"Jesus," Bas breathed, moving his body to block Drew's.

"You see what you've done?" Alexei said, looking at Bas. "You see? You made me shoot him. *You* did that."

Bas swallowed, not arguing. "You are *nothing,* Sebastian. You deserve *nothing*. You forced my hand, time and again. Refusing to work with me, disrespecting me. You made my father betray me. You took everything from me."

He shook his head frantically, eyes wild.

Down on the floor, Cam began sobbing. "Stay with me! Kendrick Cortland, if you love me, *stay with me.*"

Alexei smiled at Bas and turned the gun on Drew. "And now I'll take everything from you." He shrugged almost apologetically. "That will even the score."

"Mister McMann," Alexei called. "Step away."

Drew moved, but just as quickly Bas moved to block him. "Don't you *dare*, Andrew!" he warned.

"Move, *now*," Alexei said. "Or I'll shoot both of you."

Drew pushed Bas, forcing him aside and pinning him against the wall with the back of his arm when Bas made to move in front of him again. "Enough, Bas! Enough."

"So brave," Alexei mused regretfully, aiming the gun at Drew's head. "It almost makes me sorry to do this to you, McMann. But you picked the wrong man to fall in love with."

Drew's eyes widened as they all realized that Alexei wasn't bluffing this time.

Bas struggled against Drew's hold, trying to wriggle in front of him, but Drew held him back with a strength Bas hadn't known he possessed.

"No," he told Alexei. "I didn't." He turned to look at Bas one last time, his brown eyes resigned and full of love. "I picked the best possible man. And I have loved him my entire life."

"No," Bas screamed. "No!"

He bent his knees, ducking beneath Drew's arm and freeing himself just as the pistol crack echoed across the small space.

CHAPTER TWENTY-ONE

"*A*nd what happened next, Mr. Seaver?"

The FBI agent watched Bas with calm, sympathetic eyes as he scribbled notes on a paper, but Bas couldn't answer. He looked down at the hospital scrubs he'd been given to replace his bloodstained clothing and picked at the material on his thigh. He looked up at the brightly colored posters on the waiting room wall.

Still, the words just wouldn't come.

"He's just doing his job, Bas," Cam whispered, voice heavy with fatigue and sorrow. "Answer his questions. It'll be okay."

Bas looked at his brother, at the dried blood that still matted his hair and caked beneath his fingernails. He looked like an extra in a horror movie.

And still, Sebastian wouldn't speak.

Because what had happened after Drew had held him back, after he'd screamed and the gun had gone off, was the single most terrible moment of Bas's life. And in a life where both of his parents and his fiancée had died together in a plane crash, where he'd been threatened and nearly bombed, that was saying something.

He'd already been sobbing by the time his knees hit the floor, and he'd yanked Drew down to shield his body before Alexei could get off another shot. If they both died, he'd reasoned, so be it. It would be better that way.

He'd been dimly aware of shouts behind him. Of someone - Damon? - rushing toward Alexei. He didn't care. Not about any of it. Not anymore.

He'd known in an instant that Drew was gone. The amount of blood and gore on his face - in his hair, soaking his tuxedo - was beyond what any human could stand to lose. He'd dropped his head to Drew's chest, his own breath coming in painful gasps, and screamed all of his grief and rage into Drew's flesh.

What the hell was he going to do? A selfish thought. He'd always been selfish. But Drew had known that. Had loved him anyway. There would be no one else in his entire life who would ever know all of his flaws and all of his weaknesses the way his best friend had.

He had wasted so much time. They both had. *So* much fucking time.

Ask me when this is over, Drew had said.

We'll go to an island when this is over.

When it's over, over, over.

And now… it was.

But there was no point to it anymore.

"Why did you do that?" he'd whispered against Drew's shirt. "I hate you so much." *I love you so much.* "Hate you." *Love you, love you.*

"Bas?" Cam said, bringing him back.

The agent with the kind eyes was still watching him. "We can finish this later," he offered.

Bas nodded. Later, when he'd vented some of the emotions that choked him, maybe he'd be able to speak.

As the man walked away, Bas lifted his eyes to Cam. "Shouldn't you be with your boyfriend?"

Cam nodded. "I will be. Damon's in there now, and he'll come get me as soon as Cort wakes up."

"The surgery was a success."

"So they say. Through and through. We'll have to put up with his *just a flesh wound* jokes until the end of time."

Bas huffed. "I owe him at least that much."

"You know what he'll say to that, right?" Cam said gently. "There's no debt when it's family."

Bas lifted his chin. *Right.*

"You know I love you, right, Cam?"

Cam frowned. "Of course I do. You're my brother. It's your job."

"Nah," Bas said. "Not just because you're my brother. I admire the hell out of you. I'd want to be your friend even if we didn't share DNA."

Cam looked surprised, stunned even, and Bas realized that, like so many things, he'd waited too long to say this.

"Mom and Dad would be so fucking proud of you," he said, smiling just a little as Cam's eyes filled with tears. "At the confident guy you've become. You're the best thing they ever did for me, and that's the truth."

"Oh, shut the fuck *up*!" Cam complained, thumping Bas in the thigh with his fist. He swiped at the tears that rolled down his cheeks. "God, I have cried enough tears today to last me for the rest of the year."

"No shit," Bas said, taking a deep breath. A knot in his stomach loosened. "The rest of my damn life."

Cam gave him a soft smile. "You wanna talk about it?"

Bas nodded and looked up as the kind agent reappeared. A man wearing the same elegant blue scrubs as Bas trailed behind him. "But not to you."

"M'kay." Cam stood and stretched. "I'll be with Cort if you need anything." He winked at the man in scrubs, and gave the agent a thankful smile as they walked out together.

The man in the heinous blue scrubs walked forward until he stood directly in front of Bas.

"Are you speaking to me yet?" he whispered.

Bas looked up, past the borrowed clothes, past the white bandage on his cheek, to the brown eyes - strong as whiskey, sweet as honey - he'd spent precious minutes thinking he'd never see again.

"Always," he told Drew. He stood up and Drew fell back a pace, but Bas grabbed his hands and yanked him forward. "I will always speak to you, even when you piss me off and terrify the shit out of me. I will always want you, even when you absolutely destroy me. And you will always be my best friend."

"Even when you hate me?" Drew teased. "Seriously, who thinks their boyfriend is dead and whispers '*I hate you*'?"

But Bas wasn't ready to joke about it yet. Wasn't sure he ever would be. "Maybe the kind of guy whose boyfriend pushed him aside and was ready to take a bullet?" he growled. "Andrew McMann, you have no idea what I thought when I looked at you, when I saw you covered, head-to-toe in blood. My life ended in that minute, and I..." He choked on the words and shook his head.

"Hush," Drew said. "Hush, baby. It's okay."

Bas blew out a breath and wrapped his arms around Drew. "Yeah. It is. But Jesus Christ, that was a close call. If Ilya hadn't gotten Cort's gun in *that* second? If he'd hesitated before pulling the trigger?" The very thought still made shivers dance up his spine.

"But he didn't," Drew said soberly. "I feel so awful for him, Sebastian."

Bas coasted a hand up and down Drew's spine, thrilling at the warm solidity of the man in front of him. *Alive, alive, alive.*

Unlike Alexei, whose blood had been spattered all over the tiny supply closet... all over Drew. Drew had walked away with nothing more than a cut on his face from scratching his cheek on the shelving when Bas had yanked him down.

"I do too, baby. I can't imagine having to make a choice like that. He loved his son more than anything, but he killed him to prevent him from doing any more evil." He shook his head. "I don't know if I could be as strong."

The look on Ilya's face, when Sean Cook and his team had burst through the door a few moments later, would haunt Bas for the rest of his life. "I killed him," Ilya had sobbed. "Shoot me, please."

"Gary said Ilya has a concussion, and some kidney damage from the beating."

"He came?" Bas asked.

Drew nodded. "Said he was going to visit Ilya's nephew, too. Dmitri. Apparently, he's not doing very well."

Bas sighed.

They were both bloodstained and disgusting, exhausted and strung-out, with scars that might never heal, but at least they were together. That was the *only* thing that mattered.

EPILOGUE

wo years later…

"THANK YOU ALL FOR COMING TODAY!" The grin that radiated from Bas's face rang in his voice and echoed around the room. The crowd, which had been milling around the lovingly-designed community center and looking eagerly out the windows at the open field and play area in the back, hushed and turned their attention to the front of the room where a mismatched group of men stood.

Sebastian Seaver was well-known, of course. His face, along with his brother's, had been plastered all over the tabloids when his poor parents had been killed a couple of years back. Rumors had abounded for a while after, that he'd become depressed and reclusive, haunted by grief, but there was no shadow of grief on his face today, especially when he wrapped an arm around the waist of the man to his left. He was a beacon of optimism, something the crowd desperately needed.

"I know it's a gorgeous day outside, and there is a mountain of cupcakes on those tables!" Bas continued, and the youngest members of the audience glanced at one another with ill-concealed excitement.

The man on Sebastian's left rolled his eyes fondly, and his mouth turned up in a smile that softened the glossy perfection of his immaculate hair and serious brown eyes. *Andrew McMann*, the crowd whispered. *Sebastian's fiancé.* Those in the front rows heard him sigh, *"It's always about the sweets with you,"* just before Sebastian flashed him a sly smile.

"But before we get to that, I... *we*," he corrected, squeezing Drew tighter. "Want to say a few words about what this day and this *place* mean to us." Bas swallowed hard and gestured for his younger brother to step forward.

The crowd looked at Camden Seaver expectantly. After the crash, his shy manners and youthful features had roused instant sympathy in the media, but time and grief had clearly changed him. He was strong and confident, these days, the face of Seaver Technologies in the press and a force to be reckoned with. But watching him squeeze the hand of his husband, the long-haired, green-eyed man who looked like a surfer in a suit, the crowd had to wonder whether he'd been honed by sadness or strengthened with love.

"Like many of you, we've been through a lot over the past few years," Cam said, searching the faces of the audience. "We understand how overwhelming life can sometimes be, how insurmountable problems can seem, and how difficult it is when well-meaning people suggest that you should somehow pull yourself up by your bootstraps. But we aren't meant to go through life alone." He gave his husband a rueful smile. "Isolation only compounds the problem. Each of us needs to know that there are people we can count on."

The man on the far right stepped forward. He looked far younger than any of the others, with his slim body and model-perfect face, but his dark blue eyes glowed with vibrant intelligence. *"That's Senator Shaw's son, Cain! The one who came out just a couple of months before his father stepped down from the Senate,"* someone said. *He's even cuter in real life!*

Cain smiled shyly, and a blush crept over his cheeks. The man on his left, tall and broad-shouldered, seemed to choke on a laugh, and a strand of gray hair fell across his face. He elbowed Cort Seaver and rumbled, "Kid's got a fan club." But there was undisguised pride in his voice, and when Cain turned to glare at him and hiss, "Damon!", the loving smile he provided in return spoke volumes about their relationship.

Cain shook his head, exasperated, and faced the audience once more.

"For many of us, including many of the kids here today, there is no perfect happy ending," he told them in a low voice. "The truth is, losing a loved one, a home, or a livelihood isn't a minor setback, it's a life-changing event. Sometimes it isn't possible to put the pieces back the way they were, or to go back the way we came. Instead, we need to define a new life for ourselves. We need to find a new way home. Our goal, with this Center is to make sure everyone in our community has the resources they need to do that."

"Because the other truth is," Bas said, stepping forward once again. "That although our tragedies change us, they don't have to define us. We are more than the sum total of our losses, and there are powerful lessons that we can learn from the challenges we face that can help us shape the world for the better." He looked at his brother and brother-in-law. "We learn to make the most of every day we're given, and that sometimes we need to strip away our preconceptions of the way things *should* be." He gave a warm smile to Cain and Damon. "We learn that we're some-times stronger than we believe ourselves to be, and that ulti-mately *we* have the power to forgive when anger is holding us back." Then he glanced down at the man by his side. "And we learn that sometimes happiness is waiting in plain sight, if you open your eyes."

Drew leaned his head on his fiancé's shoulder for a brief moment, then took a breath and stepped forward himself. He looked at each of the men standing next to him as he spoke.

"We also learn that sometimes the best families are the ones you create for yourself."

Damon wrapped an arm around Cain's shoulder, and Cam grabbed Bas's hand before leaning against Cort. It was clear to every eye in the room that these men *were* family, no matter their origin.

"And that's why I'm so happy to be here today with my family to celebrate the opening of the McMann/Seaver Family Center. This organization is not only our way of honoring the people we've *lost* - namely, my sister Amy McMann, and Levi and Charlotte Seaver, who were all deeply committed to helping others - but of pledging our help to the community in gratitude for all that we *have*."

Bas nodded, grabbing Drew to pull him back against his side. "And with all that said, I think it's time for us to get out there and *eat!*" The crowd applauded wildly, and most of the kids rushed for the doors. "Hey! Someone save me a cupcake!" Bas called.

"YOU DID GOOD, SEAVER," Damon said. He moved around to clap Bas on the shoulder, Cain still tucked against his side. "Excellent speech."

"Thank my speech-writer," Bas said, ruffling Drew's hair because that was his favorite pastime. "I'm becoming reconciled to having a lawyer in the family."

Drew rolled his eyes. "The only reason you *don't* like it is because I don't let you change the rules of every game halfway through."

"Preach," Cam said wryly, darting a glance at his husband. "And this is our *lives*, Drew." He flashed the titanium wedding band on his left hand and shook his head sadly at the black engagement band on Drew's finger. "Think carefully, my friend."

"Oh, please! Just because I have *creative solutions* to problems," Cort sputtered, tickling Cam's ribs.

"*Thank* you," Bas said, throwing up a hand. "Someone understands. Sad that it's you, Cortland, but still."

"Hey, that's *Seaver* now," Cam reminded his brother. "Cort Seaver, henceforth and forever. So if you're gonna mock him, do it correctly."

"He'll always be Kendrick to me," Bas said, batting his eyes at his brother-in-law.

"And this is the shit *I* married into," Cort said, eyes to the ceiling. "But does anyone pity *me?* Noooo. Somehow they think the sexy, intelligent husband makes up for it."

"Could you stop your bitching?" Damon demanded. "You're all giving Cain the wrong idea. He's gonna change his mind."

"Change his mind about what?" Cam asked. "You mean…"

"I asked him to marry me last weekend," Damon said proudly. "Down at Eli's cabin with Chelsea and Molly there. We went for a sunset picnic."

"And you said *yes*?" Drew demanded. "To *this* guy?"

Cain laughed and wrapped both arms around Damon's waist. "In my defense, there was beer involved. But nothing is going to change my mind," he told Damon. "You're stuck with me."

Drew laughed.

Cam put a hand on Sebastian's arm. "I think Mom and Dad would be proud of this place. Amy too."

Bas nodded. "I think they'd be proud of *us*. All of us."

"I do too. I sometimes feel bad, knowing that SILA is still out there... that the organization that was responsible for their deaths is still doing nasty shit."

"Like my dad," Cain said grimly. "He stepped down from the Senate when he turned over his evidence against Alexei, but the deal he made meant that he avoided prosecution."

"Nobody blames you for that, baby," Damon said in his rough voice. "And you know I'm never going to be a fan of your father's, but he's trying. In his own way."

"I can't quite forgive him," Cam said honestly. "But I think... I think I can see that he was doing what he thought he had to do. I don't hate him, though. He saved our lives, in the end. And God knows, I would never blame *you*."

"Same," Bas said. "Honestly, I don't spend a single minute thinking about that shit anymore. Gary's still in touch with Ilya, and I have as much faith as I can that he'll honor his agreement." He shrugged. "I meant what I said in that speech... it's our choice whether we let anger hold us back. We could *maybe* have kept pursuing SILA, but at what cost? There was no objective *right way* to do things. Life doesn't work like that. We did the best we could. We found the right way *for us*. We found love and kept it. We found ourselves a home."

"Yeah, we did," Drew agreed, lifting his hand to Bas's cheek and loving the way Bas nuzzled into the caress. "And we'll keep finding it. All of us. Together."

ACKNOWLEDGMENTS

This book could not have happened without the combined efforts of some truly remarkable people!

First, Amy Wasp, thank you for loving my boys even when I didn't and reminding me not to pull the punch! Thank you Jennest and Bryce, amazing techies and even better friends, for schooling me on botnets and zero-day events. Thank you, Kara Kelley, for the brainstorming and for being patient when I'm too in love with words. Jane Henry, thank you for the discipline and inspiration you always, *always* provide. And Hailey Turner, thanks for the cats and for writing a torture scene so epic I needed to memorialize it in this book. :)

Leslie Copeland, thank you for the great beta and the head pats, which were badly needed. Ann Attwood, thank you for another thorough proof in a tight turnaround! Thanks to Shanoff Designs for the lovely book cover (and her patience!). A huge THANKS to all of the lovely ARC readers who have shared their enthusiasm and taken the time to post their reviews!

And, finally, thank you to all of you for picking up a copy of this book and choosing to spend some of your time with my boys. I appreciate each and every one of you.

ALSO BY MAY ARCHER

The Easy Way

The Long Way

M/F WRITTEN AS MAISY ARCHER:

The Boston Doms Series

ABOUT MAY

May lives in Boston. She spends her days raising three incredibly sarcastic children, finding inventive ways to drive her husband crazy, planning beach vacations, avoiding the gym, reading M/M romance… and occasionally writing it. She's also published several M/F romances as Maisy Archer.

For free content and the latest info on new releases, sign up for her newsletter at:

https://www.subscribepage.com/MayArcher_News

Or you can find her online at:
mayarcher.com
may.archer.author@gmail.com
www.facebook.com/clubmay

Made in the USA
Middletown, DE
26 April 2018